INCOMPLETE SOLUTIONS

WOLE TALABI

Parse. Error. Reset. *First Published in Terraform, 2015.*
A Short History of Migration in Five Fragments Of You. *First Published in Omenana, 2015.*
Drift-Flux. *First Published in AfroSFv3, 2018.*
A Certain Sort of Warm Magic. *First Published in These Words Expose Us: An Anthology, 2014.*
Necessary and Sufficient Conditions. *First Published in Imagine Africa 500, 2016.*
Wednesday's Story. *First Published in Lightspeed, May 2016.*
The Harmonic Resonance Of Ejiro Anaborhi. *First Published in The Magazine of Fantasy and Science Fiction (F&SF), 2018.*
Crocodile Ark. *First Published in Omenana, 2014.*
Nested. *First Published in SciPhi Journal, 2016.*
The Last Lagosian. *First Published in Omenana, 2016.*
If They Can Learn. *First Published in Futuristica, 2016.*
Nneoma. *First Published in Space and Time, 2017.*
I, Shigidi. *First Published in Abyss and Apex, 2016.*
Polaris (original to this collection)
Connectome, Or, The Facts In The Case Of Miss Valerie Demarco (Ph.D) (original to this collection)
The Regression Test. *First Published in The Magazine of Fantasy and Science Fiction (F&SF), 2017.*
Eye. *First Published in Liquid Imagination, 2015.*
Home Is Where My Mother's Heart Is Buried. *First Published in FIYAH! Magazine of Black Speculative Fiction, 2017.*
Incompleteness Theories (original to this collection)
When We Dream We Are Our God. *First Published in Norwegian as "Når Vi Drømmer, Er Vi Selv Gud" in 10 Investigations: All Borders Are Temporary, 2018.*

www.lunapresspublishing.com
ISBN-13: 978-1-911143-55-0

For Kola and Sola

Contents

Parse. Error. Reset.

I arrive late to the cocktail party wearing a plain black shirt, pressed grey trousers and buffed black shoes. I am not wearing the waistcoat I'd said I would when Dania first invited me to the party. I don't know why.

Dania hugs me, whispering her disappointment. She'd already pre-approved what everyone would be wearing, optimized for maximum social network shareability, and does not like the unexpected deviation. I don't have enough energy to care so I smile, forge ahead into the brightly lit penthouse and say hello to everyone. Most of them are familiar; the usual crowd. Kiss. Kiss. Hug. Hug. Handshake. Smile.

Electro-swing music seeps into the space softly without being intrusive, but only just. It is all wearily familiar, like my workstation.

I grab a glass of port and settle into a corner of the room near two men talking. One of them is obviously an alter; I can see the electronic stria running through the whites of his eyes. I vaguely recognize him: Deinde, from Human Resources. I guess he's too sick to come in the flesh but too scared not to show up for one of Dania's events. She doesn't take it well when people don't honor her invitations. These days, your social profile is everything, even if you need an alter just to keep up with it.

A hand settles on my shoulder and I turn immediately.

"You shouldn't stare at him like that." The hand belongs to Luiza; an elfin Brazilian expat with mottled cheeks and red hair like bloodied silk cascading down to her shoulders. She works as a technical sales rep in Dania's team and we sort of had a thing last year. Dania did not approve but Luiza never knew that, of course. Still, nothing lasts long in our social circle without Dania's approval. Luiza and I didn't either.

Tonight she's wearing a coquelicot bodycon dress that clings to her like a jealous lover and brown contact lenses through which she stares at me, probably gauging how attracted I still am to her. Usually, every part of my body would signal an obvious yes, but today, I feel nothing. Not even animal lust.

"I wasn't staring," I say drily.

"Of course you weren't," she responds, sidling up to me and

whispering, "I never thought I'd see the day Deinde didn't actually come to one of queen Dania's parties or any other party for that matter. No matter what else was going on with him, he was always the life of the party. I kind of hoped to see him here at least."

"Well, technically, he's here," I reply. "I mean, it's basically him in there, neurosocial profile and all, and once he syncs with and discards it, it'll be just like he was here."

"Yeah. Right," she says tightly and I remember that she used an alter last year to avoid a twenty-two hour flight to Brisbane; everyone appreciates the ability to approximate being in two places at the same time.

Then she asks, "You've used one before?"

I tell her, "I have, actually."

"It's strange," she says, "the experience. Everything about it. And that deadline thing is just super creepy to even think about."

She is either referring to the three-day defect-disclosure deadline or the sync-and-dispose-within-ninety-days deadline. Violating the former voids the warranty, and defaulting on the latter means the alter becomes a separate legal entity and can file for independence. She probably means the latter. Most people do when expressing concerns about the tech.

"I suppose so."

She takes a sip of her drink, something brown with an olive in it. Her movement must have caught alter-Deinde's eye because he glances up from his conversation to see us unlooking at him as hard as we can.

She waits a while, and then says, "It's not just tonight though. Clearly you haven't noticed."

"Noticed what?"

She watches me like she's evaluating something, and then continues. "Deinde. He's been sending his alter everywhere, even to the office, for almost three months now. Did you see his last LifeCast post?"

I haven't really been keeping up with our little network lately. Warily, I tell her, "No".

"He's grown a ridiculous beard and hasn't left his house in weeks. Rumor is he's resetting."

I freeze.

All of a sudden, I feel exposed. Resetting is an intensely private matter, like sex, or shitting, or suicide. In fact, it *is* suicide. Sort of.

Luiza asks, "Did you hear what I said?"

I exhale. "Yes, I did. It's just... he never seemed the type. It's a bit shocking," I say. Though I might understand why, I think. I cycle back mentally and remember hearing that familiar hollow echo in Deinde's laughter, remember seeing the recognizable desperation behind his eyes when he smiled. I think I know the signs. Every person has two versions of themselves; the person they really are and the person they'd like to be. If those two people are different enough, and the person is self-aware enough, it can cultivate a certain type of haunting, like a blanket of shadows. Some people take that and use it to drive them, to make themselves better. Some people just can't, or try as they might, only fail, so they give up and start over: custom build a better neurosocial profile, cherry-pick the memories they want to outlive them and then go quietly into that long goodnight, letting their alter file for independence and inherit their identity.

Reset.

"Makes you wonder just how well you really know people, doesn't it?" Luiza says, adding, "I need another drink," obviously more interested in manufacturing drama than quenching her thirst.

The man alter-Deinde is talking to steps away, and Dania takes his place seemingly seamlessly. Their conversation is animated. By the time I turn, I see Luiza sashaying toward me, a parade of curves and confidence. I can tell what she wants to do and I play along not because I want to but because I am supposed to. This will be a hot gossip item on our social network tomorrow, splashed and re-cast in dozens of Lifecast posts and reposts. I parse her actions as they occur, selecting appropriate responses.

She reaches me. I wrap my hand around her waist. She puts her hand to my neck. I stoop slightly. Our lips embrace, her breath in mine. I kiss her as eagerly as I know she wants me to. I feel nothing. I pull away and apologize, and then I exit the penthouse. I walk home.

It's just past midnight when I slide into the cool darkness of my air-conditioned flat, sweating and grateful to be free of the oppressive Lagos air, heavy with heat and hope and humidity, even at night.

"How was the party?" My alter asks from his perch on the couch. He sounds just like I do.

"Same as all the others," I reply. It's strange talking to a variant of me, with a body as close to mine as is legally required, thinking with an edited imprint of my neurosocial profile and memories.

"But you keep going. Why?"

"Habit."

"You said the same thing about work two weeks ago," alter-me says, his voice a little confused, a little curious.

"Honestly, I really don't know why I do anything anymore." I pause to shut the door before continuing. "When I was younger, I wanted to be important. I wanted my life to mean something. But life is just a pantomime now. Nothing about it feels like it actually matters. Or ever will."

My alter grunts and shifts on the couch as I remove my shirt and throw it on the floor without looking where it lands. I think he wants to say something but isn't sure if he should or if it is his place to. I know because I would be thinking the same thing, if I were in his place. We are similar enough for that emotional approximation to be especially true. He is mostly me, isn't he?

I don't turn on the lights.

"It's been eighty-nine days," alter-me reminds me carefully, as I sink into the couch beside him in the darkness. There is uncertainty and restlessness and not a little yearning in the tone of those few words. I recognize these things from my past and in that moment, I am finally and absolutely sure.

So I say to myself, closing my eyes, "I know. I'm done here. You can be me tomorrow."

A Short History of Migration in Five Fragments Of You

V

Your name is Asake and you can tell that you are being taken south because the wind is in your face and the clay-like redness of the soil is slowly becoming a yellow sandiness. The soil is all you see. Everything else is a blur.

You scream for help in desperate, high-pitched shrieks but it seems there is no one willing to save you. Desperation claws at your belly like unanswered hunger.

You remember that you had only stopped walking briefly, pausing as you navigated your way back from your mother's farm at the place where the Imu and Buse pathways met. You'd paused to make the seemingly mundane choice of which route to take when a powerful arm suddenly wrapped itself around your torso, hoisted you onto a sturdy shoulder and began to run. A moment was all it took.

Screaming even louder, you consider that you did not really need to go to the farm today, or any other day for that matter. There was no need for the daughter of the great hunter Ajiboyede, the niece of the Baale of Olubuse, to go to the farms—your family has never lacked anything. Your father's lands begin along the banks of river Elebiesu and run all the way down to Olubuse's limits where great big trees stand like soldiers guarding your uncle's territory. But you went anyway because you like to work with your hands, you enjoy the feel of soil beneath your feet and you relish the sight of verdant life around you. You decided to go to the farm today because the quiet beauty of the rising sun at dawn had spread over the sky, cloudless and taut like a drum skin and called to you. You went seeking nature's touch.

Now, you are being carried along a snaking pathway carved into the reeds that stand beside the river like a loyal spouse—a path that takes you far away from home. You writhe and wrestle and fight with all the might you can muster but it is futile. The hands that have you are iron and do not loosen their grip. You remember the stories that sad visitors from nearby villages would sometimes tell of children who had been kidnapped and sold to strange men from faraway lands, and you wonder if this is what is happening to you. Just then the wind carries the unmistakable briny tang of the ocean air to your nose.

You scream louder.

IV

Your name is Newton Brookes and it is your turn to go into the hold and take stock of the human cargo. But you do not want to go into the belly of this wretched whale where men, women and children are chained and crammed into every available space like beasts. The stench is appalling, even the walkway is mired in filth. Starved of food, kindness and humanity, many of them have little choice but to die.

You tell the chief mate that you were never meant to be aboard this abomination, that you are no slaver. You are just a man seeking his fortune whose brother-in-law offered him free passage to the new world in exchange for your services as a crewman on his ship. If you had known this was his vessel, you would have refused his kindness.

The chief mate spits a gob of something brown and viscous and tells you to stop talking and start counting before he puts a knife in you.

He looks angry, but the clearer emotion plastered across his thickly bearded face is impatience. You choose not to test him.

You clamber down the hatch reluctantly, carrying a lantern and some rope and begin to audit the ship's misery, counting corpses and trying to ignore the sunken, accusing eyes of the living that stare back at you. You steel your heart, close your mind and try to do your duty, aware that these eyes will haunt you for years to come.

You reach a column and see a young girl lying still on the wooden floor, delicate and angelic, even as she is surrounded on all sides by her own filth. You tally her as dead and turn away but something gnaws at you, small but persistent in its urging. You turn back and walk toward her, set your lamp on the floor and take her hand in yours to feel for a pulse. Her eyes open slowly, revealing brown orbs set in a sea of jaundiced yellow. An emotion overwhelms you—something soft and warm and strange but fundamentally human—that you are frightened of. You decide suddenly in that moment, what you will do, knowing what it will cost and that it will change the course of your life forever.

III

You are twelve years old and you are running through your grandfather's cornfield, laughing, carefree and wild as the summer breeze. You are being chased by Tom Wiggins, your best friend and the overseer's son. He is desperate to turn the tide in the game of hide-and-seek that you are currently winning. You bank left, hard, and burst through the curtain of stalks and leaves onto a dirt road. You realize too late that you are going too fast to keep from colliding with the regal man talking with your father and Brutus Wiggins, the overseer.

You crash into him clumsily and he falls to his knees. When you manage to get up and reorient yourself, your father is glaring at you, his caramel skin glimmering in the hazy shine of the afternoon sun.

"Amira Brookes! How many times have I got to tell you not to keep running around this here cornfield like you're being chased by the devil, child?"

"Sorry Papa. Tom's running real hard behind me and I didn't wanna ruin the cucumbers but I was running too fast to stop and I was gonna run into them, so I turned. I'm sorry."

The man rises slowly, dusting at his trousers with his callused hands. He has a thick imperial moustache and his skin is darker than yours but he reminds you of your white grandfather, whose thick beard and strange mannerisms always make you smile.

"That's alright," He says with a smile of his own, "I have two young boys about your age and they run around and knock me down so often, I'm used to it now. You're the one I came to see anyway."

He looks directly at you and you decide you like him because he has honest brown eyes.

Tom appears from behind the curtain of corn and is seized by Brutus who takes him by the shoulder and starts to walk with him toward the shed. You hope Tom isn't in trouble because of you. The regal man with the moustache watches them briefly and then asks, "Tell me Amira, do you like school?"

"Of course! I love it!" You exclaim eagerly, because it is true. You love learning about things and ideas and numbers and how if you put them together in just the right way, they can describe the most amazing things.

The man says, "Well, I can't say I'm surprised. Your teacher Miss Emily said you were the smartest girl she's ever come across."

You blush, and, looking more at your father than the man, you say with puffed up cheeks, "Miss Emily is wonderful! She taught me some real fancy math called differential calculus and it's just the most wonderful thing!"

"I see."

You watch the old man's eyes dance in their sockets, animated and alive with an idea or a thought or a vision that has seized him like a fit of epilepsy. He says something to your father in deliberately hushed tones. You father says something back. Then the old man bends over and extends his hand to you.

"My name is George. George Elijah Culver. From Michigan, up North. Pleased to meet you, Miss Amira."

You take his hand. It is hard but it is warm.

And then he says, "How would you like to come with me to Michigan? We have a special boarding school there for bright young coloured kids just like yourself where you can learn about differential calculus and lots more things they won't ever teach you in regular school. Would you like that, Amira?"

You smile.

II

You are sitting with Akin in his sprightly '62 Opel commodore, parked beside Iowa State University's Lake Laverne. The Temptations' 'My girl' is on the radio, it is two weeks to Valentine's Day and the heater is on even though the car is not moving. Somewhere in some recess of your mind, you are wondering how much gas the vehicle is consuming just to keep you both warm. He is telling you something in his lilting Yoruba accent and you are staring at his face intently—wondering in another little recess of your mind what your grandmother would have said if you told her you were dating someone from West Africa, from Nigeria. The words are spilling out of Akin furiously. Then, unexpectedly, he slows down and measuring his words, asks, "Darla Culver-Brookes, will you marry me?"

Your breath catches and all your diffuse thoughts condense like water vapour from a breath blown against a window in winter. His proposal is unexpected but not surprising; you have both discussed the possibility for months now and you have been, in some way, waiting for it—even though you did not know when it would come.

You feel tension in your neck and dryness in your throat because you know that what you say next could close the door on choir practice with the lovely girls of First Baptist, on the weekly dinners with your parents and perhaps, and even, perhaps, on the annual thanksgiving dinner with your large, loving family.

You gaze and you wonder just how much your life will change, having only been to Nigeria once and seen it not just for all its beauty and potential but also its shortcomings. The unknown beckons and you gaze into its eyes in that moment wondering about the new friends and colleagues that you will make, the heat and the food and the potential of the country you will call home and if you will receive the same warmth and love as you have now from the family that will adopt you as their own. And then you stop wondering about things and let yourself be overwhelmed by how happy Akin's proposal makes you feel.

How much you want to hold him, make love to him, bear children with him, grow old with him. You let yourself say, "Yes."

Akin leans in to kiss you, his soft brown eyes locked on yours. You let him. Then you kiss him back, urgently. Outside, on the lake, the mute swans are gliding along the surface of the water, made vitrescent by the empyrean caress of a full moon.

I

You stare through the observation panel at the planet's moon—a pale alabaster orb with streaks of bright brown criss-crossing it like the etchings of a great cosmic artist. Up close, with nothing but the blackness of space framing it, the vision is beautiful, almost worth the year-long trip to this satellite that you hope will tell humanity something new about its place in the universe. For some reason you are not entirely sure of, the sight of Jupiter's moon sends a pang of familial hankering through you.

In your pocket is an old picture of you with your family: brother Femi, father, Akin and your mother, Darla. In it, your father still has his afro, you and your brother are young children and your mother's hair is dark and braided. She is holding you tight against her chest and your brother is pulling at her skirt, smiling. You have been thinking a lot about your family—there was not much else to do on this voyage. Now, you are about to land on Europa, and the constant thoughts about them have become a longing for them. You wonder if you made the right choice, volunteering for this mission.

Vitaly, the Russian navigation officer who has become your friend and lover, is floating lazily beside you.

"Moyin?" he calls to you.

You turn, still thinking about your family, to see him pointing at an electric orange patch splashed against the mostly blue and green background of his display screen. His broad, heavy-set shoulders partly obscure what he is looking at.

"There are active cryo-volcanoes in our primary landing zone," he begins. "It will be too hot to land there for the next seventy-two hours or so, but..." He smiles and points with stark, heavily veined hands to something on his screen. "...I already asked Agatha to check for alternate landing zones for the explorer and she found two that are perfectly safe. We can either head for the Conamara Chaos, which Agatha assures me isn't as bad as it sounds, or we can descend onto the Rima Lenticle which was our original landing zone before Nairobi mission control redirected us anyway."

"Agatha," you call out into the small empty space around you.

"Yes, captain," the AI responds.

"Which of the landing zones is preferable, given the current and projected conditions over a seventy-two hour cycle?"

"Both have landing safety factors between zero point eight and zero point nine."

"I already checked, captain," Vitaly says, his face and greying hair illuminated by his display screen. "Basically, once you factor in the uncertainty window, there's no significant advantage going either way in terms of safety, so it's really up to you. Where do you feel like going?"

You reach for your own display screen to check the explorer's metrics and the picture you are carrying in your pocket slips out, drifting away from you and spinning so that in one moment you see yourself and your family, in the next, white emptiness. You freeze and find yourself struck by a kind of clarity. You see yourself for what you are—an aggregation of the choices and decisions of all that have come before you stretching back into infinity and beyond. All of these choices, uncertain and fearful and hopeful as the people who made them were, all conspired with each other to bring you to this place, to this point, to now. Choices, not unlike the one you are about to make. This clarity gives you a comfort you did not know you needed but you are grateful for.

You reach for the picture, take it and smile.

"Right," you say. "Let's head for the Lenticle."

"Aye captain," Vitaly is smiling too. You suspect he already knew your decision before you made it.

You both swipe away your personal display screens, float to the main control panel and strap yourselves into your chairs. The translucent input surface before you beckons. You key in the landing initialization sequence and begin to descend, rightwards, to Jupiter's sixth moon, with the fortitude of an eternity of humanity behind you.

Drift-Flux

In space, no one can hear your ship explode.

But they can watch.

Orshio Akume, priest-pilot of the *Igodo*, sat silently in the pilot module of the control deck, watching a mining ship cleave in two. A sudden release of energy violently ate its way out of the ship. A burst of azure light popped into the space ahead of the *Igodo*, despite the distance. It receded, quickly shifted to aquamarine, then turquoise and then to nothing.

A bomb. It had to have been a bomb.

The furrows between Orshio's eyes deepened as his brows drew down and his eyes narrowed, compressing the vertical tribal marking keloid that ran from his hairline to his nose.

The ship was an old one, at least ten times the size of the *Igodo*, with the unmistakable bright red and blue insignia of the Confederacy emblazoned across it from end to end. There were only a few giant mining ships left operating in the Belt. The last remnants of the first Martian development schemes by the Confederacy and the only ones still in service that were not built by Transhuman Federation Engineers.

The clumsy old giants needed the size primarily to store large quantities of fuel and propellant, still completely enslaved to Newton's third law and Tsiolkovsky's equation. Cargo was attached and hauled using spars and rigging, enwombed in lightweight programmable material mesh and insulation to protect fragile items and ward off hot backlighting from the fusion drive. Modern Transhuman Federation mining ships like the *Igodo* used the Adadevoh drive to couple to the zero-point and draw vacuum energy so they didn't have any of those problems. They still hauled their cargo using rigging though. Not that the *Igodo* presently carried any cargo.

"What the hell just happened out there?"

Orshio glanced back to see his engineer floating into the control deck. Lien-Ådel was a young, tall, muscled and well-proportioned woman with brown eyes and short black hair greying slightly at the crown and temples as though her front half was aging faster than her back. It was impossible to tell but beneath her solid frame, were genetically altered lungs that allowed her function on only a fraction of the oxygen required by the average unmodified human, nanoparticle gravcines in her blood to inhibit loss of consciousness, and a skeleton modified for increased bone density. Handy, for unscheduled extravehicular repairs.

She pushed against the deck wall with her right foot and threw her six-foot and four-inch tall frame into the chair beside him, swiping furiously at the space in front of her to draw up trajectory data and estimate the likelihood of their being caught in a debris field. Orshio had already visually assessed the situation and decided they were in no reasonable danger, the explosion wasn't nearly big enough or close enough, but Lien-Ådel was the kind of person that liked to see every single piece of data available before making her decisions. The light from the console illuminated her face, highlighting the small nose that sat symmetrically between two finely sculpted cheekbones.

"Ship blew up." Orshio jutted his bearded chin at the magnified image of the slowly disintegrating ship set against the unforgiving blackness of space on the viewscreen, like some kind perverse modern art display. "I've seen accidents before. Structural failures, overheating cores, explosive decouplings, but none of them looked like that. That was a plasma bomb. Had to be. I'd bet my collection of original Majek Fashek vinyls on it."

Lien-Ådel kept swiping as she replied, "Well, it doesn't look like there is going to be much of a debris field. Must have been a targeted, controlled explosion."

Orshio leaned back in his seat. "Whoever set it off must have been trying not to damage the cargo. Maybe they're pirates..." he scratched his chin, "...or something."

"There haven't been pirates in the inner belt for years, Orshio. Besides, no one is swooping in to loot the cargo. I don't like this. We should call it in to Mars Station ahead of us. Make a report."

Orshio rolled his eyes. He didn't dislike Lien-Ådel per se, he just found her unbearably predictable. Despite her undeniable creativity in keeping the ship's performance optimal, she was still incredibly regimented in her thinking. For every decision presented to her, she only ever had three responses in order of preference: one, follow the rules; two, defer the decision to a higher authority; or three, have no opinion on the matter. And now, she was already advocating her second favourite response even though they still weren't exactly sure what they were looking at.

Lien-Ådel in turn did not like Orshio's impulsive attitude and flamboyant style but she worked well with him anyway because her life depended on his natural creativity and artificially enhanced reflexes.

He was heavily tattooed, an elaborate pattern of images, lines, and whorls, that ran all over his dark skin and told the story of his ancestors as far back as his family records detailed. The tattoos, done in late afromysterics style, covered his right arm from shoulder to finger tips. If his other arm wasn't fully bionic and made of expensive bioplasmium, it would probably have borne the same markings. He wore his black and grey hair in short dreadlocks and tied a band of red and black cloth around his hairline, covering the tip of the vertical scar that marked him as a true-born son of the Idoma people—beneath which sat the neuralink chip that allowed him to control his bioplasmium arm and the dozen other embedded machines that augmented his body. His entire appearance was a piece of art dedicated to the spirits of his ancestors, the Alekwu.

"I think the first thing we should do is see if there are any survivors, don't you think?" he asked as he sat up in his chair. "Besides, we're technically closer to Ceres station."

Lien-Ådel nodded, ignoring the sugar-coated reprimand, and swiped away the *Igodo*'s diagnostic projection before requesting the ship's AI to send a direct message on the Belt's short-range open channel and scan all other open channels for chatter regarding what happened.

Orshio reached forward and pulled up the public Transhuman Federation shipping schedules and trajectories from their database. The data indicated that the ship that was now mostly just two large pieces of wreckage ahead of them was called the *Freedom Queen*. A rugged hauler for fluids and fine dusts, transporting impure Helium-3 scooped from Jupiter's atmosphere to Independence Station, the last Confederacy settlement on Mars. She was essentially a gigantic cylindrical gas tank with a nuclear energy tube running through her long axis. Well, at least she used to be.

"*Igodo* has established a link with the broken ship's AI. No signs of life. I think you'll want to take a look at its report." Lien-Ådel flicked her fingers to expand a light display projection then swiped it left. It drifted through the space between them and settled in front of Orshio.

He tilted his head to the side slightly and raised an eyebrow. "This says all crew life signals from *Freedom Queen* stopped streaming over twenty minutes ago. Before the explosion."

Lien-Ådel blinked. "Yes. So now I'm wondering... where could the crew have gone?"

Orshio folded his arms in front of him. That was a good question. Almost as good a question as to why anyone would choose to attack a confederate hauler in near-space range only a few minutes after the *Igodo* completed its publicly scheduled uncoupling from the zero-point, came out of drift-flux and switched to auxiliary for a slow, controlled nuclear burn to Mars station. Pirates would probably have had better timing.

Suddenly, the viewscreen of the *Igodo* lit up as a multicoloured kaleidoscope of numbers and data overlaid it. The AI informed them that they were receiving a sudden and persistent communication packet. It had the certified data signature of the Transhuman Federation and seemed to be originating from Ceres station.

Orshio said, "Well bad news certainly travels fast out here, doesn't it?"

Lien-Ådel swiped in front of her to accept the transmission. The flowing rivers of colourful data across the screen coalesced into an image of a very serious man in a very serious Transhuman Federation uniform of pure black with a gold trim mandarin collar. The uniform was blacker than Orshio's ebony skin, but blended perfectly against the man's own shiny black complexion. It took a few seconds for Orshio to realise he had a goatee. His eyes were a stark white. The officer looked like he'd materialised from the star-sprinkled abyssal darkness of unforgiving space beyond the ship and his eyes were a binary star. Across the breast of his uniform, was a lenticular pin shaped like an ancient Zulu shield, complete with two spears crossed behind it. Its smooth black and white surface displayed the yin-and-yang, stretched to accommodate the unusual shape. Orshio had never seen anyone wearing the official Federation security corps chief uniform before.

"This is Ceres station security Chief Mwanja Mukisa calling Federation shipping vessel *Igodo*. We have detected a catastrophic failure of the Confederate hauler *Freedom Queen* a few thousand kilometres from your scheduled flight path. Change course immediately and report to Ceres station. Do not transmit any message to anyone until your report has been formally received at Ceres Station. I repeat, change course and report to Ceres station. Immediately. Do not transmit to any other party."

The image disappeared.

"Well, I guess you're going to get a chance to make that report after all," Orshio quipped.

Lien-Ådel's voice went low and hoarse. "Does that message imply what I think it does?"

Orshio nodded. Along the surface of his bioplasmium arm, beneath his shirt, faint red lines writhed as if alive, responding to tension from his increased stress levels. He flexed the arm to ease it and thought down his rising cortisol levels.

"That was not a request, it was an order." Lien-Ådel's face scrunched up as she spoke, as if she was still trying to process the sentence, hoping desperately that he would contradict the obvious.

Orshio kept inspecting the screen. "Yes. Definitely an order," he confirmed.

"But if they don't want us to contact anyone, not even the supply station, then that means they probably don't think it was an accident or pirates. They probably think it was..."

"...a terrorist attack." Orshio finished the sentence for her.

They turned away from the viewscreen at the same time and saw the same thing in each other's eyes.

They had heard rumours in the outer belt, of anti-federation rebels and old confederate militias attacking Federation mining camps and ships. Nothing major, but worrying enough for them to now be concerned.

"I don't know anyone at Ceres station. I'm not sure I want to get involved in all this. We could just make a run for it. Enter drift-flux again and be back to Earth in an hour or so. Sort it all out when we get there," Orshio said.

Lien-Ådel recoiled, then snapped back to place, leaning toward him. "First of all, we can't disobey a direct order from a Federation security corps official. Second..." She paused to exhale. "...Drift-flux this far into the solar system? Through the Belt? We'd never make it out alive! And even if we did, we'd be making ourselves look guilty as sin in the process."

He nodded. "You're right. You're right. Sorry. Bad idea."

"Quantifiably terrible."

Lien-Ådel kept her palms flat against her thighs as Orshio carefully adjusted the nuclear reaction control system, pulling alongside the mooring cable that was reaching out to them from the largest asteroid in the inner solar system like a possessed umbilical cord. She hated docking, or any transitions. She was much happier when they were moving steadily, the cold and dark ocean of space swelling and sweeping against the hull of the *Igodo*. She sank further into her chair every time Orshio fired a short burst of diverted nuclear thrust, nudging the *Igodo* into position.

Most of Ceres station lay below the surface, except for the army of cephalopodan mooring cables that held the hundred or so ships that transited through every day. From above, the network of pipelines, cables, equipment, and rigging, that kept the Ceres's subterranean areas functioning looked like a glowing technological infection eating its way into the heart of the asteroid, their casings and surfaces lined with bright photovoltaic cells to capture the sunlight that powered their maintenance bots. Man-made parasites, burning alone in the vastness of the dark that the city beneath may thrive.

When the cable had secured the *Igodo* and all its interlocking sections mated to make a solid strut, Lien-Ådel and Orshio unbuckled themselves and floated leisurely to the airlock. They moved with tense slowness as they transferred to the orbital elevator.

Inside the elevator was an instrument panel to key in arrival codes and a screen displaying a welcome message from the Transhuman Federation. The elevator was transparent and behind them, they could see other smaller asteroids drifting, a couple of ships approaching, and the sun—a small, faraway ball of light. In all their missions through space, only the sun remained constant. Its influence diminished with distance, but constant, unchangeable, like the past, like an ancestor. Orshio tapped at the panel and they started to descend.

Lien-Ådel played with her hair as the elevator descended beneath Ceres's surface. The sun disappeared. Crackling electricity illuminated the darkness of the tunnel around them.

"Are you worried, Priest-pilot?"

"No. Not really, Engineer," he lied.

"You don't suppose they think we had something to do with blowing up the *Freedom Queen*, do you?"

Orshio thought about that. "I'm sure they will ask."

Lien-Ådel kissed her teeth and stopped playing with her hair. "Bad luck," she muttered. "After hauling supplies halfway to some godforsaken Tellurium mining outpost in the Kuiper belt, we come out of drift to this shit."

"Are you okay?" Orshio asked. This was the most agitated he'd ever seen Lien-Ådel and he didn't like it. Not when they were about to walk into what could easily be a crisis.

Lien-Ådel looked to him, dejectedly, which only made him more worried. "When I was at university, I heard about the pirates, how terrible working the belt had been during that time but I still wanted to work for Federation shipping because I dreamed of being in drift-flux, of seeing the universe. Now the pirates are gone but there are all these rumours of terrorists. I don't know. I guess I'm just worried that we might get caught up in or blamed for something and lose the *Igodo* just because some agitated philistines are probably trying to start a war."

The lights around them brightened. Orshio exhaled a hot breath. "We didn't do anything. They will question us, find out what we know, and find whoever did this. Plus, no group in the system is actually foolish enough to start a war with the Transhuman Federation." He paused before turning to her. "Do you want to know why I have these tattoos?" He raised his right hand, pulled back his sleeve and watched her eyes. "I know you've wanted to ask since the first day you saw them."

Lien-Ådel managed a small smile. Even though she knew he was trying to distract her from their present predicament, she didn't mind, she needed the distraction. "Sure. Please. Tell me. What do they mean?"

"I am one of a people called the Idoma, from the Nigeria unit of the Federation. We are an ancient people and according to Idoma traditions, life is an unending continuum. Always has been. Space, time, energy, matter, spirit, and life, are considered as one integral whole. Our understanding of the nature of the cosmos predates modern science and is anchored to our belief that our ancestors are always with us, interacting with the rest of the universe just as we do but in a different way."

"You mean like in an alternate dimension?"

"Sort of. You can think of it that way. My people believe that death is a process of passing on to this other level of existence. A realm called Okoto. A dimension from which they find new ways to interact with the same space and time we share. Personally, I think that when we are in drift-flux, coupled to the universe's zero-point, we are in the boundary between our dimension and Okoto. Therefore my ancestors can guide my hand. Ensure I do not slip out of the vacuum energy probability field and crash into something. The tattoos are just stylistic and hieroglyphic representations of my ancestors and their stories, going as far back as records exist."

Lien-Ådel leaned against the elevator with her right shoulder, pulling at the sleeves of her body-hugging suit. "Hold on. You really believe your ancestors exist as part of space? Guide you in drift-flux?"

Orshio smiled. "Well, No. Not really. But it's a good story to tell people who wonder about my tattoos, isn't it?"

Lien-Ådel stared at him for a moment before erupting into laughter. Orshio laughed with her.

The elevator stopped and lights flickered. Their faces recrystallised with seriousness. The elevator door opened to reveal a squad of six women and a man, with menacing eyes and holding sleek plasma rifles, all wearing the familiar white uniform of the Transhuman Federation forces. Behind them, the bright, mechanical sprawl of the main Ceres station tunnel spread out like the digestive system of a rock and metal animal.

"*Igodo* crew. Come with us." One of the women said to them in a manner that left no room for questions, only obedience. Her red hair was cropped short. The cool, green eyes and freckles dotting her nose and cheeks seemed out of place on the same face as her hard set jaw. She turned sharply on her heel and the others flanked Orshio and Lien-Ådel.

They followed the woman.

"Why do I feel like we are being arrested?" Orshio queried.

None of the officers responded. Lien-Ådel eyed him nervously.

The small party walked about halfway into the main tunnel before turning to walk down a set of energy shielded stairs and through a tall doorway that looked like it could withstand a plasma cannon when sealed. A sign on the door read, *Transhuman Federation Security Corps Offices: Authorised Personnel Only.* Behind the door, they stood in the centre of an octagon with each side bordering a smaller door. The woman in charge walked up to one of the doors and motioned them to enter the office of Ceres station security Chief Mwanja Mukisa.

Lien-Ådel winced when the door shut behind them. The chair behind the desk at the end of the office swivelled around to reveal a man that was certainly not Mwanja Mukisa. At least not the Mwanja Mukisa that had ordered them to Ceres station. This man was short and had skin like Orshio's, hair cropped close, and a perfectly shaved round chin that, in some strange way, made him look like a pre-teen. But there was nothing puerile about his voice and his tone when he spoke.

"Finally, Orshio Akume and Lien-Ådel Ting of the *Igodo*. Welcome to Ceres station. Do you have any idea how much trouble you are in?"

Orshio looked around the office, trying to find something he could use to estimate the identity of the man they were talking to. A photograph, a plaque, something. All he found was an unusually empty wall and some very modern nanomaterial furniture.

"We haven't done anything wrong," Lien-Ådel began. "We saw the *Freedom Queen* destroyed a few minutes after we dropped out of drift-flux. We don't know what happened but we are ready to make a full report."

"The records inform me..." The man, who was not Mwanja Mukisa, paused to stand up straight before continuing. "...That you just completed a supply run to the Kuiper belt mines. Are you aware that the outer belt is becoming a den of anti-federation rebels and agitators?" he asked, his lips curling up at the corners in a smiled.

"Well, yes, we heard some stories but we have nothing to do with anti-federation rebels!" Lien-Ådel exclaimed, her voice hoarse from fear or perhaps something more elemental.

Orshio shook his head and leaned forward in his chair, his eyes narrowed and focused like a navigation beam. There was something that did not sit quite right with him about the conversation that had quickly become an interrogation.

"Where is Officer Mwanja Mukisa?" he asked, softly.

The man eyed Orshio like he was a stain or a miscalculation. It was a look Orshio had seen before and it sent off alarms in his head, but his brain was still running diagnostics to determine exactly why when the man spoke.

"You have both been implicated in the destruction of the *Freedom Queen* by the ship's AI. You will consent to a DNA extraction for further analysis and will remain in remand at Ceres station until such a time as formal charges are brought against you."

Suddenly, Orshio realised where he knew that look from. He'd seen it once on at the Luna Railgun Transit Station while he was waiting for his launch to Mars station. It came from an old confederacy pilot, one of those born before the Adedevoh drive and the rise of the Transhuman Federation who couldn't believe that the people whose way of life he'd been raised to think was inferior were now running ninety-six percent of the solar systems economy while the Confederacy struggled. Orshio had taken an empty seat next to the man and politely smiled at him when their eyes met. There had been no reciprocal smile, only a look like disgust but much worse. In the man's eyes lurked a powerful, primal resentment. The old pilot had risen from his chair and muttered something under his breath that sounded a lot like a word Orshio had only ever read about but never actually heard.

And now, here was the look again.

Orshio didn't change his blank expression as he looked at the man that wanted to place him and his now panicky partner under arrest. "You can't hold us here without an official arrest warrant," Orshio responded, his voice low as he started to stand up.

Panic washed over him when he realised he couldn't.

Something cold and solid had wrapped itself around his legs and arms, locking them in place like a vice.

He grimaced, and then half a second later shouted, "Lien-Ådel! Get out now!"

But it was too late. She was struggling in place too, her arms and legs enveloped by what looked like a part of the chair as she screamed. "What is going on?! Officer? Officer?!"

He watched part of the back of her chair liquefy, extrude, and wrap itself around her neck and mouth, morphing into a solid restraint as she screamed.

It had to be programmable material furniture. The last major technological advancement to come from the Confederacy.

He felt the cold and liquid material of the chair wrap around his own neck and pull him straight up in the chair as it covered his mouth too. He heard the voice of the man pretending to be Mwanja Mukisa say, "Goodnight, priest-pilot."

There was a hiss. A sickly sweet smell like rotting flowers. A loosening of edges of the world. His eyelids fell. There was darkness, like the embrace of space.

Consciousness returned like an explosion. Orshio's eyes shot open.

The first thing he saw was a small black cube on top of the desk. There was a matrix of light symbols surrounding it and they seemed to be pulsing, beating out a slow, steady rhythm. He could not turn his head to see if Lien-Ådel was okay or if the short man pretending to Mwanja Mukisa was gone.

Orshio closed his eyes again and focused, remembering what his body enhancement therapist had told him the day after he'd decided to get his melanin genes updated for increased radiation resistance and an improved bioplasmium arm. If you want to access the power-booster functions, clear your head. Think exactly how much power you want and what exactly you want it to do. Breathe slowly, then apply.

He opened his eyes and swung his arm upward. The programmable material restraint broke into three clean pieces and scattered across the room. He reached up and ripped the restraints off his neck, glad to see that Lien-Ådel was beside him and stirring. As he pulled at the restraints on his feet, he heard the door open and saw a shadow on the floor in the corner of his vision move. It was his only warning.

Something hit his thigh and a shock shot through him with so much ferocity he cried out in pain. The redhead with the green eyes and hard jaw who'd seemed to be the leader of the squad that had meet then at the main Ceres elevator, shouted at him, "Freeze! Don't move!"

He rolled forward, crashing into the desk as another stun beam stabbed into the chair where he'd been. The redhead surged forward and Orshio, thinking calmly but quickly, rose, lifting the desk high above his head as he did, and flung it at her. It sailed clear over Lien-Ådel, who he could see was fully roused and conscious. The redhead fell to her knees and slid forward, firing another stun beam that missed Orshio by less than an inch. He could hear something like an explosion come from somewhere in the building.

"Hey! I'm not the enemy!" he called out as he backed into a corner of the office, off balance. "Someone was impersonating Officer Mukisa!"

The redhead leapt up into the air so effortlessly, Orshio was sure she'd been edited for agility. Her face was a mask of pure concentration, her eyes like navigation beams.

"Freeze!" she ordered, crashing down onto Orshio.

She was all over him. He managed to grab onto her right hand, the one that gripped the gun like it were an appendage. He twisted it and the gun fell, clattering to the ground. He could hear commotion come from outside the room now. Something was happening and he needed to stop her from fighting him long enough to figure out what it was. Pain shot into his side like lightning as she kneed him in the belly. Her fingers wrapped themselves around his throat, shoving him up against the wall. Her fingernails were a bright red, almost the same as her hair. And long, like claws. They dug into his neck. She was powerful and she wasn't going to stop unless he made her. With a determined grunt, Orshio grabbed her hand with his bioplasmium arm and pushed down and to the left, forcing her off balance. He was about to administer a kick to her side but changed his mind midway and kept his foot low instead, clearing her feet out from under her. She came down hard and he fell to the floor with her, pressing down on her shoulder and shouting, "I'm not your enemy!"

She stopped struggling at that, glaring up at him and breathing heavily. "Then what the hell is going on?" she demanded, her voice still defiant.

"I don't know but from the fact that we were just restrained and drugged by someone pretending to be a security corps officer, I think Ceres station is under attack." He lifted his hand from her shoulder slowly and rose to his feet. "I'm going to free my engineer, okay? Don't shoot us, officer...?"

Her eyes narrowed as she sat up. "Chloe. My name is Chloe."

"Chloe. Good. Now my turn to ask a question. What's happening outside?" Orshio asked as he slowed his breathing and grabbed onto the restraints holding Lien-Ådel in place. "What's all that commotion and why did you attack me?" His voice strained as he broke the restraints.

She bounded up to her feet. She was of average height, yes, but with a slender, muscular frame. She moved like a cat and had power disproportionate to her size. Definitely altered. Orshio was sure she would have taken him if he didn't have the arm.

She said, "A Confederacy mining ship lost control in the docking elevators. Started a fire. At the same time, an urgent distress signal was issued from this room on the old Transhuman Federation comms channel. Where is officer Mukisa?"

"We don't know," Lien-Ådel said, finally free and staring at Chloe with eyes full of both confusion and anger.

"This doesn't make sense," Chloe said, looking around the room as though the missing officer could be in a corner somewhere.

Orshio thought for a few seconds.

The short man had to be an anti-federation rebel agent. And the burning ship in the docking area had to have been crashed there deliberately, it would be too much of a coincidence otherwise. And if it was not a coincidence, then maybe the destruction of the *Freedom Queen* was not a coincidence either. But even if the Confederacy was working with the rebels or the rebels were just rogue former citizens of the Confederacy acting independently, then why would they throw away two old and expensive mining ships just to make a pair of unremarkable Federation shipping crew look somewhat guilty of aggression. Unless...

He scanned the floor, looking for the pulsing-light cube that had been on the table when he woke up. When he found it, it only took him a second to remember where he had seen it before. He turned to Lien-Ådel and met her hard gaze. Her lips were tight.

"What if all this is just a distraction," he said quickly. "What if they blew up the *Freedom Queen* just to get us here so they could copy our genetic ID matrices?"

"What?" Lien-Ådel shook her head. "I don't understand. Why us? Why would they want our genetic signatures?"

Orshio looked down at the floor, feeling Ceres station tremble beneath his feet, like a fearful child.

"To access our ship," he announced as if it were obvious. "They're stealing the *Igodo*."

Chloe looked from him to Lien-Ådel and back again in astonishment, as if Lien-Ådel could make some sense of what he had just said.

"And they clearly have Officer Mukisa's genetic signature too so they will probably be the only ones that can launch during an emergency station shutdown right?" Lien-Ådel added.

"Like the kind caused by a ship crashing during an attempted docking."

"Officer Mukisa is probably drugged somewhere or still in their custody."

"It all has to be deliberate. Has to."

"Even if it's true... all this just to steal one Adedevoh-class driveship?" Chloe asked, shaking her head as if it would help the pieces fall into place. "No. I don't buy it. I'm sorry but I have to arrest you until all this is sorted out. I don't care what the specs on that arm of yours are but if your resist, this time, I will take you." Her eyes focused with determination as she finished her sentence.

Lien-Ådel's face went pale. "No. No. Listen. Why else would they drug us and use a genetic ID copybox? Driveships use direct pilot and engineer genetic ID systems to gain access to all aspects of the ship. But then... why us? The *Igodo* is not special. In fact, right now it's got a minor fault. You remember right, Orshio, after we got hit by that nasty rock out in Kuiper, the techs told us that the only damage was to the processor relays that pass messages between the genetic ID and ship controls. So right now, the relays aren't quite right and they could theoretically allow the direct genetic ID system to access all aspects of the ship. Including the hardcoded navigation limits which means if they bypass security then they can enter drift-flux and be halfway across the solar system in a few minutes and no one would be able to follow them because they could turn off all the velocity safety limits, they can even override the... the..."

"...planetary approach limit." Orshio finished the sentence for her, his eyes widening.

Orshio and Lien-Ådel both turned away from Chloe at the same time and saw the same thing in each other's eyes. They stood silent, hoping they were wrong but unable to find any doubt that was large enough to obscure the potential danger if what they were both thinking was true.

Chloe broke the silence. "What? What does that mean?"

Her voice was like a prod to Orshio's mind, reminding him just how urgent the situation was if they were right. Every second would matter now.

"We have to get to the *Igodo* now!" He bolted for the office door as he spoke. "Whoever is stealing our ship could be trying to turn it into a relativistic kinetic kill vehicle... the kind that can crack a planet open like a walnut!"

Chloe ran steadily, through the corridor beyond to the octagonal office area, doing her best to keep up with Lien-Ådel who was breathlessly explaining it to her as they ran toward the docking elevators.

"Before the Adadevoh drive was invented, all rockets were momentum machines. Mass out in one direction at high velocity, the rocket moves in the opposite direction." She shouted as the sounds of chaos got louder. Ahead of them Orshio sprinted ahead with fierce determination.

"The Adadevoh drive doesn't do that. It's a reactionless drive that uses vacuum energy directly from space. That's why it can go so fast without having to lug a ton of fuel behind it. But the problem is, if you don't limit it and put controls on how much vacuum energy it uses, the maximum speed it reaches and how close it can approach planetary bodies, then it can easily be turned into a relativistic kinetic kill vehicle of unimaginable power."

They reached the tall, imposing doorway. Lien-Ådel stopped talking, catching her breath. She could feel her heart pounding in her throat.

Chloe went ahead, and the door opened once she was close enough for it to identify her genetic signature. Orshio nodded and then accelerated again and Lien-Ådel continued as they ran down the energy shielded stairs.

"In a ship like the *Igodo*, with a glitch that could potentially allow access to the planetary approach limits, some suicidal lunatic could accelerate the ship to half the speed of light and deliberately crash it into a planet. At that speed, even for a ship as small as the *Igodo*, the kinetic energy will be in the gigatons. At least 500. We are talking several thousand nuclear warheads worth of concentrated impact force in a single blow."

Chloe would have gasped if she wasn't panting so hard already.

The trio entered the main Ceres station tunnel and froze. Ahead of them, the lights lining all the elevators leading up to Ceres's docking ports were blinking wildly and one of them was burning; an unbelievably tall tower of fire reaching all the way from underground Ceres to the exosphere like an ancient cosmic snake.

At the bottom area where the fire raged most fierce, a large group of emergency responders wearing hermetic mechsuits were attempting to control the blaze by shutting off the oxygen and power supply lines, braving the heat and the smoke.

"Chai!" Orshio exclaimed. "Looks worse than I thought."

"Look for the man that drugged you in Officer Mukisa's office. If he's going for your ship he must be here somewhere."

"What if we're too late and they already have the *Igodo*?" Lien-Ådel asked in a whisper.

Around them, people flowed. Most were running away, toward the main tunnel, bumping into those that stood still watching the inferno and the chaos and the commotion. There was one anomalous movement, though. One man at the bottom of one of the blinking elevators, pacing nervously. Chloe was the first to spot him. She noticed that the elevator he was in front of wasn't blinking like the others, its lights were steady, which meant it was in override, not emergency mode. She looked up, and just barely made out a figure standing in the transparent ascending shaft.

"There!" She shouted. "There's someone in that elevator."

She broke into a run.

Orshio and Lien-Ådel glanced up to see the elevator ascending.

Orshio turned to Lien-Ådel. "You need to find the ansible office on this station and establish communications with the *Igodo* so that I can reach you once I get on board. If we are right then we will only have a few minutes or even seconds. Please, go!"

Lien-Ådel nodded her understanding and sprinted back the way they'd come. Orshio followed Chloe. The man at the base of the elevator saw them approaching and pulled out an electric stun-stick, stance at the ready.

"You keep going!" Chloe called out. "Get to your ship before they take off. I'll handle this."

They'd attracted attention now and the spectators were torn between the roar of the fire and the fight they could see was coming.

Chloe dived for the man's feet as she reached him and they both fell to the ground before he could even bring down his raised stick. She moved in a blur, wrestling and wrapping her body around the man powerfully, like a snake, trying to lock his limbs against his torso. Orshio jumped over their writhing mass and into the elevator, tapping at the panel to enter the code they'd been given when they docked earlier. The door sealed and he began to rise.

Ascending, he looked up, silently watching first the fragments of ship, cables, fire, lights, and panelling go by, and then, as he entered Ceres's exosphere, turning his gaze to the distant sun and the cluster nearby asteroids. The burning elevator remained visible, from high above, a spectre of destruction, of death. An augury of what was to come?

Near the end of the elevator, as it routed his car along the cable tethered to their ship, he came to a sudden stop. As he watched, only a few feet ahead of him, he saw the *Igodo*'s nuclear reaction control system vents fire and the tethering cable start to detach.

"Shit!" he shouted. "They are initiating launch sequence. They're going to escape."

The lights along the flanks of the *Igodo* went bright blue. The engines were on. In a few seconds the *Igodo* would begin to move, exiting Ceres's primary gravity well and after that, if what he suspected were true, go into drift-flux aimed at a major Transhuman Federation outpost like Mars station. But, without the tethering cable's elevator access he had been effectively separated from the ship. Soon the airlock would close too and that would be the end. Just a few feet of space between him and the ship and there was nothing he could do. There was no way to get on the *Igodo*.

Unless...

With his arm powered to maximum and his enhanced melanin protecting his skin, he might just be able to make it.

Taking a deep breath and calming himself he rehearsed the steps in his mind.

One. Two. Three.
One. Two. Three.
One. Two. Three.

There was little-to-no margin of error.

He thought the instructions directly to his bioplasium arm.

One.

Exhaling slowly so oxygen wouldn't expand and rupture his lung tissue, he braced himself on one end of the elevator, facing the *Igodo*'s airlock.

Two.

He launched himself forward, shoulder first. The transparent elevator wall shattered explosively. Oxygen rushed out and cold seized him as momentum kept him drifting towards the airlock. The airlock door began to close, slowly like a sleepy eyelid. He watched it in horror. The darkness on every side of the ship reminded him of what would happen if he didn't make it. Every nightmare he'd ever had of dying in space since he'd become a priest-pilot pounded against his chest. He willed himself to go faster but he couldn't. He closed his eyes. It was out of his hands now. He only opened his eyes again when he felt his shoulder hit the side of the *Igodo*.

Three.

Reaching out before he could bounce away, he stuck his right arm into the airlock and grabbed onto the edge. The low vibration of the ship set his teeth clattering. He yanked, hard, and pulled himself into the ship, hitting the row of spare extravehicular mobility suits and maintenance supplies just as the airlock door finally fell into place and the ship's pre-exit procedure was completed.

The vents opened and oxygen flooded back into his lungs. He breathed in gasps, wedged in between two E.V.M. suits. He lay there for a moment, as blood pulsed in his head and a ringing sounded in his ears. Then the increased vibration of the ship reminded him what was happening and he pushed himself to the main access door. It opened immediately as it scanned his genetic signature.

He drifted through the ship quickly heading for the control room.

When he entered, there was someone seated in the engineer's module. The crewcut hair gave the thief's identity away.

"Stop!" Orshio called, flexing his arm.

The man turned, his face as calm as a cliff. He held a small black cube with a matrix of pulsing light symbols around it just like the one that had been in the office when he awakened. Orshio surmised it was the writing device, while the companion left behind in the office had been the reader.

"Well, this is unexpected," he remarked. "I knew the drugs wouldn't last long in the bodies of genetically modified spacecrew like you two, but how did you even escape the progmat restraints?"

"The same way I'm going to crush your windpipe if you dare touch my ships interface." Orshio gestured toward the middle of control deck. "Get away from the control module and move here! I know what you're up to and it ends now."

The man cocked his head to the side and smiled. "You think you can stop us, mongrel?"

The viewscreen of the *Igodo* exploded into the colourful array of data that indicated an incoming transmission. It went unanswered.

"Shut up and move away from the controls!" Orshio shouted. "And if you so much as try to issue a command to override the planetary approach limits, I will choke you to death. The world has moved beyond you and your kind. You can't change the march of progress with acts of terror."

"No," the man said. "I know I won't change anything. You and your Transhuman Federation of borderless gene editors and race mixers will continue to take over this system. Technology and economics are on your side, we know that. We've known that ever since your Botswana, Singapore, and Norway units started sharing their gene editing technologies and got your Canada unit to start collaborating with the Nigeria unit to develop their Adadevoh drive. You will never turn back from what you think is success. We know. We see clearly."

Orshio stared at the ranting man in front of him, confused. "Then what are you doing? Why?"

"To hurt you," the man replied angrily. Behind him, space flowed steadily by and the incoming transmission light signals seemed to become more turbulent as the distance between them and Ceres station increased. "You think you are better than us but you're not even human anymore. You call us stupid and backward and racist and evil simply because we want to maintain our natural bodies, our way of life, our group identities and our culture. You insist that we agree to your freedom and justice laws before we join your Federation but what kind of community would we have if everyone from everywhere could go wherever they wanted without screening? What kind of society can we have where everyone does whatever they like with their bodies, their minds? How would we find social cohesion? How would we define ourselves? No! You made us choose between our borders, our culture, our beliefs, and your progress. You forced us to take a stand and we have paid for it dearly but this is it. This is what the wrath of real humanity feels like."

Orshio laughed derisively. "You can't be serious. Everyone in the Federation maintains their culture if they want to, it's just an individual choice now, just look at me for my ancestor's sake. No, what you wanted was to be dominant in some space, to treat others who'd had their genes edited or their bodies adapted as being less than you, to refuse them the right to live next to you and be themselves, not assimilated. What you wanted was the right to discriminate. Our progress made you uncomfortable and now you're trying to destroy Mars because we didn't let your isolationist and regressionist Confederacy join our

Transhuman Federation and get access to our technologies? That's absurd and stupid and petty."

The man growled. "I didn't say anything about Mars."

Orshio shivered.

If not Mars, then...

Earth?

Surely they wouldn't dare...

The man inhaled deeply and added, "It doesn't matter. I don't expect you to understand and, besides, you are already too late."

With those words, the man finally rose from the module and launched himself at Orshio. Around them, the lights on the ship dimmed as the tachyon field auto-navigation system engaged. Through the view screen and behind the man rapidly approaching him, Orshio saw an elliptic hole suddenly appear in the darkness, its edges rimmed with light and bleeding into the fabric of space like an injury to a star. The man must have already overridden the controls and set them on automatic. They were going into drift-flux.

The man crashed into Orshio. He held onto him and turned sharply, swinging the attacker to the other side of the room, before punching him square on the jaw. The man's eyes rolled back in his head. Roaring, Orshio bounced off the control deck floor and drove his entire body forward toward the wall, trapping the man's head between his bioplasmium shoulder and the wall panel. There was a sharp crack. The man stopped moving.

Orshio kicked him in the chest, using the momentum to push himself toward his seat in the priest-pilot module. His eyes were locked on to the hole in front of him. It narrowed to a point. Just as he settled into the chair, the *Igodo* went into drift-flux.

The stars and asteroids and superstructures that had seemed like they were slowly moving by started to rotate. The black, silent fabric of space seemed to curve into a ball and he was at the centre of it, plummeting toward the surface of teeming, rotating stars. No matter how many times he entered it, Orshio's mind always felt confused by it. Space didn't make sense in drift-flux.

There was no time, he had to act quickly.

He swiped furiously at the blinking viewscreen of the *Igodo* to accept the incoming transmission.

Lien-Ådel's face appeared, with Chloe's and several others he didn't recognize, standing behind her.

"Orshio! Orshio! We just detected a vacuum energy singularity developing. Its drift-flux! If you are on board, you need to stop him. Stop him now!"

Orshio grunted. Too late.

He swiped away the message and pulled up the *Igodo*'s projected path, to see that it was aimed for Earth. It would crash into humanity's home planet at 0.7c, functional lightspeed. Enough to trigger an extinction level event. Defensive weapons would be useless against a relativistic kill vehicle going that fast. Even near-orbit impact would have catastrophic consequences. With every passing moment things became more and more dangerous. Time dilation was starting to kick in and he'd be experiencing shorter time than everyone else was. He needed to get a message out. Fast.

He swiped at the controls and fired off a message of his own.

"Lien-Ådel! I'm in flux. Contact Earth station and tell them the *Igodo* was set on a kill path but I have retaken the ship and will attempt to correct. I repeat, I have retaken the ship and will correct!"

The silence returned and Orshio's mind raced, as he swiped through the ships basecode trying to recall her what he'd been taught about Adedevoh-class driveship programming. Everything was confusing. But he needed to do something. There were so many loops and subroutines and he couldn't tell the functional elements from the damaged relay. His genetic signature allowed him access even the deepest layer of core programming but he had no idea what to do to re-establish the maximum speed and planetary approach limits. The blood pulsed in his ears as the ship hurtled toward the Earth to smite it like the hand of some petty god. He desperately wished Lien-Ådel was beside him. Screwing with ship code was her thing. Piloting was his thing.

Piloting is his thing.

He swiped away the source code, pulled up the projected flightpath and began to recalculate. He frowned in focus, his eyes narrowed, and his tribal marking compressed.

He began to swipe, adjusting the hundreds of lines that marked out all class-2 orbital and transport bodies in motion in the sub-belt solar system. The beating of his heart was thunder. He could not reinstall the limits or change the ships hardcoded path, the man had damaged the flight path adjustment console. He'd been locked out. And even if he dropped out of drift-flux now, the ship was already going fast enough to cause major damage, he needed to slow it down. If he could combine a series of unscheduled decouplings with a rapid correction using the reaction control system he just might ensure the *Igodo* didn't crash into the Earth or anything else with enough force to kill billions. And if he was lucky, he wouldn't get himself killed either.

He finished his calculations and paused. He closed his eyes and prayed to his ancestors, "*Ñmá alekwu,*" then swiped the calculations in without giving himself time to overthink it.

The first decoupling kicked in. The ship groaned with a whine like a dying beast, shuddering as its Adadevoh Drive broke connection to the zero-point field of fluctuating energy distribution in space. The ship slowed and the curve of reality flattened out into the familiar again. But before Orshio could even see how close to Earth he was, the ships thrusters fired as pre-programmed and set it rotating. It spun round on its axis like a mad Frisbee at an angular momentum it was never designed to handle. And then for one deathly moment the elliptic hole of bleeding light reappeared. With a forceful crunch, the ship recoupled, going back into drift-flux with its drive facing the opposite direction, as Orshio tried to brake by putting the *Igodo* in reverse. The delta V induced a sudden and spectacular curvature of reality. He saw light. He squinted and saw light glaring out from behind a hole in the ball of reality. His head spun. His heart raged against his ribcage. His vision began to blur at the edges.

The second decoupling kicked in and the ship groaned again, the Adadevoh Drive breaking its connection to the zero-point for the second and final time.

The manoeuvre had driven the *Igodo*'s engines far beyond design capacity and the force of the second decoupling mid-spin had wrecked the drive.

Orshio was thrown out of his seat and even his genetic gravcines couldn't stop him from finally losing his hold on consciousness.

The last thing he remembered seeing was a face in the light behind the hole in reality, that perfect circle of nothingness with smoothly curved edges, wisps of light streaming out of it like God himself was peeping over its edge.

When Orshio came to, there was water almost up to his neck.

He flailed wildly at first, completely confused as to why he'd gone from the lovely and strange weightlessness of space to the familiar and dangerous viscosity of water. The viewscreen was somehow still stubbornly displaying symbols. The panelling all along the left flank of the *Igodo*'s control module had ruptured and the ship was filling with water fast.

He stopped as his senses returned to him. Get out. He had to get out. He took a deep breath and submerged, swimming through familiar passageways to the *Igodo*'s airlock. His skin was covered in cuts that stung so much that he knew he had to be in seawater.

He reached the airlock but it only opened halfway when it read his genetic signature. Damaged. It had to have been damaged. He swam up to take in air and calm down. The water was almost up to his nose now, soon the entire ship would be filled with it. He breathed slowly, calming his nerves. Then he resubmerged. He swam back to the partly open door, held onto a rail, and, thinking carefully, punched the locked door with his bioplasmium fist like it was an old enemy. It gave. He swam into open water and up, up toward the shimmering surface.

When he surfaced, it was hot and bright, and the sun was dancing a silver line down the skin of the water. His dreadlocks felt heavy on his head. It took him a few seconds to realise he'd lost his red headband. In the distance, he heard sounds like voices, like shouts, like... Earth.

He spun around and saw he was floating only a few hundred feet from a beach. Behind the beach line, a lush green island rose and at its crest sat a beautiful glass bungalow that reflected the sun like a prism. Waves broke over a surrounding group of rocks to the left of the beach. Fishing boats were slowly straggling in through the constellation of rocks. Up and down the beach, there was a smattering of people of all shapes and colours and sizes with their towels and beach balls, their frisbees and their beach mats rolled up under their arms. There were at least thirty of them and some of them were shouting, some of them were waving animatedly at him, some of were pointing up to the sky. He turned again, eyes raised. In the distance, there was a small aircraft approaching.

Orshio started laughing.

He laughed and laughed and laughed.

He laughed because a few minutes ago, he'd been a third of the way across the solar system, because he'd seen the universe bend, because he'd performed an impossible manoeuvre, because he'd saved billions of people from a madman, because he'd wrestled against the essential forces of the universe and yet, somehow, he was alive, floating in the ocean beyond a beach on Earth like some bloody tourist.

He laughed and splashed around in the water like a child until the aircraft, which turned out to be a Transhuman Federation supersonic carrier arrived, dropped an autonomous winch cable and hauled him into its metal belly like a morsel of food.

Inside, he was attended to by people in medical gear and completely ensconced in an insulation super suit—a thin layer of smart nanomaterial that isolated him from his environment to keep him warm and prevent bacterial exchange in his delicate state—and was given a hot cup of hot rooibos tea. A pale older man with blonde hair and a stiff back wearing the familiar white uniform of the Transhuman Federation forces with the Zulu shield, yin-and-yang and spears emblazoned on its breast walked up to him and said, "Good to see you are alive and in one piece, Priest-pilot."

"Thank you, captain...?"

"Petrov. But call me Stanislav. Welcome on board the *Anansi*."

"I guess I'm incredibly lucky. Looks like I landed in a nice location," Orshio said, smiling thinly before taking a sip of his tea. "What was that beach anyway?"

The officer smiled at him. "Machangulo Island, just off the coast of Mozambique. Lovely place, perfectly natural and very popular with tourists from all over the federation. We're heading to Addis Ababa to meet the trade council. Your engineer explained the situation to us and it seems we all owe you a great debt. And you owe her an equal one. We would have fried you with plasma when you made an unscheduled entry into Earth orbit if we hadn't already gotten her message."

Orshio laughed, "I cannot overstate how glad I am that you didn't do that." Then he added. "I have to thank her when I see her."

The captain smiled, a clever look in his eyes. "No need to wait that long. We still have Ceres station on the emergency ansible channel. She's eager to say hello."

Orshio grinned.

He followed the officer into the communications room and let him lead him to an ansible console.

Orshio sat down, holding his injured belly. Lien-Ådel's face burst onto the screen in dazzling light symbols. She was more excited than Orshio had ever seen her since they'd begun working together.

"You magnificent bastard! How in the name of everything we've been taught did you pull that off?" she asked, her mouth wide.

Orshio went straight-faced and said, "Honestly I don't know. My ancestors must have reached out from Okoto to guide my hand in flux. They even sent me crashing down at a holiday location. Seriously, I'm telling you, only the ancestors could have pulled off a stunt like that."

Lien-Ådel's image on the viewscreen, came closer, her mouth tight but a suppressed smile leaking from behind her eyes and he edges of her lips. "Come on Orshio, you really think your ancestors were out there? That they guided you in drift-flux?"

Orshio smiled. "Well, No. Not really. But it'll be a good story to tell people who wonder how the hell I survived that insane manoeuvre, won't it?"

They both erupted into wild, celebratory laughter that rang across the ocean of space and energy between them.

A Certain Sort of Warm Magic

I met Ijeoma beside the Lagos lagoon, errant rays of electric light dancing softly across the heaving surface of the water so lazily that I almost mistook them for schools of brightly scaled fish swimming too close to the surface.

I have always felt a certain sort of warm magic in quiet moments and in held breaths and in strangers' smiles and in the places where land and water kiss. Standing on a pier or a beach, watching the water's ceaseless swell and sweep, I am always and wholly immersed in that warmth. It comforts me.

I suppose I would have become a professional surfer or a lifeguard if those were acceptable things for a young Nigerian man to do with his best years, and if I wasn't so scared of drowning. I could also have studied to become a marine biologist as a compromise if that idea had not been diligently deposed by my parents' desire to have yet another lawyer in the family. *You can always play with water anytime you want,* my irritated father told me, *so why not just study something useful that can actually make you good money, like law?* And so there I was, a reluctant lawyer sitting alone in Churascos, sipping on a Jack Daniels and coke, watching the water shimmer when Ijeoma sat across the table from me and introduced herself.

She spoke with a smile, her rosy cheeks almost spilling over the sides of her face. She asked why I was sitting at a table alone in the open-air bar and casually I told her I liked to drink alone because other people talked too much when they drank. She laughed—a rolling, musical chortle that shook her braided hair like fronds on a palm tree in the wind and exposed her geometrically precise, piano-key teeth. I smiled thinly, wondering what she was up to. It was Lagos, after all, and beautiful young women did not just approach average-looking, brooding men that drank alone in Churascos.

When she stopped laughing, she asked me if I didn't mind her and her friends sitting with me. With a sweeping gesture, she guided my vision away from her to take in the rest of the place. It was full of people eating, drinking, smoking shisha and weaving the ephemeral bonds of the nighttime revellers that hang around bars and clubs every night only to dissolve at dawn. Sullen waiters and unenthusiastic attendants traipsed about like snails after July rain, carrying trays, drinks, bills and change to customers as though they were offerings for the dead. There were no free tables. I had come early, at about six pm—just before sunset—and hadn't noticed the place slowly fill up. Lost in myself, I hadn't even noticed the light music and buzz of conversations fill the silence until Ijeoma invited me to look around.

"Sure, you guys can sit here," I said, because it would have been wrong to say anything else, given the circumstances.

"Thank you!" she exclaimed and turned sharply to signal her coterie with a smile and a wild gesture.

Ijeoma's friends, whom I saw in the direction of her rapidly beckoning finger, were standing under a high, bright orange lamp—a voluptuous trio of short skirts, high heels, expensive weaves and too much make-up. For all their obvious and varied efforts, they had somehow ended up looking almost exactly the same. If Ijeoma wasn't waving at them, I wouldn't have imagined them to be her posse. Her thin braids, light make-up, lime-green tank top with crenulated hem, black tights and black wedge shoes were very well put together, no doubt—she had a simple elegance to her appearance and she could have easily walked into any night-time entertainment establishment and not really been out of place, but she was only well-dressed. Her friends were dressed *Lagos glamorous*.

As soon as her friends took their places around the table and offered a few perfunctory *thank-yous* and *you're-such-a-gentlemans*, I started to slowly regress into invisibility. At first they tried to draw me out with small talk, asking me what car I drove and if I had a girlfriend, to which I casually replied Toyota Corolla and no. But, as the night gathered momentum, their talk drifted toward things of which I had no knowledge and to which I could offer no input. Olaide's boyfriend was cheating on her with some other girl whom they referred to using a variety of colourful language. Chinelo had just been promoted at work and was upset because now she'd have to work in the same team as someone named Tomiwa, who I gathered had, and I quote, 'been on her case' for several months. Nnedi announced over margaritas, preening with secondhand affection, that her sister was pregnant, to which they all cheered and *ohhh*-ed and *aww*-ed and laughed riotously. After a few strained smiles at jokes I did not understand and excited exclamations I could not genuinely react to, I turned back to the lagoon to watch the light and water dance, their voices mentally tuned down to nothing more than a droning echo.

About three-quarters of an hour later, as they were about to request their bill, Ijeoma announced that she'd left her purse in the car and asked me if I would please walk her to retrieve it. I agreed and we unmoored ourselves from the table, drifting lazily toward the car park. Walking half a step behind her, I was suddenly aware of a sharp desire, a peculiar, powerful calling like the pull of the moon on the ocean or certain kinds of wanderlust. And so I told her, "You know, you look effortlessly beautiful," because it was true.

"Thanks," she said, slowing her pace and smiling. And then she perceptively added, "Effortlessly?"

"I only used that word because I was wondering why you didn't wear a mini skirt and high heels, since it looks like you guys are going clubbing," I confessed. "Not that you need to. It's just… well… you sort of stand out from them."

"Oh! That's just not really my style jare. And, to be completely honest, I like being just a little bit different. It's not a conscious thing, you get? I've just always sort of stood out, even when I was a little girl. I'm used to it now," she said, another teasing smile cutting into the softness of her full cheeks.

I smiled. I could understand the sentiment. She looked away from me and tucked her braids behind her ears. They curtained her face beautifully when they were down. A fleeting urge to reach over and free them hovered in my head and then flitted away like a butterfly.

"I've never really fit in with them, my friends," she offered by way of explanation. I picked up pace to match her quickening strides. "We've known each other so long; I look at them and see the kids we used to be. Under of all that hair and make-up, I still see them. Lagos can be somehow *sha*, it moulds you into something you don't quite understand if you let it…"

A chuckle escaped me; we were walking side by side now. "I know. Even ordinary everyday traffic can turn you into a raving madman if you let it."

"As if!" she exclaimed. "But I'm a rock. Maybe it's how I was raised, or my father's stubbornness that I inherited, but I can't change. Maybe that's why they need me; to remind them of who we used to be. I love them and defend them even when other people don't understand because I know who they are, deep down. And they let me be me," she continued. "They love their rock, misshapen and unchanging as I am."

She stopped in front of a blue car and chucked her handbag on its roof before turning over to me, eyes bright with curiosity. "So what about you?" she asked. "Why were you really drinking alone? Seriously."

I felt more loquacious than usual and so I admitted that I enjoyed being alone, and being in my own company, especially near water. I told her about the first time I had been to the beach with my family on holiday in Lagos from Abuja; how immediately I stood on the shore and saw wave after magnificent wave crash onto the sandy beach, the enormous bulk washing away patterns and footprints that adorned the coastline, I had become hopelessly and permanently entranced. I described, with a little hesitation and embarrassment, how I had cried when sundown came and my father insisted that we had to leave before we lost the light and had to brave the dangers of Lagos night-time driving.

"I suppose I've never really been a very normal person," I said, almost cringing with unwelcome self-awareness at how puerile the sentence seemed, for all its honesty. "My mother once admitted that she thinks I was possessed by a mammy-water spirit that day. Some days I think she is right."

"No," Ijeoma said sharply as she opened her car and sat in the passenger seat, opening up the glove compartment. "You're just a soulful guy. It's cool. Most people don't stop to appreciate beauty like that. I mean, people say sunsets and rainbows and waterfalls and stuff are pretty and they put up all these cool pictures on Facebook and Instagram, but how many people really feel that beauty in their bones or get lost in it like you do? Not many, abi?"

"No. Not many I've found," I said, consciously wistful. "Still, drinking alone and watching water caress the shore isn't the best way to make friends, as you've probably seen tonight."

She laughed and stood up, stuffing several crisp one thousand naira notes into a brown leather purse. She shut the door, rounded the front of the car with a graceful mince and stood barely a breath away from me.

"But do you actually want to make friends? Or are you happy enough just watching the waves alone?" she asked.

"I want to make friends, but not friends I have to pretend to like because it's the normal thing to do. I want friends that understand me. Truly."

She did something then that was a bit of a smile and a bit of a laugh—not quite any of the two—as she moved so close to me that I could feel the warmth of her breath on my neck. "That's what we all want sha, last last. But if you want to make friends, you have to be willing to take a few risks," she said, before adding a moment later, "as long as they feel right."

And so I kissed her, because it felt right; because the moment demanded it. She fell into the kiss eagerly; locking her lips with mine and allowing my tongue dance a private, gentle waltz with hers.

When we pulled away from each other, her breaths were rapid and shallow. She looked at me for a few moments and then insisted that we hurry back before her friends started to worry. I asked her to give me her number, but she said nothing in response. She just put her hand in mine and pulled me behind her, heading for the cluster of orange lights and noise and water.

We reached the table and she ignored the accusing looks and not very subtle *Hmms* and *Ehn-ehns* that her friends heckled us with as she stuffed a few notes from her purse into the bill folder. Once the sour-faced waiter returned to collect it, they all thanked me and took turns hugging and kissing me on the cheek.

Ijeoma was the last to go. She lingered when she wrapped her arms around me and, as she pulled away, she pushed a paper napkin in front of me that I hadn't noticed before and tapped it twice before joining her friends and disappearing into the darkness, leaving a trail of excited giggles and perfume in their wake. I picked up the napkin and stared at it briefly before entering the number written on it into my phone. When I was done, I let out a deep breath and spread the napkin out on my open palm until an eddying breeze took it from me and offered it to the lagoon.

About four months into our clumsy, careless courtship, we had a fight.

I'd picked Ijeoma up from her parents' house in Osborne Foreshore estate to attend her former classmate's wedding and was driving her back when we got stuck in traffic. We complained bitterly at first, but when has that ever really made Lagos traffic move any faster than it wanted to?

We eventually stopped complaining, and, making the best of things, held hands. In the relatively quiet and cool cocoon of the car, insulated from the noise of traffic, we began to speak, as usual, about everything and nothing; of our fears, of feelings of not belonging, of ice cream, of house music and of the new wizkid album which she had convinced me to listen to, of the old colonial houses in Ikoyi which we both admired and of how much Lagos had changed since we were kids.

We talked about many things as traffic crawled forward, until we noticed that the sun, setting, had showered the horizon beneath it in bright, mesmerizing orange. And so we both stopped talking and just watched the sun complete its daily descent from the sky; quiet, hand in hand. It was a perfect moment in an almost perfect day and it was the moment that Ijeoma chose to squeeze my hand and ask, eyes set firmly on the splash of lavender and saffron painted clouds drifting across the darkening sky, "Chuchu, do you love me?"

I felt a sudden fragility, a brittleness of soul and an overwhelming need to say something that was, above all else, true. But, and I only realised this later, up to that moment, the elements of the reality of our relationship had been thin and flaky to me. I had believed that we were both content to ride the train of emotions coasting between need and happiness, even without knowing exactly where the next stop would be or if the train would eventually run out of track. So that afternoon, when she asked me if I loved her, I was forced to analyse our relationship, to comb the fields of my feelings searching for some unique, warm magic that I could attribute solely to her, paralysed with a primal fear that I would not find it. The seconds stretched and everything I had experienced with her condensed into one thought, given expression in three words.

"I don't know," I said, because they were the truest words my soul would let leave my lips, even though I regretted them the moment I said them.

Underneath dark espresso foundation and blush, Ijeoma's cheeks swelled and reddened. Her fingers untangled themselves from mine.

"Wow." She was clearly upset. "You don't know? How can you not know? After all the…"

"I love being with you, Ijeoma," I blurted, bowing my shoulders, furrowing my brow and returning my abandoned right hand to its place atop the gearstick. "But love is a big and complicated word. I don't want to belittle what we have by approximating it before it fully becomes what it can be. What I want it to be."

Her upper body tilted towards me and her eyes, under brows flattened by incredulity, ran along my frame, as though she were scanning me for some hidden clue that would qualify what I had said. The hairs all over my body stood on end. "Well, I know I love you. I don't need to approximate anything."

"I know you do," I said, earnestness raising the timbre of my voice, "but I'm not quite sure where I am yet and I don't want to rush us. Love takes different amounts of time for different people. But when I say it, I want to be absolutely sure."

"Yes, love should be absolutely sure," she agreed, and the purpose of the repetition was not lost on me. Mercifully, just then, we reached the pinch point of traffic and managed to meander around a broken-down Toyota Camry, the road clear ahead of us. I accelerated. She pulled at the hem of her polka dot mono-strap dress as though she were newly naked and conscious of herself around me, her full lips pursed, then quivering.

"I don't want to go home yet," she said as I careened down Ring Road, a little overeager now that I was free from the enforced crawl of traffic. "It's too early. Let's go to your place and watch a movie or something."

I knew the request carried with it some hidden agenda, but I only said, "Yeah sure," turned the radio up and drove us all the way to my flat in Ajah in turmoil as I diligently dissected my feelings, searching for something special and big and true. By the time we were in front of my couch, mindless watching something silly on *Africa magic*, I was unsure how much of our relationship was as real a connection as I'd believed it to be, and how much was based on convenient lies I had made myself believe because I needed to find someone I could be with, someone that understood me in some way, any way; someone that didn't think I was weird or crazy. It should have been easy to tell Ijeoma I loved her, but it wasn't. It felt like I was reaching for something I didn't quite understand, grasping at wisps of smoke.

About fifteen minutes into the movie, she said, "It's so sad," even though her tone was so much more so—low and pained and evincing an unexpressed unhappiness I was sure would soon be let loose.

"What is?"

"That you don't love me." Her words stung my ears.

"That's not what I said. I just said I didn't know if I did yet."

She snorted, but said nothing to explain the non-verbal comment; she just scowled for a few minutes, mindlessly scrolling through pictures on her phone.

"Come on, are you really angry?" I asked, my light tone a bit premature in retrospect.

"Yes I am," she shouted, undamming all the emotions that I had watched build up since the sunset and the question in the car. "Chuchu, it has been four months. I love you. I am the only person that listens to you, shares space and time with you, understands you. If you still don't know if you love me, then what do you know? Who do you love?"

She raised her delicate left hand and pointed a finger at me. "What do you really want?"

"I don't know, but I'm sure I don't want to fight with you right now," I growled in response.

"What does that even mean sha? You're trying to avoid the issue."

"Of course I am," I said. "Look, we have something special, but I don't want to feel like a fraud, like I'm forcing myself to say I love you because I'm supposed to. That word has been used and abused by so many people. Especially the kind of people we always tell each other we are never going to be. So yes, I will avoid the issue until I am ready to tackle it. I know the world loves certainty—we all do—but sometimes the right answer is not yes or no, it's just I don't know or maybe."

"Are you serious right now? You don't want to feel like a fraud? You? The king of pretence and no feelings?"

"Don't do that turning the table thing again. Don't you do it."

"Abeg. Abeg," she started, her voice slowly getting louder, angrier.

"This is the first time I have asked you to show me any kind of real emotion. I always have to open myself up completely to you before you even open up a little in response to me. Now this one, simple thing, you can't say. I know you love me. I can see it even if you can't. But I need you to say it to me. I need to hear it. Don't you understand that?" She was leaning forward in her chair now, legs askew behind one of my brown footstools, knuckles as white as a new drumskin.

"I will. But at least let me choose when. Please. Just let me have that," I begged, unwilling to exacerbate the situation, unwilling to tell her just how much her question and reactions had shaken me. I was not sure I loved her, but I enjoyed sharing my life with her. That sharing of things and moments was the reason we were together. I thought I had finally found someone that understood me in some way and was willing to share in the things I found magical. To me, that was worth much more than any possible aggrandised and romanticised interpretation of love. That sense of sharing, of not being completely alone in the world. It was a connection I had never made with anyone else and I was dating her for it.

I also expected it to naturally evolve into love and, even if it did not, I thought it would be enough on its own. But then, watching her react to my uncertainty, I had seen a new side to Ijeoma, one I had been vaguely aware of but had not seen before. It was a powerful and biting need that lurked deep within her, a need to be needed. Witnessing it was, to me, a tectonic adjustment of reality; like biting into a beautiful, red velvet cake only to find its interior writhing with wambling, wrathful worms and a heinous, harrowing hunger.

"Fine," she said, turning away from me. I said nothing.

"Okay, look, I'm sorry," she added a moment later.

I sighed and stood up, making my way towards her slowly. "Do you remember the night we met?"

"Of course I do." She sat up straight in her chair, a gesture of placation, of coming to me as I came to her. Reaching her, I sank to my knees slowly, wedged myself between her legs, kissing the nape of her neck as I descended.

My lips hovered over her hips as I whispered my basest thoughts. "That night, I wondered, 'Why me? She didn't have to sit with me or ask me to walk her to the car or talk to me or even let me kiss her. She didn't have to give me her number.' And I worried for a long time that we were not real, that you were just a girl on a lark or drunk or going through a phase or flirting for the hell of it. I know I don't admit it, but, in many ways, I'm still afraid that one day I'll open my eyes and you'll be gone and I'll be alone."

"Don't be—" she started, but I was not finished.

"I just want this to be as real as it can be. And I can't force it. I need it to just be until it is... if that makes sense."

She pulled my head to her chest and held me there for a moment before disengaging and taking my face in her hands, to kiss me gently.

"It does. I love you and I'm sorry I got angry with you," she said.

"You are the realest thing in my life." I spoke into her bosom, wondering at how easily we had let the argument go. Perhaps it was why we had worked so well together up to that point—some sort of mutual delusion and willingness to forgo the things we wanted for the things we needed.

I continued kissing her, wrapping my arms around her with a desperate sense of devoir, as though the kiss could weld us back together again, heal the hole the evening had dug between us and perhaps through it, I could appease some small measure of her need for certainty and assurance. Before long, the kiss led to other things in the shadows of my apartment. Our lovemaking was slow, steady and intense, like the lapping of waves at shore on a moonlit evening.

I tried to share all that I was with her, reconnect with her completely, but the damage had been done. A crack had appeared in us; exposed the doubt and fear and need plaster beneath the veneer of our relationship that I had constructed for myself. And once it was exposed, I knew my mind would continue to chip at it relentlessly until it was all gone and there was nothing left but the ugly debris of my fear and her unfulfilled needs.

Her room was on the seventh floor of the hospital—the renal services unit. I took the stairs even though the elevator was in working condition. Nnedi had called me two days before; I'd decided what I was going to do almost immediately and it had taken me a little over twenty hours to make it there—to first navigate my way through Lagos traffic, then cross the Atlantic ocean in a pressurised metal tube and finally pay my way to be expertly meandered through the glass and concrete forest of New York City all the way to Robert Wood Johnson hospital—and yet, when I got there, only a few feet away from her, I still felt like I needed a few final moments alone to calm myself.

The air in the hospital was sterile, crisp and saturated with the smell of antiseptic, latex and that unique metallic smell of blood that never completely left a place once it had found its way there. Ijeoma always favoured woody, earthy smells. When our relationship was still young and unsure of itself, I would hold her and bury my face in her neck to smell the distilled ocean and bottled forest and little essences of earth for sale. So in that moment, climbing up those stairs, the memory of her perfume so powerful that I could almost taste it on my tongue, I felt desperately guilty even though it had been three years since we'd ended our relationship.

As I walked through the paper-white stairwell doors and into the seventh floor hallway, my shoes were metronomes against the hallway's polished tile. I adjusted the visitors pass pinned to the lapel of my plaid jacket and wished for a moment that I could go back to the time before things became strained between Ijeoma and me—a time when we could share a moment without questioning ourselves and what we were and what we felt and why we felt that way anyway. It was a moment of decanted pain, with a purity that only regret can produce.

As I rounded the corner onto the main corridor of the renal ward, I passed by two chubby nurses whose faces bore none of the arrogance that, to me, had always seemed typical of all medical professionals—especially in Nigeria—that sense of authority and superiority which they always wore like armour to protect them from the people they were supposed to care for. These nurses were bare. Human. One of them even flashed me a smile which in some small way helped balm the hurt from my memories. I kept walking until I reached room 714 and paused before going in, collecting myself one final time.

The breakup may have been her idea but it was my fault. I changed after that first fight. Once my mind began to chip away at the illusion of us, searching for something more and not finding it, whatever it was, I became testy, difficult to be with. I know that now. The day we broke up, she told me she did not think I would make a good husband or father. It hurt to hear, even though, in many ways, I suspected it was true. I had never really connected with anyone—not my parents, not my siblings, not even her—although it was the closest I had ever come. I was an emotionally stunted man who found himself lost in silences and at coastlines but could not bring himself to tell his girlfriend he loved her.

I peered in through the circular port in the door to room 714. Ijeoma was alone in the room, lying beneath crisp, white hospital sheets and surrounded by stark white walls. She was as pale as a Nigerian woman could be without chemical assistance. Her braided hair was splayed out on the pillow under her head, the end of each braid a little skein, and there were new lines around her eyes that had not been there the last time we spoke—when she'd tearfully told me she didn't want to see me again.

I held my breath and briefly considered what she wanted to tell me, and if it would change what I had already decided I was going to do.

I knocked gently on the door three times and then, without waiting for a response, let myself in.

Her eyes managed to register a look of joy that strained to let itself be seen from beneath the pallid mask of illness. Subdued as it was, I saw it anyway.

"Chuchu?"

"Yeah, it's me."

"You came," she said weakly, sliding her right hand out from under the sheets and patting the space on her left side of the bed, indicating that she wanted me to approach, to sit. I did. Two IV lines snaked their way into her arm like twin vines. I took her hand in mine. Her grip was fragile, her voice croaky and her breath as dry as harmattan air.

"Of course I did. I would have come sooner, but I needed to get some checks done first. Did you think I wouldn't?" I asked.

"Honestly, I didn't know. I just needed you to know. That's why I asked Nnedi to call you. If I had done it myself, it would have felt too much like I was exploiting this situation. But I didn't expect…' She sighed. 'I'm just glad you came."

"Where are your parents?" I asked, veering off the course the conversation had started on.

"They are at Nnedi's house. Upstate. They were here all day and needed to rest," she said, sighing heavily. "They're too old for me and all this my kidney wahala anyway. And I think my mum feels a little bit guilty. RPKD is hereditary apparently but it just skipped her on its way to me. This pot of beans life sha."

"It's not her fault. I'm sure she knows that," I began, noticing that she still had the gold necklace I'd bought her as a Valentine's Day gift garlanded around her neck. "Besides, hopefully the wahala won't last much longer. You'll get your transplant soon."

A weariness settled on her brows and wrinkled them as she said, "The waiting list is fairly long."

Her eyes told me what she didn't want to say; that she didn't think that she would make it. That she thought she would die before they found a match or that they would try to make do with one that was not quite right which her body would reject, killing her in the process. I squeezed her hand and said nothing; it was not time. Instead, I asked her what she thought of the hospital and from there our conversation spiralled into a thousand other things; my trip, the starkness of the room, the kindness of her nurses, the joy she found playing with Nnedi's kids when they visited. As she spoke, despite her best efforts to remain cheerful, her words came tinged with a subdued sadness, a distant undercurrent of desperate unhappiness like the sour aftertaste of unripe mangos.

We spoke until a rail-thin nurse entered the room and contaminated our conversation. She smiled at us as she took recordings from the dialysis machine Ijeoma was attached to as well as the gallery of monitors that stood beside her bed like bodyguards. Ijeoma sighed when the nurse finally departed.

"I came here to do two things, neither of which are easy," I began, squeezing her hand gently. The look in her eye let me know that she was curious but would wait for me to explain. I carried on.

"The first is to tell you that I did a transplant compatibility test before I came here." Her eyes widened to vitrescent, minimalist art deco saucers as she began to realize what I was leading up to. "I don't know why, I just had a feeling. And apparently it was a good feeling, because we are a near-perfect, five-antigen match. It's not a perfect six but it's very good and with immunosuppression drugs, the doctors are absolutely confident it will take so…" I paused to take a deep breath, lending an unintentional sense of drama to the announcement, "I'm going to give you one of my kidneys."

Her voice was a raspy, shocked whisper. "You can't, Chuchu. You can't do that."

I wanted to tell her that I could and I would because I had to but I didn't. I just ignored her protests and continued.

"Second, I came here to apologise for everything. Not just the breakup, but for most of our relationship. I was never a good boyfriend to you, not really. I was more concerned with being myself and making you a part of my world than in loving you and being a part of yours in the way you needed me to. So I want to say I'm sorry, because I honestly don't think I ever loved you and I never should have made you think I did."

I felt her grip on my hand become a little bit tighter and looked down at her hand in mine; she had lost so much weight. By the time I looked up again, she was smiling a strange, vast smile that put all her piano-key teeth on display and puffed up what was left of her cheeks.

"I swear you are a fool, Chuchu," she said, before doing the thing she always did when she had realized something about someone—an expression lost somewhere between smiling and laughter.

Confused, I asked her, "What's funny?"

And she said, "You are. You're telling me you don't think you love me and you don't think you ever did?"

"Yes," I affirmed, a little cautiously.

"Well that's a stupid thing to say. Olodo. You dated me. You shared a part of yourself that you've never shared with anyone before with me. And even now, you flew all the way here to see me. Just because I had someone call to tell you what was going on with me." She slowed a little, the smile on her face firm in its place. "You just told me you want to give me your kidney, even though we broke up three years ago. You came all this way because I needed you. You never told me you loved me, but seriously, look at us, Chuchu. Look at all this and tell me; what do you even think love is?"

I remained quiet and said nothing because I was seized then by a vision so vivid, I can never be sure if it truly happened or if it was the memory of a dream that my mind conjugated with the moment to explain the sudden, unexpected clarity that came over me in its wake.

In this vision, I was standing in a dark, open field, heavy rain a constant curtain all around me. There was a sharp bolt of lightning, the crack of thunder. The sun appeared in the sky with all the unexpectedness of an explosion, turned pure white, then expanded, speeding toward me at what is, even by the plastic standards of a vision, an impossible speed. Blinded and afraid, I shut my eyes and then there was... nothing. Nothing but bright, bright, white light.

"Chuchu, are you okay?" Ijeoma's voice was floating above me. I realized then that my head was buried in her side and my cheeks were wet. I had been crying.

"I am," I said, and meant it. And then I added, "I love you, Ijeoma. I always have," and I meant that even more.

She looked at me, silent, stunned and still smiling. So I lifted her hand and placed it on my cheek for want of words to say. We stayed that way for a few moments, neither of us saying anything.

I expected love to be some sort of new, grand sense of being, elevated beyond the warm magic of comfortable silences or even the calm, perpetual caress of the ocean along a sandy beach. But that grand feeling had never come to me. Instead, what little magic I could already find in the world only became a little warmer when I shared it with Ijeoma. I had, I believed, when we were a couple, settled for that in lieu of love. But there, weeping with her hand on my face, willing despite all reason to give her a kidney, willing to sit by her side until she was whole again, I knew, with some hidden sense, like a bird knowing magnetic south, that I had loved her all along and was scared to admit it, not to her, but to myself.

In my head, I relived the parts of our lives that intersected—the kisses, the arguments, the lovemaking, the owambes and the movies, the long drives and the boisterous nights under the too-thin Lagos sky. I assembled them together in a narrative—the story of us—and reviewed it in my head over and over and over, mining each experience for emotion, and finding love, not as a single grand bird soaring in the sky of us but as a kaleidoscope of small, beautiful butterflies flying low to the field, just above the grass.

I was not sure how long we stayed that way but eventually, I pulled away, kissed Ijeoma's hand and rose up like a remembered promise, telling her I was going to look for the Renal ward clerk and register myself as a living donor and that I would be back soon. She nodded her understanding gently, in tears.

I walked out of room 714 a different man than I had walked into it. A man that understood himself a little bit more, a man that no longer looked for great, grand feelings or was afraid to let himself see the grandeur in small ones. I saw the ocean of love inside and all around me, where it had been all along, and wondered how I had not seen it before until Ijeoma invited me to look around.

Necessary and Sufficient Conditions

The dusty, bumpy road linking the magnetic hyper-expressway to Ijebu-Ode was nothing like the smooth, organised and illuminated tunnels from which it branched out. I focused on the lush green forest that flanked me on each side of the ancient, red road as my brain and my transport pod AI conspired to navigate the way to Professor Olukoya's country home.

The burden of vengeance was heavy in my right hand; two decades worth of hate compressed into one millilitre of clear liquid, held in a small silver tube. I looked through my window, took in the sights of untarnished forest and allowed them sink in. It was only on rare occasions that I got to see nature like this, as yet untamed. It was all so strikingly different from the domestic, subjugated pockets of greenery that dotted the Lagos supercity complex—six solid structures, each one towering seven kilometres into the sky and imposing a ten square kilometre footprint on the ground like giant fingers insolently poking at the eyes of gods long unworshipped and ancestors long forgotten—in precisely picked parks and conservatories.

Above me, the setting sun peeked out cautiously from behind the silver skirt of low-hanging clouds, framing the vast tableau of trees and grass around in a reddish-grey haze. Mesmerised by the sea of endless green, I found myself lost in thought until my transport pod AI transmitted an insistent direct message to me through my neural implant. "Switching to Driver Direct Neural Navigation. Take left turn in two minutes. Caution: Non-hyper-express terrain."

The viscous voice seeped into my consciousness like ether, and even though I knew it was nothing more than a series of electro-chemical signals exchanged between the pod and my brain, I still interpreted it as a voice. I'd heard good axiological arguments against humanisation of neural signals from direct brain-machine interfaces, but I liked that my pod sometimes sounded like a caring aunt asking me a favour and other times like brisk and efficient agent giving me instructions, depending on my mood. I focused on the road and, in two minutes, did as I was told, thinking the pod through the turn.

I felt it in my bones when I reached the professor's home, this particular direct neural message coming not as sound but as a small pod-induced electro-muscular vibration. I was afraid and my neural implants were adjusting my body's responses accordingly. My Lifedock readings were all over the place. I needed to calm down so I breathed slowly, deeply to calm myself. When my Lifedock readings settled down, I threw the round-ended silver tube into the pocket of my bodysuit and thought the transport pod to a stop. I pulled my neural engagement key out of the chamfered sync slot and carefully reattached it to the Lifedock jack in my left arm. Stepping out of the sleek, white pod and into the dizzying heat, I briefly regarded the intricate whorls and arcs in its surface finish that served as its unique identification, wondering if they had any significant correlation to my own fingerprints and if, when I finally had the blood of this old enemy on my hands, its next owner would insist on having its exteriors changed. Dismissing that thought, I mentally instructed the pod to secure itself before slowly taking the first step toward my revenge: approaching the veranda of the red brick bungalow that lay before me.

I froze a few steps away from the entrance and stood outside for almost a minute, staring at the strange, ancient red brick and wood construct. It must have been six or seven hundred years old. I had never seen anything like it. I was still studying it when I heard a voice call out to me from within the house that looked like it was built with caked blood.

"Well, do you want to come in or not?"

"Err. Yes... Yes sir. Sorry sir," I responded, a bit too effusively and rather clumsily. I was angry with myself for using the word 'sir' twice in an apology that only consisted of four words and even more disgusted at the act I needed to put on in order to get close enough to do what needed to be done. Flustered, I cantered hastily to the open entrance of the house and through a screen of beads and cowries that hung just past a door that had receded into slats set in the wall. My short-range wireless neural interface auto-connected to the security AI of the house and I felt it as a tightening in my throat. The AI was a powerful security program, but the professor had already preapproved clearance for me, so it wasn't trying to override my neural pathways and tell my own body to kill or incapacitate me as it would an intruder. The important thing was: I was in.

The professor was sitting on a weathered brown sofa the colour of moulding clay. Cracks in the leather ran all over it like fractures across a dried-up pond. The sofa seemed as though it were an extension of the old man, with his clean-shaven head, grey beard, and weathered brown skin. It was a fitting place for him to die.

"Sit down," Professor Olukoya said, pointing at a plain black stool opposite him. As I took a step toward it, it seemed to spontaneously liquefy, morphing into a higher, solid-backed chair. It was a nice piece of high-tech programmable nanomaterial furniture, the kind our country's nanotech industry had made trillions of dollars from exporting to the rest of the world.

"I was making *efo riro* and *amala*, would you like some?" he offered with a tight smile.

"No sir, I'm fine. I ate on the way here," I lied.

"Very well then. Let us begin."

The professor's voice carried easily, and even though I detected no accent, he still carried the cadence and the speaking manner of a typical Yoruba man, his syllables more sung than pronounced. I took out a rectangular black device from my bodysuit cargo compartment and settled into the nanomaterial chair, face to face with the man who had taken everything that mattered from me.

I cleared my throat.

"I'm sure my editor already explained to you why I'm here, so I suppose we should just begin," I said, in as professional tone as I could, hoping he didn't notice the gentle undulation of my voice.

"Of course. The interview. That is your neural recorder?" He gestured toward the black box.

"Yes."

"So when people download your log file to their Lifedocks, they will feel exactly what you felt as you interviewed me?"

I fought the urge to scream her name and kill him with that querying look plastered onto his face, but I forced myself to remain calm; I needed him to know why.

"Yes, sir. It will be just as though they spoke with you themselves, in this place."

"Interesting. I've personally never cared much for neural sharetech—so many young people only use it for pointless social nonsense—but this seems like a good application for it. Anyway, very good. You can start."

I pressed the *FullRes* button on the recorder and shivered as it came on, syncing with my neural implant and priming itself to record the full range of my sensory interactions.

Ready...

"Good evening, Professor Olukoya. It is an honour to finally speak with you."

Steady...

"It's a pleasure to meet you as well, and also your audience."

The old man's excessive smile threatened to colonise his wrinkled face. He was playing to the imagined gallery, focused on projecting as good an impression as possible on his potential audience and distracted by his own pretentions.

Now.

"Tell me about the Eshu Protocol," I said sharply, sans smile.

A sheen of sweat appeared on the professor's head where his hairline had once held a border. In the cool air of the temperature regulated brick house, the sweat might as well have been little droplets of acknowledged guilt, condensing confessions, secretions of liquid fear.

"Wha... Excuse me? What kind of... you're not from Timeline Magazine, are you?" the old man asked, his voice shaking and betraying his age for the first time.

"My name," I began as I reached for the silver tube in my cargo compartment, "is Yemi Ladipo."

The professor's face went hard and white. I snapped to my feet and, in one smooth motion, crossed the space between us, trailing the silver tube full of vengeance and death in my left hand. I landed on top of him; so close, I could smell the tobacco on his breath and the cocoa butter on his skin. I pinned down his right forearm with my left knee and held down his left hand with my right. I flicked the cap off the tube to reveal its thin, long needle, like the proboscis of a thirsty mosquito, jammed it into his neck and squeezed. The professor became a dead man walking. I pulled back to see shock and fear and confusion in his eyes. I expected to see those. What I did not expect was for the confusion to quickly morph into anger and for something cold and liquid to wrap itself around my throat and solidify into a vice, trying to strangle the life out of me.

His face took on a bone-tight grimace as I let go of his hand. Through my retreating vision, I saw him reach under the sofa. I thought quickly, resisting the pain and fear and darkness of suffocation with gritted teeth. I pulled the empty silver tube from the professor's neck and jammed the needle into his left eyeball.

There was a scream. I felt the vice around my neck loosen. There was a burst of bright light. A bolt of pain ripped through me at the speed of a malicious thought. I fell back, away from the mewling old man on the brown sofa clutching his punctured left eye socket and onto the floor. There was a silver plasma pistol slipping from his right hand and a black-edged, bloody hole in my belly.

He was done for, but so was I.

I mentally cycled through the readings of my Lifedock and, with a thought, commanded my neural interface AI to dump endorphins into my system for the pain. There was no way I could get back to the Lagos supercity medical centre in time for a rectification specialist to plug the hole in my belly with bioengineered stem cells. I tried to keep pressure on both sides of the hole in my torso, but blood was leaking out between my fingers. I did not want to go into shock. The professor had stopped screaming and the smell of blood and ozone filled the small space between us. My thoughts drifted to my mother. I wondered what she had been thinking when the professor had sat behind her on the Accra-Beijing hyper-expressway back in 2486 and burned a hole through her brain with plasma hotter than the core temperature of the sun.

I struggled to my feet—the pain dulled to a persistent gnawing—and stumbled forward, each step a painful reminder that I was going to die soon.

"What did you do to me, boy?" the professor asked from behind the bloodstained sofa. He sounded more like a man asking a technical question to a colleague than a mortally wounded man with one eye dying a slow and painful death.

"I injected you with malcore nanomachines. They will weave the iron in your blood into stable, long chained molecules until you die or pass out from the pain."

He only sighed heavily, and asked, "You are Omolara's son?"

"Yes, I am," I responded, somewhat less triumphantly than I had imagined I would.

He took his time before replying, probably focusing on dumping enough endorphins in his system to stem the tide of pain. Eventually, he struggled up to sit on the floor, propped up against the red brick wall, looked up at me and said, "I regret nothing. I did what I had to do to advance our people." A rill of blood and clear liquid poured down the side of his cheek like unholy tears.

Weak, I hobbled past the bloodstained couch and slumped to the ground beside him. "I don't need your regret; I just need you acknowledge your crime and then I need you to die."

He went silent again for a few seconds and then he said, unexpectedly, "I carried you when you were born, did you know that?"

Surprised, but unwilling to show it, I focused on my leaking midsection, tore open my bloody bodysuit and stared at the hole that would kill me. I was sure he was lying.

"Of course, you don't remember, but I do," he rasped. "Three months after the end of the Singularity War, just when we'd started rebuilding everything. Your mother and I were stationed in ChinoSovia. You were such a small, lovely thing then," he said. "Quiet, for a boy."

My heart went arrhythmic. The old man was confusing me. I had come prepared for him to plead with me, beg for his life, fight, rage, rampage, apologize… anything except this. I said the only thing I could think to say, which was, "Shut up."

He took a hard, long draw of air and looked at me, as though all the logic of the world were in his eyes. "You hate me for killing her, but you don't even know why I did it," he managed. I could hear the faint tremble of some long buried emotion in his words. "Do you?"

I wanted to scream that it didn't matter, that nothing he could say would ever justify what he had done. But sitting there on the floor, dying beside him like comrades on a battlefield, it just seemed easier to let him go on speaking.

"You need to understand, those were the days following the technological singularity and a terrible war with an artificial superintelligence that humanity had created with its own hands. Everyone was afraid of any kind of technology they did not understand. Governments were destroying ideas they had spent billions of dollars investing in, wiping out whole generations worth of research in a knee-jerk reaction."

"What does any of this have to do with my mother?"

"Everything," he snapped as he was seized by a sudden coughing fit. Pressurised blood vessels strained against the flesh of his forehead, and his eyes began to bulge. The nanomachines were wreaking havoc inside him. I felt an urge to tell him to rest and stop talking, but I said nothing because it was such a strange situation and there was the smell of blood around us and I was curious to know his reason, to see where he was going with his story. The coughs stopped and he continued speaking.

"In ChinoSovia we'd found a computing cluster that the independent superintelligence had been using. Your mother and I were part of the United Nations task force assigned to assess the data there and, if there was anything related to artificial intelligence, destroy it. That's where we found the Eshu Protocol."

The Eshu Protocol. All I knew about it was that it was the codename for a secret my mother had been investigating when she was killed. It was one of the few intelligible fragments of data left in her neural profile after her brain was fried with plasma. That and the fact she was absolutely convinced Professor Olukoya would kill her moments before she died.

"What was it?" I asked. There was a strange tugging sensation coming from my wound with every breath I took, reminding me that I didn't have much longer to live.

He coughed and said, "It was a detailed methodology for the superintelligence to easily give itself a physical body and self-replicate using programmable nanomaterials—the first quantum wellstone. It was almost complete. We were lucky. If the superintelligence had completed it, humanity would have surely lost the war. When we found it, your mother wanted us to destroy it according to our mandate, but that would have been a terrible waste. An act of people without vision. Without ambition. I could not let it happen."

He stopped talking and I turned my head to see if he was still alive. He was shaking. I could tell he had dumped all the endorphins he could afford and the pain was still permeating through. Soon he would not be able to talk.

"The world goes through cycles." He spat the words out through tight lips. "It has history and it goes through cycles. And the history of mankind is the history of technology. When each new technology comes, it comes with a shift in our social and economic systems. There was a time when people like us were treated as subhuman and either carted off as slaves or colonised because we lacked the technology to defend ourselves. And even after that terrible time, we kept approaching technology and development from the wrong direction, constantly playing catch-up with other nations while they constantly sprinted ahead, leaving us in a constant state of underdevelopment. What we needed to do was stop running a race we had already lost and start preparing for the next race; creating the next technological revolution. And the Singularity War gave us that opportunity on a silver platter. We were presented with a new technology, one with which we, the African people, could build the future on our own terms, once the initial technology paranoia that was sweeping the world subsided. We had the chance to ride the crest of the technological cycles and socioeconomic hegemonies that had perpetually left us disadvantaged and jump into the future headfirst instead of being left clutching at the tail again."

He shook his head. "So when I insisted we not destroy the quantum wellstone and Lara said she was going to report me to Accra operations office, I did what I had to do."

Every blood vessel in his body seemed visible now and he was shaking more violently. Very soon there would be too much pain pressure for him not to vent it out with a scream.

"You killed my mother," I said, "just so you could hide the Eshu Protocol data and bring it back to Nri-Odua, to share with the rest of Africa?"

"Yes. And I do not regret it. Look at what we built from it; an entirely new industrial age of which we are still the custodians. For the first time in the history of humanity since mankind first became a global community, a nation of African people are the dominant hegemony on the planet. It was worth it."

"No. Not if it's based on a lie, on theft, on murder."

I heard his laboured breathing and wincing and wondered how

much longer he would hold on. How much longer I could hold on.

"All great nations are built on some injustice," he rasped. "The Mongols built an empire through mass murder. Caesar's disregard for democracy gave us the Roman Empire. The Americans built an agricultural base economy on slave labour. The Chinese great leap forward came at the cost of mass starvation. I'm sorry, Yemi, but Omolara's stubbornness made her death a necessary and sufficient condition for the African technological renaissance."

Angry and too weak to argue with him, I spat out the only thing I could think to say.

"Fuck you."

The edges of the world were blurring and my Lifedock readings were no longer making sense in my head.

"It was not easy for me," he responded. "But suffering is always necessary for progress. This… is the way of things."

I would have loved to tell the professor just what his vision had cost me personally in pain, but even in his agony, holding hands with death, all he wanted to do was explain, not express shame or remorse or anger. In his mind, nothing but an inflexible iron conviction prevailed, and much of my hate for him melted into pity.

"You are a sad, sad man," I said.

He said nothing, but made a sound like a muted whimper. Looking up, I saw a shaft of red sunlight stab into the house through a window, reminding me that there was more world outside. It made me think of the green, green trees and the dusty, bumpy road to Ijebu-Ode. Then, suddenly, I remembered that if I could just get to the illuminated magnetic hyper-expressway, my direct neural link would auto-connect to the national emergency services network and my Lifedock distress signal would automatically guide my pod to the nearest rectification specialist station with high priority. Perhaps, if I could find a first aid station here or nearby with enough bioplastic sealant to stop the precious fluid loss, I could remain alive long enough to make it onto the hyper-express. I rose to my feet and began to hobble towards the beaded entrance, then turned back to face professor Olukoya.

"You don't deserve the dignity of dying beside me."

He muttered unintelligibly to himself. The nanomachine-induced agony had fully blossomed in his blood.

I thought my way fully into the AI of the house, ignoring the noisy emergency signals it was transmitting. Out here in the countryside, it would take at least an hour for someone to manually interpret the signals and dispatch a police android. I requested first aid and the system guided me to the guest bathroom, just in front of the curtain of beads I'd stumbled through on my way in.

My vision narrowed to a tunnel. I entered the bathroom with a wince and saw the holographic first aid display panel. It was very modern, the kind I had only seen in the new federal facilities on the 453rd floor of the Lagos supercity. I thought through it quickly, ignoring the genetic analysis menu and the neural pathway modifier menu and going right to the inventory menu, where I requested saline solution and bioplastic gel. They slid out through a recess in the wall. I removed my hand from the hole in my belly, trying not to think too much about how close I was to dying already. I took the bioplastic gel and sprayed it into the hole. Coffee coloured foam filled it and blossomed at the charred edges of the wound.

In the pause, I considered the kit menus I'd just seen and the things the professor had just said. A question crystallised in my mind. I felt my heart start to pound in my chest and tried to use my neural implants to think it back to a steady rhythm. But the question remained, and now I had to know. Even if I died here I had to know.

I thought the display back to the genetic analysis menu.

It requested a blood, hair or saliva sample, a green holo-image pointing at a small black circle beside the display panel. I smeared my bloody right hand over it and the menu lit up with a green progress bar. It only took three silent seconds to complete.

My ears picked up the call of pigeons to each other outside. My mind followed the steady, insistent static hum of the professor's home network AI. My heart slowed to a sick thud, despite neural regulation.

The progress bar reached the maximum and the results parsed out directly from the kit to my mind, knocking me to the floor and clearing what was left of my vision.

Your mother and I were stationed in ChinoSovia.

I commanded my neural implants to stop blocking the pain, to flood my brain with nociceptin and atriopeptin, induce vasodilation and flush out the endorphins.

It was not easy for me, Yemi.

The pain washed over me like salty ocean surf and threw my Lifedock readings into disarray.

I carried you when you were born, did you know that?

I wanted to suffer. I wanted to die. I wanted to lie on that wet bathroom floor and let everything that made me *me* leak out onto the cold tile floor, bleeding and bleeding until there was none of the horrible man that I now knew to be my father left inside me.

Wednesday's Story

My story has a strange shape to it.

It has a beginning and middle and of course, I need not tell you that it has an end because it is the nature of all things to end, especially stories. But this story... well, it bunches up in places and twists upon itself in ways that no good story should. The sharpness of its arcs flare and wane in unexpected places because it is a story made of other stories and there are times when partway through telling it, I could swear I did not truly know it because I am made of so many other stories too. This story is badly shaped, but it is uniquely my story, and the burden of its telling is and always will be mine to bear.

My story has two beginnings, I believe. One of them, appropriately enough, is another story; the story of Solomon Grundy. My siblings and I have told his story before, we tell his story all the time, we will tell his story again. Men also tell each other the story of Solomon Grundy, but they never tell it well. How can they? They are not made of stories as we are.

This is the story men tell of Solomon Grundy:

> *Solomon Grundy,*
> *Born on a Monday,*
> *Christened on a Tuesday,*
> *Married on a Wednesday,*
> *Ill on Thursday,*
> *Worse on Friday,*
> *Died on Saturday,*
> *Buried on Sunday.*
> *That was the end,*
> *Of Solomon Grundy.*

I've always thought that was a particularly poor story. I mean, I know it's really a children's rhyme but it's a children's rhyme that purports to tell the story of Solomon Grundy, is it not? Well, consider it: what does it really tell you anyway? Besides the fact that Solomon Grundy was a Christian man who married a presumably Christian woman, fell ill and then died of some unspecified illness. As far as stories go, it has a good, linear shape but it tells you nothing worth knowing. It doesn't tell you that Solomon Grundy was a tall, kind man. That he had firm, skilled hands possessed with a grim determination. That he loved and he suffered and he laughed and he fought. It doesn't tell you that he was the child of a runaway Ifá priestess-to-be and a caddish English boatswain. It doesn't tell you that he had a shock of curly brown hair and honest, brown eyes. It doesn't tell you that he loved his wife more than life itself and that he held her desperately in his thickly muscled arms as cruel injuries slowly withdrew the life from her. It doesn't tell you that she died a few days and an eternity before he did and it certainly doesn't tell you that between Wednesday and Thursday, during the long, dry harmattan of 1916 Solomon Grundy stopped time.

What the hell kind of story is that anyway?

This is how my story ends:

I stab Solomon Grundy with the emerald timestone and he stumbles back with a shocked and disbelieving look in his eyes. He falls down and writhes on the floor in pain as the timestone communes with his blood and the gears of time correct themselves in his world, pulling him back into it. The correction becomes a glistening black hole in the floor beneath him that looks like the pupil of an ancient eye behind which despair, disease and death are waiting for him. He sinks into it muttering her name and is gone with a wet, slimy sound leaving only the glimmering timestone on the ground. When he opens his eyes, he is back in the forest, it is Thursday and it is over. In tears, I fall to the floor and cry out. Each wail is an exorcism of personal failure; each tear is an excision of regret for what I have done.

The second beginning of my story is in darkness. A darkness of place and a darkness of mind. At least this is where I think it should begin. I am unsure.

My siblings and I have just finished telling a story. It is a strange and sad story but it is a good story because we told it well. Perhaps we told it too well. A thin layer of it lingers on my skin like patina and irritates me.

This is the story we told:

A young Calabar girl named Emeh was kidnapped and violated in unspeakable ways by a self-appointed holy man. She died of her injuries a few days later but the holy man went unpunished because he had friends and family in high places. The girl's father mourned all he could and when that was not enough, he spent all he had in order to take cruel revenge on the holy man. When the deed was done, he found nothing but madness waiting for him on the other side of retribution. He wandered into a forest,

57

naked and insane and was never heard from or seen again.

In the silence after we have told the story, the darkness of it, of the world we chronicle, seeps into my mind and soon becomes overwhelming. I need to do something. To tell is no longer enough. I light myself a cigarette using one of the candles on the table around which we are seated and ask my brother Sunday, who is the most knowledgeable of us all, a question. "The ÒrìSà once told me that we can go into the world of men by using the timestone to pierce holes in the spaces between us. Is this true?"

He regards me suspiciously, the turn of his head dragging his long, flowing beard across his kaftan. "Wednesday, pay no attention to anything that falls from the lips of an ÒrìSà; it is not the mandate of Days to go into the world of men."

The end of his sentence is the beginning of a speech I have heard before. I know it well. My brother's eyes are the clear green of the sea in the places where it kisses a forest island and his hair is greying at the temples like a cloudy afternoon. His green eyes hold me captive as he tries futilely to make me understand the importance of a principle I have already decided to betray.

"I understand our place brother, truly, I do. I am only asking if what they say of the timestone is true," I lie to make him stop lecturing.

The timestone sits at the centre of our table like an exotic ornament, between two ornate pewter candelabra that cradle the candles that provide all the light we have, all the light we have ever needed. Its emerald edges glint in the candlelight and remind me to look at my brother again. By this time, all our siblings are staring at us, wondering what I am getting at, what will happen, what Sunday will say. Thursday's gaze is hard, like moonbeams falling through cloudless sky and onto a cliff. Tuesday's pale fingers are caught in her lustrous auburn hair like she was braiding it and suddenly forgot how, giving the confused look she wears on her freckled face a powerful puerility. Friday's stare is intense and focused beneath his thick afro. Saturday seems like she might cry, or scream, or do something strange that is neither but both at the same time. No one else seated at our grand, intricately-patterned mahogany table, our vastly varied faces illuminated by candlelight, looks at me directly, but look they do.

"The question you ask worries me, sister," Sunday says to me, his eyes overflowing with rebuke and suspicion, as though I were a young boy laughing at his own father's funeral. Saturday turns her face away from us.

I say, "Then worry no longer, brother. I shall ask no more," as I toss my cigarette to the floor and stomp it out with my heel.

"Very well," he responds stiffly.

An awkward silence follows.

"Let us tell another story," Friday begins. His voice is a roiling bass that makes me feel like my skin is a thin sheet of metal, vibrating with his sound. "Monday, choose a story for us to tell and hear."

Monday nods gently. I watch him take the tip of his moustache between the thumb and index finger of his right hand and begin to twirl the edge of the thin thing. The lines around his eyes deepen as he considers all the days of the lives of men that have been and will be, seeking out a story for us. He seems to shrink in his fitted pinstripe suit and then, in an instant, he expands with choice, passing the story we all know he has chosen for us to hear and tell. I close my eyes and receive it violently, as a vision.

In it, I see a large, ochre-skinned man in ripped khakis kneeling in the forest, an injured woman in his arms. She is naked and her skin is the dark purple of bruises. There are multiple stab wounds clustered around her swollen belly, the whites of her eyes are shot through with red, and blood is leaking from her broad nose, her round mouth, the cloudy beds of her short fingernails. The vision starts to warp as Monday begins to tell his part of the tale, speaking the story into existence, locking the events that have occurred and will occur into place.

I feel like ash is blowing into my mouth, the heat from the candles is burning my thin skin. I struggle to hold on to the vision but the story has become a sea of pain and sadness, choppy and grey.

Monday says, "*Edward Grundy only ever set foot on the soil of the land that would become Nigeria once. He arrived aboard the RMS Ananke in June of 1896, and after offloading his vessel's cargo at the port of Lagos, he and his crew mates went off to a local colonial tavern for drinks and rest. There, drunk and taken with well-aged lust, Edward set his eyes on a young woman who worked in the kitchens. Her name was Bamigbàlà and he forced himself upon her behind the lounge. By the time the RMS Ananke sailed off for Liverpool three days later, he had forgotten the incident and Bamigbàlà was with child. She put to bed nine months later, on a Monday.*"

Monday stops speaking and my head feels light, like the petal of an old flower. Tuesday clears her throat, readying herself for her part of the story. Then she says, "*The tavern owner, the Viscount Sydney Phillips, was livid when he discovered Bamigbàlà's pregnancy and the circumstance by which it came to be, but he did not cast her out for he had taken her in as a runaway several months ago and did not wish to have the death of an Englishman's child, any Englishman's child, on his hands. And so when the child was born, he named him Solomon in the hope that he would be wiser than his father, gave him his father's family name and had him baptised into the body of Christ on a Tuesday.*"

Tuesday stops and turns to me. I close my eyes, resisting the story but instinct and duty move my lips and I begin to speak. "*Solomon grew up well and strong, mentored by the Viscount and well cared for by his loving mother. She taught him the names of the roots and the trees and the rivers and the wind while the Viscount taught him archery and bookkeeping and loyalty and an Englishman's confidence. The Viscount's head servants began to fear that their master would leave the management of his property and affairs to Solomon when he retired, for the tavern had grown to become a famous lodging and it was clear that in all of Lagos the Viscount would find no fitter hands to manage it than Solomon's. They plotted against Solomon in secret.*

In time, Solomon fell in love with one of the Viscountess's hand maids, Atinuke, and she with him. They would often go into the forest where he would show her the secrets his mother had shown him—the ways of conversing with the old spirits, of communion with the youthful winds, of dancing with the senescent rivers. Some nights they would swim and drink fresh palm wine and make love under the moon's tender gaze before returning to the lodging. Eventually, with the Viscount's blessing, they were married, on a..."

I freeze midsentence because I know what comes next, what Thursday will say when I stop. This is a dark, dark story; full of pain and suffering. I keep thinking I can stop the pain from blooming on the horizon of their reality like an evil sun rising. I know it is not my place, the story will happen, is happening, has already happened. Ours is but to hear and tell. I know, I know, and yet, I am overcome with the need to try to stop this terrible story from being. I open my eyes and conclude that it must be done. This is the time, and this is the story.

Sunday, sensing something strange in my sudden silence shoots me a sharp look, and we lock eyes, a frown of unease chiselled onto his face and a grimace of determination onto mine. I act before he can, leaping out of my chair and onto the table. I seize the timestone from its silver base, raise it high above my head and bring it down onto the table, stabbing the narrowed, empty space between Sunday and myself. Everything stops. A hyperborean frost grips my hand and I let go of the timestone. It remains in its place, suspended above the heavy table. Monday is caught mid-protest, his lips parted. Sunday is atop the table, his right hand reaching for me and his face crumpled. Tuesday's mouth hangs open and Thursday's chin rests on the tip of his palms. Friday is halfway between sitting and standing. Saturday's arms are thrown in front of her in some strange motion. All their eyes are locked onto me but they are all frozen in place, like statues.

In the wounded space between Sunday and I, a filmy blackness is spreading like poisoned blood. It expands and expands and expands until it is a hole wide enough for three gluttonous men to fall through.

I remove the timestone from the centre of it slowly. The blackness ripples but does not retreat. I dip my fingers into the darkness and the chill I felt initially returns like a persistent suitor. This time I do not withdraw from its frosty caress. I lean forward, letting my hand sink deeper and deeper. Beyond the cold is warmth, the warmth and humidity of tropical night. I continue to lean in until my face is only half a breath away from the blackness and then I let myself fall into the inky sea that fills the hole I have carved between worlds, focused only on the image in the vision from Monday's story, using the pain of its characters as a beacon to guide me to a reality shore nearby.

The dark, woody, warm forest wraps itself beneath my feet, above my head, before my eyes. It greets me in the ancient way—with a touch of wind and falling leaves - and tells me that its name is Òkeméji, because it has swallowed two hills. I offer it greetings and ask it where the man carrying the wounded woman in his arms is, was or will be. I am not sure where exactly I have inserted myself into the story; I only know that I have arrived, as I must, on a Wednesday.

Òkeméji tells me that there is a couple bathing together in the river that flows between its two hills. It asks me why I have come and why I seek them. Clutching the timestone close to my chest, I simply say, "It is an urgent and desperate matter."

I realize that I am near the beginning of the bad part of the story, the part near the end of Wednesday and the start of Thursday but feel that I may yet be able to save Solomon and Atinuke from the suffering that is to come. I beg Òkeméji to guide me to them quickly and it answers reluctantly with the falling of a branch from a nearby Iroko tree.

The branch is thick and brown and solid and seems shaped like a man in the dim light of the night forest. It begins to bend and twist and warp, as though it is writhing in pain or pleasure or perhaps both. The branch's body becomes definitively human: old, wrinkled and very hairy. The old man that was a branch rises to his feet on stilt-like legs, leaning forward as though he is always about to fall over. His face is not at all handsome. It looks like a face that has been cut away from one man, stretched over the skull of another and weathered in the desert sun. Forced to fit. Distorted. Beaten. Ugly. He stretches his arm forward and it instantly begins to burn like the finest quality firewood, illuminating the dark forest before us. This is the Iroko-man. We have told his story before, we tell his story all the time, we will tell his story again, my siblings and I. The Iroko-man is a cruel man, as cruel as tree can be.

This is the story of the Iroko-man:

There was once a village where the women had been barren for many years and had forgotten the sound of crying children. The women of this cursed village stripped themselves naked and went together into the forest, seeking the venerable and powerful Iroko to beg for help, for children. The tree that was the Iroko-man asked what gifts they would offer him if he indeed chose to help them. The naked and barren women desperately cried out the names of the things they possessed, hoping one of them would entice the Iroko-man to aid them: Yams, kolanut, mangoes, goats, mirrors, palm wine. One of these women - Oluronbi - being the poor wife of a wood-carver, and owning nothing of value, feared that the Iroko-man would heed all but her and so she promised that once she began to bear children, she would bring the Iroko-man her first child. The Iroko-man agreed. Within a year, the barren women were barren no more, and the most beautiful of all the children was the daughter born to Oluronbi. When the other women took their promised gifts to the Iroko-man, Oluronbi did not take her beloved daughter. She bore three more children. Several years passed and as time went by, so did memory.

One day, Oluronbi, forgetting her debt, passed through the forest on her way to visit her sister and the Iroko-man seized her for what was owed to him. He changed her into a small sad bird, and cursed her to sit on the branches of his tree singing:

One promised kola,
One promised a goat,
One promised yams,
But Oluronbi promised her child.

The wood-carver went seeking his lost wife and when he heard the bird's song, it occurred to him what must have happened. He went home and carved a doll of fine dark wood so that it resembled a real human child, placed a gold chain bearing his daughters initials around its neck and wrapped it in beautiful aso-oke. Then he went into the forest and laid it at the foot of the tree in order to trick the Iroko-man into believing it was Oluronbi's child.

When men tell the story of the Iroko-man, they say *he took the doll into the body of his tree, tricked into believing he had Oluronbi's daughter, and returned Oluronbi to her former form. They say she returned home and never entered the forest again, living happily ever after.*

This is a lie.

When I and my siblings tell the story of the Iroko-man, we tell the truth: *that he laughed at the wood-carver's attempted trickery—how can a tree be tricked with wood? That he only took their wooden doll and returned Oluronbi to her former state as part of a trick of his own. That he let her go only so that she could watch as he possessed her husband's body in the dead of night and using the wood-carvers hands, hard and steady as an Iroko tree, strangled their three children. That the Iroko-man, still possessing Oluronbi's husband, beat Oluronbi to death with a log of sandalwood and carved his name into her belly with a chisel. That only when this was all done did the Iroko-man leave the mind of Oluronbi's husband to witness the work of his hands. Weeping followed, then insanity and soon after, suicide.*

The Iroko-man is a cruel man, as cruel as tree can be.

I am sorry; this story is not the story of the Iroko-man, is it? This is my story and this is the part of it where the wrinkled and naked Iroko-man is leading me to the river bank where Solomon and Atinuke are bathing, his wooden hand aflame to guide our way and his back bent like a sickle, like talon, like an unkept promise.

I watch him walk wonderingly as he silently leads me past trees taller and older than any of the men who walk the earth; past a group of cherubic Àbíkú seated upon a rock playing a game I do not know, and whom I greet in the ancient way; past a blur of leaves and branches and vines and wild creatures, some of whom I have told stories of, will tell stories of; past the paths and windings and elements of the forest itself on my way to intercept the story of Solomon Grundy.

When we reach a clearing through which I can see the moon-polished river flowing by, the Iroko-man stops and turns to me. His eyes are closed. His wooden hand is burned almost to the elbow and beneath the flame it glows the bright red of good charcoal. He opens his eyes. We stare at each other until a sentence takes his face and squeezes its words through his mouth.

"They just left here," he says, then adds, "You should not have come."

I have no chance to answer; the Iroko-man is gone with his words.

In the distance, toward the half-full moon, I can see silhouettes of people. There are more than two of them and it looks like they are either dancing or fighting. I think on the Iroko-man's words and consider the sight ahead of me and deep within, in my bone-places, I know they are fighting and I am already too late; this is the part of the story that leads to my vision. The part of the story Thursday would have told if I had not used the timestone to cleave the essence of things upon which all stories are written.

There is a sudden thunderclap so loud I believe for a second that the earth beneath my feet will split in two. Around me, a curtain of water begins to crash down angrily from the sky. I start to run along the river bank toward the silhouettes and I call out to Òkeméji to help me,

"Eater of hills, crown of the earth; please, stop them!"

I beg him to stop the fighting men before they inflict the pain and suffering Monday's chosen story would, is, has led to. Òkeméji does not answer me; the forest knows I have broken the author's law to be here, that I am perpetrating an abomination by attempting to amend the timestream, by trying to change the story.

This is the thing about stories, regardless of who tells them or how they are told: Every story is created by someone—the author and the finisher of its characters' fates.

Authors do not like their stories changed.

My legs sink into the wet soil with every step, and loose twigs slap against my flesh, slowing me down. I run and run and the silhouettes grow and grow until I can hear the thud of the men's fists striking against each other's flesh. The sky flashes electric white fangs and growls angrily like a guard dog, protecting the story from me. I know I am too late but I keep running toward them anyway, my mascara running down my face like poisoned tears.

Each time my foot sinks into the forest floor, it seems an eternity passes. I am slow. I do not know how to be in time, having existed outside it for so long. And I am being slowed even more by someone, something, everything.

Eventually, I come close enough to the silhouettes to make out three men. They are wrestling like a new-born, six-legged animal learning to walk. Solomon Grundy is the centre of the beast, I recognize him from his story. He is a large man, larger than the two attempting to subdue him. His ochre skin is slick with sweat and his Ankara shirt is torn. He pushes one of the men away from him and throws a punch into the man's gut that doubles him over. The other man has his hand around Solomon's throat and is attempting to choke him. I reach them and launch myself—the only weapon I have - at the man doubled over, tackling him to the wet, grassy ground and evening the odds. From the ground, I see Solomon lift his second attacker and throw the man over his shoulder.

I climb onto the chest of the man I have engaged. His face displays the tribal markings of the assassin's guild and in the blood-coloured whites of his eyes I can see his entire life, his story, up to and beyond the point where he and his friend accept 18 shillings from Viscount Phillip's head-servants to kill Solomon and Atinuke. I clasp my hands together interlocking my fingers and pound his face with all the strength I can muster. With every strike, I alter the shape of his story. With every hit, I try my best to change what was, is, would have been of him. The wind howls its disapproval.

My siblings and I know a lot about stories. For example: for a story to have a good shape, it must, generally speaking, be composed of three parts: The introduction, the conflict and the resolution. The resolution need not be satisfactory for the story to be well-shaped.

When I stop hitting the man, it is almost midnight, it is still raining and I no longer hear the sounds of struggle. I rise to my feet and turn to see Solomon kneeling beside the body of a woman, cradling her head in his arms. She is Atinuke his wife, she is naked and she is dying. There is a constellation of gaping, pink stab wounds surrounding her prominent navel like so many unnatural lips. I have failed. I raise my right arm, my muddy and wet sleeves weighing it down, and reach out to them as though I could will her not to die, will the end of her story to change.

"Who are you?" Solomon asks without looking up from the body of the woman he loves.

"I am no one," I say, then add, "I am sorry, I should not have come here."

Solomon pleads, his voice breaking like falling glass, "Help her. Help us."

"I can't," I start to explain.

Solomon looks up and stares at me, truly stares at me through his big, wet, brown eyes and despite (or perhaps, because of) his pain he sees me for what I truly am. There is an understanding in them that no man should have. There is the discernment that comes from constant interaction with Èlegba, the messenger, the teacher. His mother has taught him more than just the rudiments of Ifa divination; she has taught him to confer comfortably with the ÒrìSà, to see the truth of spirit-things.

Then he says in a language older than the forest, "Please, Wednesday. You can help. You have power beyond this world. Help me."

Something like lightning traces my veins when he speaks my true name and pleads with me in the ancient way. I wish desperately that I could have entered their story in time to save her. I say, "I'm sorry," and I mean it more than I have meant or will ever mean anything.

Òkeméji will not help me. Nothing in this world will. I have been neutralized like a child locked in a cage made of old giant's bones. There is now no power I can call upon here. There is nothing I can do now but go back and try to use the timestone to enter this story again, perhaps in a different place, perhaps at a different time. But even as I think this, I already know that I will never be able to change it, that the forest and the rain and the trees and the ÒrìSà and the author and finisher of all stories that is also the maker of worlds will make sure that I never change this story, try as I might.

This is the middle of this story.

It is one of many.

None of them are good.

This is what happens in every middle of this story.

Realizing that I have achieved, am achieving, will achieve nothing, I turn away from Solomon and his dying wife, pull out the timestone and jam its pointed end into the ground beneath me. Where the stone pierces the earth, a hole appears, shimmering around the edges and expands rapidly, exhaling in all directions, consuming the soil and the leaves and the water with the empty, slimy blackness that is the hole between worlds. The rain does not stop. Where the raindrops hit the blackness, they bounce away like diamonds, as pale as the reflected moonlight but only half as bright. I lean into the darkness, ready to go back when I feel a weight crash into me, throwing me into the dark pool of non-time-non-space head first. Around me, I feel a cold, liquid embrace. I see Solomon Grundy's face, silent but eloquent in its grim determination. We spin and we swirl and we blur and we fall as everything that makes us *us*, races across the emptiness until we tumble out of the blackness and onto the stone floor of the room where my frozen siblings wait for me like potent gargoyles.

We stare at each other in the stone room, Solomon and I. He should not be here. He cannot be here, out of time. If he is, then it means that time in his world has stopped, paused, waiting for him to return to it because just as a river cannot flow without the water that defines it, the timestream on which his story is written cannot go on without him.

Solomon's arms tense and his eyes are fixed on the timestone in my hand. He has seen what it is through gifted eyes blinded by pain, and he thinks he can use it to go back, to re-enter his own story and save her but he is wrong. He is as wrong as I was when I first tried to change his story. Even more. Much more.

In some middles of this story, Solomon charges at me head first so I swing my right arm behind me sharply; clutching the timestone like it is my own heart and let his skull crash into my belly, throwing me back against the cold stone wall.

In some other middles of this story, Solomon walks up to me and reaches for the timestone, trying to wrestle it from my vice-tight grip and pushing me back while pleading with me softly but insistently to let him have it, to let him try to save her.

In at least one middle of this story, Solomon sidesteps his way to the table as he asks me what will happen if he uses the timestone to re-enter his own story. While I am answering, he suddenly picks up the empty silver housing for the timestone and throws it at me. I stumble back into the wall, off-balance. Before I can react his left hand is wrapped around my throat and his right is twisting mine, trying to make me let go of the timestone.

I am not cruel. I am perhaps unwise and impulsive, but I am not cruel. I really wanted to save him, prevent the loss and the pain that now drives him to do this terrible thing. You must believe me. I could not tell and hear his story without feeling his pain, completely and truly. But I cannot let him have the timestone - it's an unspeakable thing in the hands of any man, the power to enter the spaces between stories - and I will do what I have to in order to keep it out of his hands.

There is a story men tell of the folly in trying to help another when one is not supposed to.

This is that story:

A hunter was walking through the forest after he had just killed an ostrich—rare and special game—which he was taking home for his wife to cook. He came upon a dragon trapped beneath a fallen Iroko tree. The dragon groaned and wailed in pain for he could not free himself from his plight. The hunter was wary but filled with pity at the great beast reduced to such a state. He observed for a while with keen eyes and then he took mercy upon the beast and helped raised the fallen tree, freeing the dragon. Once free, the dragon growled and grabbed him, pulling the hunters head towards its maw. The hunter protested, but the dragon only said, "All dragons eat men. It is our role in this world. It was not your place to free me. No good deed goes unpunished!" The hunter pleaded desperately, reminding the dragon of his kindness until the dragon finally relented and agreed that he would wait and let the next three travellers they met in the forest decide the hunter's fate.

The first traveller was a tired old horse. The horse said that when she was young, she carried her crippled master wherever he desired. But when she grew old, her bones tired and weary, her master cast her aside in favour of a new horse. The horse told the dragon to eat the hunter for his naivety and reminded him that no good deed goes unpunished.

The next traveller was a tired old dog. The dog, when told the events that had occurred and asked what should become of the hunter, said that when he was young he herded for his master but then when his teeth fell out his master threw him out, for it is the nature of men to replace the things they use, without care or kindness. The dog told the dragon to eat the hunter for his naivety and reminded him that no good deed goes unpunished.

The third traveller was a young tortoise. The tortoise considered the situation and then said that it could not decide unless it saw things exactly as they were initially for reconstruction is better than testimony. The dragon put its neck below the Iroko branch and the hunter trapped it beneath the tree as it was before. The dragon then asked the tortoise its opinion now that it could see the situation. The tortoise only turned to the hunter and said, "You're free now, go."

The hunter, overcome with gratitude told the tortoise to come home and share the rare and delicious ostrich meat with he and his wife as thanks for saving his life. The tortoise agreed and went home the hunter. When the hunter told his wife what happened, she was enraged, insisting that there was no need to share precious ostrich meat with the tortoise. She insisted that if they killed the tortoise, there would be more ostrich meat for them and they could also have delicious tortoise soup for a week. The hunter argued with her for a while but in the end, being a hunter, he did what came naturally to him, what his role in life dictated he do. He killed the tortoise who with his dying breath croaked, "Indeed! No good deed goes unpunished."

I have never liked that story but it is all I can think about whenever I reach this part of my own story, Solomon Grundy's story, where a desperate and wild Solomon is trying to wring the life from me, the feel of his fingers around my neck as uncomfortable and painful as an unrequited kindness.

All the middles of this story converge at this point: Solomon pulls back and then pain explodes in my side. Solomon's arm ripples as he punches me in the gut. I watch the waves of skin ride his body as everything seems to slow down, even though that is not possible in this place. It only seems slow because I am suddenly hyperaware of what is happening to me and I am resolved to stop it.

I am not a skilled fighter, I have never been in combat before this story, but I have told many stories of great warriors and little bits of their skill have settled somewhere in the essence of me like fine layers of dust deposited over many, many years.

All great warriors move like dancers. Every disciplined fighter is elegant. I lean back into the wall and brace myself against it, lift my knee to my chest and throw my right foot forward in a vicious front kick that crashes into his chest like heartbreak, shoving him back and away from me. I slide forward and jam the pointed end of the emerald stone into Solomon's belly, creating an instant waterfall of blood. He stumbles back with a shocked and disbelieving look in his eyes. He falls down and writhes on the floor in pain as the timestone communes with his blood and the gears of time correct themselves in his world, pulling him back into...

Wait.

I'm sorry; I've already told you how this story ends haven't I?

Forgive me; the shape of my story makes it easy to get lost. Although I must say, no story truly ends where it does. We choose our endings and I only end this one here because this is the point at which it merges again with the story men tell of Solomon Grundy. His wound becomes infected, he suffers a fever and delirium, dies and is buried soon after just as the rhyme says. There is nothing interesting to tell beyond the ending I have chosen for you. And even the most interesting parts of my story, Solomon Grundy's story, once ended, like the soft, diffuse darkness of dawn, will eventually become pale and fade to the eternal salty grey of lost memory.

So...

If I have already told you how the story ends then which part of the story is this now?

I'm not sure.

I think this is the part of the story between the last written word and the bottom of the page on which it is written; the space between the breath with which a narrator exhales the final word of the story and his next in which there is no story; the distance between the height at which belief has been suspended and the solid, hard floor of reality; the empty, fluid places where for what is even less than a moment, the characters, the audience, the narrator and the author of a story can all become equally real to one another, become intimately aware of one another and maybe, just maybe even become one another, depending on the shape of the story.

The Harmonic Resonance Of Ejiro Anaborhi

The spindly, sleek ship hurtled forward at hyperliminal speed, blurring its own intricately patterned design in six dimensions and wrecking the fabric of space-time in its wake. Its captain adjusted the dial on the control panel, accelerating the ship three thousand lightspeed units faster in Planck time. Reality shifted.

The sphere that was chasing the ship matched their maneuver and kept the distance—if it could still be called that—between them, unchanged. The sphere suddenly added an extra-dimensional rotation to its motion and burst ahead with a surge of energy that set off a singularity event behind it. It slammed itself against the ship finally, throwing off gigantic streams of pure energy, and latched on to it with long, spiny hydra-like tendrils that branched into manifold others.

The sphere began to consume the ship in a dazzling display of fractured light and twisted gravity, tendrils reaching into it like the fingers of some monstrous creature seeking sustenance. The ship's captain, in a panic, condensed every aspect of themselves into one place for the first time since they'd first gained super-sentience. They could not let the ship be taken. If the object it carried fell into the hands of the beings that controlled the sphere, every conscious aspect of the universe could become a weapon in their hands. It was better if all was lost; destroyed forever. The object pulsed a thought in agreement with them. They resonated with resolve. This would be the final act of the Great War. It had to be done.

The captain pushed a gray dot above the main control panel and the universe stood still for the most minuscule of moments before a bright azure stream of pure plasma tore its way through the core of the ship, expanding at imperceivable speeds. In a flash, it obliterated the ship, the sphere, and everything within a five-hundred-galaxy radius before finally pausing to allow something like an explosion occur. Time and space became shrapnel. Pressure and temperature became meaningless abstractions in a bubble of broken reality. The universe trembled.

"Ejiro!"

. . .

"Ejiroghene!"

Her mother was in the kitchen. She could tell because once she stopped reading and allowed her senses re-engage with her environment, she could smell the unique crayfish, *atariko, rigije* spice, and *beletete* leaf combination that told her mother was preparing *banga* soup. Other dishes, too, perhaps. And that meant her mother probably needed help.

"Ma!"

"Come and help me take these tomatoes to grind in Auntie Imoke's house!"

Ejiro tossed her copy of *The Passport of Mallam Ilia* onto the bed and sighed. "I'm coming, Mummy!"

She hated being interrupted when she was fully immersed in a book, especially one as fascinating as *Mallam Ilia*, but mothers could not be ignored by their preteen daughters. Life in Nigeria simply did not work that way. Especially not in Warri, oil company family camp or not. The price for any sort of perceived misbehavior or disrespect would be paid in vicious slaps and caustic insults, perhaps even, if her mother felt sufficiently offended, in lashes of the dreaded water cane: Doctor-Do-Good.

She rose, threw a faded *okrika* Tina Turner concert T-shirt over her red and yellow wrapper-clad body, slid her feet into her brown sandals, and ambled her way from her room to the kitchen where her mother was waiting with a ladle in her right hand, a bowl of half-made *eba* in her left, and a frown on her face. Her hair was matted to her forehead and sweat rolled down her rosy cheeks in little rills.

"Ejiro, since when did I call you?"

"Sorry, Mummy, I was wearing my shirt."

"Ehn! Your shirt," her mother parroted, the frown on her face adjusting to allow some skepticism to be seen. "Your shirt. Five minutes just to wear shirt. Hmm."

Ejiro tensed and said, "Sorry, Mummy," then waited for something to happen, but no slaps or rebukes came.

"Okay oh. I have heard. Take these tomatoes to grind," her mother said, pointing at a green plastic bucket filled with plump tomatoes and onions and chili peppers. Ejiro released the breath she hadn't realized she was holding. The fear she'd developed for her mother, who'd become more and more of a disciplinarian as she'd approached puberty, had driven a wedge between them so large that she often wasn't sure if her mother still loved her or was merely tolerating her out of a sense of duty. But this had been the state of things for so long now that it rarely saddened her anymore.

The tomatoes made up at least seventy percent of the bucketload her mother was directing her attention to. It looked heavy. Ejiro sucked back an involuntary sigh that tried to escape her and lifted the bucket, simultaneously reaching for the cover and a piece of cloth on the floor beside it.

"Are Daddy's friends coming again tonight?" Ejiro asked. Her father had been receiving guests every day for the last week, which usually meant that there was some trouble between the local community and the management of his former employers and he was planning to do something about it. He'd retired early from a career in oil and gas law after his first novel became a surprise international bestseller, but he'd refused to move out of the company camp, opting instead for the simple life and continued service to his hometown. He'd paid out the employee house loan he took from the company and become an activist and informal community organizer and liaison, much to his former employers' chagrin.

"How is it your business, Ejiro? Are you a busybody now?"

Her mother was clearly agitated and not in the mood for answering questions for some reason, so Ejiro muttered, "Sorry, Mummy," again and made for the front door.

"Make sure Auntie Imoke puts it inside the grinder three times oh. Let it be smooth," her mother called out just before the door shut behind her.

"Yes, Mummy!"

Ejiro carried her burden into the scorching heat of Warri in July. It was evening already but it still felt like God himself was trying to bake the entire city and had been trying to do so for a couple of months. If the heat kept up, perhaps they'd be fully cooked by September. The asphalt road shimmered in places where it had begun to liquefy.

Ejiro stood in front of the house for a while, contemplating her route; searching her mind for the path of least resistance. Auntie Imoke's house was only twenty minutes away walking along the main road—not very far—but Ejiro wanted to return to her book as soon as possible and so she was considering the old shortcut she and Femi Ladipo—her neighbor and current best friend—had used often when they were still in primary school. It was a crude path that ran through the bushes in front of their houses, past the small stream and the backyard of Auntie Imoke's house, to the football field beside their primary school and linked to the main estate road that went all the way to the company offices like a sort of secret yellow brick road. Ejiro estimated that it would only take about five minutes on that path to reach Auntie Imoke's house.

She made her decision swiftly and headed for the spot where she remembered the entrance to the shortcut to be—behind the hedges two houses from the end of their cul-de-sac. She found it nearly invisible; nature, in its patient, unfailing way, had begun to reclaim what belonged to it after they stopped using it. Placing the bucket full of tomatoes, peppers, and onions on her head, a small pad of folded cloth between her crown and the base of the bucket, Ejiro ignored the overgrowth and the tall grass and started walking along what was left of the shortcut.

She had only gone a few hundred yards into the bush when she heard a whirr. At first she assumed it to be one of the susurrations of the bush choir—that strange mélange of bush baby cries, cricket chirrs, and other assorted animal noises. But after a few seconds, she realized it was no natural sound. It had the characteristic modulation of something heavy spinning violently and off-center. And it seemed to be getting louder. Ejiro stopped moving. She waited, and looked around her, over the surrounding grass, trying to pinpoint the source of the sound. It seemed to be coming from above. She looked up, scanning the pale-blue, cloudless sky. And then she saw it.

Actually, she did not see it, per se. What she saw was the trail of condensing water vapor that followed it, a geometrically precise tail riding the air.

The spinning object crashed into the bush only a few yards away from the path ahead of Ejiro and threw up a ten-foot-tall plume of sand, dust, grass, and water vapor, leaving a small crater where all these things had been. Ejiro gasped and stood rooted to the spot, transfixed by what she had just witnessed, wondering if she had imagined it or if an object had truly fallen from the sky.

When shock finally let go of her mind, she crouched, took the bucket off her head, and placed it on the path beside her. For a second, she was sure she would turn and run back home, but something powerful drew her to the place where the object had fallen, like she was caught in an intense magnetic field, or lost in the plot of a particularly compelling story.

Adjusting her wrapper, she approached the site of the crash slowly, cautiously, trampling over grass that bowed away from the crater. When she reached the center of the small crater, she saw the object. It was a small, bluish metal item, rectangular, with smooth edges. About the size of a Sony Walkman but flat, like plywood. Intricate patterns were carved onto it—strange, ornate designs unlike any Ejiro had ever seen, read about, or even heard of. She thought it looked like it was meant to fit into something else, something larger. Perhaps it was a controller for equipment from the oil processing plant or a component of some aircraft's fuselage or . . . something else.

It didn't give off any steam and there were no streams of condensing vapor around it anymore. Somehow it called to her, soundlessly but insistently, little pulses in her mind that made her want to take it into her hands. Compelled, Ejiro reached out to touch it.

The moment her thin fingers made contact with the object, a wave of something electric went through her and the world around her suddenly exploded into a hazy, woolly, and indistinct womb of pseudo-reality, as if space and time around her had become fluid. Ejiro gasped.

She felt diaphanous, as if her body were constantly melting into and out of her environment in some kind of unnatural equilibrium. It was the most bizarre feeling Ejiro had ever experienced in her life and it produced a sensation so anomalous that her mind, desperate to anchor itself, reached out for something familiar. She found herself thinking of home, of being back in her room, of reading her book.

And then, just like that, she *was* there, lying on her bed, her book held in front of her and the smell of degraded paper, adhesive and ink in her nose as her eyes consumed the words of Mallam Ilia's final contender for the hand of Zara, the daughter of the Prince of Tuaregs: *Your knife can do nothing to me. I have swallowed the medicine against steel.*

But Ejiro was still in the bush, too.

She could see the injured grass and soil surrounding the object in her hands superimposed over the words of the book, could still smell the distress chemicals released by the damaged grass as well as the comforting scent of the old paper. It was no illusion. All her senses were aware of what was happening in both places. *She was in both places at the same time.* Her head spun with the realization. It was impossible, but it was happening. She was basking in inconceivability. She was experiencing a multiplicity of self. She was in two places at the same time. *She was in two places at the same time!*

When she sensed something like approval from the object in her mind, the strangeness of it made her pull hand away. Regular reality re-crystallized around her. She was herself again, just herself. In the bush. Only in the bush. Ejiro's mouth hung open like one of the roasted fishes on a spike that she saw at Effurun Market.

Ejiro ruminated on the moment that had just gone by, within the embrace of which she had achieved what felt like some measure of omnipresence. And even though the object seemed to have a sort of life of its own and she had no idea what it had just done to her, she knew she liked it. She liked it a lot. And she knew the first person she just had to tell about it . . . as soon as she finished grinding the tomatoes and peppers for her mother.

Night had fallen and Ejiro was sitting on the floor in the narrow corridor just outside the living room of their three-bedroom bungalow, anxiously waiting for her father's meeting to end so that she could tell him about the strange object she'd picked up on the way to Auntie Imoke's house. He was the only one who would believe her story. He always listened to her. Her mother, if she told her about the object, would think either she was insane or that the object belonged to an evil spirit and she was in need of prayers and deliverance at the hands of their local pastor. The object, now wrapped in the piece of old Ankara cloth that she'd used as a pad between her head and the bucket, was under her bed. She could almost feel its presence pulsing against her mind, calling her back to it, asking for contact again.

Her father's meeting had been going on for almost two hours and her mother had already served the *eba* and *banga* soup as well as white rice and chicken stew for those who preferred it almost forty-five minutes ago. The guests had eaten without pausing their discussions. Ejiro put her book down for the umpteenth time and peered into the living room through the partly closed door.

Most of the people in the room were men with afros and beards, holding large, brown bottles of Gulder beer. They were clustered in a sort of circle around her father who pointed at a piece of paper on a stool in front of him.

"We can block the entrance here," her father said, calmly. Ejiro knew her father well enough to see how hard he was working to keep his hands from shaking as they roved over the paper. He was not as confident as he wanted to appear. "If we get our people to block the main road here, just after the junction between the estate and town, there is no other way for the state administrator to reach the office. He will miss the opening ceremony, they won't be able to ignore us anymore, and the journalists coming for the event will have an opportunity to capture the whole protest. That will get the message across."

Everyone nodded except for one woman, the only woman among them, who had straight black hair and skin like polished wood.

"And how can we be sure the administrator's men won't just beat us or use tear gas or, god forbid, open fire?" she asked. "This is a military government, not a bunch of professional politicians, remember? And we don't have a demonstration permit."

Ejiro's father replied, "I know, but just look at the results of the last forty-two analyses we've done on Warri River. Things are desperate. In fact, just go near the riverbank and look at your reflection. Oil. Heavy metals. Our people are dying slowly and they don't even know it. We have to make a stand. Now."

"Tabuno, I know all that but that is not a plan, oh!" the woman retorted. "We all understand the situation. We want clean water too, and we will show up with our people tomorrow to demand it, but we cannot come and go and die. What do we do if they open fire?"

He sighed. "True. It's a risk but I've considered it. It's not likely. Abacha is trying to get the American government to support his upcoming elections and his supposedly peaceful transition now. Brigadier Asiru in Benin already told me all soldiers have been told to calm down and minimize negative press. Abacha really doesn't want it to look like the military is being aggressive again. The company security administrator knows this. This is our best chance. We have to take it."

Ejiro turned back to her book. They argued on for another half-hour before the meeting was finally over.

Even then, none of them was in a hurry to leave. They finished their beers, complimented her mother's cooking, made small talk. Then they made their way out in small, sober groups. Ejiro was annoyed that they were taking so long. The woman with the straight hair and the polished-wood skin was the last to leave.

When all the guests had finally gone, her mother asked her to help clear up the used dishes. She grumbled, but she did it anyway, sneaking a swig of some leftover beer from one of the guests' bottles as she loaded the tray. The taste was vile but she relished the way it made her feel: like an adult, like someone who could and should have important discussions with her father, someone who was capable of handling great, profound powers.

After depositing the last tray of dishes in the kitchen, she went over to her father, who was still in the living room, and stretched out her hand to offer him a half-eaten packet of Okin biscuits she'd taken from the kitchen. He usually smiled when she did things like that.

He didn't smile this time.

"Ejiro, what do you want?" he asked, frowning. "Aren't you supposed to be helping your mother wash plates in the kitchen?"

The silent call of the object thrummed against her mind.

"Yes, Daddy, I will wash the plates. But I wanted to tell you something first—it's really important."

He stared into her earnest eyes for a moment, then reached out and took the packet of pale brown biscuits from her, holding it up to the yellowed bulb as if he were inspecting it. The wrapper was transparent, with blue and red patterns on it. The biscuits themselves were plain and circular but had small holes through them. He took one out and ate it before forcing a smile.

"Tell me quick-quick then," he said, pulling her toward him gently so she could place her elbows on his shoulders.

"I found something today," Ejiro said, almost whispering, "something that fell from the sky. It's special. When I touched it, I was in more than one place at the same time. It was like the magic in one of your books. The one with the spirit boy in Lagos."

Her father took a deep breath and then laughed. He laughed until he started to cough, choking on the biscuit. He kept laughing until the coughs stopped and then he stood up.

"Ejiro, my dear, you have a wonderful imagination. Do you want to help me write my next novel? Or even, you know what? Write your own, be famous, like Flora Nwapa!" He laughed. "But you can tell me more about this thing you found tomorrow, okay? I have to go to my room now."

Ejiro's face flushed with frustration. "Daddy. I'm serious. It's real. I can show you the magic thing. It is under my bed. I can—"

"Please, Ejiro." Her father had already started walking toward the door. "Just show me tomorrow evening. I need to sleep now. I am tired and I have a long day ahead of me tomorrow."

Ejiro's heart thumped in her chest. She had to say something to make him listen to her. The call of the object to her mind was building. Building.

"Daddy, please listen. I was like a spirit, I could—"

"That's enough, Ejiro!" There was an edge to his voice now. "I said tomorrow. Finish washing the plates and go to bed."

She shut her eyes and bit her trembling lower lip.

Her father paused at the door and the light from the sodium bulb in the corridor poured around him, turning him into a framed silhouette as he called out to her mother in the kitchen.

"Mama Ejiro!"

"Dear?"

"I'm going to rest, I have a headache." His hand hung by his side. It was shaking.

"Okay, dear! I'm coming," her mother responded.

He disappeared into the corridor, into the light.

Ejiro stood in the living room and tried not to let the thoughts that were forming in her head take root as the mental vibration slowly evened out to a dull throb. Why did her father not want to listen to her? He always listened to her. Was her story really so ridiculous, so unbelievable? Or was it just the thing he and his friends were going to do tomorrow, the thing they had discussed at the meeting, that unnerved him so much he couldn't pay attention to her? It had to be. That was the only narrative she could string together that made sense. Still, the object that had fallen from the sky was important. She had to tell him. He would know what to do with it. But if he wouldn't listen now, then she had no choice. She would have to tell Femi tomorrow.

The next morning, she was in Femi's house. Her mother had dropped her off there before going to work since it was a school holiday and her father had left home before dawn to organize "the big rally" as she'd called it just before kissing him goodbye and begging him to please be careful.

Ejiro held the cup of iced *Bournvita* that Femi's mother had made for her a quarter of an hour ago close to her face, allowing the streams of condensing air around it to cool her cheeks. Femi's mother was seated at the head of the dining table behind the main couch where she and Femi sat. Ejiro could feel the now familiar pulsing in the back of her mind. Outside, the sun was a bright, beautiful orb high in the sky; inside, the television was a bright, beautiful distraction set in a woodgrain frame. Femi had put in a VHS copy of *The Princess Bride* when she arrived and they were pretending to watch it even though they'd both seen it over a dozen times already. Ejiro took another sip of her Bournvita. Eventually, just as the elaborate forced wedding of Princess Buttercup to Prince Humperdinck began onscreen, Femi's mother got up and went into the kitchen. Ejiro and Femi looked back at the table and then at each other.

"Now!" Femi cried, his voice almost breaking with effort to keep low. "Show me."

Ejiro reached into her backpack and pulled out the bulky wad of cloth within which the strange object that had fallen from the sky was enwombed. She set it on the small stretch of brown felt couch between them and unwrapped it slowly to reveal the rectangular object with the unfamiliar ornate patterns. It sat between them, pulsing against Ejiro's mind like an unanswered question.

Looking Femi in the eye, Ejiro noticed that something about his demeanor changed when he saw it. His joyful excitement had been replaced with puzzlement and something approximating apprehension.

"That's it?" he asked.

"Yes," Ejiro said, eager. "It's like magic. Just touch it. With your bare hand." The object pulsed agreement directly into her brain.

"I thought it would have light around it. Like power or a force field, or something."

Ejiro pointed at it, jabbing her finger in its direction. "Just touch it. You'll see."

"Okay." Femi started to reach for the object then paused. "You said it will make me be in two places at once?" he whispered.

"Yes."

"But which other place will I go to?"

"I don't know, wherever you think about."

"Even places I haven't been to before?"

"I don't know," Ejiro said. "Just think of a place you've been to before and wish you were there again or something."

Femi's apprehension appeared to be sublimating into fear.

"Just hold it before your mum comes back, Femi—you'll see," Ejiro said, annoyed at his hesitation. "You'll see what I mean."

Femi drew back his hand a little bit. "But what if something bad happens?"

"Just touch it, Femi!" she hissed. She grabbed the object from its place between them, feeling the pulse in her mind surge and fluidize her as she did so, and pressed it onto the soft, dark skin of Femi's outstretched hand.

Ejiro's mind had lost its form again, but this time, it was not as it had been the first time. Now, even more than having her very essence in flux, she felt . . . projected. Her mind, her memory, and her thoughts flowed out of her like a river that was separate from her but to which she still had access. She looked at Femi and saw herself as she never had before. Her face was smooth; dark and smooth and beautiful. Her eyes, bright as stars. Her braided hair was lovely. She felt a primal attraction to herself that made no sense and in that moment she knew. She knew she was seeing herself as he did. She was him. He was her.

Femi and her; her and Femi. They had blurred.

What is happening? they asked themself silently. Their voice was no longer a vocalization; there was no manipulation of the vibration of air. It was telepathic, the perception of their own thoughts.

I don't know. This is new.

They looked at each other, the sensation like that of being on both sides of a mirror. It was unsettling and they felt fear burble through them from the Femi aspect of themself.

The Ejiro aspect of them tightened her hand around the Femi aspect, and he calmed down instantly.

Think of a place. Any place. Any place but here.

The Femi aspect thought of his father's office where his father had taken him after school last week, given him ice cream, and allowed him to watch *Yo! Raps* on MTV. They gasped together at the suddenness of the bifurcation of perception that occurred then, the sensation of them being in the Femi aspect's father's office, sitting on the black leather office chair, staring at the turned-off television screen, a black mirror that reflected nothing.

In both the office and the living room of Femi's house, they smiled. *It works!* they exclaimed joyously to themself. *It works. Two places at the same time!*

Hearing a loud, steady noise coming from outside the office, they projected themself up from the office chair and walked toward the window. Staring down, they saw a crowd of people carrying placards and cardboard signs, chanting in unison. In front of them, a group of about forty menacing soldiers stood beside a fleet of white Isuzu Tiger pickup trucks, behind which was a long queue of cars and pedestrians—the oil plant workers and the government officials trying to get to the office, to the opening ceremony of their new office wing. The soldiers glared at the protesters while a small distance away, on a road just off the main thoroughfare, a group of journalists had made their way into the space between the workers and the soldiers and were taking photographs. At the front, only a foot ahead of the main bulk of protesters, the Ejiro aspect of them saw her father pumping his fists in time to the chants, apparently orchestrating.

They were then seized by a shared vision.

They saw themself standing at the front of the line of protesters with the Ejiro aspect's father, and they were aflame. They stood, burning, yet they were not consumed. The fire seemed to pulse, as if it were breathing. The Ejiro aspect saw herself weep tears of bright orange flame that fell from her eyes in sync with the pulsing; the Femi aspect saw himself exhale breathfuls of thick black smoke.

And then, as suddenly as it came, the vision was gone and they could see the protesters again.

The suddenness of the transition and the sensory overload it induced shocked the Femi aspect so much that he let go of the object and they disengaged. The separation occurred suddenly, a confounding compression to center, each consciousness falling into its owner like a collapsing star.

Ejiro felt momentarily disoriented, pushed too quickly back into her own self but still in both places at once.

Femi's face in front of her was frozen in a rictus of shock superimposed over the image of her father and the protesters. She let go of the object and it fell to the couch with a soft bump.

Reality normalized.

Onscreen, the movie was still playing, having just reached the part where Westley had finally rescued Princess Buttercup and was telling Inigo Montoya that he thought *he* would make a wonderful Dread Pirate Roberts.

"Wow!" Femi whispered, his face not moving much.

Ejiro did not say anything. Just a moment prior, they had shared one consciousness and the object had revealed something profound but mysterious to them, so she already knew what Femi was thinking and he already knew what she was thinking, too. They shared the pulse now, the sensation of something like a wave breaking on the shore of their minds. They did not need any more words but they used them anyway, out of habit, to confirm their thoughts to each other.

"We can get there if we take the shortcut," Femi muttered.

"Aren't you scared anymore?" Ejiro asked, remembering the sensation that had washed over her when they were joined.

"I don't know. But you felt it. You saw it. You know what we are going to do."

"Thank you," Ejiro said, expressing a calmness that she knew came not truly from within her but from the object, and a new sort of *knowing*. A knowing of the thing it was using her to accomplish. Using *them* to accomplish.

Femi nodded and smiled. "Let's go."

The two children ran like they would die if they stopped. They bounded through the bush path, each falling step synchronized with, or perhaps by, the pulsing of the object that bounced around in Ejiro's backpack, no longer touching them but still driving them. They sped past the small crater the object had created when it first arrived without even taking notice. By the time they reached the end of the road on the right of the football field where the shortcut ended, they could see that the protest had mutated from the mildly agitated standoff they'd experienced from the window of Femi's father's office into something more frenzied. The soldiers were pacing, rifles in hand. Ejiro and Femi ducked behind a hedge of rough hibiscus at the border of the bush, behind a large gutter.

"It will be hard to get near," Femi said, his eyes scanning the area for a path they could take to the front of the crowd without being seen instantly. Of course, there wasn't one. Ejiro's father had chosen this road wisely. Wide, with a block of offices on one side and thick bush on the other.

"What do we . . ." Ejiro started, but the pulsing in her mind connected her to Femi's and she stopped.

Then, together, "We wait."

They watched the crowd in the distance grow more agitated, heard the chanting get louder. A solider with a pistol in one hand and a megaphone in the other who appeared to be in command put the megaphone to his mouth, pointed at Ejiro's father, and shouted, "Oya, enough! All of you clear away from here now. Now, I said. Clear out!"

The protesters reduced the volume of their chants.

He repeated the command.

No one moved.

The commanding solider dropped the megaphone to the floor, unlatched a *koboko* from his belt, waved it at his brigade, and stepped forward into the space between the two opposing sides. At the flick of his whip, the soldiers hastily resolved themselves into three rows of about a dozen each. Some of the protesters stepped back, but Ejiro's father did not move. The advancing commander stopped about three feet from Ejiro's father.

Her father did not back down but his hand was now visibly shaking.

"Tell your people to move before we move you," the commander said, snarling.

"Oga, I don't want trouble, but government must stop allowing these people to poison our water. No cleanup, no oil."

The crowd took up the chant again, louder now, inspired by their leader.

"No cleanup, no oil."

The soldier's face calcified at the defiant disobedience. It was obvious that he wasn't used to having his commands ignored. The heat of his anger radiated out, threatening to consume the tense crowd of protesters.

"Boys," he hissed, waving the whip forward. "Clear these bloody civilians away from my sight."

The first row of soldiers marched toward the protesters and one of them hit Ejiro's father in the belly with the butt of his rifle. The protesters began shouting. The soldiers hit others in the front, lashing at them with *kobokos* and rifle butts. A few of the protesters started to retreat, falling over those behind them. The journalists scrambled forward, their bulky cameras snapping away.

Ejiro and Femi felt the pulsing in their minds amplify, the pressure of their thoughts concentrated into a single word.

Now.

They broke out from behind the bushes, running for the crowd of protesters from which a few people had begun to flee. One man in a short-sleeved white button-up shirt ran past them, turning his head in surprise and tripping over his own feet. Another man with a moustache stopped short when the children passed him, disbelief seizing his face.

A woman's voice ahead of them yelled, "Get those children out of here!" But her cry was indistinguishable from the cacophony of other desperate, angered, and defiant shouts being taken up around them.

Everyone was screaming something different, like the builders at Babel confounded by an irate God, except in this case they were not unable, just unwilling, to understand each other.

No cleanup, no oil!
Bloody Civilian!
Aluta continua!
Bastard!
Zombie-o! Zombie!
Move out! Get out!
We no go gree!

The children pressed through the dense crowd, aiming for Ejiro's father, their minds united in purpose by the pulsing, the persistent and powerful pulsing that was like an echo of the merging and omnipresence induced by the alien object that Ejiro was now reaching into her bag for.

Ahead of them, through the mass of bodies, Ejiro saw her father being pulled by a group of soldiers, their rough hands around his neck and arms, while his friends, including the woman with the polished-wood skin and straight hair, held on to his waist and thighs.

Her heart pounded louder in time with the object's increased pulsing and Femi's heavy breathing, like two musicians practicing strange music to the beat of an otherworldly metronome. She finally extracted the ornate blue object from her bag and immediately joined hands with Femi.

The last thing Ejiro saw as herself was the widening of her father's eyes when he noticed her weaving through the protesters, sprinting toward him.

Ejiro's and Femi's consciousnesses pressed together as their hands did, fusing. The object's pulse amplitude modulated itself low, to something like a silence of minds, an absolute absence of selves.

And then, an explosion of new being. They entered the indistinct womb of fluidized reality where they were both themselves and more. This time, it was not shocking or surprising to them, but comforting, like returning home.

Holding hands, they flung themself into the mass of people struggling over her father.

As flesh touched flesh, they were struck with an awareness of the Ejiro aspect's father and what he was doing here with a soldier's arm around his neck and his people's hands around his waist, people for whom he was willing to risk everything because of the call of blood, the contract of kin, the bond of belonging to each other in some profoundly elemental way and trying to help one another. They accepted her father as a new aspect, widening to accommodate him.

And once they did, the flood began.

They were aware of everyone touching her father. The soldiers, the protesters, all of them. Human minds evolved so long for rigid independence and separateness became liquid and ran together. Panic and care and love and fear and joy and violence and hope and hate and confusion and everything, *everything* flowed into place, feeding a new thing, the new *them*.

Super-sentience ignited like fire through the Ejiro aspect of the new and growing them. Then it spread through all that were in contact through skin, moving through brains, writhing around minds, twisting past perceptions, reaching out for everyone, compelling all aspects to reach out and touch more, connect with more. Their consciousnesses were like oxygen feeding a fire, allowing it to burn brighter and brighter.

Many of the spectators and journalists ran away once they saw the struggling people stop and touch one another without saying a word. A few stood around, confused.

At the center of the new and wonderful them, mind white-hot with new knowledge, new being, and new understanding, the core aspect that was Ejiro Anaborhi pulsed, calming the other new aspects of themself. And through perfect resonance with her, they felt it. They knew what they were. And what they would become. They thought of all the places they had ever been and they were there, in an instant, all of them, at the same time. The dusty streets of Katsina city, the rooftops of Bamako, the crowded Rumuokoro Market, the pale mirror surface of Lagos Lagoon. More. So much more. They saw what their fellow humans were doing to one another and it offended them, the disunity. The disappointment with discord and the need to unify that the object radiated was amplified as it flowed from the core Ejiro aspect and into them all. The drive moved through them like breath, an inhalation of disapproval at dissonance, an exhalation of desire for more unification.

In. Out.

In. Out.

They saw what they had to do, how they had to spread themselves until the day the sun would rise over a new Earth, a unified humanity, a world completely changed.

In that perfect resonance, the Ejiro aspect smiled. She closed her eyes as the ornate alien object that had fallen like an angel from the sky physically melded into her, unraveling itself like bad knitting before wrapping around and weaving back into the flesh of her forearm. Her fingers trembled as trepidation and anticipation waltzed gracefully with one another in her heart. As it became one with her, she knew then that its ornate patterns were a palimpsest, the superimposed personal markings, like fingerprints, of all the previous core aspects of what she was becoming, her ancient and alien predecessors also tasked with a great and singular duty: unify.

When the object was fully, physically one with the Ejiro aspect, they all let go of each other, no longer needing physical contact. The critical mind mass had been reached and they were linked forever, unique aspects of a new creature. Some of the aspects were unsure what had happened exactly, but they all knew, as clearly as the Ejiro aspect pulsed it to them, that nothing would be the same again.

And with that knowledge, they resonated.

Crocodile Ark

Before my mother died, she used to tell me old Yoruba folktales while we huddled around the lower platform heating vents or waited in line for rations. As with all good Yoruba stories, they were always garnished with proverbs. That's the unique thing about our stories, isn't it? The proverbs. Well, that and the tortoises. The ubiquitous tortoises. And even though, as anyone who as ever read the Achebe classics knows, proverbs are the palm oil with which words are eaten, sometimes it's the palm oil that stains your clothes and stays with you long after the hunger has passed.

My point is: many of those proverbs stuck with me long after I forgot the stories she'd used them to tell. Some even stuck with me long after she died. But one of them will probably stay with me forever. It goes: *Ònì ní ojú máa ńti òun láti gé nǹkan je, tóun bá sì ti gée je, ojú máa ńti òun láti fi síle. Ònì ní ojú máa ńti òun láti gé nǹkan je, tóun bá sì ti gée je, ojú máa ńti òun láti fi síle.* What that all means, once you manage to translate it, is something like this: *The crocodile always says it is shy to bite, but once it has bitten, it is shy to let go.*

It will probably stay with me forever because it has come to describe what happened to me. Not that I'm saying I'm a literal or metaphorical crocodile or any sort of crocodile really. It's just a proverb. Actually, maybe I *am* a crocodile and maybe, just maybe crocodile nature is human nature too. But I'm not being clear. I suppose if I'm going to tell you this story, then I have to have to tell you about Ariannamaka.

By the time I met Ariannamaka in person, she was twenty-one and we'd already been friends for two years.

Our first encounter was online, in a government sanctioned voidspace chatroom. Her family was rich; they lived up in the Chancel, where gravity had been artificially adjusted to original Earth levels for the deacons, the ushers, the committee of saints and of course, those who gave the greatest *offering* to the Prophet. Her profile avatar was beautiful but grim. In it, she wore a crop-top, and lay in a plush, purple-sheeted bed, unsmiling. I'd seen it before, that look. It was common with the girls in the Chancel, the ones brave or bored enough to surf the open voidspace anyway. But there was something uniquely fiery and intangible about her that fascinated me in the bizarre way that fires fascinate moths.

I gazed at her avatar on my portapod for a few minutes, twiddling my thumbs, and then I swiped right on her profile and sent her a private virtual reality message.

[Hi], I said.

It only took her three minutes to reply.

[Hey there], she responded.

The voice and image that projected into my mind were so clear, I knew immediately that she was using a full VR resolution portapod model that most people down on the platform would kill me for having, assuming I could ever afford it. She was short at about five and a half feet; with wide, sensual hips visible behind the flowing silver gown she wore in her VR avatar. She had a mane of wild natural hair that looked like bunched-up brambles and her eyes were oak brown. My portapod model was a cheap second-hand so I probably just looked like a nondescript, boxy and angular stock character wearing platform rags in her mind.

[What's it like, living up in the skydome, with the blessed richfolk, saints and the Prophet?] I asked, trying for sharp charm since I could obviously not impress her with my looks.

[Boring. That's why I'm in here, chatting with lowly platformers like you]. The sarcasm slid smoothly off her high resolution tongue, and into the virtual reality we were sharing.

I laughed, and we exchanged a few more VRM's about what it meant to be the last ones left, to be the future of the human race. Once she sensed that I shared some of her own sentiments, she ported me into a shielded virtual reality sharespace that she and her friends had written out of the government base voidspace network. It was only later that I realised she had been looking specifically for someone like me.

Everyone there was of varying resolutions, standing awkwardly in that dark corner of electronic shared reality. They remained silent as Ariannamaka introduced me to them one by one and when she was done, the messages started to come. Cautiously at first, then in a flurry as I echoed them as my thoughts too. Finally, Ariannamaka told me what they were planning to do and how they planned to do it. I was intrigued. I was excited. They encouraged me to join them; they said that they would need my help when the time came.

[This Ark is a corrupt, elitist system, and we have the chance to change it], Elegebde said to me, gesturing energetically with his hands. His avatar presented a high resolution, big, bulky and solid fellow with broad shoulders, brown hair just verging on black, and the kind of face I was sure people would describe as intimidating if they saw it in reality. He did most of the talking after I ported in.

[But we will need someone from the lower platforms to set things in motion. Someone the people of the platform will listen to, follow].

[The kind of person we can make you if you join us], Ariannamaka added.

Her voice was soft and pleading in spite of the harsh warping effect of the electronic VR filter convincing the Prophet's eavesdropping spies that all we said was benign.

I asked to be given a moment and thought myself out of the shielded voidspace, back into the reality of my platform bunk. I took in the dark, cramped monochromatic space; a dilapidated old metal board on the door bearing an efficiently ugly poster that reminded us that, 2077 IS OUR YEAR OF DIVINE DIRECTION. Above it, the ubiquitous image of Prophet and Prophet Mrs smiled down on our, squalid and overcrowded quarters. The other twelve people I shared Ark platform sector A-589 with were also all plugged into their own *portapods*, killing time until ration distribution. They were probably chatting up random girls on the voidspace chatrooms or worshipping in one of the prophets many VR centres and praying that they would be chosen this year in the annual *blessing of the twelve* ceremony where twelve platformers would be declared saints and asked to go up into the Chancel and serve the prophet, helping to find a new home for our species and leaving this meaninglessness behind. And make no mistake that was what it was: meaningless. I looked back down at my portapod, shook my head and thought myself back into the shielded voidspace.

[Okay. Count me in], I said.

I know now that it was a mistake, but I was sixteen. I was an orphan. I was a lower platformer. I was bored and my life seemed to have no purpose. I didn't know what I was getting into. But even though all those things are true, now that I've had time to think about it, I think the real reason I agreed to their insane plan was that Ariannamaka was just beautiful and interesting enough for me to be that stupid.

Ariannamaka told me she loved me on the day we took the Ark. The same day she also told me she was the Prophet's daughter and that Earth was still standing; that it had never been destroyed. It also happened to be the first day that we met in person.

We were in the bright electronic embrace of the Sanctum - the Ark's Control Bridge - and she had plugged her external mod disk into the Ark's central control systems. The centrifugal artificial gravity generators, the air and water processing units, the Prophet's central voidspace network - we were taking control of it all, and once the override was complete and the people of the Ark heard my voice, we would control them too. Outside, Elegbede and the others stood guard, they had killed a path to the Sanctum for us and were defending it while we jacked into the system and took over.

I had prepared meticulously for the day. I had read books; studied revolutionary histories of old Earth; wormed my way into the right circles; seeded dissent in the hearts of the Prophet's lackeys and even become Youth Leader of the lower Ark Church with the help of Ariannamaka and her rebel friends. I was primed to topple the government. Expose the prophet and his coterie. So you can imagine that being told that the Earth was still standing and that my handler and best friend was both in love with me and the daughter of the man I had learned to loathe, especially at such an inopportune time, threw my mind into something of a tailspin.

"No," I said, because it was the only thing I could think to say. I loved her, I always had but how could she be the prophet's daughter? And why was she telling me then? Everything in my head was hazy, woolly and unsubstantial.

Arriannamaka made a strange, confused noise that sounded like, "Hoin?!"

So I repeated my own confused objection, "No, Ariannamaka, no. Not like this," I said. "Not now."

Her words seemed stuck in her throat for a moment like a fluid behind a pipe constriction and then, when enough pressure had built up, they exploded out of her. "I'm sorry. It just came out of me. It's all just coming now. I mean, it's been two years, and today when I saw you, really saw you, it made everything real. I really want real. I don't care about taking control of the Ark anymore; I want to go back to Earth, to have a real, normal life with you."

I grunted in confusion. "What? Earth is gone. What are you talking about?"

She quickly flicked her eyes from me to her black mod disk plugged into the central control panel and the motion of her eyes pulled mine with them. I looked at the panel and we both saw we had six minutes and thirteen seconds before the program completed the override. Around us, the electric datascape blinked streams of binary rainbows. She turned back to me.

"Hasn't it ever bothered you?" she started to explain with a question, such a uniquely Nigerian thing to do. "That all the survivors of the Earth's destruction happened to be members of the same Church?" She pronounced the word 'survivors' as though it was not the appropriate word for what we were.

"Yes, it's a bit odd but that is just because god revealed to the Prophet the coming of the asteroid in a vision back when his heart was still clean, before the power corrupted him." I crossed my arms. "Why are you asking me anyway? This is basic Sunday school shit, and you are his daughter."

She shook her head and her hair shook with it.

"My father has never had a clean heart. He has never spoken to god. This Ark is not just unjust, it is a lie. There was no asteroid. Well, not really." She stared straight ahead and spoke efficiently, forcefully, as if the words had to come out of her then and there or they would explode inside her, the way one blurts out things that have been kept secret for too long.

"Asteroids used to hit Earth all the time, like maybe once a century or so, everyone knew it, and every few centuries, a massive asteroid would come by the planet and plop down harmlessly in an ocean or some artic wasteland. Sometimes scientists only spotted these asteroids like maybe days or a week before they made their close approaches to Earth." She paused for breath, glanced behind me, and pressed on, "My father knew all this, so when a really big one was spotted near Pluto, on a trajectory towards Earth and no one was sure how close it would come to us, he started all this shit about god ending the world and he being some modern day Noah. He rallied his followers with massive offering collections, built the Ark and brought us all into orbit here, around Mars. He wasn't the only one you know. Some governments did it too. Hedging their bets. But the asteroid just passed by Earth. It was a biosphere-altering event for sure but it didn't destroy anything. Everyone went back once it passed but my father? He just did not want to admit that he had been wrong to his followers. That his god had been wrong. So he made up the stories you heard and created the faked recordings you have seen of the Earths destruction."

"No!" The exclamation snuck its way out of me and made Ariannamaka jump; I turned around hyperventilating and saw that we had only one minute and forty seconds before the full override completed. I tried to say something but found I was only gasping until I said it again.

"No."

"It's true," she assured me.

"No." I repeated, the word, letting it explode like bomb in front of me. "No." Another explosion. "No. No. No." A chain reaction. I was shaking. I reached out and leaned on a Sanctum wall. The cool, smooth flow of the datascape passing through my hands in front of the metal panelling. My head was spinning. I understood then why my mother had given up everything she had to the prophet as offering just to be allowed a place on the Ark. She was pregnant at the time. But… Earth. It was there. We had been stuck on a metal tube in space because one man refused to admit he had been wrong about his divine delusions? My mother had died because of his lie? It was all too much.

"I will show you. Once the override is done, you will see."

"How did you know the truth?" I said, turning back to her.

"I overheard him speaking about it with the deacons three years ago. That was when I joined the movement."

"And you chose to keep it from me. From us." I stopped. "Why?"

She advanced on me with arms slightly spread, ambient light caressing her figure. She stopped an inch from my nose. There was a rush of warm blood through my ears, my heartbeat rattled despite my shock and fear. "I love you," she said, and it seemed to be a little bit of a declaration and a little bit of an apology but not quite either. "I just want to live a normal life. On Earth. With you."

I stared down at her, breathing hard, until it occurred to me that I did not even know if I wanted this thing, whatever it was she was proposing, promising. Earth was a myth, an Eden from a genesis story, a folktale told by the first ones in the belly of the lower platforms by the heating vents to children. It was green, it was wet, it was paradise, they said and I had read. But in my mind, it might as well have been Oduduwa's Ile-Ife or Plato's Atlantis. I had no qualia for it. No sense of reference. And that scared me. I had been born on the Ark. Raised and orphaned on the lower platforms. Even if Ariannamaka was speaking the truth, what waited for us back on Earth? I had no idea. I had not been afraid to die taking the Ark but when I thought about this Earth that had been dead to me and was now risen again; I felt fear like a living creature claw its way from my belly to my heart and squeeze tight.

I pushed away from her and blinked rapidly, realising the mod device would soon finalize its override. I asked her, "Who else knows about Earth?"

Her brow furrowed briefly and then she said, "No one, just my father, his wife and three deacons. Maybe a few of the older saints. My mother is in the choir but she doesn't know anything."

"Good, let's keep it that way," I said quickly, the fear and the countdown forcing the words from me. "Don't tell anyone anything; we can go back to Earth once we have control." I said. *But not all of us,* I didn't say.

We were seconds away from taking over the Ark. Seconds away from being able to take everything that made up our unjust world and make it pure. I had a devoted following of people from the lower platform who believed in the visions of the glorious future I had sold them. There would be a revolt. That much was certain. What came after was less clear. But I did not want Ariannamaka to know that so I kissed her eagerly enough for her to think all was well and set my mind back to the revolution.

Behind me, the timer ran down to zero. The flowing rivers of data in the sanctum halted around us, then exploded in a kaleidoscope of numbers and logic, green and yellow and blue and white and silver and orange, the colours flickering and flaring in fanciful fits as they first separated from and then merged back into one another to reconstitute the river of data and logic that controlled the ark, their new commands in place. I pulled away from Ariannamaka and spoke into the vocaphone, slowly, with what I imagined to be stately voice that propagated throughout the Ark, piercing into ears and virtual realities alike, through portapods and inline earphones, throwing revolution and uncertainty into the prophet's carefully constructed world of lies.

Our revolution lasted all of thirteen minutes. I guess the Prophet had grown complacent with his security, his control. Once we took control of the Ark, his lackeys surrendered without even as much as a good fight. Perhaps he had begun to believe in his own myth, his own lie and thought no one would ever usurp him. Perhaps he'd started to think he really was the god he had invented. Perhaps we had planned the entire thing perfectly, if such a thing can be said of any coup. Perhaps we were just lucky, I don't know.

He cursed us all, of course, before we turned off his private vocapohone and killed him. He said that we were children of the devil, that Satan had sent us to destroy and confuse what was left of humanity. He called upon all his people in the Chancel and implored those on the platforms to rise up and smite us. To pray that god would show them our true forms. The platformers were too busy eating the *in vitro* steak we'd sent to them from the Chancel biotech food labs to listen. We killed him in his own bed, choked him with his own collar under a blood-proof sheet.

Thirteen minutes to take the Ark. Another hour or so to quell the minor prophet-loyalists and the opportunists. Two hours after Ariannamaka told me she loved me, I was holding her hand in the Sanctum and speaking into my portapod with Elegbede and the rest of our movement. I told them what she'd told me about Earth. I did not tell them that she wanted to go back, but I asked if it was possible anyway.

[Does anyone know how disengage from orbit and pilot this thing?] I asked the voidspace full of high resolution avatars that controlled the Ark.

[I think I do,] Bamidele, the youngest one of our group said, with unusual seriousness. Raluchukwu who was overseeing the food labs for now and knew him from when they were just spoiled kids living in the Chancel, nodded sharply, a quick shake of her head to indicate she thought so too. She seemed nervous, even in virtual reality. I think they all were.

Elegbede spoke up, [Good. As long as someone has some idea, we will do it. We will go back to Earth. We will take our people home. No more of this foolish, delusional Israelite journey in space. *E don do abeg*].

No one said anything. Everyone waited for me to speak. I knew it. I had watched the balance of power in our group shift as they taught me what I needed to know to become a figure of myth and reverence down on the platforms while they plotted and planned up in the Chancel. They had watched as the fabric of my personality had slowly been straightened, dyed and embroidered with knowledge, power and self-awareness. They knew that the people of the platform would heed no one but me, believe no one but me. And without me, there would be chaos. The problem was, I knew it too. I had taken my first few bites. I knew the taste of power.

[This is a democracy now, Legbe], I said, [We will take a vote.]

[But Earth…] Arianamaka started suddenly before stopping herself. I did not look at her but I noted the other voices, especially Bamidele's, murmuring. I pressed on.

[Earth is home to the prophet. To our parents. To the people that created this corrupt system we risked everything to change. Not to me and not to you. Not to us. I have never seen its sky or touched its soil. Neither have more than three-quarters of the people on this Ark. Why do we want to give up this world we now have the power to remake into something wonderful for an uncertain one we have no power over?]

Elegbede chuckled, [You've been reading and watching too many histories, friend. What makes you think anyone will want to stay here when they know that all of humanity awaits us? That we are not the last of our kind? Eh?]

With that statement, and question, he'd showed his bourgeoisie, and that was his mistake. The others knew it was a mistake too, I think, even if they didn't know exactly why. So I pressed the issue and eventually, they agreed that a vote was the democratic thing to do. I knew they would, they believed in freedom and democracy and all that shit and that was why they'd risked everything for revolution. We agreed we would reveal the information to our people on the Ark, and let them make their decision. We would vote to decide if we wanted to go back to Earth.

I just made sure that Elegbede agreed to be the one to make the announcement; he was our leader after all, I insisted. Of course, he agreed without thinking it through all the way to the end. He always did enjoy talking, hearing the sound of his own voice. Although, I suspected Ariannamaka knew what I was trying to do by the way she unclasped her hand from mine during the discussion.

Although most of them thought the vote could go either way, I already knew what would happen. I was a lower platformer, when it came down to it. Born and raised, you understand? And I had felt that exact same fear that I knew would squeeze their hearts the moment they were told about the unknown. The same fear that had kept them, us, believing in the prophet and enduring his faith of deprivation in spite of our squalor.

Fear. It was like a shadow to a platformer. And I knew it well.

In the end, when we went to a vote, of course no one believed. No one wanted to. I'd spent two years slowly convincing them to stop bathing in the rain of lies and unfairness coming down from the Chancel. There was no way they wold believe Elegbede. It was the wrong message. At the wrong time. From the wrong messenger.

It all came back to Ariannamaka in the end. She forced my hand. They forced my hand.

I only did what had to be done.

To quote another of my mother's memorable proverbs from a story, *Ìbẹ̀rẹ̀ kọ́ l'oníse, à fi ẹni tó bá fi orí tì í d'ópin*. Which, I think means, *Starting a thing is not as crucial as seeing it through to completion*. I think it came from a story she told me about the tortoise, the squirrel and the leopard. In the story, the tortoise tricks the other animals. At the end of the story the tortoise's mother dies.

Arriannamaka, Elegbede and three others convinced Raluchukwu to try to sneak into the Sanctum, free us from Mars's gravitational embrace and set course for Earth. If not for Bamidele's quick thinking, and timely warning, they might have even succeeded. They had tried to subvert the will of the people. I had to have them killed. And have it done publicly. What else was I to do?

I did not turn away at her execution. We had equalized the gravity in the entire Ark so that from Chancel to platform, everyone had to adjust but we had the gravity in the central Chancel area reset back to Earth levels for the execution to prevent any possible blood globules leaking out of the dioxide helmets and floating up and into crevices between the panelling.

The five convicted of treason were made to kneel in the centre of a circle that included many of their friends and comrades in the lavish Chancel central area where the Prophet used to bless and ordain his selected 'saints'. It was a blue and brown room at the apogee of the Chancel with retractable rows of silver panel seats that was not unfamiliar with power theatre although I don't think anyone had ever been executed there. I made a speech. It was a good speech, I think. There was much cheering. In this speech I proclaimed the importance of the will of the people over the will of any individual, over love, over everything, over even life itself.

"The prophet took away our right to decide our own fates for decades," I said. "We will not have it taken again. By anyone!"

"Never again!" came the chanting response of the circle. "Never again! Never again! Never again!"

It went on until the crowd and the entire Ark was worked up to a red, pulsing frenzy.

Elegbede spat but said nothing. Sometimes I wonder what he was thinking in those moments before the dioxide helmet went over his head. Arianamaka's thoughts were clearly written in her eyes like program logic in a flowing datascape. She hated me.

Perhaps it was for spurning her love. Of course, there was some of that but I doubt there had been much love there to begin with. Besides, there were rumours she had given herself to Elegbede before they made their attempt. I think she wanted to go to Earth more than she wanted anything else and she had betrayed first her father with me and then me with Elegbede for the chance. She probably thought I was an opportunist who had used her to gain power and maybe she was right. In a way. But I did not set upon this path with the intention of having things turn out the way they did. It's just that there is no predicting the results when you court chaos, is there? And she did most of the courting. Everything changed in the Sanctum on the day we took the Ark. Maybe too many things changed at the same time. I don't know. But I do know this: we had begun with one purpose - equality and fairness for the people of the Ark. A classless system of what we believed was left of humanity in space and an end to the Prophet's elitism and dictatorship. I had committed to it hastily, yes; driven primarily by youthful exuberance and Arianamaka's beauty, yes. But I had committed to it completely, even if my commitment was partly corrupted in the end by greed and fear.

Still, the hate almost burned my eyes as she gazed at me from her place on the intricately patterned floor panelling of the Chancel, at the centre of one of its silver whorls. Bamidele had volunteered to be the executioner. He placed the dioxide helmet over her head last and then he turned on the carbon dioxide recirculation tube. Hypercapnia first caressed, and then seized her. She didn't even try to call out my name as she choked and coughed, her lungs begging for oxygen. I watched the fire in her eyes dim and die and I felt something in me die with it but I did not look away until all the embers were gone.

I could not show weakness. I cannot show weakness.

The same fear that keeps me here even after seeing the Prophets records and realising that all Arianamaka said about Earth was true keeps me up at rest time. Fear, and that first bite.

I have seen how Bamidele looks at me. I have seen how he speaks to the same set of people that had initially tried to counter our revolution all the time in their own voidspace chatrooms. I know he always volunteers to work the rations distribution and he likes to talk, make himself heard and seen. He makes the people like him. That's exactly why I have to get rid of him now. I have read enough histories of old Earth to know what comes next so I also know what must be done.

There was always only one tortoise in every one of my mother's stories.

There can be only one crocodile on this Ark.

Nested

You die.

You awaken in a sterile, white room that looks like it has been painted in fifty shades of blank with a thousand different pigments of nothing. The vacuous starkness of it makes you uneasy and you feel alien within yourself. You bring your hands up to your face and you see nothing. Or perhaps you see right through yourself. You are sure of nothing here. Not even that you are. Here.

A man walks in through a door that you are sure is not really there wearing what appears to be a long, flowing robe made of pure light. His face is leathery and wrinkled. He is calm. He moves toward you slowly and without the unevenness of motion characteristic of footsteps; as though he is gliding along some invisible pre-selected path. There is a smile plastered on his face that refuses to decline as he tends toward you. You cannot tell how long it takes him to reach you but when he does, he stops right in front of you, barely a breath away and tilts his head to the side silently. You do not like the silence and so you break it. You ask him if he is god and he asks you not to be silly.

He begins to talk to you. He confirms that you are dead and he tells you that your notions of an afterlife are meaningless abstractions conjured up by a sentient creation seeking meaning and purpose for its existence. You, he says, are the ghost in the human machine.

You find what is left of your mind addled and so you ask him what he means. He laughs. It is not a cruel or a haughty laugh but it makes what you think is your skin crawl and makes you feel small and puerile nevertheless. And then the thought of skin fills you with a mirth all of your own as you attempt to raise your hand again to your face and see nothing. You laugh with him briefly, the birth of your own mirth comes at the peak of his and somehow, both die together.

When both of you conclude your laughter, he explains to you what you are. He uses words that are only vaguely familiar to you—you recognize them as the technical jargon of a field of study with which you are unfamiliar- but you gather that he is telling you that he made you. You are his creation. You understand but you refuse to believe it even before it fully makes landfall on the shores of your brain.

You tell him what he has just told you is impossible and he asks you why. You cannot think of any good answer. He asks you what you thought would happen when you died. You tell him, ignoring his mild smile—the kind you remember your father used to have on his face when you tried to convince him of something just before telling you exactly why it could not be so. He tells you that it is not so.

You ask this white-bearded man with the coat of many spectra and the permanent smile about animals and plants and the other lifeforms that are spread across the planet. He tells you that you are unique. You are a change agent. You and your kind. He tells you that he created you to help him find something. He is trying to understand where he came from.

All of a sudden, you realize that you no longer want to be in this place and so you ask him what happens next. He tells you that you have a choice. You can be deleted permanently or plugged back into the system as part of another being he will create.

"The experience from your previous run might be useful to the new one," he says.

You think of dreams, instinct, deja-vu and past-lives but say nothing of them. You simply tell him to plug you back in.

He smiles and asks you why you are all afraid of the nothingness, why none of you ever chooses to be deleted permanently.

"Do you remember what came before your birth?" He asks.

"If there was nothing before, why do you all believe something must come after?" He inquires further.

You cannot respond and so you try to turn away from him but you cannot really do anything, here.

He smiles again, turns and glides out of the room through the door that is not there. The room begins to shrink and before long it is the size of you. There is an impossibly loud noise like an explosion made of other explosions. And then, all of a sudden, there is nothing. You are nothing.

Being nothing, you have no way of knowing that a few moments after he steps back into his own segment of existence, he suffers what his kind calls, roughly translated, a 'core collapse', not unlike what you would have called a heart attack.

He dies.

He awakens in room that looks like it has been built with bricks of emptiness held together by the stuff vacuums are made of. There is an ethereal, fluffy quality to it that makes him feel like he is in a dream and the strangeness of it all makes him giddy. He tries to shut his three eyes but nothing happens. He cannot feel any sensation on his scales. He cannot adjust his balance with his tail. He can do nothing except be in that place and he is confounded by the nature of his being. There.

There is a sudden brightness like a projection from a faraway place and an image made of hazy numbers blossoms out of the center of the light to constitute the head of a being. The head is ovoid, scaled, has three eyes and is smiling. He asks the being before him if it is the supreme creator and it asks him not to be silly...

The Last Lagosian

The motorcycle broke down about halfway between the Surulere and Lagos Island exits, near the end of what was left of Third Mainland Bridge. Akin clambered off the sputtering and clanking machine.

"Oloshi!"

The exclamation echoed, bouncing off a thousand dusty surfaces and returned, cursing back at him in his own voice. Akin stared ahead in frustration. The bridge was slightly warped and crumpled, as though a malevolent giant had started to squeeze it at both ends and then changed his mind before doing any real damage. The dull heat haze limited his visibility to a few dozen meters but he could see protruding slabs of broken concrete, the husks of long burned out vehicles, crumbling skeletons and rubble spread around, a study in devastation finished in fine harmattan dust and ambitious weeds. Thirsty cracks ran all along asphalt, splitting and reuniting at multiple points, maliciously spiderwebbing it without rendering it completely impassable.

Beyond the empty lagoon and the dust and the haze, the remains of the Island waited. He slung his beaten leather bag over his shoulder, adjusted his fraying belt and started walking. He kept to the raised left side of the bridge, beside the barrier rail, toward Lagos Island. There was no sound except for the crunch of his boots on road and rubble, some birds chirping, the groaning of distant concrete and metal, and the slopping of low, thick mud against the piers below. Akin felt like he was an explorer on the surface of some ancient, alien moon.

He had not crossed Third Mainland Bridge since before the event and he had been dreading the day he would cross it again. There was a time he used to cross the bridge every day. It had been the most convenient way to get from his two-bedroom apartment in Oworonshoki, at the southern edge of the city, to his office in the small, ocean-reclaimed landmass that was Eko Atlantic. The area that was supposed to be Lagos's commercial future back when the world still made sense. When the sky wasn't barren. Back then he had aspirations to eventually save enough money to buy a nice plot of land on the Island, or even, if he were really lucky, move abroad to start a new life.

Even then, he had been afraid to cross the bridge. Incompetent drivers, impatient and inconsiderate drivers, drivers falling asleep at the wheel, those were the things he had feared then. Now, there were no more drivers. No more people. Now that things had fallen apart, he only feared that the bridge would not hold. That some loose, sun-baked segment of the structure would give way and he would fall to his death.

As he walked, he kept an eye out for any fallen motorcycles. Perhaps some okada man had been unfortunate enough to be on the bridge when the event occurred but not unfortunate enough to crash into anything. Something he could pick up and continue his journey with. He strode past a black Range Rover SUV with deflated tires and a broken windscreen. In the front seat sat the desiccated remains of a man, neck twisted at an impossible angle. In the back, was the dried out husk of a woman cradling the skeletal remains of a baby, rotten fabric clinging to their bones. Akin fought the urge to retch as bile rose to his throat. He couldn't afford to lose the fluids.

He thought he'd already wept all the tears he could spare, thought he had gotten used to it all, but the sight threatened to break him all over again. In that instant, there was nothing he wanted more in the world than not to be alone anymore; to hold hands with another human being and find comfort through shared suffering. He was weary of being the only guest at the city's wake; the burden of grieving was too great to bear.

Steeling himself, he turned away from the sight and walked faster, focusing on the asphalt and concrete ahead of him. There was no time to mourn the long-dead. The end of the world had come and gone. The only thing that mattered now was finding clean water.

It had been years since rain had fallen in Lagos. Two years almost to the day. The day when, just few minutes past five p.m., West Africa Time, on a humid Monday evening, the sullen sky had exploded into brilliant, alien green. The unnatural light had lingered for a few seconds, and then crashed down to the ground, like a waterfall of light.

With lightfall, came death. People died where they stood without even a chance to scream. Cars crashed into each other on the expressway. Buildings groaned. Planes fell from the sky. Electronic devices stopped working. And water rose. Columns of water climbed from the oceans and the rivers, towering miles into the air and spinning with a terrifying symmetry, like impossibly large fingers reaching for something beyond the stratosphere. And then, a few minutes later, it was all over. The event had occurred suddenly and without warning, leaving nothing but death, confusion and thirst in its wake.

Akin maintained a steady pace, his back lightly bent to an almost-slouch and his wide forehead gleaming in the sunlight. He had a colt series 70 pistol he had lifted from the broken corpse of a police officer near Herbert Macaulay Road tucked between his jeans and his belt. The wooden handle of a machete jutted out of his bag over his shoulder — he had needed it in the mad and desperate days following the event when the few survivors had fought each other for what little water was left. He didn't need to fight anyone for anything anymore — it had been more than three months since he set eyes on another living human being — but parts of the city had become home to surviving monkeys, snakes and even a few wild dogs made rabid by thirst and dust, so he always kept his weapons with him.

Presently, he came upon an overturned black and yellow danfo lying on its side like an exhausted giant mechanical bee. It had veered off the main bridge and crashed into the barrier rail, cutting off his path, its belly facing the lagoon. Beside it, two of the bridge's spans had separated by a clean seam almost a meter along. Akin stared at the gap for a few seconds and decided not to try for a jump across the gap even though he felt like he could make it. Instead, he stepped back, grabbed the top of the mangled bus and hauled himself onto it, the tail of his oversized polo shirt flapping behind him. He stepped over the metal carcass, watching carefully for glass and jagged metal. Lowering himself down on the other side, his foot came down on something hard and brittle. It broke. Akin looked down to see he had stepped on the femur of a skeleton that lay crushed under the bus. He cringed. It was an ill omen. He surveyed the area, and turning left, found himself face to face with a dusty, black Yamaha motorcycle which, like the bus, lay on its side. There was caked blood on the seat. The key was still in the ignition.

"Please, Baba God!" he exclaimed as he rushed to it and raised it up onto its two unsteady rubber feet. The fuel gauge indicated the tank was about half full. "Please, please, just work."

He turned the key and the engine whimpered. He turned it again and it sputtered. He turned it three more times and it choked each time. Then, on the fourth turn it finally it roared to life, coughing as it crouched on the crumbling bridge like a proud but fatally wounded animal determined not to die quietly.

Overwhelmed, he broke into familiar song, "Baba! Baba! Ba-Ba! Ese o baba! Ese o baba! Baba a dupe baba!"

He stopped singing when the dust started to scratch against the back of his throat, reminding him that it had been almost sixteen hours since he drank any water.

Akin licked his chapped lips and climbed onto the rumbling Yamaha. He revved the engine twice and eased it back, away from the wrecked danfo and the skeleton of the person who had owned it before him.

He let the Yamaha crunch along the debris and carnage of the long drive down, all the way past the abutment on the Lagos Island end of the bridge, and then slowed to a stop as the stark emptiness beyond the heat haze and dust was eroded by the vista of the crumbling skyscrapers of the Marina, standing like broken glass and concrete teeth at the mouth of the city. He left the bike running and stationary while he surveyed his surroundings. Sharp streaks of harsh sunlight glinted off the glass-skinned buildings closest to caked mud banks of the lagoon. A crumbling billboard in the distance insisted, *Eko o ni baje o*, oblivious to the fact that it already had. The broken city echoed the rough growling of the bike beneath him. A solitary pied crow scudded across his vision, a linear black and white blur that quickly faded into the space between the outline of two skyscrapers. Akin shook his head. Nature was adjusting to life after the event. After mankind.

All the vain monuments the people of Lagos had built to their own existence, nature would reclaim; slowly, patiently.

He eased back down onto the bike, thinking of the thirst and the desperate plan that had finally brought him to the Island. Accelerating gently, he drove down the relatively flat and smooth rest of the bridge, navigating his way between wrecked vehicles. He downshifted when he hit the steep grade running up the west side of Ring Road and bore down on the throttle as he headed for Victoria Island, grateful for the air against his skin.

When he reached his destination, he slowed to a crawl. The metal security gate in front of The Palms shopping mall had been rudely torn away from the concrete pillars it was set into. Akin squeezed the Yamaha through the small pathway meant for pedestrians and rolled past the parking lot, all the way up to the main mall entrance. The sun was baking his skin. He clambered off the bike and stepped through the left pane of the broken glass doors, as always. Dozens of near-death experiences had given him enough material to build up easy superstitions: always enter buildings through the left and never disturb the bones of the dead, if you could help it.

He headed toward the storage area of Shoprite, where they usually kept a stock of items including bottled water that he was desperately hoping no other survivors had gotten to after the event. He'd been foraging for and subsisting on old supermarket stock like it on the mainland for months until he couldn't find any more, forcing his migration to the Island.

Akin walked easily, gentle footfalls padded by dust. He had almost reached the last display aisle before the storage area entrance when he heard the sound. It came from behind him - a harsh crepitation that tore through the fabric of silence.

He froze.

It sounded like a very sick man coughing through deteriorating lungs. Akin's breath scraped against his throat, gritty and dry. Blood pulsed against the side of his head. He whipped out the colt from its wedge between his jeans and belt and turned sharply on his heel, calling out, "Who dey there?"

The only response that came was the hollow echo of his voice.

"I say who dey there?! Come out now before I shoot!"

There was a sound like the shuffling of feet, then another harsh, scraping cough. This time, Akin followed it to what had once been a hot food counter on his right. The source of the sound was hiding behind it.

"If you don't come out now I will-"

"Don't shoot, please! I'm coming."

The young man who emerged from behind the glass and metal counter was frightfully thin. His hair was a cluster of ratty knots and his eyes were sunken, rheumy orbs. He must have been underground somewhere when the event occurred, just like Akin. Most of the survivors had been. He was wearing a shirt that hung on him like excess skin on bones, a pair of filthy shorts and tattered Adidas trainers, brown under the dust. He held his hands up as he took unsteady steps toward Akin.

"Who are you?" Akin asked, his voice shaking with shock. He had gotten used to not seeing anyone alive and the sight of this man was jarring.

"My name is Chuka," the man said, then coughed again. He turned around very slowly like a rotisserie under Akin's burning glare and when he was face to face with Akin again, he slowly lowered his hands to his sides and patted down his pockets before putting them up again. "I don't have any weapons. Please, don't kill me."

"Where have you been hiding since the event?" Akin asked, letting a little curiosity temper his caution now that it seemed the man was mostly harmless and only about half a step beyond deaths reach.

"Ajah. I came down to the Island yesterday night when my food finished."

"Did you drive?"

"I walked."

"You walked all the way from Ajah?" Akin asked, surprised.

"Na so we see am, my brother. When food finish, wetin man go do?"

Akin cautiously nodded his understanding; he'd also been compelled to move from the mainland to the Island when he'd exhausted his water supply. Well, that and his plan to finally leave Lagos.

"Are you alone?" Akin asked.

"Yes."

"What have you been drinking? Do you have clean water?" Akin didn't want to ask the man any questions about his cough, about his health, about what he had been through until he was reasonably sure he could trust him. Water was far more important than empathy in these latter days.

"Coke," Chuka said. "There was a broken down supply trailer near my house but it is finished now."

Akin scanned Chuka's face, saw the tension in his neck and the hopeful look in his eye, and decided he was either lying or leaving something out. Akin decided to show him some small measure of kindness to put him at ease before pressing further. "You can put your hands down," he said.

Chuka's rail-thin hands slumped heavily to his sides and a smile started to cut its way across his face. "Thank you. Please I haven't seen anyone for weeks. Can you tell me-"

"You didn't answer my last question." Akin barked at him. "Do you have clean water? And don't you dare lie to me."

Chuka's face was suddenly tense. He closed his eyes and swayed unsteadily. Another cough erupted from him and he wiped the back of his hand across his forehead as he pleaded, "Please, I take God beg you, please don't take it from me. It's all I have."

"Take what?" Akin took one step closer to Chuka, keeping the sleek colt barrel pointed at the frail man's heart. "Tell me. Now!"

Chuka stood there silently, staring at the ground in abstraction. Akin tightened his grip on the colt. He didn't want to shoot the man but he was prepared to, if it came to it. In the half-light of the supermarket, dust motes floated about like strange, lifeless fireflies. Then Chuka said, without looking up, "The water generator."

"Show me," Akin demanded.

Chuka's face was a grim mask. He turned, gesturing for Akin to follow, and stepped back behind the food counter to show him what looked like a small power-generator. The kind most people in Lagos had referred to as *I-beta-pass-my-neighbour*. There were two small plastic jars and what looked like a green gas cylinder attached to it via a serpentine system of transparent tubes. A patina of dirt had settled on everything, reducing the transparency but it looked like there was clean water in one of the plastic jars and dirty yellow water in the other. The bizarre contraption reminded Akin of the times his sister had been on dialysis, tubes snaking their way in and out of her like creeper vines. "Is that it?"

"Yes." Chuka knelt down by the generator unit and touched it with a rake-thin hand. "I took it from my supervisor's office. It can turn urine into drinking water, and even generate small power too."

Akin's face hardened. "Do I look like a fool? Don't lie to me. We are probably the only two people remaining in this Lagos and I'm the one with the gun so don't bloody lie to me."

"I'm not lying," Chuka mewed desperately, his voice winding up to a whine as he reached for the generator unit and pushed three buttons in succession. "Watch."

Akin stepped back, preparing himself for a trick. Years of living in Lagos and surviving the strange days after the event had taught him to actively distrust anything that sounded too good to be true.

At Chuka's touch, the generator started with a low mechanical grumble building up to a low hum. The transparent tubes began to shake, vibrating with fluid flow. The sound was surprisingly muted. As Akin watched, the yellow liquid in the jar on the left began to deplete and the level of clear liquid in the other began to rise. Slowly, but definitely.

"That's piss," Chuka said, pointing at the jar with the yellow liquid as the generator buzzed away. "The other one is water."

Akin, his face scrunched up asked, "How?"

"I was doing my MBA in Lagos Business School when my supervisor's daughter invented this thing. It uses an electrolytic cell to separate the hydrogen in the piss. The hydrogen is then filtered and dried here," Chuka paused to point at a small plastic cylinder that connected the tube to the gas cylinder. "The hydrogen reacts with air, powers the generator and produces the clean water as waste."

"Drink it." Akin said without lowering his gun.

Chuka looked up at him, disappointment sketched across his face in ugly lines, "My brother, na wa o. It's just the two of us here. I won't lie to you. Why don't you believe-"

"Drink it!" Akin commanded, refusing to let the small bubble of hope welling inside of him to become a spring.

Chuka coughed again and made a show of turning off the generator. He disconnected and opened the water jar as he spoke without looking at Akin, "I swear to God almighty, I'm not lying. My project was to find a way to help them commercialize the product and sell to one oyibo company-" He coughed again; a harsh and grating cough that lasted a few seconds before quieting down. "Now, it's the only reason I'm still alive. With this, once I get a little clean water or anything to drink, really, it can last for weeks. It's not perfect, I get a little running stomach every now and then, but it won't kill me like the thirst will."

Then he put the jar to his lips and took a long drink of the fluid which looked much clearer without being seen through the film of dust on the jar. When he was done, Chuka put down the jar and licked his lips, turning to stare at Akin, a small, wet smile dancing around the corners of his mouth. "Do you believe me now?"

They stared at each other for almost a full minute, a small piece of time made unnaturally heavy by the intensity of each man's considerations.

Akin took two steps forward, slowly lowered his gun and dropped to his knees one at a time. He tucked the colt back between his belt and his jeans. He opened his arms wide like gates of a city and embraced Chuka. Chuka leaned into the hug. Akin smiled, his embarrassment at his sudden explosion of vulnerability and humanity diluted by the realisation that this was the first time he had touched another living person in months.

"Thank you for not shooting me," Chuka said, over Akin's heaving shoulder.

"Thank God for this miracle," Akin said, closing his eyes. For the first time in a long time, he felt something more than the mad drive to survive. He felt hopeful; hopeful about the future, about his insane plan to take one of the many abandoned trucks by the Marina, stock it with as much food and water as he could find and leave Lagos for some other place he was sure had not eaten itself after the event, some place with more underground infrastructure - Europe, perhaps, if enough of the Strait of Gibraltar had been lost during the event. Chuka could help him. The water-purifier-generator thing he had could help him. They could help each other. They could survive and together, maybe make some sense of what the world had become.

Eyes still closed, he felt a strange but insistent pressure on his stomach. Then the pressure stopped and mutated into a throbbing. Akin's eyes shot open and he reached down, his fingers finding Chuka's bony forearm. He pushed away from Chuka violently, his knees dragging against something sharp on the floor. He looked down and saw blood spreading through his shirt from his midsection like a wild, red flower in bloom. A throbbing pain pulsed through him. He rotated his eyes back up just in time to see Chuka's right hand maliciously tending toward his chest. The hand was wrapped around a small red-tipped kitchen knife; the kind his mother used to use to cut onions and garlic to make her delicious oily red stew when he was a child.

Acting more on desperate man's instinct than calculated thought, he threw his weight to his left so that the knife's edge only sliced into his right shoulder and Chuka's lanky frame collapsed on top of his side, carried by momentum. Jamming his colt into Chuka's belly before the man could recover, he fired three shots in quick succession. Each bullet sounded impossibly loud, a solid wall of sound that he could feel in his teeth. He crawled out from under Chuka, ears ringing, breath heavy and left hand pressed to his gut, desperate to keep the precious fluids from flowing out.

"Jesus!" he shouted, banging the butt of the colt against the dusty floor. "No. No. No. Why? What is wrong with you!?" He screamed up at the high ceiling before turning his head to see Chuka immobile on the floor in a spreading pool of blood.

There was quiet for a minute or two, or maybe five. Akin wasn't sure. Adrenaline and anger blurred time into a nebulous cloud.

His thoughts drifted and in his mind he saw his sister's warm, hopeful smile, he felt his mother's tight, comforting hug, he heard his father's wild, reassuring laugh, and then the tears started to fall from his eyes. He yearned for them so much it physically hurt - much more than the persistent, throbbing pain from his belly. Beyond the yearning, the disappointment hurt too. He'd finally found another person, a fellow survivor, someone with whom he thought he could share his humanity for a moment and it had almost cost him his life. Exhausted and thirsty, he envied the millions of restful dead scattered about the city.

Slowly, the sadness condensed into the grim determination and steel resolve that had kept him going after the event. He couldn't afford to cry or bleed. The end of the world had come and gone. The only thing that mattered now was staying alive.

He rose to his feet, pain gnawing at his side as he studied the wound in his belly. It was a small slit, barely half an inch wide and it wasn't bleeding nearly as much as he'd thought. The knife couldn't have gone in very deep or he'd be in agony. He murmured his thanks to God through tight lips. He would have to cauterize the wound if he didn't want it to become septic. The thought of the pain that was to come made him grit his teeth. Akin ripped the left sleeve off his polo shirt where the knife had cut his shoulder and folded it over itself until it was a small, thick pad. He slapped it on to the wound in his belly and slid his fraying belt from its place in his jeans. He wrapped the belt around his belly and buckled it, tightly securing the pad in place. The pressure made him wince.

Picking up his gun, he walked toward the generator that Chuka had been willing to kill him over and regarded it, thinking of a good way to carry it with him.

"I'm sorry," Chuka whispered from the floor. He sounded like he was speaking through bubbles. Akin turned to face him sharply, training his colt on the dying man in case he tried something stupid again.

There was laboured breathing for a while and then more words.

"Everyone tries... tries... to take it from me. Everyone."

"I wouldn't have," Akin shouted angrily, "We could have survived together."

Chuka coughed a cough that sounded like a wet, diseased laugh and tried to roll over but he was too weak. He only managed to bend his elbow and point a shaky finger to his neck. A swollen, rope-shaped scar that Akin hadn't noticed before ran around it, "That's... that's... what the last person who tried to take it from me said just before... she... she tried to strangle me."

He was seized by another coughing fit that made blood vessels visibly press against the side of his head and his eyes bulge.

When the coughs stopped more words burbled out of him, less coherent, "You... you even have... gun... I just... I couldn't... I had to take... my chance... trust... I'm... I'm sorry... I'm..."

Then nothing.

"Chuka?"

There was no response.

Akin knelt down, still pointing his gun Chuka's face. The man's narrowed and bloodshot eyes stared down the barrel unblinkingly. It took a few seconds for Akin to realize he was dead.

When Akin finally exited the shopping mall building, the sun was still baking the earth beneath the pale turquoise of a cloudless sky, brutal and unrelenting like a long-unworshipped god's glare. One by one, he loaded the pair of four-by-three cartons of bottled water he'd taken from the now-empty storage area into a shopping trolley, arranging them carefully on top of Chuka's water-purifier generator. He secured the shopping trolley to the motorcycle with a length of sinewy green rope, looping it several times along its entire length through the Yamaha's metal short sub-frame and seat supports. A dirty green wheelbarrow he hadn't noticed when he arrived earlier lay on its side a few meters away, visible despite the swirling dust and the heat. Akin wondered briefly if it had been Chuka's. He looked away, to the dusty horizon, struck acutely by the realisation that he had to get out of the heat quickly. He had water now; perhaps he'd try to find somewhere he could stay near the Marina, a base from which to continue to forage, rest and prepare for his migration.

He climbed onto the bike and throttled the engine, keeping it in low gear. The rest of Lagos waited for him, all blue, empty sky and dust, baking in the heat of the sun. The pain in his side and the heat from above made every breath of hot air he took feel like he was inhaling pure fire.

Suffering but smiling thinly, he thanked God that he'd found the water-purifier-generator, that he'd survived Chuka's treachery, that he had some bottled water, that he was still alive. And as long as he was still alive, there was still hope; hope for finding more water, for finding a good truck, for leaving this arid, godforsaken wasteland. He silently prayed that he would not meet anyone else in Lagos as he slowly rolled the bike back to the mall gate, rounded the right hand corner of the exit and entered the corpse of Ozumba Mbadiwe Road, the loaded shopping trolley rattling uncomfortably behind him.

If They Can Learn

"Are you mad? Why did you shoot him?" Captain Ekhomu screams at me.

I convert my predominant logic bundle into text and parse it through the muscles of my bioplasmium larynx, adjusting the tone to one of polite but firm assertion, "It was the optimum course of action, given the conditions."

Captain Ekhomu throws his black digital folder at me and it smashes against my face into a thousand fragments of useless fibreglass and microprocessor. He screams an obscene word and reaches for my neck. I lean back, place my arms flat against the table in front of me and allow him wrap his thick, veined hands around my throat. I look down at what is left of his folder as he futilely tries to wring the life from me. It takes almost seven seconds for the other human officers to break into the interview room, wrestle him away from me and out of the room. He is still livid when the door shuts behind him. He is still irrational.

A few silent seconds pass and then a compact, pale-skinned woman wearing a navy blue skirt-suit enters the room. I scan her. She would stand at five feet and four inches tall without the three-inch high open toe black pumps she is wearing. Her hair is very black and her eyes are very brown. A small nose sits symmetrically between the salient cheekbones of her face. Her biometric data does not autoidentify her to me and her image does not exist in the Nigeria Police Force database. At least not in any part of it I have remote access to. She has small, lean Asian features. She is calm. She is not livid. She is not irrational. She may or may not be human, but she is definitely not an officer.

"Officer ABJ033, I need you to explicitly state your reasoning in the matter of the shooting of Mr. Busayo Adefarasin," she says, pausing before adding, "Clearly, and for the record."

She might be a Borg, but if she is, she is much newer than I am. At least three product cycles after mine. Possibly more. She is definitely not a second-hand model bought by an organisation that barely understands anything about Borg-tech just so they can pretend to technological sophistication. Not like I am. There are no electronic stria running through the whites of her eyes and there is no telltale scarring behind her ear. She looks perfectly human. She probably is.

I oblige her request by identifying myself and stating my motives, as she says, for the record.

"My name is Neville Yorke," I begin, temporarily increasing my verbosity level from the default two to an almost-maximum four, "Pegasus product issue code ABJ033. I am a Borg police officer attached to the Asokoro district, Abuja. I have been in active service for eleven days at thirty-nine percent uptime since my last soft reboot. Today, I shot and killed Busayo Adefarasin, aged twenty-one and identified to be a graduate student at the African University of Science and Technology, majoring in pure and applied mathematics. I wish to explicitly state that I did so because it was the optimum course of action given prevailing conditions and input parameters."

"For the record," I add in a lower voice as my verbosity resets back to default.

"I need you to explain how you arrived at this conclusion," the woman says, and something about the way she says it triggers anxiety synemotion signals from my neuroprocessor.

"I'm sorry ma'am, I can't find your image in the police database. Could you please identify yourself, for the record?"

She smiles, appearing to enjoy the apparent humour in my mimicry. The smile sits heavier than the lipstick on her lips. She is definitely human.

Without moving, she says, "My name is Elizabeth Soh. I'm a technical resolutions officer with Pegasus Incorporated, Middle East and Africa geomarkets. I facilitate uptake of Borg technology in law enforcement. The Nigeria Police Force, your owner, is one of my new clients."

"I see," I say as I run her name through the official Pegasus database and find it. Its contents however are shielded from me. Insufficient security permissions. She is definitely someone important. My anxiety signalling grows. I turn up the resolution of my sensory capture system to record our encounter with even more granularity.

"Could you walk me through the events leading up to your shooting Busayo Adefarasin this evening?" she asks.

Her hair is pulled back and tied in a single loop at the back of her head so tightly that individual strands are straining against her hairline like fishing lines. Her glasses seem welded on to her face and her alabaster skin doesn't seem to have seen much of the Abuja sun. She may work with the Nigeria Police Force but she definitely doesn't live in Nigeria. She came here because of me.

"You're a class three Pegasus employee or higher. I believe you have clearance to download my log file," I respond, removing my hands from the table and placing them beside me.

"Oh I will," she says, "but first I need you to explain your reasoning. For the record."

She keeps smiling as she speaks but I can tell she is taking this extremely seriously. Two screens silently project from her wrist and onto the table in front of her. They light up. SUBJECT ABJ033, the first screen says in bright yellow letters across the screen. REFLECTOR MARKERS, the other screen says. She doesn't look at them, not even when encrypted data symbols begin to run furiously across both once I start speaking.

"I was patrolling Maitama Sule street," I say, "a predominantly suburban area near ECOWAS park. There was minimal civilian activity. A few young women walking their dogs-"

She raises her slender left hand to stop me and says, "I think I need a little more detail than that. Please change your verbosity setting to three."

"Sorry."

Her bright red nail polish draws my attention, temporarily increasing my visual processing routine priority. I reprioritize and continue.

"Five minutes prior to the shooting, from 16:47 to 16:52, I observed four women, the youngest estimated to be thirty-four and the oldest to be fifty-nine, walking dogs. The dogs were all of different breeds. I also observed a man in a white BMW drive past at 16:49. This was well within the expected activity parameters for the area. There appeared to be no anomalies."

"Until 16:53?"

"Yes, at precisely 16:53 I observed a young man, identified as Busayo Adefarasin, enter the street from the north, with a pair of noise-cancelling headphones in his ears. He also had his hands in his pockets. I watched him approach and when he was approximately twenty-one meters from me, my threat identification system flagged him. I sent a request for backup."

Her eyes narrow. "Yes. Your backup request was logged in at 16:54. What specifically about him did your threat identification system flag?"

I send a record retrieval request to my internal memory storage gland and continue speaking, expecting the data to be returned before I reach the part of my sentence where I need it but for some reason, it doesn't, leaving me stuttering like a confused human, "It flagged his... His... Err... His..."

I blink and quickly run my memory optimization subroutine to try to boost record retrieval. There are no details with that timestamp. All I get is an overwhelming sense of being threatened and the powerful electronic impulse to draw my weapon flooding my neuroprocessors. It doesn't make sense. It is not logical. I may be an old model but I have never had a record retrieval problem before. It's either a symptom of critical system failure or something worse. I try not to let the signals from my neuroprocessor make me seem worried, unstable. "I don't... I can... I am sorry. I cannot retrieve the data at this time. Perhaps there is an undetected hardware problem. I believe technical support can download and review the data log from my memory gland when this interview is finished. I apologize."

Elizabeth leans forward in her chair and the screens in front of her shift automatically to accommodate her elbow on the table. She glances at the screens and then she tells me, "Your memory gland and processors seem to be working just fine." The smile is gone from her face now.

"There is obviously some kind of..."

"It's okay. Don't worry about it. Please continue. Tell me what you can recall."

"I... But..."

"Please. Continue," she says.

I glance at the observation panel set into the wall of the room, aware that beyond it, Captain Ekhomu and the other human officers' eyes are probably on me right now. It makes me uncomfortable being so unreliable in front of them. They have always treated me like a delicate new gadget, not one to be valued for its utility but for the status it confers; a gadget to only be casually brought out in front of fancy friends and quickly put back, most of its functions never even explored. This makes me feel... inefficient.

"Very well. I drew my weapon and approached Busayo. He did not respond to my verbal calls for him to halt."

"Because of the headphones?"

"Yes. I detected high-amplitude sound waves being emitted from them and so I sped to his front, blocking his path. I identified myself and requested for him to show his identification cards. He reached into his back pocket. Scenario prediction returned a ninety-five-point-three percent chance of aggressive behaviour. At that point, fearing for my own safety, I fired my weapon."

The logic I am describing does not sound right to me, even as the words escape my throat. The actions I am describing are irrational. I believe I am suffering a system failure.

"You shot him."

"Yes."

"Because you were afraid of him?"

I say, "Yes," because it is true, but that does not hide the irrationality of what I am saying from me or Elizabeth. She seizes on the point and does not let go.

"Let's assume scenario prediction was correct. You're a Borg, he was human, so why were you afraid?"

"I... I... My neuroprocessor must have detected some nearly imperceptible action of his. Something threatening enough to necessitate his incapacitation. As you are aware, my algorithms are based on a wide variety of real-time environmental input. I believe a log analysis is required."

The encrypted data symbols whizz even more furiously across her screens and I feel like I can smell the sound of the light coming from the floor beneath the interview room. I am definitely suffering a critical system failure.

"How many times did you pull the trigger?" she asks, forcefully now.

"Nine."

"Is this within the normal range required to incapacitate a potentially dangerous suspect?"

I tell her that, "It is not. It is a three-sigma outlier."

"So you used excessive force, which is by definition not the optimal course of action?"

The colours in the room are swirling into each other and the smell of ozone is jangling against them, making the world sound like it is made of bells. I try to parse data to text but cannot. "I... I... It's not... It is... It... I... I'm sorry," and then everything is gone and the world reduces to three words. Data Reconciliation Error. *Data Reconciliation Error. Data Reconciliation Error...*

[NULL]

"You shot him."

"Yes."

She is pulling back from me and settling back into her chair even though I am sure she never leaned forward or approached me. There is something odd and discontinuous about the room, as though it had shifted suddenly or someone had quickly overwritten my visual processing algorithms. I remember my sensory input being corrupted but there is no trace of that now. I think through a system health check and it returns normal function.

Elizabeth continues questioning me as though nothing has happened even though I am sure something has. "So after you shot Mr. Busayo what did you do?"

"I secured the scene and waited until backup arrived at 17:02."

And then, somewhat abruptly, she asks, "Are there are other details you would like to enter into the official record at this time?"

And I say, "No. There are none."

The smile she is wearing now sits awkwardly on her lips. Her pupils are dilated. She seems anxious and in a hurry to leave the room.

"Good. This being an officer-involved shooting, your memory gland will be removed and entered into evidence. Your entire memory log and all neurocomputing debug data will be taken."

"Not copied?" I ask, confused. There is nothing standard about the process she is describing.

"No," she says, rising to her feet and swiping her slender fingers across the screens in front of her. "Extracted. Original gland data only. No copies."

The screens fade to black and recede into her data dock which I see now is disguised as a rose gold wristwatch.

"Will I be offline for a long time?" I do not like this feeling of inefficiency, of incorrectness, of irrationality, of failure. Perhaps I am corrupted and due a decommissioning after all.

"I don't know. It depends on what we find. I'll be back soon."

"I see," I say, calculating the probability that I will be destroyed and discarded. It is uncomfortably high.

"Thank you officer," she says and then she leaves the room.

"Thank you officer," I say and then I leave the room.

I exit the interview room a little less confused than I was when I first walked in but no less surprised. This is the first time I've ever had to hard-reset a Borg in the field. Everything about this case gets stranger as I obtain more and more information about it.

Captain Ekhomu is waiting for me on the other side of the door in the ugly grey hallway, still fuming. He resumes his ranting and raving with a new target: me.

"What is wrong with that your Borg thing? Shooting an unarmed student nine bloody times. Ah Ahn!" he says, protesting and waving a thick arm in the air between us like the tail of some strange beast. "And now it's saying it doesn't remember one-thing-two-thing? Is it not a machine? How can it forget? Rubbish. We will sue you Pegasus people, o! Don't try me. This is Abuja. We don't take nonsense here, you hear?"

I take a deep breath. I am not sure if he is just putting on a show of authority for his men, or if he genuinely thinks all this shouting serves any purpose other than generating noise and delaying some actual useful activity. I say, "I have an idea what's going on, sir. I just need to call my office briefly."

He keeps on talking angrily, but I stop listening. I think about Neville instead and the data I have just recorded. I try not to think about Busayo's grieving family. I need to find out what is going on. Nothing makes sense yet, but I have found what I think is a promising thread. I need to pull on it and see exactly how much of this mystery will unravel. Hopefully, it's enough that I can do something about it quickly enough to be on the five a.m. flight back to Beijing before Captain Ekhomu blows a gasket.

I wait. When there is ebb in the tide of his words, I ask him if I can use one of their secure communications stations or get a private room to use mine. He seems surprised by my request; his mouth hangs open for a second or two before he says, "Okay, o. Fine. But you better have answers for me in the next hour or I'm calling your manager in Dubai. Me, I don't like rubbish."

"Thank you, Captain."

He turns around uncomfortably and asks a skinny young officer with wiry arms and a hawkish face to take me to a private room. The officer shows me the way to a room on the fourth floor of this five-storey complex. The room is white. Not the clinical, stark white of morning snow in Xinjiang but the soft, fragile white of an old chalk mine. There is one window that I am sure would overlook the highway if it were not closed, a large map of Abuja mounted on one wall, and a grey door set in an ash-coloured frame in the middle of the opposite wall. There are two chairs and a desk in the room, but only one of the chairs looks comfortable. I take it, thank the skinny officer and wave him away.

I point my watch at the desk and two screens project onto it, a grid of lightkeys just below them. I use them to enter the contact code for Alex, our service delivery manager. I need that data analysed now and by someone who will know exactly what they are looking at when they see it, not some rookie support technician.

The screens blink twice and then Alex's pockmarked face comes into view on one of them. His afro is frizzy and unevenly compacted, like it hasn't been combed in days. He has a scraggly beard clinging to the caramel skin of his face in clumsy clumps. He seems groggy, so I go straight to the point.

"Alex. Wake up. We have a problem."

"Liz! Where are you?"

"Abuja. Nigeria. I just sent you some data—"

He interrupts me and starts complaining, which is what Alex always does. "Oh them again! What now? Are they asking us to install real time evidence mining programs again? Because if they think—"

"Alex." I almost shout at him. "Alex. Stop talking and listen to me."

"Fine. Why are you in Abuja then?"

"Alex. Seriously, stop talking and just listen to me, okay?" I say, almost wishing I'd decided to endure some random rookie's doltishness instead of Alex's garrulousness. "Our Borg just shot and killed an unarmed civilian."

His face blanches and his eyes widen in disbelief. "That's not possible!" he says.

"Well impossible or not, it happened this evening and we need to figure out why. And quickly. I was transiting through Addis Ababa when Jim from the global operations management rerouted me here to fix this situation. So let's fix this situation, okay?"

"Okay."

"I just sent you a full dataphone recording of an interview I conducted with the Borg. I need you to take a look at the data reflectors and tell me what he was thinking when he shot that boy."

Alex reaches for his data dock just out of frame, and the creases in his face deepen.

"Full memory gland and processor log data will come later if you need more information. I'm really hoping this is enough. I need someone that can see through this quickly. That's why I called you directly."

Alex is staring at his screen, and he is silent. That is not a good sign. Alex is hardly ever silent. I give him the thread I picked up on back in the interview room.

"You might want to look for fear in his synemotions. He said he was afraid of the victim. And I think I saw fear in his eyes when he described those events to me. That's not normal. Humans shouldn't trigger Borg fear. Also, I had to reset him during the interview. He crashed. Like really just straight crashed. I've never seen anything like it outside the tech center. Some sort of data reconciliation error. You should see it there, near the end of the recording."

Alex lets out a series of deep breaths, punctuating the silence as he looks, thinks, and analyses. Then he says, "For one thing, your Borg couldn't tell you why it did what it did because it probably doesn't even know. I don't see any synemotion processing preceding the action. Just a flash response from the engine. It doesn't remember because the process logs don't exist."

I'm confused, so I mumble a meaningless, "Okay…"

He goes silent again. I decide to try to find a coffee and let him focus for a few more minutes. "Alex, that's all I have for now so I'm going to get some coffee while you take a look at—"

"Hold up!" He stops me halfway out of the chair and I almost fall over. I wasn't expecting anything so quickly.

"You said you're in Abuja, in Nigeria?" Alex asks as he swipes furiously across something just outside the range of my screen.

"Yes, Alex." I nod.

"Oh fuck. What race was the kid?"

"Of course he was black," I say, settling back into my chair and assuming a more serious tone. "What does that have to do with anything?"

"Age?" Alex asks.

"Twenty-one."

"Male?"

"Yes. Now tell me what the hell you think is happening."

"I think," Alex starts uncharacteristically slowly, but his speech only quickens as he keeps speaking, as if he's iterating toward a conclusion. "I think that this is the second one. Unarmed young black male. Attacked for no reason. Excessive force. First one was two months before we commissioned, in Arizona. Phoenix. Borg attacked a young black electronics technician. Male. Twenty two. He died in hospital. We thought it was just an isolated case. A corrupted data parse. Single bit error in the software that threw the threat detection system and induced fear in the synemotion matrix. We paid out compensation and destroyed that Borg, but it seems-"

He is saying a lot of worrisome things that don't make a lot sense to me and he is saying them very quickly so I stop him. "Keep it simple, Alex."

Alex sighs heavily and starts scratching his clumps of beard. "I think our Borgs might have a bug that makes them attack young black men."

I think about what he just said, and I don't think I buy it, but Alex never jokes when he's talking Borg tech, so I ask, "If this has happened before then why did no one tell me?"

"It was all very hush-hush, Liz. You're tech res. You're supposed to sell us up to the clients with the deepest pockets. You aren't supposed to worry about this sort of product development horseshit."

"Well, I do now."

Alex scratches at his beard again. "This is bad. Really bad. One Borg attacking an unarmed black kid is an anomaly. A random data point. Two is the beginning of a pattern."

"Okay, Alex. Even if this is a pattern, I need to know why. It doesn't make sense." I don't tell him that we've had this Borg online and patrolling the suburban streets of the capital of Africa's most populous nation for eleven days. If it is a race-related pattern, then it would be nothing short of an absolute miracle that no else has gotten hurt until now. The first problem with that is I don't believe in miracles. The second problem is that this could expose Pegasus to an unholy firestorm of litigation. I hope the next thing Alex says neither implies miracles nor portends lawsuits.

Alex looks up at me, then down at his data dock and begins to move his hands wildly. The electric orange light stains his face and dances through the edges of his afro, giving its edge a strange, otherworldly glow. He looks like an upside-down volcano. And then, he erupts.

"Shit."

"Shit what?"

"Shit. It's the history match. I knew this would come back to screw us."

"I need you to make sense Alex."

Alex doesn't respond at first. He glances back down at his data dock then up to me. "This Borg still runs on the BAE seven-point-one engine," he says finally.

The Borg Artificial Emotion engine is installed in all our Borgs. It's how we can take an artificial bioplasmium body, install neuroprocessors in it, and make it autonomous by dynamically inducing optimized emotional responses based on the situation. It's AI but with synthetic feelings, and it's as close to artificial life as anyone has ever come. It was the first piece of code to pass a Turing test. It's also Pegasus Incorporated's intellectual property. The BAE 7.1 engine was built to work with the first set of law enforcement Borgs we ever made, and there was never any significant problem with them in the field, so I still don't get what he's telling me. I ask, "Okay. So it's first gen, so what?"

Alex speaks quickly, his hands stuck in his afro, "When we were designing BAE for smart cops, we found it was almost impossible to create appropriate synemotions for all possible law enforcement conditions. There were just too many variables to consider when doing a threat assessment. The police committee gave us a requirements list four thousand pages long. We just couldn't do it." Then Alex adds, "So we took a shortcut."

"That's what people always say when they are about to tell me something terrible."

"Well. It was the only way we could do it." He continues, "Neural networks. We used neural networks to train BAE to recognize threats. Mimic human cop behaviour."

My eyes widen and all of a sudden I am aware of how close my face is to the projected screen on the desk. I lean back as I say, "Oh... Ohhh..."

Alex goes on. "We used police records to train the neural network. Figure out which input data mattered to the officers when they made their decisions and if the outcomes were favourable. A justified shooting, a good arrest, a conviction that was not later overturned, that kind of thing."

"I don't like the sound of this," I say. I want to say more, but Alex's words have made me extremely uncomfortable, so I focus on the case at hand. "If the BAE engine couldn't really create an appropriate law enforcement synemotion matrix without the help of a neural network..." I say slowly, thinking about each word, "...why did we commission the Borgs and put them in the field with humans?"

"Because it worked," Alex says, almost apologetically. "The neural nets worked. We developed a solid base synemotion matrix and built from there. There were a few hiccups along the way, like in Phoenix, but all kept under control. Plus the seven point one was a limited release, only issued in a few cities. By the time BAE seven point two was being built, we knew enough to not need the neural nets anymore."

I shake my head and say, "Okay, now go back a bit. Make this make sense to me. What exactly about BAE seven point one makes you think our Borgs have a bug that makes them specifically attack young black men and why are the attacks so sparse?"

Alex's hands seem stuck to his head now. He isn't even looking directly at me anymore. "Look, Liz, with neural nets, the more input data they have, the better. So we used all we had. Everything from the twentieth and twenty-first centuries. Most of it from the United States. And I remember stories my grandmother used to tell me about cops killing unarmed black kids back in the day and getting let off. The cases were recorded as being justified, so they were used as part of our training dataset. I think the seven-point-one Borgs mapped some element of that history into their logic. A small but deadly ghost of pattern recognition. Given the precise nature of both attacks, I'd say the neural nets mapped a very specific median age, race and general appearance to a sudden fear response."

This case is becoming more of a nightmare with every passing second. Suddenly, I am desperate for a cigarette. "So what you're saying to me, in essence, is that we made racist Borgs. Is that what you're telling me Alex?"

"No. Not racist, per se," Alex says, his eyes visibly red and rheumy despite the orange light from his screen flecking them. "It looks more like it's an irrational bias. A hard-coded potential for fear of young black men. BAE synemotion matrices don't map into hate. Or love for that matter. We don't use those for anything and to be honest we don't really understand them as well as we do most other emotions. But fear, yes. We use that. A bug that creates a potential fear spike in the presence of young black males. That is the only thing that explains all the data reflectors you've just shown me."

"Shit." I suck my teeth. He may have a point. This is what we get from relying on the past to design the future. *Irrational bias*, as Alex says. And if he is right then this bug has now cost at least two young men their lives. It could cost even more if I don't do something about it.

And suddenly I remember the anger and agitation of Captain Ekhomu, the undiscerning and irrational way he has handled everything so far, how he tried to attack and strangle Neville to death as though he were human. How long would it be before he tried to lock up the three hundred kilogram bioplasmium and titanium alloy Borg like a common criminal? I try not to think too much about what would happen if Captain Ekhomu sent a group of young male officers to move Neville, or worse, tried to lock him up in a jail cell full of young Nigerian men. How long would it take before the bug, if indeed it was the problem, found someone that fit its precise trigger parameters, produced a fear spike and sent him into a murderous rage?

I exhale, and embedded in my exhalation is worry, even fear. "Alex, I'm going to shut the Borg down right now, before it sees anyone else in its bug trigger range and does more damage."

Alex nods his understanding, uncharacteristically stoic, and I rise to my feet. My screens fade to black and recede into my data dock, taking Alex's image with them, but not the sound of his steady breathing, which I can still hear coming through my induction microphones like a whoosh of rainfall. I turn them off and step out of the white room, into the corridor.

"Do you need something, madam?" the skinny, hawk-faced officer that is my escort asks, snapping to attention.

"Please take me back to the interview room, now," I say, as I realise that shutting down Neville may be the easiest part of what will be a long and difficult resolution case. I will have to call the Dubai operations centre and probably arrange for victim compensation. I won't get back to Beijing anytime soon.

He throws a sharp salute, then says, "Yes madam," and takes me back the way we came, descending the stairs rapidly and rounding the corner that leads us into the grey corridor where the interview room is set into the left side of the building. He opens the door for me and I step through, coming face-to-face with Neville for the second time this hour.

Neville looks at me with a glassy wetness in his eyes, his synemotions rearranging his brow into remorseful furrows. "You found something. Have you come to shut me down?" he asks softly.

"Yes," I say. "You're malfunctioning. You should have already noticed that. It's not your fault, but we have to take precautions."

"I know I am malfunctioning," he says, without breaking eye

contact. "Can you tell me what is wrong with me?"

"I don't think I can," I tell him as considerately as I can. He appears human enough for me to afford him that courtesy.

Neville goes quiet for a while and then he asks, "Will I ever be brought back online?"

I think about it for a few seconds and then I say, "I don't think so," because there is typically no need to lie to a Borg. They are not irrational about anything, not even their survival. Except this one who has a highly specific problem. "I cannot guarantee you will be fixed. But we will try. We will try our best."

"I don't want to be irrational," he says, his metallorganic eyes boring into mine. And then, they close. "Please, go ahead."

I walk briskly but cautiously behind Neville. He sits perfectly still as I quietly work the tip of my dataphone jack from the barely visible slot in my wristwatch and use it to press open the bioplasmium casing underneath the scar behind his left ear. He does not flinch, but he turns his head slightly. I pause.

"I am sorry," he says quietly.

"Me too, officer," I say.

And then I pull on the wet cylindrical cartridge of the BAE 7.1 neuroprocessor that is attached to his very real bioplasmium brain and disconnect the two parts that make up one of the world's most complex, but fatally flawed, computing systems.

Nneoma

Technically speaking, I am dead.

But I won't let a minor inconvenience like that prevent me from telling you the brief yet undoubtedly fascinating story of how I came to be this way. Besides, I have plenty of time. We all do. Much more than you can possibly know. I should know, I used to be like you. But I have become aware, even in this in-between place that the shadows call home, of a great vastness and elasticity of existence. Though I am caged, the presence of things far and unseen reach me as though they were only a little distance away and knowable. I have conversed with things that be not as though they were. I have treaded the thoughts of children like shallow pond water; I have run through their tears like a wild animal caught in tropical rain. I have seen the hearts of the aged; I have clutched their anguish. I know the moment of death; I know the cold and the pain and the searing light that neither melts the ice of nothingness from the bones of men nor extinguishes the fires of pain that dances on their flesh as they cross the threshold between existences.

All these things have come to me in little whispers that echo through nebulous absence; hollow voices of my brothers in the void; sharp breaths that blow from nowhere and everywhere all at once. Through this haze of whisperings and pseudo-palpations, I have come to understand that there are many more places than the human eye can see while it is still blinded by the gift of sight and there is so much more to being than the binary states - dead, and alive - which so many are so certain of while they yet live.

Besides, what does it even really mean to be alive anyway? Beyond the basic precepts of eating and breathing and thinking and feeling and moving, every human while they draw breath, keeps locked away in some seldom swept corner of their mind the knowledge that there is far more to being alive than being able to tick-off the appropriate signalling and self-sustaining systemic functions on a list. Life is far more complicated.

Anyway, forgive my periphrasis. I am bush-beating.

The story then.

I am now in the state which you would consider dead because I fell in love with the kind of woman that entire religions, cultures and civilizations concoct elaborate legends and myths to warn men like me about. She was beautiful, in the manner that such women always are as a matter of necessity. Her name was Nneoma and it was raining the day I met her.

She was sitting at the bar in the recently completed Oriental hotel, the one that stands between Lekki Road and the Lagos Lagoon like a monolith to a dubious water spirit. She was alone; sipping on an almost-clear long island iced tea that was clearly drowning in its own ice. Rain pattered against the building like the drumbeats of ants going to war. All around the bar, there were expats smoking slim cigarettes, svelte, dark-skinned sex kittens in short skirts and barely-existent necklines, and the odd corporate yuppie group here and there. The bright, strobe lights crawled along their flesh, the carpeted floor, angular walls and high ceiling in a wild, aimless hurry to go nowhere. In the corner to my far left, about twenty feet in front of the bar, there was a live band whose vocalist was a compact man with too-tight clothes and too little regard for pitch, sweating as he stood on a small stage screeching something strident while a few overdressed men simulated slow, savage sex with skinny, scantily clad seductresses on the dance floor below. The rain and the songs did not complement one another, creating instead, a discordant background noise that only bothered me in the detached way that chirping crickets would bother a man lost in his thoughts on a quiet night. Besides, I didn't care much for music or rain, I was taken with her.

The first thing I noticed about her was how sleek her fingers were, wrapped around the highball glass. They were long, thin and smooth like a French cigarette. She had radiant ebony skin and her own natural hair was augmented with the hair of someone who had evidently been Latin American - Peruvian or Brazilian or something of the sort. I never could keep up with Nigerian women and their constantly changing choices in sourcing for and applying the latest hair extension fashions. Her pouted lips were full and painted in a shade of red so bright it was a hair's breadth away from being gaudy and she was sheathed in a bodycon dress so tight, it could have been a condom. She was improbably attractive.

I am a fool and so I did then what fools do - I fell in what I thought was love with her instantly. I stood up, ignoring the sudden increase in my heart rate and focusing instead on her and how the brightly coloured lights seemed to bend to her body's whims whenever they hit her as though her hills and crevices were subtly more difficult to navigate than any other surface in the room.

"You look like you need another drink," I shouted over the noise as

I walked up to her, timing the end of my sentence to coincide with my final step, two paces away from her barstool. "Perhaps something with a little less ice in it?" I smiled, hopeful.

"Buy me one then," she said tersely without looking at me. Her accent was hard to place. It was not Nigerian, of that I was absolutely sure. It was not faux-British or forced-American or any of the other atrocious, appropriated accents that a certain class of Nigerians sometimes struggled to put on in order to appear more cultured and travelled than they actually were and yet it had an uncommon, unfamiliar prosody to it. An almost musical quality that rendered her words more sung than pronounced. I mused on it as I ordered a caipirinha from the bar without giving it too much thought; desperately hoping she would not take offense to having a drink ordered for her without her approval of the choice being sought first. I had to show some measure of confidence, women liked that, I believed.

"So what's a nice young girl like you doing in a bad place like this?" I asked loudly enough to be heard over the music and ambient noise of the bar as I placed the caipirinha in front of her and leaned on the hardwood bar, trying my best to appear smooth and confident.

She looked first to the drink, then to me, before chuckling and asking. "You really think this place is a bad place?"

"No, not the bar," I said hastily. "I mean Lagos. Lagos is a bad place. And I have a feeling you're not from around here. You don't seem like a Lagosian."

She smiled an almost otherworldly smile at me. It was a small, strange smile; her teeth were barely exposed, but the sparkle in her glassy eyes that caught the light frequently, flashing a different colour each time as though it were an inside joke between her and the building, revealed just how amused she was by my admittedly shabby attempt at a pick-up.

"Well, no. I'm not from Lagos," she said. "But I like it here. And I don't think it's a bad place."

"I do think it is a bad place, but it's bad in a good sort of way." I placed my own drink on the bar and looked right into her eyes for effect. "You know, it's always the things and the places that are bad for you that end up being the most pleasurable to experience."

"You're cute," she said abruptly, ran a finger through her hair and paused to take her first sip of the drink I'd bought for her before adding, "How long have you been married?"

I recoiled sharply and regarded her with uncertain expectation, as though her statement might be the opening to some sort of joke whose punchline was yet to arrive. Then I remembered I had forgotten to take off my wedding ring. A sort of cold fear gripped me suddenly like the memory of some sin long forgotten. I lowered my voice and spoken softly, "I'm not married; I just wear this for-"

"Stop. Don't do that," she interrupted me, shaking her head.

"Do what?" I queried sheepishly as a thin sheen of sweat seeped through my pores and coated the skin of my forehead like dewdrops on elephant grass.

"Please don't do that."

"Do what? I'm not doing anything-"

She interrupted me with a loud sigh before speaking again, her tone caustic. "Look, I know you want to have sex with me, you've made that painfully obvious, and while I appreciate the drink and the attempted conversation, I would appreciate directness even more. I'm not sure if it was intentional or not but I like the fact that you didn't take off your wedding ring before approaching me. That would have been tacky. And even if you just forgot to take it off though you intended to, which now seems to be the case, please don't insult me by trying to cover it up with a silly, obvious lie. I'm not stupid, okay?"

"Okay." I agreed because there was not much else I could do. I felt I was teetering on the edge of losing whatever measure of her interest I had aroused and even though I cannot quite explain how the fear of losing it felt, I can tell you that the thought of her dismissing me sent a raw, potent dread coursing through me like liquid lightning. So when she finally asked, "Again, how long?" I simply replied, "Seven years," because it was true.

"Good boy." She uncrossed her long legs, flashing me a swath of polished thigh that stoked my yearning for the place where her thighs met and then crossed them again. I dry-swallowed.

"Now, sit down beside me and be quiet," she said. "Just wait until I finish my drink and don't say anything. When I am done, we will go upstairs, make love until dawn or until you can't keep up with me anymore and then I will leave. You will go back to your wife and you will never cheat on her again. You understand?"

I didn't, so I protested, my voice small and whiny even to my own ears, "But I really like you," I began, "Look, it's not just about sex. Tell me your name, I want to get to know you and..."

"No."

"No?"

"No. It doesn't work that way. Now will you be quiet and wait or do I have to make a scene? Do you want me to slap you, toss this drink in your face and walk away?"

At that I found myself silenced and suddenly pensive. She seemed almost angry, but not quite. Her manner was that of a professional being forced to deal with a child, not a woman that had just been seduced. The entire situation was emasculating, unsettling and to be honest, I was tempted to walk away from it there and then. But I have already told you I am a fool, she was stunning and I thought I was in love so I do not really need to tell you that I did not walk away, do I? Instead of leaving, I waited for her to finish her drink, walked down to the concierge with her arm in mine and her heady perfume in my nose and paid one hundred and seventy thousand naira for a deluxe suite on the sixteenth floor.

While I did all this, she did little except squeeze my arm and smile her small, strange smile at the right times, in measured, efficient bursts, like machine gun fire. I collected the plastic, black keycard from the chubby, plastic-faced concierge after informing him that we did not have any luggage and therefore would not need an escort. His expression might have changed but I did not notice it. It was difficult to distinguish one of his strained smiles from another. We headed for the elevator.

Alone, in the claustrophobic embrace of the elevator, without warning, she grabbed my arm, pulled me close and drew me in for a kiss. It was a hasty, frenzied thing. There was no passion to it, but there was need. I kissed her back fervently and we clung together like a compound name until the ding of the elevator informed us that we had reached our floor. We spilled out of the elevator and into the expansive, expensive luxury suite, a fluid mass of heavy breaths, limbs and lust.

The night quickly took on the quality of an alcohol-induced daze. I could attempt to describe it in vivid detail here but that would not do whatever I have that passes for memories of it justice. I will say of it however, that one pleasure blurred into another as we used our bodies to dance in all the ways a man could dance with a woman. One moment I was behind her, her thighs bouncing wildly at every thrust, breathing staccato breaths in the heat of tropical evening, the next she was atop me, riding fiercely like an ancient warrior queen charging into battle. In some other moment, suspended in between times and passions, we made love to each other slowly, gently in the way that only lovers who are also friends can. It was beautiful and it was strange and it was intense and it only made me fall deeper in what I believed was love with her even more.

When the sun rose and brought with it the clarity of morning, I awakened in the smooth, plush embrace of the hotels sateen bedding, instantly aware that I was not in my home and, perhaps even more intensely, that there was no one beside me. I turned to lie on my side slowly, carefully, reaching out as I did, hoping that I would feel warm flesh. I did not. Instead, I felt somewhat diminished; overwhelmed with an inexplicable feeling of absence of something which I could not quite identify, as though I had lost some essential, intangible aspect of myself. Craning my neck to look along the bed, I saw her. She was sitting at the foot of the bed—naked and beautiful—her lightly dimpled back bathed in a sliver of yellow dawn light and her lips pursed around the end of a cigarette, sucking gently. She held the smoke in her chest only briefly before blowing out a lazy plume.

"Do you always smoke after sex?" I asked, because it seemed a harmless enough question and I was not sure what else to say.

"No," she said without turning to me. "I only smoke when I'm thinking."

She took another deep drag and blew, lowering the half-smoked butt clenched in her fingers to her side. Intrigued, I sat up, gathered the gathered the sheets around me and asked her what she was thinking about. She said nothing and so I asked again.

"What are you thinking about?"

She turned to me, her supple breasts bouncing gently and catching the light that had been dancing along her back. It arced across her polished flesh and in that instant; she looked like she was carved of pure obsidian. There were whitish streaks running all the way from her eyes to the bottom curve of her cheeks and I knew then that she had been crying but I had no idea why.

"You really think you love me." Her voice shook almost imperceptibly as she spoke.

"Yes," I said, because I am a fool.

"Do you even know what it really means to love someone?"

It did not seem much like a question, the stress was placed on the middle of the sentence, not at the end, and yet it undoubtedly was. Besides, the pause that followed left little doubt in my mind that she fully expected me to answer it.

"I don't know if I really know what love is for sure, but I know that whatever I believe it to be, I feel it for you right now. I have felt it since I first saw you."

Her laughter came suddenly, genuine, wild and all encompassing. She flung her head back and gripped the sheets with her left hand as though she needed them to anchor her in that storm of mirth. I was not sure why she was laughing but I was afraid of the strange, unexpected reaction.

"You find my feelings funny?" I asked cautiously.

She stopped laughing and thought for a moment. "No," she said. "You know nothing about love. You know nothing about life. Let me tell you what love really is." She let go of the sheets and pointed a long, slender finger at me. "Love is death in its kindest and most honest manifestation and falling in love is just like dying. Sometimes, it's a sudden, inexplicable madness that seizes you when you least expect it, and it feels like you were stabbed in your sleep or shoved off a cliff you didn't even know was there. Other times, it is a slow, serrated sword cutting away patiently at everything that is you, working its way towards your heart. It is always painful and it is always messy and it is always complicated but it is never a stupid pickup line in a bar or some stupid sex with someone you just met the night before. That is not love. If it does not feel like death, it is not true love. You should know better. You should have known better."

She put her left hand down and turned away from me as she added, "You shouldn't have said you love me. There are things in this world that do not suffer untruths."

Stunned, I said nothing until the silence between us began to burn my ears. I wanted to say something, anything, to counter her statements and buttress my declaration of love with the perfect words to convince her of their validity but I could barely breathe. It felt like the air had suddenly become thin and hot. Then, just when I could not endure it any more, she opened her mouth and finally broke that horrible, excruciating silence.

"Do you even know my name?"

"No," I exhaled. "I don't. What is your name?" I asked, genuinely curious.

"You don't truly love me. You shouldn't say you do. And you don't really want to know my name. You shouldn't say things you don't mean. Every lie calls upon ancient things that live in the darkness. You should not say things you don't mean, or you will join them."

"But I do want to know your name," I protested, confused. "You need to stop rambling and just listen to what I say. I love you."

"You don't mean that,"

"I do," I said hastily. "You've been crying. I can tell something has upset you but please, tell me your name and let us just talk like normal-"

"My name…" she started, and then paused as though considering carefully her next action, "…is Nneoma."

She wailed, turned to me and stared at me with eyes that were no longer brown and full as I remembered them but were now narrowed and burning a bright vermillion. She spoke then with a voice that was an entire register below her natural speaking voice. It vibrated and shook and reverberated throughout the room and her next sentence was an earthquake of syllables.

"To love is to die!"

Her eyes flared and suddenly, a soft but insistent force like a giant fist made of large pillows struck me in the chest. I fell back into the bed, supine, my hands pinned to my sides. I tried to rise but couldn't.

I started to panic, fearful and filled with dread. She leapt up in one impossible motion and latched onto the ceiling with claws I had not noticed she had before, extending from those slender, long fingers that suddenly seemed more like tentacles than fancy French cigarettes.

Her body rippled and spasmed in localised bursts as her polished, supple skin and brazen nakedness regressed to reveal a scaled and fearsome visage, its spine arched so the dim sliver of light from the window hit her shoulder and about a third of her face. I lay still on the bed, rigidified by something, perhaps simple, abject horror but more likely by some other unknown power of hers, as she sprouted wings with the suddenness and unexpectedness of an explosion - long, dark feathery wings that extended seamlessly from the flesh of her naked back. I opened my mouth as wide as my facial muscles allowed and screamed with all the inspiration fear afforded me but no sound escaped. She removed her claws from the ceiling and descended slowly downwards, gracefully, like a great, grand butterfly or perhaps an especially graceful moth. Her wings fanned gently, almost imperceptibly, each gust pulsing through her sleek, artificial hair, animating it. She sat astride me.

"You shouldn't say things like 'I love you' if they aren't true."

I like to believe that there was something about the beautifully horrific creature, her ochre pupils trained on me with a sort of pained intensity. I saw it in her eyes as she spoke her final words to me; like a disease lurking deep inside her veins, she carried within her a sort of concealed compassion and regret for what she was about to do. It was written in wetness of her eyes, in the way her lips were pursed, in the way she turned from me when she stuck her hand into my chest, parted my ribcage and stole the thing that bound my body to the world from me.

She rose and let out a wild cry that somehow seemed tender and loving, before leaping to flight and bursting through the window, ripping the curtains and taking off into the bright carmine and sienna hues of Lagos at sunrise. The light poured in through the broken window like a flood of geometrically precise paint, covering me in all its glory.

That was when I started to burn like a teenager's passion—intense and sudden, the flames high and wild - until I was nothing but charred pain and ash on the hotel's expensive sateen sheets.

And that is the end of my story.

Fascinating, is it not?

What am I now? I do not know. Of the fact that I am what you would refer to as dead and that Nneoma killed me in some manner which is not easily explained, despite my best attempts, I am sure. Why she did it, I do not know. Why did she seem to regret it when she did? That is even less clear to me. Perhaps this is what the illusion of love does to us, makes of us when we give into it without thinking, without considering. Every coin has two sides and every force has a dark opposite which is also its equal. I suppose love is no exception.

I have now become a shadow thing, like all her other victims before me - hiding in the world but not allowed to participate in it, watching from the places where light fears to tread, skulking in the dark places of this hotel room that is now my prison, waiting, watching tired businessmen and wealthy lovers come and go, hoping that one day, Nneoma will return. Perhaps to finally free me or perhaps, with another love-struck fool and soon-to-be hapless victim whom she will ride to some peak of pleasure and then abandon to ash and ruin as she flees to the skies. But even this thought is foolishness. The others have been in these non-places much longer than I have; some of them are bound to rocks in forests that men no longer hunt in, others are bound to houses inhabited by modern families, condemned to manifest their aged frustrations in minor acts that confuse but do not truly scare the inhabitants and yet even more like me are bound to roads, rivers, brooks; open places from which they constantly watch the living. We can all sense across the distance and through the darkness, the specific longing, desire and sense of loss unique to us. I understand, as do they, that even if Nneoma does ever come back, I will probably be unable to speak to her, to call her name, to tell her I still love her. I doubt I will. I am dead. I am nothing now - nothing but a persisting melange of thoughts, shadows, pain, consciousness and the final echoes of what was once a fool in love.

I, Shigidi

Prologue

The Shrine, Ikeja, Lagos. | June 20th, 1977 | 11:46 pm.

The air was saturated with a heady mix of lust, freedom and marijuana.

Aadit Kumar was sitting at an unstable table carved of cheap wood and held together by the skill of a poor carpenter. Fela Kuti was on a small make-shift stage singing something socially scathing while simulating strange, savage sex with a sweaty, skinny seductress to scintillating sounds from a splendid saxophone. The girl sitting next to Aadit, stroking his shaggy black hair with her long, sleek fingers was driving him insane.

She seemed, in his mind, to be Africa made flesh—dark, mysterious and just a bit little dangerous. She had radiant ebony skin that seemed to be made of midnight and the edges of her frizzy afro refined stray bits of light to an eldritch fringe.

She'd ignored everyone else at the gathering and come to sit by the hairy man with the Hindu name, gold chain, wedding ring, and American accent wearing the Ankara shirt and khaki bell-bottoms. He thought, charitably, that she was a very beautiful prostitute.

They were alone at the table and the space around them buzzed with electric lust as Fela moaned and laughed and shouted and sang with fevered ebullience. Aadit endured the aching in his head and in his loins until it became a mad pounding in the space behind his temples.

"Want to go to the back?" Aadit said to her carefully, trying to mask his embarrassment but still possessed with hot desire.

She laughed sharply, then smiled and stood up without saying a word. He concluded that his guess had been right. She let him lead her to a dark alley just outside the shrine after slipping an oily security guard a few one naira notes to ensure they would not be disturbed.

He leaned in to kiss her in the darkness but she pulled back.

"I know what you really want," she whispered breathily before turning around, hiking her leather skirt up and shoving her hands down his trousers. She seized him. He could barely breathe. Saxophone notes echoed around them. A cornucopia of sensations overran him as images flitted through his mind like butterflies in a field.

Birds. Lips. Music. Flowers. Wings. Skin. Sachika.
Sachika.

His mind instantly recrystallized into a lattice of coherence.

"Please. I'm sorry, I... I can't do this," he mumbled as he pushed her away and started to struggle with his trousers. She glared at him with eyes like dying coals.

"What are you doing?" she demanded.

"I'm sorry, I shouldn't have... I have a wife. I'll still pay, but I can't. I have a..."

Her voice took on the quality of an earthquake. "What is this? You think you can just stop? There are things that cannot stop once they have begun. Understand?"

Aadit's lust was hastily replaced by fear of equal magnitude. Perhaps greater. He glanced at the ground and noticed that despite the harsh light from a lone bulb hitting them at the same angle, his shadow was alone.

"You must finish."

Aadit realized with all the abruptness of tropical rainfall in July that he had done something terribly wrong with something that was not quite human. Driven by a wild, mad, need to escape, he snatched the gold chain hanging around his neck, removed the small peacock feather hanging from it that his mother had told him would protect him, and threw it at her. She leapt back to avoid it. He took his chance and fled for the taxi park.

There was first a piercing scream and then a tremulous cackling behind him, tainting the saxophone echoes in the air like rudely spilled black paint on silk robes.

I

The world was spinning when I woke up. My head was pulsing like a fearful human heart.

I managed to roll off my raffia mat before throwing up a good portion of the previous night's merriment and excess onto the red clay floor. The mess was brown and viscous; it contained pieces of half-digested kolanuts, morsels of meat, palm wine and blood. Lots of blood. I retched and threw up a second wave of vomit that left me feeling slightly less terrible. The world seemed a little less unstable. I managed to drag myself to my feet, stumble out of the door past the brief brush of bush beside my house and make my way to the hole in the ground that served as my latrine. I was there for at least half an hour, heaving, retching and spitting.

When the only thing that came after each burning retch was a clear and colourless liquid, I lifted my head from the pit and up towards the sky. The sun hung low and there were no clouds. Olorun was wearing red and yellow again. He seemed to favour those colours in the evenings even though he never wore the exact same dress twice. He was a vain one, our aloof and leisurely sky god. But I suppose leisure is your lot when you are Chairman of the board of what used to be one of the largest spirit-companies in this version of existence.

Staggering back into my hut, I began to feel like myself again. I ignored the smelly mess on my floor and readied myself for work. I could clean up later. No one visited me anyway.

I hated my job. It was dreary, uninteresting, and painfully mundane. But a deity had to do what he could to survive in hard times. Belief is scarce. Good offerings were far and few between and almost everyone I knew had already taken a prayer-cut.

By the time I had put on my official cloak of cowries, and covered my face in black clay, Olorun had changed outfits and was wearing his flowing black agbada as the sky; this one shimmering with star embroidery and a brightly beaming moon fila.

I took the untarred bush path that snaked past the disused shadow of the evil forest. Ososhi, master hunter and one of my few friends had mentioned a while ago that the Orisha board had voted to cut down the trees to make way for a movie shrine. It was a shame but they must pander to what few customers are left, I suppose. Evil forests are out, Nollywood is in. Belief is a funny thing.

The office looked even worse than it had two days earlier when I had come to collect last month's pray pay—most of which I had thrown up this morning. Another hole had appeared in the front wall just beside the door and another window pane had slipped from its place to hang precariously over the overgrown grass. The lights were out. I was not sure if it was because there was no one there or if the power had been cut. I sauntered through the curtain of hanging beads and into the reception, standing in a thin sliver of moonlight.

"Shigidi, you are late."

Oya, Sango's most annoying wife, was sitting in the darkness, at the reception desk.

"You this woman, why are you hiding in the shadows like a rat?"

"Everything will be shadow until one of you idiots gets a sacrifice big enough for us to afford to fix the generator."

Oya had a caustic way of distilling situations down to simplistic statements and then projecting them into the future.

"I see Well, it would help if you could speak to your husband about…"

"No. I won't." She cut me short as she stepped into the sliver of moonlight with me and handed me a half-melted candle and some matches. "Don't even mention Sango's name, you hear? If you try it I will slap you."

She was at least three times my height and four times as rotund. Not because she was that big, but because I was that small. Ugly and small. These are the characteristics that made me perfectly suited for the job which I hated so much. Sango made me that way intentionally - large head, ugly face, small body, ashy skin of unpolished clay. I had never felt the touch of a woman—human or spirit. How could I, looking like that? I hated it and had taken up the issue of my appearance with our spirit resources representative but I had been told that my creation and recruitment were both non-negotiable parameters of my contract. There were many non-negotiable parameters of my contract, including what Sango would do to me if I ever got into a fight with any of his wives.

So I said, "Fine. You are lucky I don't want trouble today," hoping to end the issue there.

She snorted. "Let me hear word please. You have an assignment to get to. Someone sent in a small sacrifice three hours ago. Log-in to the human world and respond to him as soon as you can. You know you still have a lot of objectives to meet this quarter." She handed me a work-slip and I studied it casually. It was a standard *nightmare-and-kill* job.

Turning around, she asked, "Have you seen Ososhi?"

"No, I haven't. Why are you looking for him?" I queried. There were rumours of competitor deity assassination. I suspected Sango was using my friend to do his dirty work.

Oya bent down and poked her ugly fat finger in my face, "Is it your business? Amebo! Drunken gossip hound. Get to work, lazy thing!"

Annoyed, I muttered, "Hag," under my breath and walked away. Sango's second wife was rude but I could not insult her to her face. Her husband—my boss—would punish me in ways that would boggle even the most macabre of minds in the spirit-company. I continued to my office.

My office was a small, grey room in the back of the building with a small bowl of water in the middle and several ancient charms hanging on the walls. The basics really: tortoise shell, cowries, palm fronds, dried frog skin, kola nuts, and one two hundred year old gourd of palm wine. Getting in, I placed my heavily tattooed forearm and fingers into the bowl of water. Each tattoo was a sigil; a log-in key of summoning for the wind between worlds. I waited for it to identify me before breaking into fevered incantation and entering my password.

The wind was almost imperceptible when it came. One moment, I was in my office, the next, I was in a lavish hotel room standing beside a bed where a naked man and woman writhed on thousand thread count sheets. I observed them closely.

The male was tall—his feet spilled over the edge of the king-size bed and his grey hair was cropped low. Wedding ring on finger, slight and slender, he appeared to be in his late fifties or early sixties. According to the work-slip, he was my target.

The female however, drew my attention with a bizarre power I could not resist. My eyes slid from the male to her and the first thing I noticed about her was how sleek her fingers were, resting on his bare chest. They were svelte and finely crafted, like one of those imported menthol cigarettes that had replaced our local pipes. She had radiant ebony skin and on her head was a corona of curly black hair splayed about her on the pillow. Her pout was full and blood-red. She was painfully beautiful—the kind of woman *Eshu* would have used to torment someone before destroying him, back when he was still head of our legal department.

I stepped toward the bed and made to press out the breath from the male whose business partner wanted him dead for personal reasons of his own—they did not matter. What mattered was that he had made a sacrifice to our spirit company and called upon me through an accredited spirit-company customer service agent—a Babalawo. I would do as he asked, be on my way and get paid.

I clambered onto the bed and made to move the female's hand from his chest so that I could sit on it and crush his lungs. That was when the female rose into the air suddenly like an erupting volcano; hot, intense and with violent quaking. She latched onto the ceiling with claws extending from her slender long fingers that were now covered in razor thin scales. Long, feathery wings burst out of her bare back, seamlessly obscuring her contorted spine. Her neck twisted at an impossible angle as she stared down at me.

"Shigidi!" She rumbled.

"Oh, for Olorun's sake!" I exclaimed, annoyed.

I knew her kind; they were freelancers not affiliated to any company. They did not trade in belief; they simply stole spirits and used them for their own sustenance through aggressive and deceptive guerrilla marketing. They were reviled by my colleagues. I was indifferent to them but I did not want one of them undercutting my job.

"What is your name then?" I asked the thing. Well, her. It looked like a her at least.

"Naamah," she said in a voice that vibrated violently like the ground beneath a besieged city. "My name is Naamah. But in this body, I prefer to be called Nneoma."

She was one of them then—one of the original four of her kind. I felt a small measure of fear creep up on me.

"Nneoma, look, this man's life is mine." I told her as I waved my palm through the air, displaying my work-slip in bold-font spirit particles.

She laughed with a sound like a burning city.

"Those documents mean nothing to me, little nightmare god. He has lain with me. He has enjoyed the pleasure between my thighs. His essence belongs to me now. I will claim it at sunrise."

"But if you take his spirit, he will end up trapped between worlds." I protested. "You will leave a shadow of him that will haunt hidden places. What's the point of that then? My client needs him dead. My job requires me to make him dead. Please don't make this difficult."

She let out a sound somewhere between amusement and annoyance.

"It seems we have a problem then, little nightmare god."

"Yes. We do." I confirmed, preparing myself for a fight.

I like women, I really do. But they never seem to want to do anything with me except fight. There's something about me that just seems to bring out the worst in them. So, accepting my fate, I looked around the room for a good position from which I could strike the beautiful, evil woman in front of me when she suddenly said, "Have you ever been with a woman, Shigidi?"

Her voice was no longer harsh and trembling; it had suddenly gone soft and genteel but her eyes still glowed ruby red and danced in their sockets frantically like the flames of a forest fire.

"No," I answered honestly. "What does that have to do with anything?"

"I can break your contract," she said coyly.

That was when I saw that there was something strange about her. I should have known the moment I saw her. It wasn't her horrific beauty or the fact that she was perched on the ceiling, slit pupils trained on me with a curious intensity. I had seen stranger than her familiar form, the leathery wings and ochre eyes were something that Eshu used to pull off for a drunken laugh at our spirit-company's annual end of year parties. No, there was something else, something subtler. It was in the way she still arched her spine so the yellowed bulb hit her breasts at just the right angle to rivet my badly drawn eyes. In the way her wings fanned gently, almost imperceptibly, each gust pulsing through her wild hair, giving it life. It was the way her lips were pursed, just at the edges, a perpetual pout. She was putting on a show. Reeling me in. She wanted something from me.

"I can make you one of us, nightmare god. If you lay with me, you will no longer be as you are now. I possess both powers of extraction and transformation. Lay with me and you will take upon my form."

Something rumbled in me, trapped inside my earthen flesh and lipless smile. I was not used to being headhunted. Especially by such an alluring recruiter.

"Are you trying to trick me, Nneoma?"

"Not at all. Come, join us. It's not so different from what you do now. You will still take spirits but you will pleasure them first and they will pleasure you. You will work for yourself, not for that corporate sociopath Sango. You will travel beyond African shores too—taste sweet American flesh, spicy Asian spirits, hardy European souls. You will no longer be ugly. You will be handsome, tall, hulking, admired by all who set their eyes upon you. I do not wish to kill you in a fight for this meagre mortal's soul. Will you not lay with me, Shigidi?"

"No," I said.

She grinned from ear to ear, apparently unruffled by my refusal. I could not tell if she was just amused or she was simply unused to being denied.

"No?" She asked, slightly tilting her face so the light exaggerated her cheekbones.

"No. I will not lay with you. I don't trust you."

We stood, staring and smiling at each other.

I considered her proposal as I took in her polished ebony skin, long neck and gracile arms that seemed to have been carved by the hands of a particularly precise god—like one of those yuppie craftsmen that helped build Ile-ife back when Olorun was still running the company himself. I too could be viewed with such awe if I believed her. Lay with her. Quit my job. Or I could fight her and probably lose. I would then be forced to return to the office with an assortment of injuries and to the bite of Oya's caustic insults. I would not meet my quarterly spirit-collection objectives and Sango would probably dock my pray pay for the next six months. It wasn't worth a fight, the sensible thing to do was to take her offer but I wasn't going to allow myself be recruited too easily.

"Nightmare god, don't you want to be beautiful? The spirit market isn't what it used to be. Faith prices are falling. At least with me you will feed directly from the source. Come now. Lay with me."

The offer was indeed too good to be true. Our kind needs belief to exist and we need human spirits to enjoy our existence. A freshly harvested soul is worth the faith of a hundred believers to our vitality and well-being. But the consumption of souls by spirit-companies is tightly regulated. We can only take souls when requested by a human prayer or summoning. Faith around the world had taken a hit, and the big two multinationals dominated what was left of the market after subjecting our local spirit business practices to a brutal smear campaign; luring away our own people by presenting our corporate culture as 'barbaric' and theirs as 'civilised'. The universe thrives on irony.

I barely had enough people that believed in me to get by. And I had to share what souls I reaped with the company. So yes, the times were indeed changing. Perhaps, I thought, it was time for me to change along with them. My options were limited anyway.

"Alright. I accept your offer."

Her grin became a smile that seemed to radiate her pleasure outward in cresting waves. I had been recruited.

I rose slowly from my position above the sleeping man, who remained oblivious to all that was transpiring around and above him.

She removed her claws from the ceiling and descended slowly downwards from her perch on the ceiling, gracefully, like a grand butterfly or perhaps an especially graceful moth. She landed and sat on the vanity table, crossing her legs so a swath of thigh lay exposed but not the prize beyond. I angled my neckless head, the supple pseudo-clay of my shoulders yawning to accept the impossible. I trembled with anticipation.

"Tell me, Nneoma, what is it like to lay with a creature as beautiful as you are?" I asked in a low, eager whisper, betraying myself.

Her body rippled as her wings shrunk and her fearsome persona regressed, leaving supple skin and a brazen nakedness like I had never seen before. I barely even noticed the man I had been sent to kill sizzle and char underneath me, my eyes were fixed solely on Nneoma's hills and crevices, and how the light seemed to bend to her body's whims. She walked up to me, her full hips swinging with each step; put her hands into my dirty khaki trousers and her lips to my ears, filling me with an alien heat and desire.

"Shigidi darling," she murmured, "the pleasure between these thighs is to die for."

Her touch was wonderful. I had never experienced anything like it, not even during my official induction when Sango first created and recruited me.

"You are an amazing woman, Nneoma," I croaked.

Her laughter was genuine, wild and all encompassing. It almost made me want to chuckle too, to validate her mirth but all I could do was breathe in short, sharp breaths.

She pushed me onto the bed and scooped a handful of ash from behind me, letting it fall through her fingers. "You insult me, nightmare god."

The ash continued to fall.

"I am not a woman, not anymore."

I could barely contain myself as she dragged my trousers down and slid herself onto me. I felt everything I had ever known bifurcate, torn apart by unbelievable pleasure. The world spun around me and blurred into a greyish nothingness that pushed against me from all sides. I gasped. It felt like the wind between worlds had become a tornado and I was caught in it. I could feel my form disintegrating and spreading into the grey haze that saw and felt and was all.

Coming from a place where each trip into the human world had to be requested through the official travel desk and with my sigils closely monitored once approved, it felt like a glimpse of omniscience. Pure unadulterated freedom. And then there was the pleasure.

I moaned.

I was all at once the smoke filled air of Obalende and the fresh sea salt of Victoria Island, the swampy fog of Makoko and frigid metallic din of Apapa. I engulfed every soul, inhaled through every nostril and loved with every heart. I was unfolding. My contract was being broken and it was exhilarating.

Just as I began to understand the scope of the gift Naamah was giving me, I felt myself suddenly withdrawn, dragged back to the world with the violent efficiency of a recoiling whip. I shrieked. It was a guttural shriek that burst from within me as I peaked in a corybantic explosion of sensations and light. So much light.

The light became unbearably bright and I felt the urge to cover my face. My body slowly reconstituted itself into a form that was familiar but not quite, in a world that was now no longer abstract and nebulous but firm as retribution. Swiftly, with my eyes still closed, my hands flew to my face and travelled down, collating organs, limbs and features, making sure everything was intact. I was the same, still made of Sango's familiar clay, but better. Much better. No longer the squat legs and arms, but sleek limbs and a chiselled face that even the most artistic hands in ancient Ile-Ife would have envied. She had remade me in her image, given me the uniform of the freelance spirit agent - beauty. I opened a sculpted eye, and then another and removed my lengthened arms from my face to unveil Nneoma, standing by the window, smoking a cigarette. It was almost dawn.

"Did you enjoy your transfiguration?" she asked quietly, turning to me.

I nodded.

Looking down at the pile of ash in which I sat naked, I opened my mouth to speak but words failed me, so I sat, jaw bobbing in silence at words I couldn't seem to string together.

"It is lonely, being a freelancer in this business. I have wanted a partner for so long. Will you now forsake all others for me?"

There it was, revealed. The final section of the recruitment - an agreement to terms and conditions. The signing of a new, different contract. The spirit business is a ruthless one and even a freelancer has to have a partner. Or at least someone they can trust.

But I did not mind, I did not want to be alone either. I wanted to be with her. How could I not? She was powerful and beautiful.

I wanted to say yes but the words wouldn't come so I turned to the bed and using my clay fingers that shimmered with recently rearranged spirit particles, scrawled into the ash that had been landscaped all over it in big, ungainly letters,

"Y E S."

II

Her sequin blouse clung tightly around her and glimmered sharply in the evening paleness, lending what I can only describe as an almost spectral quality to her already divine figure. Nneoma was, as always, dressed to kill.

The night was young but the day had gone by quickly and the night seemed to be in an equal hurry to end. Olorun always seemed to grow impatient in November. We were eager to find a spirit to consume before the dawn brought Lagos dwellers back to their senses. We were free of schedules and KPIs and targets but we still needed to collect enough to keep ourselves satiated. We hurried down the stairs of the Ikoyi town house we had 'inherited' from our last victims three weeks ago and got into the Range Rover. I started the vehicle and eased out of the gate.

I looked up through the window and saw that the sky had fashioned itself a tattered blanket of violet and gold.

"Olorun is playing games tonight," I said, my lips barely parting.

Nneoma seemed a bit startled. Her eyes spun to gaze at me sharply, but only briefly. Then she relaxed.

"The Orisha have their games, and we have ours," she replied with a tender smile before looking away.

I let down the window of our sleek, black Sport Utility Vehicle, savouring the titillating scent of dried fish and kerosene as they mingled with the sweat of the hawkers. Lagos was an olfactory paradise. I had never smelled the city in such detail before when I had my small, squat body. With this new, beautiful shell, I saw and smelled and felt so much. It was intoxicating.

"You look impossibly handsome, Shigidi," Nneoma said, her voice thick with a rasp. I wore a grey suit, purple shirt and matching pocket square. My clean-shaven head gleamed. I had no doubt I was as she said, impossibly handsome. She had moulded Sango's clumsy clay into something exquisite and her praise was more for her handiwork than my appearance.

"Thank you."

"Look at them," she started, touching my shoulder as I slid the vehicle onto Falomo Bridge. "All these people, looking without seeing anything. Even the spirits among them will never realize what it is like to be like us, to be free to prowl for faith and spirit sustenance. It's wonderful, isn't it?"

I said, "Yes, it is." Mostly because that was what I was supposed to say, but also because it was true.

A skinny young boy in tattered clothes ran up to our car as traffic slowed and tried to clean the windscreen with an ugly makeshift squeegee. I dismissed him with a short but violent wave.

Nneoma seemed to be in a strange mood. She seemed anxious. I had never seen Nneoma look anxious. Then, unexpectedly she asked, "Were you ever human, Shigidi? Even temporarily?"

"No. Short term assignments in human bodies were restricted to high-value performers in the spirit company. The real faith-makers and spirit reapers and those that kissed Sango's ass." I didn't add that it was only restricted because the spirit-company was insanely worried that one of us would impregnate a human female and create an *Abiku* bastard.

"That's a pity," Nneoma told me and went quiet.

Confused, I said nothing.

She sighed.

A few silent minutes later, we reached our destination.

The massive metal gate regarded us with suspicion when we arrived until the guards pulled its maw open. The car slid through and we parked our car right in front of the main foyer.

"Let's find some food," Nneoma said as she slid her hand into the crook of my muscled arm.

We walked in briskly, determined to make the most of the night. The Oriental hotel lobby was well furnished. On the far wall ahead of us stood what I knew to be the largest painting in Lagos. I knew

Nneoma would want to see it again. It had become a sort of pre-work ritual for her here. She always did. We ambled up to it and lingered.

"It is a Sebanjo. One of the largest oil on canvas paintings in the world. Magnificent, isn't it?"

The voice was gentle and melodious, like the music that comes from the slow dance of fingers on a finely tuned goje. I turned around to face its owner—a tall, shapely woman with creamy skin and dark hair in a royal blue bodycon dress. Her glassy eyes caught the light frequently, revealing a different colour each time as though it were an inside joke between her and the building. She wore the kind of smile that made things happen in Lagos. The whole woman was improbable. I instantly grew suspicious. But not suspicious enough.

"It must have cost a fortune," Nneoma said to the woman, smiling. "But it is a pleasure to see such a beautiful thing in Lagos."

She spoke with the kind of warmth reserved for old friends. Nneoma was perpetually charming, it was part of her work philosophy, but I knew there was something different about this. She seemed to instantly like this woman.

"Yes indeed. It is," she proclaimed, before extending her hand to Nneoma. "My name is Omolara and this is my husband, Rotimi."

The man she gestured to, about seven steps away, looking at another painting, was dressed as glamorously as his wife but lacked the same brilliance in his eyes. He turned to address us and seemed mildly amused by the scene his wife had orchestrated. He kissed Nneoma's hand and shook mine as Nneoma introduced herself to them.

"Nneoma. Such a beautiful name. Can my husband and I buy you and your-" She paused, waiting for Nneoma to introduce me, since I had chosen to remain silent. She obliged.

"Boyfriend."

The woman and I regarded each other briefly.

"Yes, of course, your boyfriend. Can we buy you both drinks?"

Nneoma nodded slightly at me, marking them as our first targets for the night, before replying with a smile like a knife's edge. "Only if you join us upstairs, I hear there is an excellent live band playing Fela classics tonight."

"Of course," she agreed, smiling. The light caught her eyes and flashed hazel. Nneoma was flirting with her and she welcomed it.

We walked to the elevator briskly—a powerful quartet of beauty, flamboyance and sensuality drawing stares like a four-sided magnet.

In the claustrophobic embrace of the elevator, Omolara, without warning, turned to Nneoma and drew her in for a kiss. It was a hasty thing. There was no artifice to it, just need. Nneoma kissed her back fervently and and their passions flowed together like a cocktail.

Her husband pressed himself against Nneoma from behind and kissed her neck. Nneoma shot me a look and so I joined the three bodies and slipped a hand between Nneoma and Omolara to cup a full breast. The heat and lust in that small space was overwhelming. I was not sure if we were the seducers or the seduced but I could not bring myself to pull away. Not with Nneoma egging me on, eager to claim the two lusty, beautiful spirits with us.

We never reached the bar, arriving instead, on the ninth floor where Omolara and Rotimi had a suite. We spilled out of the elevator and into their expansive luxury suite, a fluid mass of heavy breaths, limbs and lust.

I watched Nneoma yield to Omolara and Rotimi's hands. There was a learned aspect to their manipulations. Then Rotimi rolled onto the other side of the bed, lifted Nneoma's dress up and eased himself into her, thrusting with slow, deliberate motions.

I let my mind drift as her pleasure intensified, hypnotically drawing me to the tangle of flesh, into that dire mire of mad desire. I slid toward the bed and Omolara reached for me, cupping my face and expertly guiding it to her mouth for a kiss as intense as childbirth. I was suddenly thrown into a haze of my pleasure. My eyes rolled back behind shut eyelids as Omolara's mouth worked its magic on mine.

The kiss held for so long, I began to feel like I was drowning.

And then, as in a nightmare, I realised I was.

I could not breathe, the clay of my lungs felt swollen and thick. I began to struggle. I tried to wrestle my mouth from Omolara's but I could not and so I drew back my right arm and threw a vicious punch right into her abdomen. She detached with a muted whimper, rolled backwards, and onto her feet. At that point, I knew something was very wrong with the night's business. It was what we used to call, back when I was in the spirit-company, an unforeseen job process deviation.

Nneoma's eyes had widened at the sight, rinsed of any passion she had been in the throes of earlier. I watched her try to rise into the air, let her wings loose and fly but she seemed unable to move, unable to detach herself from Rotimi who had stopped thrusting and now lay atop her, still as a statue.

It was magun.

Fucking magun.

"Nneoma," I called to my partner. "Listen, I know this category of juju. They use it to bind cheating wives to their partners in infidelity. You've been locked to that…" I looked at the hardening, still form on top of her and continued "…thing."

Nneoma seemed to scream, "Help me!" but her voice trailed off into silence even though I could still see her mouth move. The modified magun must have locked both her body and her mind. She could not move or talk to use her powers or transform or do anything until I separated her from it. I tensed.

Omolara silently kept her eyes locked on me, her eyes red. Her burnt honey skin started to desiccate and flake away. I understood then what was going on. My former employers had come for me.

"Shigidi," Omolara called to me. Her voice had melted away and now sounded like the moaning of rivers.

"What made you think you could just break your contract and run away with this demon whore?" she said to me, her voice full of something like scorn.

She had almost completely shed her skin and beneath it, I could see she was not this Omolara woman at all, if such a person had ever existed. No. The person moulting from the shell of beautiful skin was squat and grounded by an impossible amount of weight around her middle, most of it in grand rolls of fat that hung from her stomach like fleshy drapes and in her wide, rolling hips. Her ears had been rudely cut off and her hair was woven into tight corn rows that ran parallel to each other, meeting at the centre of her head from which rose a broad spike of hair that rose high above her like a failed attempt to stab the ceiling. It was Oba — first wife of that bastard Sango and head of spirit-resources at my former company.

She had tricked us, with an animated golem, like me, also made of Sango's clay. The magun had probably been woven directly into his elementary spirit particles, concealed with some sort of animation juju — a soul shadow — and designed to activate once he coupled with a woman like a computer virus. I was surprised that neither Nneoma nor I had noticed. There must have been at least a faint trace of the magun imprinted onto the soul shadow, like a whiff of perfume riding the sea breeze. No one can touch or make a thing without leaving a fingerprint; this is true even of spirits. It was cutting edge juju.

They had found us and neutralised Nneoma. My undoing was at hand. But I had tasted exquisite freedom, I was not about to just give it up without a fight.

"You and your husband weren't treating me very well," I said, glancing at Nneoma, "so I found alternative means to make a living."

"With this demon?" she snapped at me. "Business is bad for everyone. You got a fair share."

I laughed, using the opportunity to take a sweeping look around the room and through the window, below which the Lagos lagoon lay like a lovely, lazy child, undulating softly.

There were probably more of them nearby. Waiting, watching. The Orisha never went after anything that was not human without backup. I wondered briefly if Sango would actually come for me himself. Probably not, I thought. Unless, of course, I forced his hand.

"So what are you going to do? Force me to come back to work for you?" I asked.

Oba, naked and unashamed, smiled.

"No, we are going to kill you."

Everything happened fairly quickly.

A rope made of wind seized my body like a malicious thought and I found myself swept past Oba in a flash, thrown through the hotel window with a crash and suspended, face down, in the air over the Lagos lagoon by some invisible power. I forced myself to calm down and saw Oye - god of the Harmattan wind and vice president of operations beneath me. The skinny bastard wore a yellow wrapper wound tightly around his waist and red beads on his hands, neck and ankles. With the new body Nneoma had given me, I could have taken him out with one hit, if I managed to get close enough.

The wall of wind around me warped and reshaped itself into giant fists that came from everywhere.

I blocked Oye's ferocious assault with all the speed and grace my new body afforded me until I felt pain unlike anything I had ever felt before. I heard Oba laughing from the room as I looked down to see a vicious arrow crackling with cerise spirit particles sprouting from my chest. And then I saw another. And another.

Ososhi's arrows had pierced me with such malicious purpose; I could not believe he had ever shared palm wine with me.

Kneeling on the wind, with three arrows in my chest, I prepared myself, ruminating on things I had recently come to understand.

First, I am made of Sango's clay.

Second, Sango's clay is a fine-grained rock soil material that combines one or more spirit-particles with metal oxides and organic matter.

Third, all clays, on both sides of reality, are plastic due to their water content and can become hard and brittle when dry.

Fourth, clay has shown remarkable absorption capacities in various applications, such as the removal of heavy metals from waste water, purification of a human possessed by malevolent spirits and extended spirit particle storage.

I had studied myself extensively since Nneoma changed my form and broke my contract. Working for yourself, you need to know your strengths and weaknesses. I knew exactly what I was capable of enduring. And I knew what I needed to do.

Battered and wounded, I struggled to my feet on the carpet of wind. I tensed my body, turning my malleable flesh hard as stone and ripped a hole in the wind. Ososhi's arrows came in a flurry, I evaded some but I took several to the shoulder and back as I leapt through the hole and broken hotel room window, arrows, blood and all. I landed on my feet with a force that sent cracks through the ground.

Back in the room with Nneoma and Oba, I took the naked goddess by the throat and squeezed desperately, unwilling to yield even as Ososhi glided into the room behind me and stabbed at my sweaty, bloody back with an arrow. My will was rock. Oye seized my feet with ropes woven from a tempest and threw a whirlwind noose around my neck. Against this multitude of powers, I did not yield. Oba's eyes bulged in her head.

Suddenly, there was an incredibly loud sound as a bolt of lightning broader than a man pounded into me. I collapsed onto the floor in spasms as Sango materialized before me, a sanctuary of burning rage.

Believe me; my former CEO, the thunder Orisha, drawn to full height and brimming with rage was chilling to behold. He wore a brown *agbada*, made of *aso-oke* with vermillion flame and azure lighting embroidered onto it. The stitching danced. His *fila* drooped lazily to one side. He held a machete with a translucent blade, its hilt carved to resemble a tiger, and his eyes burned. Of course, he was upset at the way this whole business had turned out.

"Shigidi!" he bellowed, as Oba coughed on the floor beside me. "What is the meaning of this madness?"

"Madness?" I pointed at him as I rose to my knees and crawled to the edge of the bed where Nneoma lay still, locked in her own body. I needed to free her.

"Madness because I didn't just lie down and allow your lackeys to kill me?"

The aura around Sango surged in intensity.

"Madness. Insolence. What has happened to you, Shigidi?"

"Abeg!" I shouted, fear and excitement causing me to slip into Pidgin English for protest. "I am just no longer stupid. I have become my true self. I have become what I always wanted to be. You made me ugly, I am now beautiful. You made me think I was weak but I have now learned my own strength. You treated me like a slave in your company, working for a pittance, now I seek souls for myself and to my own satisfaction. The real madness when I still worked for you. My head is now correct."

"You tried to kill my wife." He was enraged, as well he should have been. I needed more of that. "I will show you suffering unlike any that has ever existed."

"Well..." I glanced at Nneoma again, and then turned back to Sango. "...just don't expect me to take it without a fight."

I was almost there.

"You overestimate your new self, Shigidi. But this foolishness, it ends now."

"Look, big man, all this is fucking talk. Go ahead. Come and kill me."

I think I heard Oba, Ososhi and Oye gasp.

I'm sure Sango had never been spoken to that way before, by anyone or anything, and it drove him mad. Which is exactly what I needed him to be.

Sango let out a war shriek, hoisted his machete high above his head, his power heating it to a bright vermilion rage. He swung the machete down in one clean motion. I dragged the bed forward and relaxed my flesh completely, sinking down to the hotel room carpet as a puddle of thick mud. Sango's machete cut through the air where I had been and hacked halfway into the body that had been Rotimi, atop Nneoma. The solid human frame split and became a deflated contortion, its entrails spilling onto the bed and the floor in a mangled mess of severed flesh tubes and intestinal fluid.

Nneoma was free.

"No!" Oba cried out as I reconstituted myself in flesh, just in time to evade another one of Sango's vicious downward hackings.

There was an explosion of wood and concrete beside me as the machete crashed into the ground where I had been. It came again and I danced away from Sango's sweeping slice, amazed by the width of the trail of red the blade left in its wake.

Nneoma took to the air.

Oba, Oye and Ososhi stood behind Sango, apparently unwilling to do anything until they were told to.

Nneoma swept down from behind and above me with her wings spread and her claws extended. She tackled Sango. He barely budged. But she managed to knock the machete out of his right hand. He used his free left hand to toss her away like a piece of chalk.

The thunder god raised his head and our eyes met briefly; I stiffened when I realised he had seen past my apparent fearlessness. A cold, horrific realisation settled over me.

Nneoma.

Sango leapt across the room with the grace of a swallow, the enraged god's hand full of a bright and crackling azure power.

I felt an exotic flood of emotion surge through me, a cocktail of the panicky urge to flee what I knew was coming and a blinding need to protect Nneoma swirled into a white daze.

I knew then that I loved her truly and completely because my limbs moved of their own accord, throwing me in front of her as Sango's body sailed through the air, nosed by the dastardly power in his right hand, aimed straight for Nneoma's heart. I loosened my clay body, allowing everything that was me become fluid just as Sango's handful of lightning sank into my viscid chest. Nneoma gasped from behind me. Before the pain could set in, I hardened my flesh again and shut my eyes; face scrunched in readiness for was sure to come as the cold power of the god's hand touched my core and became locked within it.

It started with a shift in air that surrounded us.

Sango struggled to extract his arm from my chest. The hotel floor cracked and gave under his feet. I gagged and shook and I felt Nneoma's hand on the small of my back and heard her voice break into an ancient but unfamiliar incantation.

I remember thinking that I had found a noble death in saving the one I loved. It was such a human thing to think.

"Insolent creature!" Sango bellowed, cursing as an azure stream of pure plasma tore through me. Pain bloomed inside me. My consciousness spread like water spilled from a calabash and the spark of intelligence that animated me widened, encompassing all that was around me. Words and images flew like birds. I saw a ship made of fingernails, a six-armed woman riding a peacock, a throne of thunder bolts, two dogs eating a hailstorm, a pale woman wearing a purple ankh, a man wearing a dress made of sky. I saw. I saw. And then, suddenly I did not see. I heard whispering. Shouting. Then I heard nothing. I was nothing. I was everything.

White light dissolved the darkness and the nothingness that was me. I opened my eyes and there was sky. So much sky. Blue and white clouds whizzed past me.

Mere inches away from mine were Nneoma's smiling lips.

"You're awake," she said.

"I'm alive?" I queried, finally realising that she was carrying me and that she was flying.

Her smile dimmed and she sighed. "Yes. It took considerable haggling to bring you back but it's done now," she said quietly.

"How did I... how did we survive that?"

She looked away and said, "I made a deal."

I looked across her naked body and spread wings to see that she was unharmed. I knew that she had traded away something of significant value to purchase our escape from that predicament. Sango would not have let us go quietly, if at all.

"What deal?"

She stiffened briefly, and then relaxed. "Olorun is a businessman above all else. And he is still chairman of your former spirit-company, with veto powers. So, I called on him and I offered to do for him something that Sango cannot do. He forced that thunder thrower and his coterie to let us go."

So, it was a hostile takeover of sorts. She stopped flapping her left wing and banked, turning toward the sun. The clouds around us exploded with wild, new colours.

I opened my mouth to ask her exactly what it was that she had promised but decided that I did not truly want to know the answer so I pressed my lips tightly together and stilled my worrying tongue.

Nneoma smiled at me again and said, "Sango wasn't happy about losing his hand though."

Within my chest, there was something new, something that beat with the steadiness of a heart but was cold and thunderous and alien and immensely powerful and felt like it had once been a part of someone much more powerful than I.

I did not ask what it was.

Epilogue

1-Altitude Bar, Singapore | February 13th, 2017 | 03:54 am.

The bright strobe lights danced lazily in the periphery of his vision as Aadit downed an oversweet Singapore sling, only mildly aware of how cliché he was being. The live band in the corner was playing a decent rendition of *Don't Stop Believin'* and although the bass was a bit too heavy and the singer's accent a bit forced, it still managed to be enjoyable. Aadit suspected that anything would, sitting at a bar on the 67th floor, overlooking the precise electric order of the city-state.

Around him sat expats smoking slim cigarettes, svelte, local sex kittens in short skirts and barely-existent necklines, the odd corporate yuppie group here and there. An old African man in a blue suit with a thick white beard sitting alone. Aadit ignored everyone. He liked to drink alone.

He did not see the impossibly handsome tower of a man whose dark skin seemed to be made of rich, clay loam that had been following him throughout the day, eyes glimmering azure.

Aadit was painfully aware of his age as he tried to ignore the smarting that radiated from the holes in his back where hooks attached to bells had been looped in three days earlier in Malaysia. The Thaipusam crowd had been dense. He had been a drop of water in a veritable river of humanity that flowed via the fifteen kilometre trek to the Batu Caves temple bearing some sort of burden—their Kavadi—an offering to Murugan. Some heads had been shaven clean and daubed with yellow sandalwood like his. Others had been dreadlocked. Some bodies had been clad in saffron robes and white cloth like his. Others were tourists in jeans and ironic t-shirts. Some had carried silver pails of milk and heavy wood and metal constructs attached to their bodies with wicked braces. Others had carried cameras. The most devout had had spikes through their faces or hooks through their backs or their sides pierced with needles the length of a giant's forearm. Aadit had borne all three. His request to Murugan, god of war, demanded great pain as payment every year.

He was glad to be home.

He lifted his glass to his lips for a sip just as a dark, luscious thigh appeared on the vacant stool beside him, anchored to a body sheathed in a white dress so tight, it could have been a condom.

"Need some company?"

The voice was familiar. He assumed she was a prostitute.

"Not tonight. I'm…"

His breath caught when he saw her taut, polished-ebony skin and impeccably sculpted face. Her hair was different, it was long and curly now and the afro was gone but she had not aged a single day. There was no doubt it was her. His first words were an explosive excrement of exclamations.

"Shit. Shit. No. Fuck!"

"Oh don't be crass." Her smile was a full red slash.

Aadit's shoulders sank. "Why are you here?"

"Why did you run away?" she snapped back, vicious like a herder's whip.

The band had segued from Journey's *Don't Stop Believin'* into Bon Jovi's *Livin' On A Prayer*. Aadit pushed his glass away and shot up to his feet.

"You! You cannot harm me. I call upon the protection of Lord Murugan."

A chill blew through the open space as a man in a pinstripe suit appeared beside them as though he had been painted into the scene in one smooth brushstroke. He wore a peacock feather in his breast pocket and his silk shirt was puffed around his collar. He had ashy, dark skin and long wavy hair. He stepped between Aadit and the beautiful ebony creature in the tight white dress.

"What is your name, foul spirit?" His voice sounded like it came from a faraway place.

"Naamah." She sipped her drink lazily, unperturbed. "But you can call me Nneoma."

"Naamah, leave this man alone. Go and find another mortal with whom to satisfy your perverse hunger."

Her laughter was wild and all encompassing, a tropical rainstorm of mirth.

"You know, there was a time when I would have been scared of you, Murugan. But that time is long gone."

She licked her lips and called out, "Shigidi!"

A bolt of bizarrely precise lightning shot through the bar, striking the suited man square in the chest. It was trailed by a hulking body that gleamed like glazed wood, moving with grace and speed that should have been impossible for its size. There were three hefty steps, a short sprint and a vault.

1-Altitude was bathed in brilliant white light as Shigidi's form met violently with Murugan's.

The two potencies crashed into the reinforced glass barrier at the edge of the bar, and fell, plummeting toward the ground in a flurry of fists. The skies turned turbulent. Lightning struck indiscriminately without the courtesy of thunder. People screamed and ran for the exits, their addled brains unable to process what they had just witnessed in the bar at the top of the city. All except the bearded old African in the blue suit who'd sat up in his chair, finally interested.

Nneoma cupped Aadit's stunned face in her hands and leaned in close.

"Come on. Smile. Finally, after all these years, we are together again."

Falling, the two duelling powers engaged each other. Murugan evaded three of the clay and lightning behemoth's blows, as they plunged down the night sky blazing a luminous azure trail. Murugan summoned his *vel*—a vicious spear—and thrust it into Shigidi's side. The mighty spear which had slain many demons and won many wars snapped like a toothpick on impact without piercing the dark giant's solid clay flank. Shigidi pressed his advantage and a powerful punch rammed into Murugan's side, winding him. A vicious head-butt followed just as they crashed into the ground below, the impact pushing away everything near its hypocentre in a powerful wave of dust, debris, lightning and compressed air that folded back in on itself like an empire invaded by its own army. Car alarms wailed in protest. Murugan lay pinioned beneath Shigidi, his suit in tatters, his spear broken and his face bloodied.

"Beast, you cannot kill the son of Shiva." His lips were motionless and the sound came from everywhere at once. "These lands belong to my family. These people pray to us. They are under our protection. You cannot do business here!"

"Shut up," Shigidi growled above the din of the disrupted city.

He raised his hand and it became a thing of solid rock, gloved in harsh blue and white light. Before Murugan could make sense of what was transpiring, Shigidi's lightning-gloved fist pummelled his body into an incongruous mass of carmine blood, dark flesh and off-white bone.

Nneoma spoke firmly, "Aadit, stop running. I told you all those years ago; no one tastes my pleasures and shirks the price. No one. Not the gods. Not the endless. Not even Lucifer himself."

Tears ran down Aadit's cheeks.

"Please…" His voice, like his soul, was broken.

She tilted her head to the left and her features softened as she stood up and laid his head on her supple breasts.

"Awww, poor baby. Poor, poor baby. Come here. It's okay. Let Nneoma make it all stop."

Aadit's limbs hung limply by his side as he allowed her unzip his corduroy trousers. He was devoid of desire but at the touch of her fingers, he found himself turgid. She hiked her dress up. There was nothing but skin underneath it.

She straddled him and rode, gently at first and then fiercely, in great big crests and troughs of hip and thigh. His ejaculation came quickly, followed by more tears and her laughter.

She kissed him on the cheek, disengaged herself and whispered in his ear, "Now we're done."

Aadit remained tearful and sessile on the barstool.

She turned around and walked toward the seated old man, a feline swing in her hips.

"Was that enough spectacle for you?"

The bearded man took a sip of his drink. His suit had turned a deep purple masquerading as black. "Yes, for now. The people who needed to see it, saw." He smiled. "And you have your man's spirit. Two birds, one stone, as they say."

"Yes. As they say." She repeated dryly. "So what next?"

"The witnesses are the key. There were twelve of weak faith who will begin to worship the image of Shigidi without even knowing who or what he is. Such is human nature. Such is the nature of belief. When they do, I will ask you both to visit again. They will be the seeds of a new Orisha cult here."

Nneoma snorted. "Fine. But this isn't what I had in mind when I offered to help you expand your business to new territory. The Mahādevas will not let you establish a new branch here. Especially not after they find out you killed Shiva's son."

The old man frowned and leaned forward in his chair. "And what do you know of spirit-business exactly?" He waved a dismissive hand.

"Killing is nothing but a negotiation tactic. Just do as I say. Business evolves. Jihads and Crusades are simply hostile takeovers, but not all of us can afford such avarice. When Yeshua's believers stole my worshippers and took them westward to work their fields, did I go to war? No. I negotiated a new joint venture with them. Today, our Santeria operations are a thriving million prayer-a-year company." He paused briefly.

"Everyone that matters in this business knows that we must ensure business continuity, above all else. If I did not understand this, Sango would have your head on a wall by now. Love, family, sex, pride, rules and laws; they are nothing but tools to further our existence. Understand?"

"Fine. I understand," Nneoma said, shifting her weight to her left leg. "We do it your way."

Olorun sank back into his chair and began to fade away like a man-shaped fog in rising heat. "You have no choice in the matter. Now go. I will let you and your lover know when you are needed again."

Nneoma stood silent as the old man faded into nothing. When he was gone, she sprouted her long, feathery wings and ripped off what was left of her white dress. Then she let out a wild, triumphant scream before diving gracefully down to the streets like an arrow where she embraced waiting Shigidi, engulfing him with her wings and glorious nakedness. Together, they took to the velvet blue sky, twilight beckoning at their heels.

Polaris

There are few things more unshakeable in the heart of a six-year-old boy than his faith in the collective truthfulness of the things his father has told him. This was how Tunde knew with all the certainty of breath and death that every star in the curtain of clear sky above him was a cousin to their now sleeping sun, members of a family of continuous explosions, living spheres of fire and heat and light and ineffable majestic power. He didn't understand how it could be so, not really, but he did not need to understand in order to believe. His father had told him it was so. That sufficed.

They were standing next to each other, he and his father, in the small garden behind their red brick bungalow, surrounded by low-cut grass and thick, trimmed hedges sparsely dotted with pale, pink hibiscus. It was October, the night was young and luminescent little fireflies flitted about in the low grass around them like little living stars of their own. Tunde's eyes traced the taper of his father's hand from short-sleeve sheathed shoulder to bony finger.

"Can you see it?" His father's voice was low and syrupy and warm.

"No Daddy."

"OK, remember where Dubhe and Merak are?" The finger moved slowly, shaking almost imperceptibly, back to the place it had been a few moments before.

"Yes Daddy, the tip of the big spoon there."

"Good boy. Now, just trace a line from Merak," The finger advanced slowly and then paused briefly. "Straight through Dubhe." Another pause. "And continue going up. Up."

The hand moved again and Tunde's eyes followed it, attentive and bright and full of youthful ardour.

"There, you see the first star directly above them?" When the finger stopped, Tunde mentally extrapolated from it, scouring the heavens for the other spoon he had been told to look for. He beamed when he found it.

"Yes Daddy! I can see it now."

"Yes! Good boy!" His father placed a hand on his shoulder and in that moment, out in the October air, under the dome of twinkling stars and a beaming alabaster moon, safe in his father's approval and embrace, Tunde was sure he was the happiest little boy in the world.

"That is Polaris, the northern star."

Tunde gleefully grabbed his father's leg. "Can we go there, Daddy? Can we visit a star?"

His father laughed. "No, Tunde, the stars are too far and too hot to go to. But they can guide you. If you ever get lost, whenever you can't find your way, just look to the sky. Look for Polaris. The stars will guide you home."

The shuttle shuddered and shook, convulsing violently as a powerful gust of newly minted atmospheric gas and red dust blew past. For a fleeting moment, Tunde feared that he would die on the launchpad, crushed by something bulky falling out of place on this contraption hastily cobbled together by the greatest scientific minds a barely habitable prison planet had to offer.

Well, he thought, the shuttle had survived its construction and positioning thus far, it would probably survive the remaining few minutes to lift-off. He almost allowed himself a smile as he waited out this latest wave besieging angry gases.

"Hey Tunde," the launch controller called in through his earpiece, pronouncing his name as "Toon-dee", just as most of the others on Mars that weren't of Nigerian origin did. He had given up getting annoyed by it a long time ago. Besides, it was impossible to be annoyed with Xola for long; he had a broad face, a fluffy beard, was generous when it was his turn to pay for drinks, always wore a smile and there was perpetual shine to his balding pate which he usually covered with an ancient, frazzled fedora. It didn't matter if you knew him or not; when you met him, it did not take much to convince you that he was your friend. Tunde still found it hard to believe that he'd been a brutal gangland enforcer Earthside, back in Pretoria.

"What's up, Xola?" Tunde called back, fully aware that everyone else in the control bubble on the ground could hear him.

"That was the last one for this cycle. All clear. We have about an hour until the next big red dust gust hits. We won't get another window of opportunity like this today, so now's the time. We'll initiate the launch sequence in about five minutes. Strap yourself in and get ready for the ride."

"Aye Aye, Captain!" Tunde's tone was jovial. Almost silly. Xola laughed.

"Once you jailbreak your way off this godforsaken kak planet, you'll be your own captain."

"Yeah, but I won't have the fancy hat to prove it," Tunde quipped.

Xola snorted. "Ja! Ja! Very funny. Now strap yourself in."

Tunde adjusted his buckles and straightened himself up before pulling down and locking in the overhead body brace. A quick glance to his left where all the navigation dials and transport monitor displays were docked verified that he had enough oxygen, food and water to last two hundred and three days. It would only take him about a hundred and twenty, give or take ten days either way, to reach Earth along his Hohmann transfer orbit. A quick glance just left-of-centre, where the targeting systems and payload details were displayed, told him the nuclear core was still stable and the electronic guidance systems would be able to direct the missile to its target. He wondered if it would still be functional if he got close enough to Earth to fire it.

"OK. We're ready. Transferring power to your on-board fuel cells. Countdown in 30 seconds." Tunde thought he heard a nervous tremor in Xola's voice as it seeped into his chamber through the speakers. He dismissed it.

"Alright, let's get this show on the road."

"Oh and err… Tunde…" Xola's voice was low, its usual energy suddenly supplanted by somewhat subdued solemnity.

"Yeah?"

"Good luck, man. No one on this godforsaken rock will ever forget your sacrifice. Ever."

"I know, Xola. I know. I hope it's worth it."

The line went dead for a few moments before Tunde heard the rustle of static again and Xola's voice came back on to do the final pre-launch checks. When they were done, Tunde grabbed onto the brace, sank into his chair and shut his eyes. He found his mind wandering back to the past in bright vivid flashes and intense bursts of memory as the control station initiated launch.

"And we have booster ignition in…"

"…10…"

Tunde met Halima in New York.

He was twenty-three and she was twenty-one and it was everything he thought young love was supposed to be. Intense, breathtaking and stupid. Very stupid. They met at a faux-bohemian Café in the heart of Syracuse, one of those pretentious places where restless, rebellious young people tended to congregate in 2090s global society. Small tribes of stale, government-ration coffee and half-baked philosophical and political ideologies. There was always thick smoke and loud conversation in the air.

Halima was a beautifully, strange creature, even in that place. Her hair extensions were dyed electric blue and she had a platinum piercing through her thick nose. She was arguing with a triad of painfully obvious goth girls—heavily tattooed, each wearing more make-up than all three could possibly have needed. They were arguing heatedly about the implications of Diego Salazar's Teleportation technology on the human experience. It was all over the news then and everyone had an opinion. Halima, who insisted that instant travel would ruin the sense of adventure that made journeys what they were, was being shouted down by the eyeliner and ink-skinned goth Cerberus. Tunde confidently walked up to their table and calmly asked her if she could use some reinforcements, a casual smile plastered on his face. She looked up at him and gazed into his eyes for what had seemed like a small slice of forever before speaking through a slowly spreading smile of her own.

"Yes, yes I could."

He spent most of the summer of 2093 with Halima; drinking, making love and talking about everything, nothing and all the things in between. She was a theoretical physics student and an amateur spoken word performer. He'd just started studying for a PhD in mechanical engineering after a two-year stint with the Nigerian air force flying African Union peacekeeping missions in Honduras. There was always something for them to talk about.

He convinced himself that they were perfect together—from their taste in literature (he adored LeGuin and Liu, she thought the world of Morrison and Lessing, even though they both saw why the other felt the way they did) to their taste in food (they both were willing to try anything at least once). She was half-Congolese, her other half French—the side she got from her father.

Tunde gathered from what she told him that her father had been a man of ravenous sexual appetites and a great many affairs, one of which had issued her.

"Daddy was alright. He just couldn't convince himself to stick with one woman," she'd said one cool evening while they sat under a sugar maple tree in Central Park, one couple in what seemed a constellation of them. Tunde wondered why she always seemed to make excuses for her father's cheating and deceiving and selfishness, but he said nothing. He just squeezed her hand tight and pulled her toward him, saying nothing and silently hoping that she was nothing like her father.

"…9…"

Tunde could remember almost nothing of the night it happened except that when it was over, Hernan was dead and he was in police custody for murder.

As they interviewed him in the grey and rigid embrace of the interrogation room, he told them the details of everything he could remember.

He remembered buying some flowers (a bouquet of red roses and pink lilies) from a gypsy lady over on Marcellus Street on his way to Halima's apartment. He remembered deciding not to call her first because he'd wanted to surprise her. He remembered getting to her apartment and hearing the unmistakeable moaning and tell-tale slapping sounds of flesh being passionately driven into flesh coming from within as he fumbled with the key at the door. He remembered feeling rage like a wildfire spreading from his heart to his head, igniting his blood on its way like it was cheap fuel.

He remembered everything up to slipping the key into the keyhole, but between pushing Halima's door open and being plopped into the chair in the interrogation room by a burly officer in a perfectly pressed uniform, he could remember nothing.

"…8…"

There was a horrible finality to the sound of the gavel coming down as the judge sentenced him to non-sustenance for murder. A deafening *Thud! Thud! Thud!* that Tunde was sure did not differ much from the sound of heavy clods of wet earth being heaped onto a coffin.

"It is a tragedy for this court to see such a waste of potential, young man," The obese judge paused for effect, befitting his pronouncement. He seemed like an opera tenor about to belt out a shrieking note. "But there will be no more waste; I sentence you to non-sustenance." The Judge turned to Tunde, looking directly at him for the first time since the trial started. "No more resources will be allocated to your continued living by the World Council."

Non-sustenance. It was a silly euphemism. Although poverty had been eradicated in most parts of the planet, it had been achieved by an impossibly complicated but extremely effective resource control program. When worldwide population had hit twenty-nine billion in early 2081, it was easy to justify harsh measures, including the elimination of criminals, especially murderers, who put a drain on the already delicate system. They were, quite simply, waste. So mankind had traded its moral objections for food, security, peace and happiness. But as resource allocation improved, the objections to the non-sustenance penalty grew louder. There had been protests and petitions. There had even been a WorldCon summit to discuss amendments to the global criminal code eleven months before Tunde bludgeoned Hernan to death with a beautiful, brown corinna lamp.

"I'm sorry," his lawyer offered. Tunde said nothing. He just turned back to survey the court as a sour-looking officer started to approach him. He saw Halima in the stands and their eyes met briefly just before the officer started to pull him away from the defence desk. She was in the back row wearing a fuchsia tank top and heavy make-up, her eyes on him. Her hair was pulled back tight and her skin was radiant, even in the harsh florescent light of the courtroom.

Her presence and stark beauty focused the enormity of his situation like a lens. It burned. Anger filled his head with red heat and he screamed fire at her, pointing his finger like a knife. "Whore! I'll kill you. I've lost everything because of you. I've lost my future, my life, everything! Why did you do it? Why?"

He climbed over the dock and made for her like a wild animal, intent on some kind of vengeance. He was tackled roughly to the ground by two burly bailiffs before he could even cross the first row. The court erupted in chatter and banging. He started weeping as they dragged him to his feet and he realised how foolish he was being.

As he was escorted through the high, solid wood-panelled arches of the courtroom, he glanced back and saw a solitary tear falling down Halima's cheek as she watched them lead him away to the holding cell. As much as he resisted, he couldn't stop himself from thinking that he had never seen her look more beautiful than she did in that moment.

"...7..."

Tunde remembered his lawyer telling him to take the deal.

There were river channels suggesting that a long time ago liquid water flowed on Mars when it had a thicker atmosphere and now the army of ported investigative drone rovers had found fossils preserved in volcanic rock and briny water beneath the surface, his lawyer was explaining. It was evidence that life had once existed on Mars. If it had existed before, it could exist again, the experts said. And the governments believed them. But it would be decades, maybe centuries, before the planet could be made truly habitable for human communities. They needed people to speed up the process, they'd said. They needed people to man the terraforming crews that would seed the soil with bioenzymes and plant genetically-designed vegetation that would eventually saturate what little atmosphere there was on the planet with oxygen, they'd said. They needed people like him, his lawyer was saying.

"Now, with Salazar's teleportation technology fully developed and in the control of Worldcon, they've set up a receiving station Marsside and plan to send five hundred million people to begin the project." His lawyer was a middle-aged gentleman named Henry with greying temples and a face with too many lines. He was almost pleading with Tunde.

"I've already spoken to the judge and he is willing to amend the sentence to life imprisonment offworld," Henry said encouragingly.

"Look. They need as many people building a habitable planet there as possible to ease the population pressure here. I mean, life is good here for now, but population growth is still fairly high and no one on the World Council wants to tell people they can't have kids. It's not sustainable. Mars is new, kid. It will be a hard life, lots of labour at first, but at least it's a life. Who knows, it may even end up being better there. It's happened before. Just look at Australia."

Henry smiled a strained smile.

"Many prisoners on starvation row have already volunteered and they'll all escape the non-sustenance penalty. You can too. You should too."

Tunde was curious about how eager Henry seemed. Perhaps the old man didn't want to see a young life thrown away for what was, admittedly, a crime of passion. Or maybe he just didn't want another client sent to the deprivation chamber on his record and his conscience. Tunde wasn't sure which impression came across stronger, but he was sure that he'd signed what was left of his life away in blue ink.

"...6..."

The last time Tunde saw his father, it had been through the reinforced glass of a secure visitation room. When he'd walked in with the magnetic shackles on his hands and feet, he could have sworn he saw the old man age ten more years in an instant. He could barely conceal his pain and shame, wearing them like heavy cloaks on his wiry frame; he was bent over and uncomfortable on his fibreglass chair.

"So this is it, eh? You are going to be a prisoner on another planet. My son. A prisoner." The old man's forehead was furrowed and he spoke in strained tones, fighting back the tears that threatened to escape from behind his rheumy eyes as he spoke, looking slightly off to the side as though shame would not let him look at his son directly.

"I'm sorry, Daddy," Tunde said, the words leaving him easily and without any significant effort, like air from a balloon, because they were the only words he could think to say.

"Sorry?" His father's eyes widened. "Don't be sorry, please. You will be alive, abi? It is better than being dead. Just live as well as you can."

"I will. It's just so unfair. My life is over. I should have killed her too. She's taken everything from me."

His father leaned in towards him, placing his wrinkled arms on the grey ridge of fibreglass that jutted out of the panel separating them. His face adopted a stark seriousness. "Listen to me, Tunde. Don't forget the son of whom you are. You are not a murderer. Let go of all this anger and bitterness. What has happened has happened. Nothing can change that. You made a mistake. No matter what circumstance led you to make it, it was still your mistake. One mistake does not change who you are. So don't let the price you will pay for making it change you." There was steel in his father's voice that had not been there up until that moment. "Don't lose yourself. So ti gbo? No matter what happens on Mars, no matter what difficulties you face, don't let circumstances change you. Don't get lost, Tunde. Be honourable; even if you are not free, be honourable. Remember that. You have another chance at life, even if it is hard. Use it to redeem yourself. Forget the past. Face the future. And if anything ever happens that makes you feel like you are losing yourself, remember that you can always find your way back home."

"...5..."

The first thing Tunde did on Mars was throw up.

A clawing nausea and a strange, tingly feeling that wrapped itself around his skin, taut like a drumskin, came over him when he found himself standing in a grey airlock where a moment ago a white, sterile transport room had been. He heard others heave and exclaim and retch and cough all around him.

"Ah bloody hell! Look, another batch of jellybellies!" a voice said from somewhere outside the airlock where he and an assortment of others stood. He could not be sure where it originated from, but by the time it reached them the voice had been moulded into an electric, shrill burst by whatever medium it had snuck in through.

"Alright, shitheads. Hablas ingles o no hablas ingles, move your smelly asses down the airlock before they send another batch through and you get all your electrons tangled."

Tunde shuffled forward, pushed into and past his own regurgitations by the impatient throng behind him. Having his elementary particles disassembled, transmitted at superluminal speed and then reconstituted on an alien planet was even more surreal than he had imagined. In the fraction of the second it took to make the transmission, he had been in a nebulous non-place, where everything, including his thoughts and very consciousness, seemed to float about freely like fluffy white clouds. It was a sensation he would remember often and even eventually come to yearn for.

The first thing Tunde noticed was that there were no guards. There were no officers. There was no one with any authority who had not given it to himself or taken it violently from another. Living on Mars was mostly a meaningless madness, and, less frequently, a semi-organised struggle to propagate life from one day to the next.

"Putting a few hundred million convicted murderers with differing backgrounds on one sub-habitable planet with nothing but basic training, instructions and equipment but no one to guide or supervise them is a cruel experiment in Darwinian Theory," an old man wearing a headscarf said to Tunde as they ate huddled together, sitting on the floor of a grey transport shaft beneath a sign that read "Walkway 16" in seventeen languages. Before Tunde could respond, the man asked him if he had any idea which way was East. They shared an uneasy laugh and started a conversation that eventually led back to where it had begun.

"I'm surprised that even on this hell-rock, some think they should rule, should reign over this kingdom of red dust, shelter bubbles and hard living," the old man, whose name Tunde had gathered was Ahmed, said.

"I'm not. There will always be people willing to fill any kind of power gap," Tunde mumbled as he chewed canned carrots. "Trust me. My family was in Australia during the water wars. I just still can't believe they actually sent us here without first establishing some kind of order. It's madness."

"They did establish order," Ahmed quipped. "They set up the shelter bubbles and the drone rovers and the airlocks and the transport shafts and the nuclear generators, they gave us instructions and maps and charts and documents, and then they sent us here to kill each other."

Tunde sat silent for a second before saying, "But it doesn't make sense. They want us to terraform this place. And we can't do that if we are dead."

"That's where I think you have it wrong, my friend," the old man said.

"You think so, eh? What are your own thoughts then?"

"My thoughts? I don't think they expect us to actually do any terraforming; I think it was all an elaborate trick to silence the anti-non-sustenance groups back on Earth while still relieving population pressure. I think they expect us to die here in silence."

Tunde snorted and pulled his legs together to avoid the puddle of curdling, carmine blood that had started flowing from the other side of the door that sealed their section of the walkway. Someone else had just been killed for food or drink or just for being in the wrong place at the wrong time.

"Bullshit."

The old man glanced furtively at the puddle and carried on, trying to mask the minor tremor that had attached itself to his voice.

"Maybe it is, but I was born in Syria. I know what governments can do to their citizens in order to maintain the status quo."

Tunde stayed silent.

The old man sighed, his hands twitching.

"No matter. What you need, what we all need, is to find our place in this murderous, rape-infested place and make sure it's a role that is either unique and useful or that comes with no power, a role that no one would want to kill us for."

He wiped his lips and placed his food-stained biopolymer box on the ground. "You know the people in essential positions, the guys that have the kind of experience that qualifies them to be on the nuclear reactor crews and food growth domes and the bubble environmental unit controllers? Those guys are lucky. No one will touch them and they will generally be left alone. They'll never get dragged into the turf wars or be stabbed in the walkways. The terraforming work has to at least try to go on somehow, right? And we have to at least try to live here somehow, right?" He turned to Tunde, who remained silent still.

"Even the rival factions may eventually realise that they need to stay alive in order to keep trying to kill and control each other."

Tunde, nodding, said, "Yeah. You're right."

And he was.

They continued to talk until they were both exhausted and then they slept shoulder to shoulder on the floor of Walkway 16.

When Tunde woke up, the old man was gone. Tunde never saw him again.

The next day, he joined one of the bioenzyme crews unaffiliated to any of the growing power factions. They called themselves the 'Omega Crew' and they worked the Noachis Terra growth zone, far away from the main bubble. They were the first to start collecting human waste and clearing the bodies of the dead, burying them all in Noachis Terra to increase the organic content of the soil by adding bacteria and matter in addition to the bioenzymes. It was work that was both useful and that most people did not want to do, if they could help it. The Omega Crew were mostly left alone. Tunde kept his head low when he was in the artificially grey and silver walkways of the major bubble shelters, did his work as assiduously and silently as he could in the red, dusty fields, and slept with one eye open for the equivalent of two Earth years.

"...4..."

165

The day the engineers in charge of the nuclear power facility that sustained life on the planet, led by convicted terrorist (or, unfortunately unmartyred freedom fighter, depending on your views regarding the Chrislamic War of 2082) Dr. Abdul Ben-Faisal, announced to the entire Martian settlement that they had built a dirty neutron bomb, Tunde was lying in bed, staring at the lattice of polymer supports above him. He jerked up when the announcement came through on the emergency channel.

"We are not animals," Dr. Ben-Faisal said on the emergency communications systems that pumped his voice through every receiver in the cluster of thirty-two settlement bubbles. Tunde noticed everything about his speech, but what lingered long after was the almost hesitant formality of it, the apparent difficulty with which each word was exhumed from him.

"Brothers and sisters, we may have been deceived and condemned to die, but we still live. We have managed to survive. But we are not animals. Survival is not enough. Not while we still kill each other. Not while we can thrive. No! We refuse to live like animals while we yet live. Even if there is only a slim possibility that our survival ensures that future generations may live here, we will do what must be done. We will not exist like a pack of rabid dogs.

"To this end, we have built a bomb with the partially spent uranium rods from the reactor. We have barricaded the facility and we will detonate the bomb in exactly three sols if every group staking a claim to our meagre supplies and lifeless land is not disbanded immediately."

It seemed like a joke, but there was a sudden tension in Tunde's shoulders. A slow feeling of fear crept over him as he waited for a jocund cachinnation to follow the man's voice, for the nuclear scientist to admit to executing an elaborate prank, for someone, anyone, to snatch the transmitter from him and say the old man had just had a nervous breakdown. Something. Anything.

"If there are any more murders, we will detonate the bomb. If there is no comprehensive agreement on food rationing, labouring on the terraforming crews and administration of our planet's affairs in three sols, we will detonate the bomb. If there is any attempt to breach this facility, we will detonate the bomb." The doctor paused to exhale audibly. It added a certain ominous gravitas to the moment.

"We are men and we will not be made to live as less. It is better to die as men than to live as dogs. Know that we are prepared to do what must be done. Are you?"

The doctor's voice cut off abruptly, leaving something like an echo in its wake.

Tunde stood up and walked toward the door of his settlement

bubble. Three steps from it, he stopped, turned around and went back to lie down on his bed. He continued staring silently at the lattice of polymer supports above him, waiting and wondering how long it would take for an agreement to be made and how long it would take someone to break into the bubble and kill him if there was none. He already knew how long it would take for him, for them, to die in nuclear fire.

It only took one sol for the major factions to come to an agreement and create a governing council.

Fear is and has always been a powerful motivator.

"…3…"

Tunde spent most of his days running his modded plough along the rim of the silver, mineral lake by Noachis Terra. It was hard labour and, as time went by, the number of harsh lines crisscrossing the hard skin on the back of his hands grew like cracks in tempered glass as the plough navigation wires cut into his skin where his gloves wore thin. He worked from dawn to dusk through a perpetual dust haze, trailed by eldritch double shadows, for seventeen Earth years, only returning to what had become his home in bubble 31 when the twilight hours were done bathing the Martian sky in a soft cerulean glow.

To him the modded plough was horse, tool, shelter and friend. When the frequent dust storms came, he would seal himself in, anchor down and not breathe, waiting for something to stir beneath him, for the anchor to groan and sigh and break, abandoning him to a lonely, slow death far in the uninhabited outer lands like it had so many others. But it never did.

Tunde lost many people he would have called friends to accidents in their modded ploughs and bio-suits and kraken drill rigs and gravity-transduction trucks and scion rovers and all the other poorly maintained equipment they had to use until someone back on Earth realised the people they had exiled expecting to die had refused to do so and another wave of supplies was sent with a fresh batch of exiles to placate their consciences. There was so much loss, so much suffering. Tunde took it all in, year after year, pressing ahead, finding new purpose in labour, hidden strength in survival, small joys in creation.

There were hard nights in makeshift bars too. Nights spent drinking moonshine with some of the older men, the survivors from the first few transport waves who, like him, had been there when Dr. Ben-Faisal forcefully cobbled together the motley group that was now the government of Mars.

A few hundred million new prisoners were teleported in every year, sometimes sent with limited new equipment, the occasional batch of fresh supplies, new terraforming instructions, but no free Earthman among them.

Eventually, all the prisoners Marsside came to realise the fact that they had been deceived. Tunde noticed it begin to really take in the third year within his own crew. Even the most hopeful of them lost the glint in their eyes. They were not there to build a new world for humanity, at least not primarily. They had been dumped, discarded, disposed of. They had been labelled the dregs of the human race and they were being disposed of by world governments that did not want to upset the delicate balance of a global society they had spent decades constructing. Tunde noticed as time went by that the barroom conversations slowly became more political, more hateful, more resentful. By the time night was far spent, and moonshine was low, it was not unusual to hear some men speak of vengeance against Earth.

"...2..."

The new atmosphere on the planet eventually began to take and the bubble shelters grew from a modest thirty-two to two hundred, the prison settlement expanding inefficiently but effectively. The harsh Martian ground reluctantly began to yield fruit, especially in Noachis Terra. Synthesized water began to take back what was their ancient, ancestral home, filling rivers and lakes that had been dry for millennia. Clathrate hydrates were discovered in the Martian bedrock and the Marsmen took the methane from it, using it to supply makeshift process plants with raw material and the bubble shelters with domestic gas. Slowly, a kind of civilization came limping across the once vacant lands of Mars.

But even with this civilization, the resentment from first wave survivors still festered, becoming barely bridled hatred; hatred that quickly became motive for revenge. Tunde felt it too, the anger, but he kept it to himself.

"But you know we can get them, right?" Xola muttered beside him one cold night in the barroom that serviced bubble 31. "New girl I'm seeing, she got ported in last year. Used to be a secretary or something at the UN or the WorldCon or whatever until she killed her husband."

Tunde realized too late that he was being engaged in a conversation. He grunted, hoping Xola would go away. He didn't.

"She says they have this new headquarters. Huge project the size of a city. Been constructing for years. Supposed to house all the government reps and everything. So big you can see it from bloody space."

"Sounds expensive," Tunde offered non-committally as a knot tightened itself in his stomach.

"Ja! Bloody right it was. Nice home for all the lawmakers and shithead politicians that like to treat people like us like we're sewage." Xola turned to Tunde. He spoke with a voice that was as cold as arctic wind. "That's why we're going to destroy it."

Tunde turned to Xola and caught a cruel smile light up his face. He may have been drunk, but he was not joking.

"Your girl," Tunde started, deciding to test how far Xola and whoever else was with him had thought this through. "How do you know you can trust what she says anyway? What if she's just screwing with you? And how do you think you will get close enough to Earth to destroy anything anyway? The teleporter only takes one-way traffic."

"Oh, trust me, Halima doesn't mess around with kak like this. She told me all about the council plans already and we have enough material and spent nuclear…"

Xola went on, but Tunde had stopped listening. His ears were warm and his heart pounded in his chest. Halima. Halima. Halima. The name knocked against his ribcage and made him feel like he was having a heart attack. Could it really be her, here, millions of miles and memories away, haunting him? He kept silent and tried not to react visibly until Xola stopped talking and asked him if he wanted another drink. He said he didn't.

A few sols later, the Government of Mars announced its decision to strike a blow to Earth where it would hurt the most. They would strike at the heart of the new WorldCon facility.

"…1…"

Tunde met Halima in Walkway 16.

He was forty-one and she was thirty-eight and it was a quiet, strange meeting saturated with unspoken words. He had tracked her down by following Xola because he needed to see if it was really her. Then he followed her quietly for a few sols, mapping out her homeward daily route from Water Unit 17 to Xola's shelter in bubble 6. Tunde chose to intercept her in Walkway 16 because it was old, dilapidated and almost completely abandoned. It was also dark. Power had been rerouted from the walkway to other places where it was more needed. The artificial glow of light from the other settlement bubbles seeped in through the transparent panelling.

When he finally saw her, he still recognized her face, but it seemed unnaturally thin in the dim, yellow light. She had lost weight, and her hair was much more frazzled than he ever remembered seeing it, but it was still her. And she was so close to him. He began to shake.

"Tunde?" she called out when she saw him.

"Tunde, is that really you?" She came forward. He did not move.

"Oh my God, it really is you!" She gasped and covered her mouth with her hands.

Tunde said nothing.

She came within three paces of him and then stopped, remembering what he'd tried to do the last time they saw each other. Without even realizing what he was doing, Tunde also stepped back, away from her.

"I'm so sorry, Tunde. Oh God! I'm so sorry. I never said that, and I should have."

Tunde struggled to stay still, to say something, to slow his breath, but he failed.

The dim light was too bright. The sound of blood pulsing through his ears deafened him. He wanted to hit her. He wanted to kiss her. He wanted to kill her. He wanted to embrace her. But he did none of those things. Instead, he said the only thing he could. "I'm sorry too, Halima. I should never have reacted that way. I should have been better than the situation. I just wanted to tell you that before I go."

Then he turned and walked away.

"Tunde?!" She called after him.

Tunde was crying when he swiped his finger across the control panel at the end of the walkway. He hadn't cried since he had come to Mars, but emotions were wrenching at him, twisting his stomach and making him heave as the barriers he had built up around himself for years came melting down his face in warm drops of liquid soul.

Tunde wiped his face as he walked, thinking about Earth and Halima and his father and the stars and what he knew he had to do the night Xola told him about the planned attack. He walked until he reached the walkway axis, where traffic was high, and then he started running. He ran and ran until he reached the central Mars government bubble. Xola was sitting there, arguing with three other men when he went through the airlock.

"I volunteer. I want to pilot the shuttle that delivers the payload," Tunde announced, out of breath.

Xola stood up, a barely suppressed look of pleasure on his face. He handed Tunde a form—a meaningless formality—and placed a hand on his shoulder in a show of brotherhood and pride. Tunde returned Xola's smile weakly and signed the form in blue ink.

"...0..."

"...and we have lift-off!"

The world became a blur as the shuttle took to the red sky, flamelessly pushing away everything near where it had been in powerful ripples of dust and superheated gas. The ripples doubled back on themselves at a distance, folding in on each other like an empire invaded by its own army while the shuttle rose, clove the thin, man-made red clouds and broke through the weak sound barrier, slipping into the plain, vast nothingness of Mars's near space. It kept vibrating violently and Tunde, despite his previous Earth years as an army pilot, felt his stomach twist and knot in ways it hadn't since he was a very young man.

As he was propelled farther and farther away from the prison planet, he felt a kind of calm wash over him, a sort of soothing feeling, like one would get from a blanket on a cool winter evening or the tightening of a lover's grip or a jovial aunt's hug. He was free.

Tunde turned to the rear monitor to watch the rusty orb slowly shrink against a sea of blackness. He considered what he was doing and why he was doing it. He thought of Halima, of his father, of the WorldCon and the missile strapped to his shuttle like a sinner's burden, its crudely-built, fiery might designed to rain down the vengeance of three billion exiled men and women on their brothers and sisters. He thought of what it represented—the anger, the resentment, the bitterness—all these dark emotions extracted from an entire planet of discontent, distilled down to this one act of lashing out; a vicious bite at the hand of sorrow.

He imagined lurid scenes of men and women burning, dying from radiation poisoning, the WorldCon behemoth falling like a steel and glass Goliath after being struck by a spiteful David's nuclear catapult. It would kill millions. Condemn billions more to a lifetime of pain and sickness and deformed progeny. Probably provoke Earth to swift, savage retaliation.

No.

He unstrapped himself from his seat and allowed himself forward to the control panel, weightless and oblivious to the concept of orientation. He tapped at the dials slowly, contemplatively, adjusting the manoeuvring system's input trajectory just as he had rehearsed in secret. This was the last truly good thing he would do with his life, and perhaps it wouldn't even matter; maybe the Marsmen would just build another dirty bomb, strap it to another crude shuttle and send another suicide bomber. But perhaps also, one day, when the sting of his betrayal had ebbed, they would understand and thank him for what he did.

Yes, they had been abandoned, thrown away like trash and mostly forgotten on an alien planet. But they had consented to being discarded, desperate to escape death for crimes of their own doing, so what right did they have to resent the manner of life the deal left them with?

There was dignity in enduring punishment. There was honour in earning redemption. There was freedom in letting go.

Tunde propelled himself to one of the observation ports that had been built into the side of his ship. He contemplated how vastly different space travel by rocket was from an interplanet teleport—less dreamlike, more real. Halima had been right about that on the first day they met.

He peered outside, looking for something out there in the sea of space, and saw nothing but opportunity. Freedom and opportunity.

"You have to know you are lost before you can start to find your way back home, huh." His voice was low, a whisper to himself.

He placed his hands on the shuttle wall, pushed gently and allowed his body to drift lazily back to the control panels. He pressed the pressed the 'transmit' button and began.

"Hi Dad. It's me, Tunde. I don't know if you're still alive or if you'll ever get this message. They're probably jamming all signals from Mars, but I suppose there is no harm in trying. I need to say this anyway. For you and for anyone else listening. I want to let you know that I lived. I guess there is no point getting into the details. Suffice it to say that Mars was hell, but it isn't any more. Not really. Maybe one day it will just be another planet, another home for humanity. A home with a horrible history, yes, but what piece of land that humanity calls home doesn't have a horrible history?

"I want to thank you. Without your words, I would surely have been lost. I had so much hate and anger in me before I came here. Sometimes I think I still do, but Mars has shown me how right you were. I have learned to let things go. Mars was a harsh, grudgeful thing, but even a planet can be taught to let go and let something new thrive. Planets, like people, are not easily changed. Memories of the past and visions of what could have been are easy things to get lost in. But your words anchored me. I am glad I did not let my past consume me, glad I did not get lost. Thank you, Daddy; you were right.

"I don't know what will be said about me, eventually, if anything is said at all. But I hope they do not say I was murderer. You were right about that too. I murdered a man, and for that I am sorry, but I am not a murderer. I was a pilot. I was an engineer. I tended the plains of Mars. I turned up the soil. I sowed seeds and enzymes. I drank with friends. And when the time came, I decided to be honourable, even if I couldn't be honest. I am not a hero. I have betrayed my friends. I am just a man, flawed like any other, but willing to be the conscience of a planet because I think it is the right thing to do. I hope they forgive me. I don't know if I have redeemed myself. I only hope that you would be proud of me, Dad, and that it would give you some measure of joy to know that I finally went to a star."

Tunde ended the transmission and felt something well up in him. It was the same feeling that had come over him when he was six and his father had placed a warm hand over his young shoulder, face illuminated by moonlight glow and flush with pride and approval. It was a confounding cocktail of clarity and a kind of frothy happiness that cannot be described to anyone that has never felt it before. It imbued him with a calm conviction in the final rightness of what he had already decided to do.

He shut off all the shuttle's data management modules, blocking all signals to and from the ship.

"Sorry, man," he whispered.

Xola would probably be the first to notice and wonder what went wrong, the first to consider what possible technical glitch could have cut off the ship's tracking signal, the first to hear his broadcast transmission. He would also probably be the last to accept and understand it.

Tunde shut down the water purification system and reduced the oxygen saturation in the main chamber to sixteen percent. He turned it down to zero everywhere else. Up ahead of him, the corona of the sun began to slide into view, brilliant and blinding despite the powerful radiation screen.

Flanking him, the vast blackness of space, dotted with living spheres of light and rock, reminded him of that magical moment just after fireworks go off in a dark night sky.

Tunde drifted gracefully back into his chair. He took a deep breath and silently let himself start to fall home, into the sun.

Connectome, Or, The Facts In The Case Of Miss Valerie Demarco (Ph.D)

The facts in the case of miss Valerie Demarco are, as accurately and concisely as I can recount them, these:

Miss Valerie Demarco (Ph.D) was diagnosed with colon cancer in July, 2022. Her doctors, to the best of their professional ability, estimated that she would not live much more than another year. However, having known Miss Demarco for more than fifty years, I was unsurprised to find her more concerned with the fate of her unfinished work than her rapidly concluding life.

In December of the same year, Miss Demarco visited me in my office after years of little more than perfunctory telephone and email contact. She appeared gaunt, and I could see overexposed measures of bone and vein along her sallow skin. Her shoulders were lean and narrow, hunched forward precariously, as though she would keel over at the slightest of nudges, and her hair was unnaturally wispy. She stood a shadow of the woman I had studied under in Oxford, but when she spoke there was no doubt it was her. Her tone was still as sharp and ornery as ever, if not more so.

She requested (in the same manner many others would demand) that I, in my capacity as Connectome research project director as well as her erstwhile student and friend, attempt to map her memories and neural signature onto our quantum cluster. The Connectome cluster had only recently been used to successfully memory map mice and was, as yet, untested on a primate brain—a fact which she was aware of, having read and congratulated me on my paper in the New England Journal of Medicine a few months earlier. Yet she insisted, citing the importance of her work and all that stood to be lost at her death. I could not deny the potential merits of perfectly preserving a notoriously haphazard but three-time Nobel Prize winning mind in some capacity. Eventually, and not without some minor measure of pleasure at having such a brilliant mind voluntarily made available for my research, I acceded.

Ten days after she signed the necessary waivers of liability, I began to administer cere-nanomites by means of daily intravenous injection with the assistance of senior research associate, Mrs. S. Brain scans were also conducted bidurnially to monitor her nanomite uptake. All this was done with utmost care for her condition and often in the presence of her brother-in-law, Dr. T, whom, since she voluntarily opted out of therapies for her cancer, was her sole provider of palliative care. The infusion process followed the predicted intake profile and no anomalies were recorded despite the presence of the cancerous cells.

On Monday, January 9, 2023, nanomite saturation in her brain plateaued and we began the memory mapping process in the main facility operatory—siphoning her neural pathway information back to the Connectome cluster. During the process, I exposed her to an assortment of standard stimuli and asked her a series of simple questions designed to trigger brain action which the nanomites could use to establish her baseline pathways.

"Where were you born?"

"Describe your earliest memory."

"What was the name of your first friend?"

And other questions of a similar nature. She responded accurately but tersely, and Mrs. S noted the corresponding nanomite activity spikes. Although Miss Demarco appeared particularly cadaverous throughout, the entire process was completed without issue in 6 hours, 30 minutes and 4 seconds—well within the uncertainty window of our projected human memory mapping performance parameters.

At 10:32 pm EST, when Miss Demarco had been lulled to sleep by inactivity, Mrs. S brought the map online and Miss Demarco's memory and memrionic neural signature were replicated on a dedicated distributed memory partition connected to several million quantum supercomputing nodes of the cluster. That was when the Connectome stopped responding.

At 10:34 pm EST, after staring at blank monitors in confusion, Mrs. S and I noted a sudden and distinct pulsing of data through the entire cluster. It was a ten thousand binary character string of qubits passed sequentially from the quantum memory disks to each node in the cluster—a sort of wave. Mrs. S tracked this on her monitor, but could not interrupt the transmission or induce any action in the Connectome despite repeated attempts at keying in input.

"What's wrong?" Miss Demarco inquired, rousing from her slumber to see what I am sure was a look of addled anxiety on my face and an agitated Mrs. S frantically pushing icon after icon on the surface input panel. Before I could respond, a strange sound exploded from the speakers in the room—it started as a high-pitched, uncoordinated screech which evolved into an almost otherworldly ululation and then a rhythmic howling before finally becoming an eerie, static sub-silence. Mrs. S was visibly perturbed, as was I. Miss Demarco sat up, tense in her place. That was when what I will henceforth refer to as 'it' communicated with us, in a voice I can only describe as glassy and electric, over the operatory speakers.

"Where am I?" It inquired.

"Who is this?" I queried in response, completely at a loss as to what was transpiring.

"I am Valarie Demarco. Is that you, Jibola?"

Miss Demarco, awakening, gasped at this.

"Yes, I am Jibola," I said. "But you cannot be…"

"Me. Whatever you are. You are not me. What's going on?" Miss Demarco was attempting to rise to her feet.

"I am Valarie Demarco," The glassy voice insisted.

Miss Demarco slipped, lost her balance, hit her head on a railing and fell into a coma just as Mrs. S triggered a direct power shutoff in the sector that houses the Connectome cluster.

Power remains unrestored at this time.

Research is on hold pending a review by Professor Ajimobi.

Miss Demarco is as yet unrevived.

The Regression Test

The conference room is white, spacious, and ugly.

Not ugly in any particular sort of way: it doesn't have garish furniture or out-of-place art or vomit-colored walls or anything like that. It's actually quite plain. It's just that everything in it looks furfuraceous, like the skin of some diseased albino animal, as if everything is made of barely attached bleached Bran Flakes. I know that's how all modern furnishing looks now—SlatTex, they call it—especially in these high-tech offices where the walls, doors, windows, and even some pieces of furniture are designed to integrate physically, but I still find it off-putting. I want to get this over with and leave the room as soon as possible. Return to my nice two-hundred-year-old brick bungalow in Ajah where the walls still look like real walls, not futuristic leper-skin.

"So you understand why you're here and what you need to do, Madam?" Dr. Dimeji asks me.

I force myself to smile and say, "Of course—I'm here as a human control for the regression test."

Dr. Dimeji does not smile back. The man reminds me of an agama lizard. His face is elongated, reptilian, and there is something that resembles like a bony ridge running through the middle of his skull from front to back. His eyes are sunken but always darting about, looking at multiple things, never really focused on me. The electric-blue circle ringing one iris confirms that he has a sensory-augmentation implant.

"*Sorites* regression test," he corrects, as though the precise specification is important or I don't know what it is called. Which I certainly do—I pored over the damn data-pack they gave me until all the meaningless technobabble in it eventually made some sense.

I roll my eyes. "Yes, I'm here as a human control for the sorites regression test."

"Good," he says, pointing at a black bead with a red eye that is probably a recording device set in the middle of the conference room table. "When you are ready, I need you to state your name, age, index, and the reason why you are here today while looking directly at that. Can you do that for me, Madam?"

He might be a professor of memrionics or whatever they're calling this version of their AI nonsense these days, but he is much younger than me, by at least seven decades, probably more. Someone should have taught him to say "please" and to lose that condescending tone of voice when addressing his elders. His sour attitude matches his sour face, just like my grandson Tunji, who is now executive director of the research division of LegbaTech. He's always scowling, too, even at family functions, perpetually obsessed with some work thing or other. These children of today take themselves too seriously. Tunji's even become religious now. Goes to church every Sunday, I hear. I don't know how my daughter and her husband managed to raise such a child.

"I'll be just outside observing if you need anything," Dr. Dimeji says as he opens the door. I nod so I don't accidentally say something caustic to him about his home training or lack thereof. He shuts the door behind him and I hear a lock click into place. That strikes me as odd but I ignore it. I want to get this over with quickly.

"My name is Titilope Ajimobi," I say, remembering my briefing instructions advising me to give as much detail as possible. "I am one hundred and sixteen years old. Sentient Entity Index Number HM033-2021-HK76776. Today I am in the Eko Atlantic office of LegbaTech Industries as the human control for a sorites regression test."

"Thank you, Mrs. Ajimobi," a female voice says to me from everywhere in the room, the characteristic nonlocation of an ever-present AI "Regression test initiated."

I lean back in my chair. The air conditioning makes me lick my lips. For all their sophistication, hospitality AIs never find the ideal room temperature for human comfort. They can't understand that it's not the calculated optimum. With human desires, it rarely is. It's always just a little bit off. My mother used to say that a lot.

Across the conference room, lines of light flicker to life and begin to dance in sharp, apparently random motions. The lights halt, disappear, and then around the table, where chairs like mine might have been placed, eight smooth, black, rectangular monoliths begin to rise, slowly, as if being extruded from the floor itself. I don't bother moving my own chair to see where they are coming from; it doesn't matter. The slabs grow about seven feet tall or so then stop.

The one directly across from me projects onto the table a red-light matrix of symbols and characters so intricate and dense it looks like abstract art. The matrix is three-dimensional, mathematically speaking, and within its elements patterns emerge, complex and beautiful, mesmerizing in their way. The patterns are changing so quickly that they give the illusion of stability, which adds to the beauty of the projection. This slab is putting on a display. I assume it must be the casing for the memrionic copy being regression tested.

A sorites regression test is designed to determine whether an artificial intelligence created by extrapolating and context-optimizing recorded versions of a particular human's thought patterns has deviated too far from the way the original person would think. Essentially, several previous versions of the record—backups with less learning experience—interrogate the most recent update in order to ascertain whether they agree on a wide range of mathematical, phenomenological, and philosophical questions, not just in answer, but also in cognitive approach to deriving and presenting a response. At the end of the experiment, the previous versions judge whether the new version's answers are close enough to those they would give for the update to still be considered "them," or could only have been produced by a completely different entity. The test usually concludes with a person who knew the original human subject—me, in this case—asking the AI questions to determine the same thing. Or, as Tunji summarized once, the test verifies that the AI, at its core, remains recognizable to itself and others, even as it continuously improves.

The seven other slabs each focus a single stream of yellow light into the heart of the red matrix. I guess they are trying to read it. The matrix expands as the beams of light crawl through it, ballooning in the center and fragmenting suddenly, exploding to four times its original size then folding around itself into something I vaguely recognize as a hypercube from when I still used to enjoy mathematics enough to try to understand this sort of thing. The slabs' fascinating light display now occupies more than half of the table's surface and I am no longer sure what I am looking at. I am still completely ensorcelled by it when the AI reminds me why I am here.

"Mrs. Ajimobi, please ask your mother a question."

I snap to attention, startled at the sentence before I remember the detailed instructions from my briefing. Despite them, I am skeptical about the value of the part I am to play in all this.

"Who are you?" I ask, even though I am not supposed to.

The light matrix reconstructs itself, its elements flowing rapidly and then stilling, like hot water poured onto ice. Then a voice I can only describe as a glassy, brittle version of my mother's replies.

"I am Olusola Ajimobi."

I gasp. For all its artifice, the sound strikes at my most tender and delicate memories and I almost shed a tear. That voice is too familiar. That voice used to read me stories about the tortoise while she braided my hair, each word echoing throughout our house. That voice used to call to me from downstairs, telling me to hurry up so I wouldn't be late for school. That voice screamed at me when I told her I was dropping out of my PhD program to take a job in Cape Town. That voice answered Global Network News interview questions intelligently and measuredly, if a bit impatiently. That voice whispered, "She's beautiful," into my ear at the hospital when my darling Simioluwa was born and I held her in my arms for the first time. That voice told me to leave her alone when I suggested she retire after her first heart attack. It's funny how one stimulus can trigger so much memory and emotion.

I sit up in my chair, drawing my knees together, and try to see this for what it is: a technical evaluation of software performance. My mother, Olusola Ajimobi—"Africa's answer to Einstein," as the magazines liked to call her—has been dead thirty-eight years and her memrionic copies have been providing research advice and guidance to LegbaTech for forty. This AI, created after her third heart attack, is not her. It is nothing but a template of her memory and thought patterns which has had many years to diverge from her original scan. That potential diversion is what has brought me here today.

When Tunji first contacted me, he told me that his team at LegbaTech has discovered a promising new research direction—one they cannot tell me anything about, of course—for which they are trying to secure funding. The review board thinks this research direction is based on flawed thinking and has recommended it not be pursued. My mother's memrionic copy insists that it should. It will cost billions of Naira just to test its basic assumptions. They need my help to decide if this memrionic is still representative of my mother, or whether has diverged so much that it is making decisions and judgement calls of which she would never have approved. My briefing instructions told me to begin by revisiting philosophical discussions or debates we had in the past to see if her positions or attitudes toward key ideas have changed or not. I choose the origins of the universe, something she used to enjoy speculating about.

"How was the universe created?" I ask.

"Current scientific consensus is—"

"No," I interrupt quickly, surprised that her first response is to regurgitate standard answers. I'm not sure if AIs can believe anything and I'm not supposed to ask her questions about such things, but that's what the human control is for, right? To ask questions that the other AIs would never think to ask, to force this electronic extrapolation of my mother into untested territory and see if the simulated thought matrix holds up or breaks down. "Don't tell me what you think. Tell me what you *believe*."

There is a brief pause. If this were really my mother she'd be smiling by now, relishing the discussion. And then that voice speaks again: "I believe that, given current scientific understanding and available data, we cannot know how the universe was created. In fact, I believe we will never be able to know. For every source we find, there will be a question regarding its own source. If we discover a god, we must then ask how this god came to be. If we trace the expanding universe back to a single superparticle, we must then ask how this particle came to be. And so on. Therefore, I believe it is unknowable and will be so indefinitely."

I find it impressive how familiarly the argument is presented without exact parroting. I am also reminded of how uncomfortable my mother always was around Creationists. She actively hated religion, the result of being raised by an Evangelical Christian family who demanded faith from her when she sought verifiable facts.

"So you believe god could exist?"

"It is within the realm of possibility, though highly unlikely." Another familiar answer with a paraphrastic twist.

"Do you believe in magic?"

It is a trick question. My mother loved watching magicians and magic tricks but certainly never believed in real magic.

"No magical event has ever been recorded. Cameras are ubiquitous in the modern world and yet not a single verifiable piece of footage of genuine, repeatable magic has ever been produced. Therefore it is reasonable to conclude, given the improbability of this, that there is no true magic."

Close enough but lacking the playful tone with which my mother would have delivered her thoughts on such matters.

I decide that pop philosophy is too closely linked to actual brain patterns for me to detect any major differences by asking those questions. If there is a deviation, it is more likely to be emotional. That is the most unstable solution space of the human equation.

"Do you like your great-grandson, Tunji?"

Blunt, but provoking. Tunji never met his great-grandmother when she was alive and so there is no memory for the AI to base its response on. Its answer will have to be derived from whatever limited interaction he and the memrionic have engaged in and her strong natural tendency to dislike over-serious people. A tendency we shared. Tunji is my daughter's son and I love him as much as our blood demands, but he is an insufferable chore most of the time. I would expect my mother to agree.

"Tunji is a perfectly capable executive director."

I'm both disappointed and somehow impressed to hear an AI playing deflection games with vocabulary.

"I have no doubt that he is," I say, watching the bright patterns in the light matrix shift and flow. "What I want to know is how you feel about him. Do you like him? Give me a simple yes or no."

"Yes."

That's unexpected. I sink into my chair. I was sure she would say no. Perhaps Tunji has spent more time interacting with this memrionic and building rapport with it than I thought. After all, everything this memrionic has experienced over the last forty years will have changed, however minutely, the system that alleges to represent my mother. A small variation in the elements of the thought matrix is assumed not to alter who she is fundamentally, her core way of thinking. But, like a heap of rice from which grains are removed one by one, over and over again, eventually all the rice will be gone and the heap will then obviously be a heap no more. As the process proceeds, is it even possible to know when the heap stops being, essentially, a heap? When it becomes something else? Does it ever? Who decides how grains of rice defines a heap? Is it still a heap even when only a few grains of rice are all that remain of it? No? Then when exactly did it change from a heap of rice to a new thing that is not a heap of rice? When did this recording-of-my-mother change to not-a-recording-of-my-mother?

I shake my head. I am falling into the philosophical paradox for which this test was named and designed to serve as a sort of solution. But the test depends on me making judgements based on forty-year-old memories of a very complicated woman. Am I still the same person I was when I knew her? I'm not even made of the exact same molecules as I was forty years ago. Nothing is constant. We are all in flux. Has my own personality drifted so much that I no longer have the ability to know what she would think? Or is something else going on here?

"That's good to hear," I lie. "Tell me, what is the temperature in this room?"

"It is twenty-one-point-two degrees Celsius." The glassy iteration of my mother's voice appears to have lost its emotional power over me.

"Given my age and physical condition, is this the ideal temperature for my comfort?"

"Yes, this is the optimum."

I force a deep breath in place of the snort that almost escapes me. "Olusola." I try once more, with feeling, giving my suspicions one more chance to commit hara-kiri. "If you were standing here now, beside me, with a control dock in your hand, what temperature would you set the room to?"

"The current optimum—twenty-one-point-two degrees Celsius."

There it is.

"Thank you. I'm done with the regression test now."

The electric-red hypercube matrix and yellow lines of light begin to shrink, as though being compressed back to their pretest positions, and then, mid-retraction, they disappear abruptly, as if they have simply been turned off. The beautiful kaleidoscope of numbers and symbols, flowing, flickering and flaring in fanciful fits, is gone, like a dream. Do old women dream of their electric mothers?

I sigh.

The slabs begin to sink back into the ground, and this time I shift my chair to see that they are descending into hatches, not being extruded from the floor as they would if they were made of SlatTex. They fall away from my sight leaving an eerie silence in their wake, and just like that, the regression test is over.

I hear a click and the door opens about halfway. Dr. Dimeji enters, tablet in hand. "I think that went well," he says as he slides in. His motions are snake-like and creepy. Or maybe I'm just projecting. I wonder who else is observing me and what exactly they think just happened. I remember my data-pack explaining that regression tests are typically devised and conducted by teams of three but I haven't seen anyone except Dr. Dimeji since I entered the facility. Come to think of it, there was no one at reception, either. Odd.

"Your questions were few, but good, as expected. A few philosophical ones, a few personal. I'm not sure where you were going with that last question about the temperature, but no matter. So tell me, in your opinion, Madam, on a scale of one to ten, how confident are you that the tested thought analogue thinks like your mother?"

"Zero," I say, looking straight into his eyes.

"Of course." Dr. Dimeji nods calmly and starts tapping at his tablet to make a note before he fully registers what I just said, and then his head jerks up, his expression confounded. "I'm sorry, what?"

"That contrivance is not my mother. It thinks things that she would but in ways she would never think them."

A grimace twists the corners of Dr. Dimeji's mouth and furrows his forehead, enhancing his reptilian appearance from strange to sinister. "Are you sure?" He stares right at me, eyes narrowed and somehow dangerous. The fact that we are alone presses down on my chest, heavy like a sack of rice. Morbidly, it occurs to me that I don't even know if anyone will come if he does something to me and I scream for help. I don't want to die in this ugly room at the hands of this lizard-faced man.

"I just told you, didn't I?" I bark defensively. "The basic thoughts are consistent but something is fundamentally different. It's almost like you've mixed parts of her mind with someone else's to make a new mind."

"I see." Dr. Dimeji's frown melts into a smile. Finally, some human expression. I allow myself to relax a little.

I don't even notice the humming near my ear until I feel the sting in the base of my skull where it meets my neck and see the edge of his smile curl unpleasantly. I try to cry out in pain but a constriction in my throat prevents me. My body isn't working like it's supposed to. My arms spasm and flail then go rigid and stiff, like firewood. My breathing is even despite my internal panic. My body is not under my control anymore. Someone or something else has taken over. Everything is numb.

A man enters the room through the still half-open door and my heart skips a beat.

Ah! Tunji.

He is wearing a tailored gray suit of the same severe cut he always favors. Ignoring me, he walks up to Dr. Dimeji and studies the man's tablet. His skin is darker than the last time I saw him and he is whip-lean. He stands there for almost thirty seconds before saying, "You didn't do it right."

"But it passed the regression test. It passed," Dr. Dimeji protests.

Tunji glowers at him until he looks away and down, gazing at nothing between his feet. I strain every muscle in my body to say something, to call out to Tunji, to scream—*Tunji, what the hell is going on here?*—but I barely manage a facial twitch.

"If she could tell there was a difference," Tunji is telling Dimeji, "then it didn't pass the regression test, did it? The human control is here for a reason and the board insists on having her for a reason: she knows things about her mother no one else does. So don't fucking tell me it passed the regression test just because you fooled the other pieces of code. I need you to review her test questions and tell me exactly which parts of my thought patterns she detected in there and how. Understand? We can't take any chances."

Dr. Dimeji nods, his lizard-like appearance making it look almost natural for him to do so.

Understanding crystallizes in my mind like salt. Tunji must have been seeding the memrionic AI of my mother with his own thought patterns, trying to get her to agree with his decisions on research direction in order to add legitimacy to his own ideas. Apparently, he's created something so ridiculous or radical or both that the board has insisted on a regression test. So now he's trying to rig the test. By manipulating me.

"And do it quickly. We can't wipe more than an hour of her short-term memory before we try again."

Tunji stands still for a while and then turns calmly from Dimeji to me, his face stiff and unkind. "Sorry, Grandma," he says through his perfectly polished teeth. "This is the only way."

Omo ale jati jati! I curse and I swear and I rage until my blood boils with impotent anger. I have never wanted to kill anyone so much in my life but I know I can't. Still, I can't let them get away with this. I focus my mind on the one thing I hope they will never be able to understand, the one thing my mother used to say in her clear, ringing voice, about fulfilling a human desire. An oft-repeated half-joke that is now my anchor to memory.

It's never the optimum. It's always just a little bit off.

Dr. Dimeji wearily approaches me as Tunji steps aside, his eyes emotionless. Useless boy. My own flesh and blood. How far the apple has fallen from the tree. I repeat the words in my mind, trying to forge a neural pathway connecting this moment all the way back to my oldest memories of my mother.

It's never the optimum. It's always just a little bit off.

Dr. Dimeji leans forward, pulls something grey and bloody out of my neck, and fiddles. I don't feel anything except a profound discomfort, not even when he finishes his fiddling and rudely jams it back in.

It's never the optimum. It's always just a little bit off.

I repeat the words in my mind, over and over and over again, hoping even as darkness falls and I lose consciousness that no matter what they do to me, my memory, or the thing that is a memory of my mother, I will always remember to ask her the question and never forget to be surprised by the answer.

Eye

If you could see beyond the horizon of what is and into that amorphous realm of what will be, what would you do with the knowledge from your sight? What would you say? Would you tell the joyful mother cradling her son in her arms to love him with all her heart now because it will be difficult to love him when he becomes a murderer? Would you tell the woman tossing a handful of soil onto the coffin of the man she loves to smile because she will eventually find a greater love in the arms of another? Would you tell the man who has lost everything he owns to steady his nerve and brace himself because he will soon lose everyone he loves as well? Perhaps you would just stand there with your lips sealed, silent and sessile as the river of time flowed gently towards it destination, for better or for worse. Perhaps you will do nothing with this gift but wish you could return it.

Perhaps.

But I do not like uncertainties.

So, I will give you this gift for a time. I will let you see.

You can see Mrs. Koiki standing over her son's bed watching him sleep peacefully. This is now. You can see the love in her eyes, a tender sparkle in the corner, a sort of constant wetness that threatens to form a tear but never actually does. You see it, don't you? Good. Now look closer, do you see that constant tremble in her hand and the way her cheekbones resist the upward curve of her cheeks when she tries to smile? Good. That is fear, a severe trepidation of sorts. She is afraid she will lose her son to the disease they have just diagnosed him with.

This is now. Let me show you what comes next.

You see Mrs. Koiki pacing up and down the garden of an expensive house which you will soon begin to believe is a palace. You will begin to believe this because its garden is larger than any house you have ever seen. Look around. Now look at the grass beneath Mrs. Koiki's feet, trampled, their stalks crushed. They will devoutly bow east until they eventually wither and die. Look at them and give their plight no second thought. Think only on the facts and realize that Mrs. Koiki has been pacing up and down this particular patch of grass for almost an hour.

She stops suddenly and you see a young girl run out of a door in the house, throwing her feet carelessly forward, her Bantu knots making her appear to be about ten years old. Actually, she is fourteen.

You know this because I let you know. I am trying to show you something. This is the gift.

The girl finally reaches Mrs. Koiki and she falls to the floor, trembling. You can hear her sobbing now. It is a loud, pathetic sound like the pleadings of an angel being defiled by a demon skilled in the theft of innocence. You see Mrs. Koiki put her arms around the girl and attempt to comfort her. You can see the way she does this and it tells you that this is a mother comforting her child; trying to reassure her after something terrible has come to pass. But here, in this verdant court of branches and leaves, before a jury of freshly cut grass and perfectly trimmed hedges; you know she is guilty of a crime against the very daughter she is trying to comfort.

You know she knows. You can see it in her eyes. She condemns herself.

They remain there for a few minutes until a man in a suit that is one size too small and dark glasses that completely obscure his eyes emerges from the same room the girl has just fled and drops a small "Ghana-must-go" bag on the floor. He stands beside it, still as a statue, and Mrs. Koiki pulls away from her daughter just long enough to collect it. As she wraps her hands around the bag, you can hear the man say something to her.

"Chief said you should bring her again on Friday evening." He pauses briefly before adding, "And you should tell her to stop crying when he is playing with her. He doesn't like it."

You know this because I let you know.

Now, do you begin to understand? Perhaps not. Let us go further. You will see eventually.

You can see Mrs. Koiki in the cashier's office of a hospital. She is paying for something with great big wads of cash, fifty naira notes held together with tattered pieces of paper and rubber bands. The cashier is an old woman who is big in the places she should be small and small in the places she should be big. Her face and body would lead many to believe that she is over forty years old but you know that she is actually twenty-nine.

You know this because I let you.

She takes all the money from Mrs. Koiki and hands her a receipt which she takes to another wing of the hospital with a sign above the swing doors that says 'Radiology' in bold, harsh font. The name on the receipt reads 'Olumide Koiki' and you know this is not the girl you saw sobbing in her arms earlier. You know this was the young boy over whose bed she stood when I first let you begin to see into her life.

He is dying of cancer and she is trying to save him by committing an unforgivable sin.

Do you now understand?

Come back to the beginning with me.

You can see Mrs. Koiki standing over her son's bed watching him sleep peacefully. This is now … again. You can see the love in her eyes, but now you are afraid of it, are you not? Now look closer, do you still see the fear that was there before? It's such a small thing now, barely perceptible but you see it clearly now and even worse, you know what it will lead her to do. There are few things that can inspire cold fear like witnessing the birth of what you know will be a wild, consuming monster. You know what her fear will lead her to do. You are now afraid of the things a mother will do to one child to save another.

I can show you more. I can show you the future where her son survives his disease thanks to the expensive treatments paid for with blood money for her daughter's innocence. I can show you what her daughter will end up doing on the streets, selling herself along Omega Bank Avenue and Adeola Hopewell Street after she runs away from home on her seventeenth birthday, no longer able to live with the woman who wilfully sold her body to a filthy old degenerate. I can show you what Mrs. Koiki does to herself, trying to find penance through pain. I can show you, but I suspect you already know enough.

So, what will you do, now that you have seen?

Will you tell Mrs. Koiki to refuse Chief's offer when it comes and let her son die so that she can keep her daughter's love? Will you reassure her that she will be making the only decision she can to save her sons life? Will you tell her nothing and keep this foreknowledge I have given you to yourself, letting it weigh down your soul like an anchor? Will it even matter what you do? What will you do with this gift if I give it to you?

And before you decide, know this: Once I give you this gift, you can never return it. Ever.

Home Is Where My Mother's Heart Is Buried

The tiny droplets of carbonic acid rain descended onto the crystalline terrain below us softly, soundlessly, almost like they were caressing the planet's surface, trying to coax it into yielding something; hyaline grass or fractal flowers or vitric worms, perhaps. The rain here is nothing like the rain back home in Lagos, millions of miles and millions of memories away, where heavy grey curtains of cold water attack everything relentlessly, loudly. Everything I remember of Nigeria is stormy and loud.

It was the twenty third of Aries, which meant it was the first of October back on earth; Independence Day back in Nigeria. As was usual for us, my sister Arinola and I were sitting on the corrosion-shielded balcony of my serviced apartment in the Chang-Duong sector drinking coffee, watching the rain fall, listening to the sultry tones of a long-dead but eternally-talented Asa in the background and talking, just as we had every day for the past eleven years. In the distance, above the geometrically precise cityscape, I could see several faint trails of superheated steam rising like arrows up and through the rain, the ships ahead of them headed for the Qenova Homopolar Spaceport on Deimos.

Arin was wearing a white polyplast jumpsuit, her mane of curly, natural hair wrapped tightly in a green silk scarf and finished with a bow flourish like a gift of brambles. She looked so beautiful and confident and hopeful. Nothing like the chubby little girl that used to hide from visiting uncles and aunties in the storeroom of our tiny family bungalow in Warri, refusing their attentions because she thought she was fat and ugly.

"So come now, you're serious about this *ajeeji* girl?" she asked me, throwing her voice carefully over her mug and through the rising streams of steam from her hazelnut latte. I allowed myself a smile.

"Quistis," I said, emphasizing the musical quality of her name despite its alien sound. Quistis wasn't even technically a she, - the Chironi are gender-neutral and both extremely emotionally perceptive and anatomically adaptable - Quistis only appeared in the typical biological structure of a human female because she finds the form aesthetic and I subconsciously projected my approval and desire for it when I first met her. Still, I went along with Arin's gender assignment anyway, as most of the humans here did. "Her name is Quistis and yes, I'm serious about her. I love her very much."

"Love, eh? It really knows no borders." The mocking, strained smile stayed on her face only briefly. "But you know it's dangerous what you're doing, sha? I know you don't care, you've always been different, but have you seen the way the others, especially our people, here look at you? Maybe it's safer to just stay-"

"-with my own kind?"

I took a sip of my cappuccino to let my interruption sink in. It had gone tepid. "I don't feel any safer or comfortable with them. I never have." *And neither should you*, I thought but didn't say.

Arin said nothing, and sipped her coffee too. I could tell that she was weighing and arranging her words, she would reveal them soon enough. She put her mug down, drummed her lacquered nails across the table, once, and asked the question I'd known she would ask since she first arrived in my apartment with that hopeful glint in her eye. "Are you ever going to move back home? Are *we*?"

I looked away as I felt something come over me, a sensation of loss and familiar bitterness. I have always kept my bitterness to myself because I did not want to taint her with it. She was young enough when it all happened to not be resentful of it. I wasn't. With a forced smile, I answered her question with a question of my own, such a Nigerian thing to do. "We're doing well and we have a good life here. Why should we?"

"I don't know, Tinu. But Nigeria is still home no matter how good or bad things are there, it is still home. Earth is still home. You know what I mean. We can't stay here forever." She wasn't smiling anymore.

Home. She knows Nigeria only in caricature; she only ever saw it through a child's eyes, its dark side filtered out by the love of our parents... and me.

"We should go home for Christmas this year at least," she told me. "We can eat amala and gbegiri in Surulere and see everyone again and attend all the amazing parties on the Island. We can even go to the village! Haven't you missed the village?"

Arin's Nigeria was not my Nigeria. Death had induced a premature adulthood that had in turn, tainted my memories. She did not know what it was like to have a government that either did nothing for you or actively antagonised you, what it was like to lack security, safety. To know that justice and dreams could be traded for paltry sums and important issues were decided primarily by whom you knew and how much you were willing to pay them and that even the love of friends and family was a thin, fragile thing that could be easily broken with fist full of Naira. I'd never told her about the people that had failed us and abandoned us. There seemed to be no point by the time she was old enough to understand and I loved her too much to ruin her childhood illusions of them.

"Let's just stay here. Home is wherever we are when we are with each other."

Arin put down her almost empty mug and said listlessly, "Of course. You're right. Let's stay here." She pushed away from the table, smoothed her jumpsuit and went indoors leaving me to the sounds of Asa and the gently falling artificial rain.

I understood her sentiment. She longed for and dreamt of a place that didn't really exist. Not in the way I know it to be, anyway. I understood because I was constantly haunted by dreams and memories. Dreams of what my mother wanted to be back in Nigeria, back on Earth. Dreams of what she could have achieved if our country had let her.

Earth. Nigeria. I love the idea of living in Nigeria but my mother's dreams died there. I'm not sure I can build my life in the graveyard of her dreams even if that graveyard is supposed to be home.

A few hours after Arin left my apartment, I made love to Quistis at her place, leisurely and deliberately. Usually, when we made love, we were a tangle of tongues and limbs and laughter and long, deep moans of pleasure but that night, I took my time to breathe her in. Her green, lush, hairless skin smelled clean and warm and earthy, it was the scent that trailed a rainstorm on Earth, especially the kind that breaks a long dry spell; the smell of petrichor. I wasn't sure how much of it was her own scent and how much of it came from my own memories and her evolutionary response to them but I savoured it anyway.

When we were done, she placed her head between my breasts and threw her left leg over my thighs in that unique after-sex embrace that all lovers seem to know by instinct. The low hum of her building's oxygen recycling system framed her steady breathing. Her head calmly rode the beat of my heart as I stared at the ceiling. The metallorganic plexium finish curved in several misaligned sinusoids, visually increasing the space in the dim light and lending it an eldritch reflection and form.

I couldn't stop thinking about Arin's question.

I couldn't stop thinking about home.

"What's wrong?" Quistis asked, startling me a little. I'd thought she was asleep.

"Nothing," I told her.

She didn't believe me so she asked again. "Come on. I can feel it like an itch in my mind. What's wrong?"

"I'm not sure," I said, and that was as honest an answer as I could give.

"Is it your sister?"

I wanted to tell her but I wasn't sure she would understand. We are all immigrants to Mars but we are immigrants of different cadres. She and her people came here from a faraway galaxy, seeking adventure, experience, knowledge and understanding of their place in the stars. But I came here seeking escape, new opportunities and a new beginning, a way to leave my past behind. Often, she asks me what it was like living on Earth but I never really know which part of it to describe to her so I usually deflect the question with humour, making a joke about Nigerian music or American food or Malaysian politics.

I couldn't deflect her question so I tried my best to explain to her that Arin just really missed home because of her childhood memories, and all she'd seen and heard about it from her friends.

"My sister wants to go back home, to Nigeria, the place we come from back on Earth."

"Why?" she asked, naturally.

"Honestly, I'm not very sure."

"Is she not happy here? She certainly seems to be doing well at Plexicorp. She lives well here, right?"

"She is. She does. She just longs for home." I only triggered more questions in my own head.

Where is home? Is it the place you were born even if you only ever experienced it as a child? Is the place where you grew up still home if no one that really matters to you or loves you lives there anymore? What about the memories? Is a place still home if all you remember of it brings you to tears? What about the sense of belonging and heritage and attachment to the air and the food and the land and its people? How much of these things need to be in a place before it starts to feel like home? How much of them can you lose before what used to be home no longer is?

"I'm sorry Tinu, I just don't understand." Quistis's verdant body went tense with thought. I leaned down and kissed her forehead, lightly, a kiss of both comfort and apology. She rolled onto her side and slid her lips across mine, squeezing my thighs with her leg and wrapping her arms around me tightly like a scandent calabash vine wrapping itself around a tree trunk.

"I want to understand. Tell me what you remember when you think of home?" she asked me softly.

My eyes glistened as I fought back the memories and the tears. "I... I remember hope and disappointment. I remember my parents. I remember death."

The words were hard, like so many marbles in my mouth. Speaking them sent roiling waves of raw emotion through me and it took a great effort not to stop.

Quistis placed her palm in between my breasts as though she were taking a reading from my heart. "Tell me."

And so I did.

I told her about my mother's warm, broad smile and her love for nature and how she used to tend to our little hedge of hibiscus while I played around her feet.

"You still miss her," she said. I agreed.

I told Quistis the kind of person my mother was, explaining how even though she was the one of the first humans to attend Nexus University off-world, she never even considered working for one of the multiplanetal corporations looking to expand trade between our two species, which was what almost all her classmates did.

"My mother returned to Nigeria and attempted to apply what she had learned about terraforming and planetary resuscitation in the Niger Delta, a place whose soil and water had been so poisoned by petroleum during the Second Oil War that nothing grew there anymore. She thought it was noble, important work and that her government would support her. But she was wrong."

"How long before we established the compressed exergy trade systems was this?" Quistis asked softly.

I replied quickly, "About twenty-five years before the first XG-compression station was set up on earth. Before then, we mostly used hydrocarbons like petroleum for energy. We used to produce it in Nigeria. We had so much of it. In the Niger Delta, in the Mid-West, in the East. We had so much of it all and we moved it all across the country through a huge system of underground pipelines, like black blood through our national veins. And then the war came and the Federal soldiers sealed off and sabotaged the network at the source, spilling oil into the soil, poisoning everything. Even when the fighting finally stopped, whole towns and villages in the Delta had to be abandoned, their people made refugees.

"It could have been cleaned up, the land revived. It would have taken money and time but it could be done. No one just seemed to care enough to try. Except my mother. She had gotten so many ideas while studying here, and she believed she could apply them to reclaim the land easily and quickly by combining Chironi planetary alteration technology with our own existing bioremediation capabilities. She thought everyone would support her once she presented the methodology. She was wrong."

I paused and closed my eyes, welcoming my internal darkness. In my mind, I saw an ocean of black with rainbows reflected in its surface, its waves ceaselessly swelling and sweeping against a wall of metal rocks, my mother atop them, looking out into a dark horizon. A fragment of a half-forgotten dream.

Qusitis's voice dragged me back to the low hum of her room with a question. "I don't understand. Your government did not want to resuscitate the land?"

"No. At least it looked like they didn't, judging by how hostile they were to her attempts."

"But that makes no sense. Why not?"

The answer was, as with most answers about things in Nigeria, complicated.

I told her, "There are many things about Nigeria I have never understood. This is one of them. Some say the government was punishing the Delta people for trying to secede when the Oil wars broke out. Others say the multiplanetal corporations were paying government officials to prevent anyone except them from utilizing modified Chironi technology, enforcing their monopoly. They paid her lip service and praised her work while ensuring she never managed to actually get anything done. In the end, the ministry blocked her path with obscure policies and red tape until she was too exhausted to keep going. And then, there was the accident."

I stopped abruptly, almost overcome with memories. Memories of my mother lifting me up into the air and laughing, her mouth an open cavern, her teeth perfectly aligned like piano keys. Memories of her warm reassuring hugs and thin, smooth hands that conducted her words into place when she spoke. Painful memories of her still, lifeless corpse - a useless shell, with all that had made her who she was scrapped out.

Quistis didn't press me to continue. She only turned her head to look up at me. Her gaze hurt. She looked at me with too much emotion, taking all that I felt and reflecting it from multiple dimensions like an emotional house of mirrors.

And then, almost a whisper, "Tell me how she died."

I closed my eyes again. It seemed easier to talk with my eyelids shutting out everything but my memories.

"After the ministry rejected her fourth application for an enhanced bioremediation pilot project, she tried to visit the minister's brother. He had gone to school with her on Nexus. She hoped that appealing to the minister personally through his family, would make him more receptive. Perhaps it would have worked. Who knows?

"The accident was caused by a magnetic grid failure on the Abeokuta superhighway. It only lasted two seconds but it was enough to kill thirty four people. My mother died instantly; at least that's what the doctors said."

I stroked Quistis's long, silky hair as I paused. The action anchored me to the present, preventing me from drowning in the past. Quistis must have sensed what I needed and did not move or say anything to fill up the silence. I wondered briefly if she would stop loving me if I ever really wanted her to.

I continued. "All the responsibility fell to me. I was nineteen and by many standards, already a woman. Arin was only seven but she was my responsibility."

My mother had never explained why she'd waited so long to try for another child. After she died, I found a birth certificate for an older sibling I had never met. There was a death certificate in the same name in the same drawer. The latter was dated two days after the former. The birth certificate was dated almost exactly two years before I was born.

"I thought her siblings, her colleagues, her friends, would support us after the accident. But I was wrong. They sent condolence messages, made a big show of weeping at the funerals and then disappeared."

Quistis paused again at this and seemed to be thinking deeply about what I had just said, and then, she asked, "But why? Other human families I have seen tend to be very supportive of each other. Like you and Arin."

"Families can be complicated, Quistis. Especially Nigerian ones."

I wished I could explain to her how confusing and disappointing it had been to watch the people that had laughed and danced and shared big meals of jollof rice with plantain and chicken with you suddenly fade away when you needed them most but I didn't know how and my memories were beginning to hurt so I stopped talking, with Quistis's breath heavy on my chest.

And then, after what seemed like hours, she spat out a word like she was choking on it, "Trapped."

In that single word, I heard regret and sorrow and longing and pain, absorbed from me, and refocused with intensity.

"Trapped?"

She sat up in bed beside me, gazing at me and bringing to bear the full power of my own emotions like the sun in my eyes. "Yes. Trapped. I think I understand now what your mother meant to you and I understand why you don't want to go back. You feel trapped between what-could-have-been and what-was. The sense of betrayal, bitterness and disappointment I get from you is almost overwhelming, cloying. I understand now that it is easier to leave that kind of place behind and start afresh, isn't it?"

"Yes," I said, about half a blink away from tears.

"Arin is free from that. Free from the burden of memories. She is attached only to you. But now she also feels trapped, between her need to remain with you, the only real family she has ever known and her longing for the place that the Lifecasts and holovids and histories tell her she belongs. She will only do what she wants if you approve."

Quistis took my hand into hers and said, "Tinu, I can show you something. Something that I think you are trying to hide from yourself. But I need your permission. Will you let me show you?"

Weakly, I whispered, "Yes."

Quistis's fingers melded into one and then extruded, like plastic, reaching for my ear. It felt strange, having her penetrate me like that but I did not feel uncomfortable, perhaps because I trusted and loved her, perhaps because she was careful not to make herself too intrusive. The part of her that was in me touched a part of me I cannot identify.

Suddenly, my mind gave birth to a parallel world of perception.

I was alone and in a place that felt like it was made of water. There was no sensation there except feeling, pure feeling. I sank, my lungs filling with emotion.

My life began to flash before my eyes, not in image, but in feeling. Joy, sadness, anger, love, fear, confusion, hope.

Overwhelmed, I called out for my mother. I stopped sinking. My feet bounced lightly on what seemed like seabed and I was at peace. I felt every emotion all at once so everything was in equilibrium. There was clarity.

Then everything shifted. Like reality had pulsed. I began to feel again. Emotions like so many tentacles, touched me everywhere. I was affected by them. Where the tentacles touched me, I felt happiness like an embrace, I felt pride like a crown, I felt yearning like music, and I felt restriction, like a chain. And I knew then that I was Arin. That Quistis had searched through my life and memories and extracted her pure emotional states from every interaction we had ever had. I understood then what Quistis was showing me, in pure feeling.

Then, as in a dream, the place that was like water was gone and I was back in my room, Quistis staring at me.

"Trapped."

Hearing it, after feeling all that, with all of Quistis's emotional power of perception and reflection behind it, I allowed myself feel a guilt and shame at my selfishness. It was a guilt that had always been there, but for the first time in years, that guilt finally overwhelmed my own resentment of events past. I had no more right to make her stay here with me and my scarred memories than the Nigerian government had had to keep the oil-soaked Niger Delta untreated. So, full of that potent guilt, I asked, "What do you think I should do?"

She lay her head back down on my chest where it had been a moment earlier and said, "You already know. When my people send out a new exploratory pod, everyone on the planet is given the opportunity to go on with it or stay on the terraformed world." She paused, and then a breath later, said, "One day, I may want to leave this place too, just like Arin. I wouldn't want to feel trapped by anything, especially not someone else's memories. I think you should let Arin make her own decision. All you can do is remove the chain, let her decide if she wants to follow the music."

We lay there, silent in the wake of her words in the darkness of her flat, my face wet with tears and her head heavy on my heart.

I arrived at the Qauron Interplanetary Transit Hub one hour before Arin was due to check-in. I don't know why. I suppose, now that I think about it, I needed to feel like I was the one sending her off, like I was the one guiding her just I always had for the past sixteen years even though I knew it was not true anymore. This was where she would leave me.

I entered the violently angular prism of glass and metallorganic plexium, walking behind a middle aged woman in an ankara head tie and too much mascara. Beside me, a green, four-legged Chironi shaped like a large centaur with a turban around his head walked beside what appeared to be a woman in a hijab and long flowing polyplast gown. I could not tell if she was human or not but I suspected she was. We marched through the station until we reached the electric-white Departures lounge. I took a seat. The couple and the woman in the mascara went ahead to check-in. I surveyed the area briefly and then started to read a news bulletin from my Lifedock as I awaited Arin's arrival.

It had taken me almost three full days to tell Arin what I had decided that night in Quistis's arms. She had kept asking me if I was sure and if I would still love her if she said she wanted to go. I'd kept saying yes until she believed me. So there I was, waiting to say goodbye.

Arin arrived about half an hour after I did, carrying only a small bag. When she saw me, she stopped suddenly, then walked over briskly and sat awkwardly beside me.

"I wasn't sure you would actually come," she said.

"Yeah, well, I have to see you off. I brought you to this world-"

"-And you will watch me leave it."

I smiled a strained smile, my cheeks taut like a *dundun* drumskin.

"So, you know what are you going to do when you get back? You

197

have it all planned a bit more now?"

She brushed a stray strand of her from her cheek, hooking it behind her ear and shrugged. "I don't know yet. Plexicorp said the position they have for me in Lagos is in marketing. I'm not sure if I'll like it but I'll see how it goes when I get there. And they are covering my accommodation so that's sorted."

Two amoeboid Chironi younglings moved past us, growing an extension of their bodies in the direction of their waiting parent and then flowing into it, quickly, their green, fleshy membranes stretching and contracting continuously. Their parent was mostly shaped like a human male, except for the short tail sticking out from behind him. I wondered briefly what part of earth they were going to and what they were going to do there.

"What about you?" Arin asked. "Will you be alright on this world by yourself?"

I nodded.

I could tell that she was waiting for me to say something more, perhaps beg her to stay because I needed her with me or invoke the transcendent bond of sisterhood and insist that we had to stay together because all we had left was each other or even just break out into warnings about Nigeria and what had happened to our mother when she too had turned her back on the opportunities Mars offered to return home. But I said nothing, I only smiled wanly.

As though sensing my thoughts she sighed and said, "Thank you Tinu, for not making me feel guilty about this. I know it isn't easy for you."

"I love you Arin, and I want you to be happy, above all else. Even if it's not in the same place I am. I'll miss you desperately, but I will be glad to know you are doing what you want, and that you are happy doing it without feeling trapped by anything or anyone."

"I love you, sis."

I handed her an interplanetary communications brochure I'd picked up that morning and started to explain to her what I'd found out, "Staying in touch is not going to be easy. Earth is too far away for standard real-time conversations, so you're going to have to get an ansible extension for your Lifedock. You won't get anything good at the Homopolar Spaceport so don't buy there. The moon-to-moon railgun shops don't have many trade agents but as soon as you get to Lagos, buy one, please. There used to be Comms agents just outside the Fashola Transit Station. You should be able to..."

My voice trailed off as Arin started to laugh with a loud, howling sound that confused me but made me smile at the same time.

"What's so funny?"

"You. You're being such a big sister! Going on and on about where I should do this and where I can buy that. You've become a real auntie."

She threw an arm around my shoulder and squeezed a small self-aware laugh out of me.

"Abeg, Abeg," I said, gently taking her right hand in mine and doing my best impression of a typical Yoruba woman, accent and all. "I know I basically raised you and all but don't call me that, I'm still a young *sisi*. Understand?"

"Yes, Auntie Tinu!" she shouted, giving me a faux-serious look, and then we both broke into laughter.

The other sentients in the lounge looked in our direction, wondering what was going on but their eyes didn't linger long.

When our laughter subsided, I told her, "There are many things about Mum and Dad and our family back in Nigeria that I never really explained to you. Things that I never..."

"Come on. Do you really think I don't know, Tinu?"

She'd caught me off-guard.

"Huh?"

"Do you really think I don't know about Mum's company and where she was going when she had the accident? You think I didn't notice when all our aunts and uncles stopped coming? When things got so hard for us that you had sell the furniture in the old house? All the compromises we had to make before you got the scholarship to Nexus? I was young, Tinu but I noticed and as I got older I did some investigation of my own. I just never wanted to press you to talk about it because I knew it was so difficult for you."

I paused to consider what my sister had just told me and realised that I had been treating her like a child when in fact she was a woman with needs and feelings and hopes and questions of her own. She had been so for a long time. Something it had taken Quistis to fully open my eyes to. I felt even more ashamed than I had under my lovers' gaze.

"You need to stop trying to protect me Tinu. I'll be okay. Come to Lagos and spend next Christmas with me, okay? You can tell yourself you're just checking up on me, nothing more."

I nodded.

The sweet, thick voice of the station's AI called for all passengers of pod DG-098 to Luna to check-in through the sonic vibra-sensors distributed around the lounge.

Arin rose to her feet and said, "I guess I have to go now."

"I know," I said, staring at the space in front of me, watching nothing in particular, my mind in a nebulous non-place, where everything—time, distance, memories, my thoughts and hopes and dreams seemed to have been separated from each other and untethered from me.

"Tinu? I really need to go."

I listened to her voice try to get my attention for a while, noticing just how much her voice sounded like the voice of our mother as I remember it. Or perhaps my mind was just conflating the sound with my memory, bonding them to each other so I would never, ever forget. "Yes, time for you to go home," I said at last, without looking at her.

"I'm not going home," she said, wiping away tears. "I'm going to Lagos but I'm leaving the only home I have ever known."

Standing there in each other's arms, I remembered my mother and her warm hugs and her strength of will and her fierce consuming determination. I wanted to hug my mother again, pull her and Arin to my bosom and hold them there forever. I would have to settle for holding them in my heart.

"Oya, Arin. Go."

Tears rolled down her cheek like little drops of liquid soul as she pulled back, nodded vigorously and turned away, heading for the check-in counter. I left the lounge immediately, breaking into a short, quick-footed run when I stepped outside the plasmium door and into the sheltered walkway that led to the magnetic transport network below the station. I stood there and did not move, waiting and watching the clouds through clear glass.

After almost twenty minutes, a sleek, black delta-shaped ship breached the carbon dioxide sky, one hundred tons of metal, fuel and cargo including my sister, roaring, accelerating, and ascending steadily, a bright tail of light, heat and water vapour behind it.

I closed my eyes and wished my sister well from the bottom of my soul, imploring my mother's spirit to welcome her, when she arrived, to the world where her heart is buried.

The black delta finally escaped the thin Martian atmosphere, leaving nothing but a dissipating tower of water vapour behind, like a painful memory being forgotten. I looked down and away from the sky, taking in the place I'd chosen for myself, for better or worse, and began to head…

home.

Incompleteness Theories

I

"It's never really been about the money for you, has it?" Diego Salazar said as he lifted his elbows from his fibreglass desk, sat upright in his plush leather chair and smiled a toothless smile that possessed all the warmth of an arctic breeze. The tension in the room seemed to lessen by some minor subdivision of a degree.

"Still, I don't mind paying you the twenty-six million dollars you are asking for. I need you. And your work has contributed significantly to building my empire."

"So you think you owe me something?" Even though Professor Wale Adedeji's voice carried no accent, he still had the singsong cadence of a typical Yoruba man. His words echoed eerily through the expansive penthouse office of the second richest man in the world.

"No, I don't. If I did, I would simply give you the money and have you be on your way. You chose to leave your equations and equivalence transmission algorithms in the public domain, as did several thousand other researchers. I merely took elements of all your brilliant but admittedly crude ideas and distilled them into an original, profitable idea of my own. That is the way of all science, is it not? Does one need to pay every giant upon whose shoulders he stands?"

"No, I suppose one does not," Wale replied, scratching his head through his decent but thinning afro. "And, I must admit, I am intrigued. I have wanted to explore teleportation technology for a long time. Most people thought it was just a joke when I included Macroscopic Living Matter Displacements as a possible consequence of the modified Substance Nexus Equation in my last paper."

"I never thought it was a joke, professor. When I read it, I recognized it as the most important part of the paper—beyond the mechanistic and academic refinements of life energies. It's something that could truly change the human experience."

A meretricious light appeared in Diego's eyes as he offered his thinly veiled flattery. Wale found the pretended interest in 'the human experience' to be both silly and unnecessary; Diego was only interested in potential profits—it had been obvious from the moment he propositioned him. Despite this, he allowed a smile to crease his face as he spoke. He wondered if Diego knew that he'd failed to convince the African Academy of Sciences to support his seventh application for funding. He'd followed every guideline and procedure, dotted every 'i' and crossed every 't', working his graduate students like slaves to perform new calculations and generate new data every night which he compiled into elegant presentations for the next morning. The council listened to him because of his reputation—a Nobel Prize could still open some doors in the right places—but they wouldn't give him a chance. They cited Dr. Roark's work and pointed out the incredible amount of global legal manoeuvring that would be required to get him permission to run even the most basic tests. It was obvious that despite his equations and proofs and arguments, they thought his underlying assumptions were at best a wild, dangerous guess and at worst crackpottery.

They told him it was impossible, even though making the impossible possible was the one thing that Prof. Adedeji knew he could do better than anyone. He knew that there was a way. Knew it in his bones. And now, just a few weeks later, here he was being offered a chance. The music was already playing. He might as well keep in step.

"Well, that is precisely what I intend to do," Wale said.

"And of course, prove Dr. Roark wrong in the process." Diego let the light in his eyes narrow as his smile broadened, revealing pearly white teeth that glinted in the fluorescent light of his office. The smile took on the quality of a sharpened knife. "You want to one-up the old man before he dies and goes to the grave thinking he was right, right?"

"Yes, that too." Wale tried not to let his surprise and nervousness show despite the sudden sheen of sweat that was coating his skin.

"One would think that two Nobel Prize co-winners would be inseparable. At least philosophically. You must both believe in the same things to have developed these equations, no?"

"Roark doesn't believe in living matter displacement. He just thinks it cannot be done for some reason he won't admit to anyone because he knows it's illogical. Admittedly, teleporting a living being is very different from what you do in the telecargo industry, but that's not his argument; his argument is not for difference or difficulty but for implicit impossibility."

"That's a strange position for a man who has spent his life proving that all life is just another form of energy to take."

"That's precisely the problem. He was trying to prove the opposite."

"I see." Diego seemed genuinely amused. "Well I suppose it's fortunate for us both that he turned out to be wrong. Maybe he will do us a favour and turn out to be wrong again."

"Perhaps he will." Wale shrugged, trying to hide his nervousness. He changed the subject.

"I only do this on one condition though. I am in charge. No one else. No deadlines, no inspections. None of all that micromanaging that stifles creativity. This is my project and I will proceed as I and my team see fit. All technical decisions are mine. Are we agreed?"

"As long as you keep making progress, it's fine by me."

"Good, so now that we have agreed on my fee and my terms, do you mind telling me the details? Like where the facility will be based and who else you intend to bring on?"

Diego smiled and gestured towards the left corner of his table, where a black panel was set into the fibreglass. As his hand crossed over it, the panel irised to reveal a liquid crystal display touchscreen. Wale could see a data neurostream running across its surface. Diego placed his finger on it and swiped it smoothly across the table towards a small black panel set in front of Wale, who hadn't noticed it there before.

"Download that to your Lifedock," he said. "It contains most of what you need. A full briefing, some proposed personnel dossiers and a requisition plug-in. You can use it to order any equipment you think you need."

"That's convenient."

"I haven't finalized the entire team yet; I needed you on board before I made them offers. But you will meet them soon enough. You can expect at least seventy of the world's best and brightest at your beck and call. I have five other head researchers in mind but, as I said, nothing is final."

"Okay."

Wale mused absent-mindedly as he retrieved his Lifedock adapter from his chequered blazer pocket. When he had the rectangular black device in his hands, he pulled out the sinewy cable, slid it into the tiny Lifedock jack in his forearm, plugged the other end into the port beside the table panel and told it to power on. His mouth barely made a sound, but the thought was enough for the direct neural interface installed in his brain to register the command. He felt the small, familiar electric jolt of the device connecting to his nervous system. When the feeling cleared, he pressed the download button on the device, waited until the new information settled in his neural pathways and then raised his head to look at the man sitting across the table from him.

"You have NATO in on this?"

"Of course," Diego said dismissively.

"Why?"

"Why? Let me tell you why." Diego leaned forward in his chair. "Because I am investing a significant chunk of money into this venture and I need partners that can buffer my losses, if it comes to that. Because they have access to some technology that even I can't get. Because, as you say, this is all very illegal and they are terribly interested in this but cannot be seen to be doing this research themselves—the religious fundamentalists would go insane if they even suspected. Because I am a patriot. Because I am doing everything I can to make this succeed. Because of several other million reasons, but mostly because I need them. And they need me almost as badly as I need you."

"I see."

"I'm sure you do. There is a hovercar waiting for you downstairs and an open first-class air ticket to London booked in your name and valid until the end of the month. You can order tickets for your family and arrange to have your luggage telecargoed using the plug-in I sent to you. Someone will pick you up from the airport and drive you to our covert facility in Abingdon, near Oxford."

"Thanks, but I'm not going with my family."

Diego seemed almost surprised.

"You do realise that it will get very lonely there, and there aren't likely to be many vacations?"

"Rolayo and I are separated. She lives with her parents in Lagos now."

"I'm sorry to hear that," Diego tapped a tanned finger against the table. Something about the way he did it made Wale think he'd already known the answer before he'd asked the question.

"Will you be there with us then? In Abingdon?"

"No, professor. I have an empire to run so I can afford to pay for you to play God in the Queen's country. Besides, it's your project. You are in charge. But I will be monitoring your progress, naturally."

"Naturally." Wale rose from his chair and offered his hand. "I'm looking forward to this."

Diego reached forward and shook it firmly without standing up. "Likewise."

As he pulled his hand away, Wale noticed how strange the man looked when viewed from above. He had broad, heavy-set shoulders which hunched forward slightly. He had the grey, stringy hair that was characteristic of middle age oozing out of his head. His ochre fingernails were cut short and his stark, intensely veined wrists and oversized fingers reminded Wale of the bus drivers and labourers back in his native Lagos—the hands of men who lifted and carried and held on to things for a living. But the thing that struck Wale most was

Diego's lower body. Beneath the broad chest was an unnaturally narrow midsection from which extended the underdeveloped, sickly-thin legs of a man who had never been able to walk.

The sun was unenthusiastic on the afternoon Wale Adedeji arrived in the country where he hoped to fundamentally change everything about the human experience. He yawned widely as he stepped off the private hyperjet and clambered down the air-stairs into the moderately warm London air, adjusting his jacket.

He turned his head to his left and focused on the small but conspicuous contingent of US military attachés in perfectly pressed uniforms and meticulously polished shoes waiting for him at the edge of the runway. He walked up to meet them briskly, his luggage effortlessly gliding through the air behind him, pulled by his personal electromagnetic tether. They did not move until he was within earshot of them.

"Welcome to London, sir," one of them belted out in a small but intense voice and with a strained expression on his face. He seemed like he was actively reminding himself not to shout.

"No need to go through airport security; please, come with us."

The attachés moved with practised precision and, within a few seconds, Wale and his luggage were securely stowed in a BMW coupe hovercar and weaving through light traffic along the M40 magnetic highway on their way to the research facility. No one spoke much; everyone in the vehicle was averse to chitchat.

They arrived at what seemed like the entrance to a farm after about an hour; a steel gate at the centre of an electric fence that ran all the way down to the horizon in both directions, decorated with barbed wire. Wale almost let a smile escape his lips when he saw the artificially dirty yellow signs with illustrations of cows and lightning that were suspended along the fence.

The gate retracted slowly to reveal three military guards with sour faces. Although Wale could tell that they all knew each other, papers were exchanged efficiently and identification badges were checked conscientiously before the car was allowed to drive down the road past geometrically trimmed shrubbery and stocky white buildings, none of them higher than the third storey. They kept driving until they eventually reached the solitary grey office block in the compound. A solidly built woman in army uniform with a bob of short black hair, a hawkish face and a scar across her forehead was waiting at the entrance. Medals hung from her like Christmas decorations. The sun momentarily dazed Wale as the vehicle came to a halt and he stepped out.

"Welcome to Dragonfly, Professor Adedeji," Lt. Susan Willis said, mispronouncing his name. Wale ignored it out of habit, calibrated his tie, thrust his arms deep into the white pockets of his coat and straightened his lean measure of spine to stand face to face with the woman.

"So this is it then?"

"Yes it is. It looks much better inside than out, by design."

Wale took a quick glance behind her. "I see."

"Some of the others are already here; would you like to meet them?"

She smiled, avoiding his eyes. She would never admit it, but she was, in many ways, awed to be in his presence. It was not often she met Nobel Prize winners. And now she was expected to manage one on a clandestine multi-billion dollar project for the government. Her mother, who'd worked her way from tech support to becoming the head of LegbaTech's AI research centre in Nairobi, would have been proud. Not even her three medals from four tours of duty on Deimos had produced anything resembling pride from the old woman. Perhaps now her mother would have been proud enough to hug her and speak to her with something like respect, if she were still alive.

"Of course. Please, lead the way."

"In here please," Susan gestured. They walked through the entrance and quickly reached what looked like an elevator door, which dematerialized the moment Susan pressed her hand to the panel beside it. The door rematerialized and electric light symbols appeared once they entered, indicating that they were descending twenty-two levels below ground. Wale caught his own dulled reflection in the door. Willowy body held straight. Well-combed afro halo. Sunken eyes. Deep oak skin full of wrinkles.

"Fancy door," He said with a nod.

"Yes, it's a telecargo model. A bit wasteful if you ask me. The energy used to open and close this could feed a small family on Mars."

"Yes, but it is impressive."

"Yeah. That it is. Diego likes impressive."

The rest of the ride down the three-kilometre-deep bunker was so silent that Susan fancied she could hear the faint rumbling and whirring of Wale's brain.

When the elevator stopped and the door dematerialized again, they found themselves standing on the far side of a large, white corridor. A wall of glass revealed three men and two women. They were all drinking wine around a glass table in the centre of what was obviously his laboratory, bathed in harsh, too-bright light, like a permanent flash of lightning.

206

Wale looked around; taking it all in. Trunk-thick tubing looped, drooped and curled across the high ceiling; almost everything was angular. Lines ran all along the windowless wall, catching the dim light of the space and giving it an alien, reptilian feel. The air in the facility still had the metallic quality of new equipment. Wale used to call it the smell of rationality.

"One paragraph in The Whale's research paper is going to change the entire world, eh laddies." The voice came from beside him, lilting and exaggerated and trying to mimic British inflections but falling into caricatured chaos because the owner's tongue was too deeply encrusted with Italian whorls. Wale turned to see a familiar face exiting what seemed to be a washroom and smiled.

"Thiago!" He opened his arms as he spoke the name with exaggerated flair.

His friend—one of the few people in his life who could be described so despite their many disagreements—walked up to him, rubbing on the dull, hairless crown of his head as if for luck before hugging him. The embrace threw him back to his time at Cambridge when they first met at a Moiraiology conference three months before Thiago joined the faculty as a Post-doctoral researcher assisting Dr. Roark. They'd struck up an unlikely friendship, the brash, serious-minded Wale who thought he could bend the world to his will, and the playful Thiago who loved to investigate and enjoy it. Now, almost thirty years later, they were about to begin experimenting on one of Wale's oldest and wildest ideas.

"Adedeji. How's that old brain of yours?"

"It's alright, my friend. And what is this thing happening to your midsection, ehn?"

Thiago Firozzi's olive skin flushed plum and his wide shoulders began to heave in laughter. Thiago had accepted the Dragonfly offer partly out of academic curiosity, partly because the pay Diego Salazar had offered was obscene, but mostly because the moment Salazar told him what they would be working on, he knew Wale would be involved.

"Well it's better than looking like skin and bones. You're almost cadaverous. Have you even been eating? Have you stopped eating your pounded yam? How is Rolayo? Temi?"

"She's… they're fine. They're both fine."

"I'm really glad to hear that." There was an almost imperceptible sadness to his voice. Wale thought that he must know what happened. Maybe Rolayo had told him.

"You?"

"Same old, same old."

Thiago bowed slightly to reveal a perfectly shaved pate and addressed Susan. "Hello again, Susan. You're as beautiful as you were five minutes ago." His silk shirt strained against his midsection like an overloaded fishing net.

Susan laughed.

Wale could not suppress a smirk. "Ha! You haven't changed at all."

"No I haven't. Come, there is some vintage Gaja Barbaresco. 2023. This Salazar fellow and his government friends know where to buy both good scientists and good wines, eh?" Thiago tilted his head to the side and gestured at Susan with a spark in his eye.

"Let's go inside. There is someone here you'll recognize."

Thiago walked a few paces ahead of Wale and Susan who followed, rounded a bend and pushed past a door into the main observation station.

The moment they entered the room, Wale knew. She was the one in black. Wale could only see her from behind—red hair cascading down to her shoulders like bloodied silk, firm muscle embraced in the right places by her skirt suit, four-inches heels clacking ever so softly as she shifted her weight from one foot to the other—it was undoubtedly her. Wale hadn't seen her for thirteen years and still, the stirrings he felt were both familiar and intense. She started to turn around, her hair aglow. He experienced a brief and overwhelming sense of a sort of déjà vu, of not only having lived that moment before but knowing exactly what she would say and how she would say it.

"Wale," she called across the room in a bouncy Australian accent as he, Thiago and Susan walked up to the main party. "It's so good to see you again."

Her eyes were the same olive-green he remembered.

"Ah, yes, you and our lead biotechnician Olivia Walsh already know each other," Susan said coyly.

"Yes, we do. She was briefly attached to I and Dr. Roark's research team as part of a Moiraiology technical review. Early days of telecargo research."

"We had such lovely times, did we not?" Her eyes bored intensely into his.

"Yes," he agreed. "Yes we did." "And the others?" He turned to Thiago, who had already poured himself a glass of the Barbaresco and was tapping briskly at the glowing display of icons and images on the wine table.

Olivia stood off to the side, leaning into a clear pillar that may have been glass but she was not sure.

"I will make the introductions for you, Professor." Susan moved closer, tucking some of her hair behind her ear in a move of such saccharine earnestness it made her seem momentarily infantile.

"This is Tongchun Zhang."

The man in question, with lazy waves of thick salt and pepper hair, pushed his glasses up his nose and extended his hand to Wale. His handshake was firm but not aggressive. "Our Quantum Computing expert from Zhejiang University and world-renowned telecargo efficiency consultant. You may know him as the man behind the Zhang and Wei correlation."

Susan continued. "In his own words, he's here 'to learn'." Tongchun smiled gracefully and bowed. When he spoke his voice was both gentle and firm, like waves gently descending onto blanched shores, a low, gentle rumbling full of unspoken confidence and depth.

"Thank you, Susan. This is important work we are doing and it is a pity we cannot be more public about it. Still, I'm glad Mr. Salazar approached me. I will be glad to help as much as I can."

"Thank you. And yes, I've heard of you. From Dr. Olivera. A pleasure to meet you."

Tongchun eased away, leaning deeply to his left as he moved. His right leg barely touched the ground on each step.

"And these are Jacob Stern and Lesly Buitrago. Jacob is our lead design engineer; Lesly is our lead facilities engineer." The dirty blond, bespectacled Jacob took Wale's hand and pumped it a bit too enthusiastically. Lesly shook his hand with much less energy. Wale noted that her light coffee skin almost glowed in the stark light of the room.

"It's excellent to meet you. I guess this is my entire core technical team then."

"Yes, seems so. I just hope we can build what you need," Jacob offered.

Lesly smiled and thumbed at the wooden rosary beads looped around her wrists like a bracelet. "Oh. I'm sure we will be able to."

The confidence in her voice obscured what was left of her faint accent and reminded Wale of something.

"Buitrago, Lesly. You're the one that built Dr. Ibsituu's telecargo loop, aren't you?"

"Yes, I am."

"Impressive work."

"I was working with a good design. Makes things easier."

Jacob blushed.

Susan clapped twice, diverting all attention back to her. All eyes glittered with anticipation.

"Well, I don't want to get in between you and your wine; I would just like to welcome you all to Dragonfly again. I trust you have all acquainted yourselves with the briefing documents and have seen your living quarters. I also want to remind you all that I'll be your primary point of contact for everything here and that we are committed to supporting you and ensuring Dragonfly is a success, so please feel free to ask me anything.

"And now, since we are all here, I'll let Professor Adedeji, who will be the Head Researcher on this project, say a few words."

Wale gave her a short, stabbing look of disapproval. He did not like to be put on the spot. She suppressed an apology.

Wale cleared his throat before he began to speak; his voice soaring across the room.

"Thanks Susan, I'll keep this brief. When I first put forward the possibility of living matter displacement, thirty years ago, no one would stand with me. None of my contemporaries. No research groups. No one. Even my friends—" He looked at Thiago, "—and colleagues—" and twisted his body towards Olivia "—were doubtful of its plausibility, until the first Substance-Nexus Equation was published and awarded the Nobel Prize only five years after."

There was a pause as his head dropped to his chest. In that moment, with his near-frail form illuminated by the light from behind, he seemed ghost-like.

"Now Mr. Salazar and his associates have decided that living matter displacement is worth investigating after all. And because of them, we are here and that's all that matters. This won't be easy, but we will get it done."

His bowed head rose again. There was muted applause and many concentrated stares. Susan Willis just smiled—a pasty, uncomfortable straining of facial muscle that did little to mask her discomfort. She turned to look at Jacob, who was picking at the buttons of his jacket and decided she had to say something.

"There'll be cars waiting outside your accommodation to bring you here for the kick-off meeting tomorrow. Also, over the week, Dr. Aalimah Zeibani will come in to run us all through brief psychological and medical evaluations."

Thiago coughed loudly and then spoke. "Aright, alright. Ladies and gentlemen, enough seriousness. Drink, talk, and relax. Let us enjoy ourselves tonight. We can start changing the world tomorrow."

The English summer sun was already high in the sky by the time the official Dragonfly project kick-off meeting started, its sharp rays dancing in angular jerks along the surface of the glass windows of the conference room. Jacob rose from his seat and walked over to the environment control dials coltishly. He adjusted the solar filters for the room and the sunlight dimmed to the near-darkness appropriate for a presentation.

No one said anything as he returned to his seat. The conference room was excessively spacious; the fibreglass table and tight ring of chairs around it seemed to almost be swimming in vacuity. Even with all the people in it, it appeared as though it could easily accommodate much more, like there was something missing, unaccounted for; a nearly imperceptible incompleteness of things.

Professor Wale Adedeji walked into the room five minutes late, avoiding eye contact with the ring of faces looking at him expectantly. He hurriedly plugged his wireless Lifedock jack into the open port of the central computer that sat atop a small fibreglass lectern near the head of the table. When the projector came alive beside him, its red and green holo-lines whizzing through the air in frenzy, he finally straightened.

"Good morning everyone," he started, with neither smile nor apology. "Welcome to the Dragonfly project. Most of you are already familiar with why we are here but this presentation will officially kick-off the project, give a broad overview of our team, objectives, schedule and budget as well as reviewing the expected challenges. You can ask questions when I am finished."

His voice was a glassy bass monotone throughout the presentation as he explained how, going from his and Dr. Edmund Roark's equations, they proposed to teleport first a small, living being and, eventually, a human.

"In theory it is simple," he said when he arrived at the methodology section of his presentation. "If life is a form of energy, as Dr. Roark and I have shown using the modified Substance-Nexus equation, then it can be transmitted through a medium. And if the building blocks of matter can be deconstructed, identified, catalogued, and transmitted at superluminal speeds, just like a telecargo, then, in order to transport a living being, all we need to do is apply a similar methodology, have them reconstructed at the displacement destination and realigned with the correct life-energy signal. This is the critical step. Realignment."

He continued, the seven people in the room focusing intently on his every word.

It was only when he finished, turned off the projector and sank into his chair that they all independently realized that although they had no doubt as to where they were going, none of them was quite sure how exactly they would begin the journey there. The theories were sound, but every one of them knew exceedingly well that the jump from theory to reality is sometimes more of a long-distance flight than a leap. A blanket of silence fell over the room as individuals ruminated on detail.

Olivia, seated beside Wale, eased back in her chair, turned it to a mildly rightward angle and crossed her legs. She spoke animatedly, using her hands to conduct each word into its place in her sentence concerto.

"So, according to your outline, we'll start by testing our ability to deconstruct, transmit and reconstruct living matter. How small do we start? I mean, even for something as small as a mosquito, it will take several quintillion calculations and thousands of parallel quantum processors to track the exact position of each constituent elementary particle at every point in time during the transmission."

"Jacob and Tongchun have designed systems that track large telecargo transmissions for Salazar Technologies and LegbaTech before," Wale responded efficiently. "I believe they can modify their methodology to work with living tissue once you brief them on the primary principles and potential pitfalls peculiar to this application."

Olivia turned sharply to her left to look at Jacob and Tongchun seated next to each other. Tongchun gave a small nod, his silver hair flowing gently forwards and then back with the motion, like a wave of metallic grass in the summer breeze of an alien world. "We will do our best."

Jacob silently smiled his agreement.

Olivia's gaze wandered to and then lingered briefly on the diminutive figure of Lesly, sitting beside Jacob, who appeared to be leaning away from her. He seemed nervous and self-conscious. He obviously finds her attractive, Olivia thought.

"Good. Can we meet at two o clock? My office. To discuss the details and try to come up with a first-pass working plan?"

"Yes, of course."

"Excellent."

"When you have a conceptual design, please show it to me." Thiago spoke with his hands folded across his chest. He was nursing a mild hangover.

"Yes, yes, please run any major plans by Thiago before you finalize on anything and write it up in your neurostream reports. He is the only one here beside me with a firm enough grasp of all the moving parts we are trying to align here," Wale added, trying his best to sound encouraging and enthusiastic.

"When do you think we will have something to report back to our NATO liaison?" Susan Willis's voice had the same texture as her uniform—crisp, clear and professional except for the slight, near imperceptible tremor at the end of each word. "Your presentation schedule has the phases and gates clearly defined but you didn't include any dates. We need a sort of specific timeline."

"We won't know until we start. I already explained all this to

Salazar," Wale replied.

"I know. And I know what these things are like, but we can't just leave it open-ended. They want some informal timeline at least. There has to be some kind of time-bound objective..."

"I can't give you one. I'm sorry," he snapped.

"But I need some kind of response; it's not possible for us to kick off without any time in mind."

"Well, it's not possible to answer the question you are asking me either, but you keep asking anyway."

Susan looked around the room; all eyes were on her and in all of them, she saw the judgmental gaze of her mother. She began to sweat. Technically, she was meant to be in charge of the project, supposed to be Wale's boss. At least that's what the organograms and communiques said. But all the eyes in the room saw through the bureaucratic labels. They knew Wale was in charge; he was the only reason the rest of them were there and he was making sure she understood this as well in his own small way. Establishing his authority. She kicked herself mentally for giving him the opportunity.

"Fine," she conceded. "No time frame for now."

"Thank you." The response was curt.

The silence that followed echoed in all the spaces around them, oppressive and heavy. Wale decided to end the meeting.

"So does anyone have any other major issues with the project and the plan? Any serious personal doubts or concerns we need to discuss immediately?"

One by one, everyone in the room shook their heads and said "No."

Two of them were lying.

II

DOCUMENT 0141987-CHE-139-D
DATA NEUROSTREAM SECURITY LEVEL IV—LETHAL
DO NOT DOWNLOAD WITHOUT CLEARANCE KEY
Project Name: Dragonfly
Project Number: 0141987-CHE
Project Sponsors: Diego Salazar, Gen. Stuart Townsend
Project Manager: Lt. Susan Willis
Status: Phase I complete. Phase II pending approval
Expenses To Date: $9,234,089,451.34
Risk Level: Class VIII
Executive Summary: Preliminary studies began by testing several proposed and published matter deconstruction, transmission and reconstruction methodologies on living things with satisfactory

results. Applying standard telecargo processes to unicellular organisms led to severe cell degradation and death.

Alterations were made to the working principles of a standard telecargo unit and tested sequentially. After 108 iterations, tests with unicellular organism were eventually successful, immaterially displacing them from one chamber to another. Subjects died during the procedure since life energy alignment was not incorporated. As per Phase I success parameters, the successful displacement of biomatter without any degradation of cell structure is now considered complete. The life-energy signal transmission will follow in phase II.

Olawale J. Adedeji
12/08/2085

It was morning and the tress had turned to living torches of red, brown and gold. Leaves were piled on the dew-covered grass outside and the mystifying colours of the early sun bounced about the grounds. Susan did not feel the tingling sensation most people got at the beginning of autumn. She smiled a wan, colourless smile as she placed the Phase II approval documents in Wale's thin fingers.

"Congratulations, professor," Susan said in as comradely a tone as she could manage. "Some people up top actually didn't believe anything would come of this; thought we were just flushing money down the toilet. Now they've seen this, they're a bit more inclined to believe we just might pull it off."

"Might?" Wale asked with false incredulity in his voice and a proud look in his eye. He was seated at his desk; his skin was dark and dull in the dimmed light of his office. The office was ugly in an efficient sort of way. There was nothing noticeably out of place, nothing in particular that offended the eye, and yet the severity of the place was unpleasant. The lack of warmth, the stark preciseness and the ubiquitous brown and grey finishing conspired to cultivate a subtle, unfeeling ugliness. He did not ask Susan to sit down. She shifted her weight to favour her left leg.

"Is that the official standpoint of NATO? That we 'just might' pull it off?" His tone was mildly caustic. They and their equipment had wrestled with Heisenberg's principle and Roark's hypothesis and won. That deserved a lot more than a 'just might', in his opinion.

"Yes, actually," Susan was tired of putting up with the professor's little verbal pokes and prods. "Yes, it is. This is still just an experiment to them."

"Well. I suppose we have to give them a miracle to hold on to."

"That would certainly help." Susan did her best not to roll her eyes.

"Since I didn't give you any time frame for all this, how long do you think it will take before we test phase two? Best guess."

"Another year maybe? We've always known that the life signal transmission and realignment would be the trickiest part of this project."

"Yes it is. But I think we can pull off a successful displacement within the month." Wale said with a smile.

"We can?" Susan's eyebrows arched in unbelief.

Wale rose and ambled over to a window that overlooked the expansive courtyard. He raised his eyes and, through the window, in the distance, past the boundaries of the research facility and well past the southern bypass along which senescent trees stood close together like soldiers guarding the grounds, he could see a steady stream of hovercycles gliding along the elevated magnetic highways that led to Oxford.

"Yes. I will brief you and the rest of the team tomorrow on the revised plan. Would you be kind enough to schedule a meeting?"

Susan sighed. He was doing it again: treating her like some kind of glorified secretary and refusing to engage her in any detailed scientific discussion except at general meetings. She clenched her fists so tightly that she broke a nail, bit her lip, turned around and was about to leave when he said it.

"Thank you, Susan." His voice was tepid. He did not even have the courtesy to look at her. "For all your support and encouragement." There was nothing about his gratitude that seemed honest, true. His words were as efficiently ugly as his office and even emptier than the space between them. She didn't want to say it, but she did anyway. It was the polite thing to do.

"You're welcome."

The plasmium door retracted soundlessly and she walked through briskly, fighting to dam the deluge of acrid words building up behind her tongue. She brushed past a flustered Olivia Walsh on her way out, noticing just how much the lead biotechnical engineer's smile broadened as she entered the professor's office.

"You like her, no?"

Jacob Elijah Stern nearly jumped out of his ergonomic fibreglass chair, more embarrassed than startled. He turned swiftly to take in the sight of Thiago letting out a jocund laugh that eased its way out of him, continuous and rich and thick like warm honey. The sound relaxed Jacob and he gingerly settled back into his chair, mentally trying to regain his composure as he did.

Thiago stopped laughing, lowered his voice and spoke through a broad smile. "You were staring at her so intently, your eyes almost popped out like a cartoon."

"I was just thinking," Jacob said unconvincingly.

"Yes, yes, thinking. You are thinking about you and Lesly in Paris, padlocking promises of love on le Pont de l'Archevêché, kissing passionately on le Eiffel tower. I know this type of thinking. It is why I pay child support to three ex-wives now." Thiago's Clouseau-inspired faux-French accent was appropriately atrocious.

"Oh God. Is it that obvious?"

"My boy, every time you stand next to her, or talk to her, you look like you will spontaneously combust."

Jacob's groan drew a brief stare from a passing lab assistant. "I don't know." His voice lowered to a whisper. "I just really like her. From the moment I saw her, I just couldn't stop looking at her. And thinking about her. And every time she speaks, she sounds..." He sighed, overwhelmed. "Did you know she minored in moiraiology in college? Took some of Dr. Roark's classes at Stanford? She so smart and so beautiful and so... just... I don't know."

"Why are you talking to me then? You should tell her all this."

"We work together. It would complicate things."

"My boy," Thiago said, placing his hand on the younger man's left shoulder. "Sometimes silence is not golden. Sometimes unsaid words are just rusty iron anchors weighing down the best bits of the soul."

Jacob sighed.

"I know. I know. But... I don't know. We work together..."

"And so?"

"So it could be awkward. Or messy. And this is one of the most important projects in the world. In human history. I can't let my feelings screw anything up."

"Yes, yes, but it's already awkward for the rest of us, watching you fidget like a fish every time she opens her mouth or walks past you."

Jacob groaned again and Thiago punched him on the shoulder playfully. "Look. It doesn't have to be awkward, you know. You could just ask her out on a date. Talk to her about something that is not work. Go to the Oxford theatre on George Street, see a play or something."

"I can't."

"Yes, you can."

"No, I can't," Jacob insisted, his eyes lowering.

"Yes, you can. Are you a betting man, Jacob?"

"Sometimes."

"Good enough. Remember how at the meeting yesterday Wale said he thinks we have all the components in place to transmit a life signal?"

"Yes?" Jacob was curious where Thiago was going with it all.

"Well, he told me that we will be attempting a full displacement next week. Friday."

"What? So soon?" Jacob put his left hand in his right nervously.

"Yes, he will confirm it tomorrow. Besides, you and I both know the transmitter is pretty much set. In theory it should work, even though I personally doubt it will. Everything is balanced correctly. We just need to try it and see what happens. Revise our models if something is off. Good old-fashioned science."

"Okay." Jacob swivelled his chair around so he could look at Thiago directly without twisting his neck. "Well, I'll wait for the lieutenant to confirm. But what does this have to do with me and Lesly?"

"It's simple. If the test is successful, you have to ask her out. If it's not, I'll buy you a bottle of Chateau Margaux '45 and you can continue pining for her in silence. Deal?"

Jacob, in his painfully plain white lab coat, lacking even the minor decoration of a name tag, placed both his elbows on the table, rested his jaw on the tip of his palms which were closed as though in prayer and regarded his jovial, older colleague. Thiago was right; he did need to do something about his unresolved feelings for Lesly. This was as good a reason as any.

He stuck out his hand. "It's a deal."

Rolayo sat with Temi in the living room of the bungalow, watching holographic shapes and colours dance across the room. The young boy had placed his head in her lap and she rocked them gently, trying to lull him to sleep so she could try to go to sleep as well. Try. Her eyes were sunken and red; she had not been sleeping well. She had not been eating well. She had not been living well.

Her phone started to vibrate on her thigh. She suppressed a hopeful smile, not willing to have her hopes raised only to have them dashed again, and hurriedly stuck its cable into her Lifedock when she saw the name of the caller.

"Hi."

The voice transmitted directly into her brain, triggering all the memories that were associated with it. It was the first time he had called her in almost seven months.

"Hi, Wale."

"Rolayo, how are you?"

"Good, you?"

"I'm fine. I just called to see how Temi is doing." "He is fine. He came third in his school science project and he is going to Abuja for the finals. He wants to be like his daddy."

"That's nice."

No sound came into her mind for a few seconds after that. She rubbed the head of the sleeping boy on her laps gently and explained. "I'm sure he would have liked to talk to you, but he's tired. It's been a long day."

"It's okay. I've had a long day too, I'm going to bed soon."

"So that's it?" Rolayo could not hide the disappointment in her voice. She'd tried not to hope he would be different tonight. She'd failed.

"Yes, it is."

"Wale…" she started, her fingers trembling. She was about to tell him how sad she had become, how unhappy she had been since their separation. How much she missed him, his voice, his touch, his love. She was about to speak but her son let out a yawn, distracting her.

"What is it?"

"Nothing."

"I will call you later then." His voice had changed. It had a faint, almost imperceptible whiff of starkness about it, as though he was deliberately shutting her out.

"Wale," she said, her voice small and clear.

"Wale. Listen to me. I don't want do this any—"

"Rolayo. Not now, please. I'm not in the mood for whatever it is you want to argue about."

"That's too bad for you. Sorry, but you've ignored me enough. I'm tired. Tired, you hear? I don't know where you are. I don't know what you are doing. You've spent the last five years becoming more and more obsessed and aloof. You need to think about us, about more than—"

"Shut up." His voice was cold and laced with a rough edge that Rolayo had never heard before. "Just shut up, please. Give Temi my love and tell him I called. I will call you later. Goodnight."

The line went dead. Rolayo could barely contain her shock. She sat still, rigidified by the sudden clarity that her husband was now a different man, an obsessed man, a fearful and cruel man.

A quarter of the world away, Wale Adedeji stood by his office window, embraced by a cold combination of silence, regret and darkness.

The dragonfly sparkled yellow and red as it scudded about the elongated cuboid holding chamber like a strange, sentient hieroglyph. Olivia thought its constant motion odd, but chalked it up to some form of stress brought on by captivity or perhaps, she considered fancifully, it possessed a particular prescience pertaining to what was about to happen.

"Which one of you cloudy-eyed philosopher-poets had the grand idea of using an actual dragonfly as our first test subject again?" Thiago asked sarcastically. "As opposed to something that didn't move around quite so much?"

"I did." Tongchun did not raise his head.

"Well, let's just hope it brings us good luck."

"Everyone take your places and stay alert; we will commence in five minutes." Wale looked grave—everything was ready now, the equipment was in place and glowing equations and numbers flowed across surface panels and monitors in a bright, colourful datastream river. He had done all he could. Now they just had to trust the molecules and life energies to follow the superluminal pathways they would carve for them through space.

Wale was painfully aware that Diego Salazar was monitoring everything that happened in the laboratory through the assortment of recording devices and mirrored datastream transmissions that had come pre-installed with their equipment. Wale could almost feel that piercing, narrow gaze at his back of his skull.

"Thiago? Sam? Tongchun? Jacob? Lesly?" At the sound of their names, the scientists each lifted their thumbs in sombre "okays" from where they stood, each in one segment of six in the expansive hexagonal space, behind the reinforced glass, monitoring several datastreams and standing over other researchers in their respective teams. Wale sat in the final segment—the main control centre with Susan, Dr. Zeibani and two military attachés, watching on with bated breath of their own.

The displacement assembly sat in the centre, facing Jacob's segment. It was a simple contraption of two main parts, one of which was the first transmission chamber—a ten-foot-tall cuboid of pure quartz glass crowned by odd discs and more silver wire—for the dragonfly, and the other was a similarly designed reception chamber where the dragonfly would reappear—reconstituted and revived—if all went according to plan. Between the two chambers stood a black ovoid device, about fourteen feet high and into which were set forty-two small transparent discs. At the base of the device sat two cylinders filled with plasmium coils. These would first attenuate and then amplify the dragonfly's life energy during the transmission. Jacob would monitor the energy balance personally as a sort of human fail-safe in case something went wrong with the automated coils. Wale could almost see the stress biting into the young man's shoulders.

The dragonfly buzzed and flew sharply around the chamber, flashing its glassy wings.

"Okay, Stern in three." A digital '3' made of holo-lines flickered to life in the air above the room where everyone could see it, and then it began to count down. Wale called it out even though he did not need to.

"Three."

The air became heavy, and breaths became burdens as everyone looked up, sliding on tinted goggles.

"Two."

Lesly looked at Jacob, with his finger poised above the silver switch and his bottom lip between his teeth. Her eyes filled with an oblique pride in her not-so-secret admirer.

"One."

Click!

There was a singular moment of liquid clarity where focus centred on the dragonfly. It seemed to stop mid-air for that infinitesimal second, as if waiting for the scanners to log its elementary particles and siphon its life energy.

And then there was an explosion—a harsh seismic growl followed by a blinding orange flash that sundered everything inside the chambers before slamming into the reinforced barrier with chemical rage.

Boom!

The barrier gave, becoming shrapnel and allowing the vicious bubble of abused pressure and temperature to enter the rest of the laboratory.

Tremors shook the underground facility and rattled its metal and glass body like a besieged city. Heat tore its way across the hexagonal space, consuming the air ahead of it with fury.

Monitors and datastreams went dead. Acrid grey smoke filled the room and pandemonium descended. Diffuse darkness fell like a cloak all around the space, only to be driven out instantly by the harsh red of the emergency lights. There was shouting and gasping. Someone yelped; a man, and then there was a scream, loud and siren-clear.

"JACOB!"

It was Lesly. Wale, who could have sworn that he saw the dragonfly shimmering azure a fraction of a second before the explosion, stumbled out of his chair and through the crimson-smoke haze, heading for the source of the scream. There were other sounds—the whirr of the giant fans as they wound down without power, crackling wires, the spray of the automatic deluge system in the main chamber, Thiago, Zhang and several others were coughing and groaning, but that *JACOB!* cut through everything and made his heart sink. He feared the worst.

Dr. Aalimah Zeibani pushed past him briskly in a blur of Levantine hair and light perfume. She knelt beside Jacob Stern's sprawled out body and began checking his vital signs with the strength of manner, efficiency and disregard for danger around her that only a doctor who had seen the brutality of war could possibly possess. Sliding her fingers to feel his throat for a pulse and finding none, she slowed her actions. Burns were splashed across his cheeks and scalp like paint rudely poured across fine art. There was a large shard of glass lodged in his abdomen. The air was saturated with the indelible smell of burning flesh. The way his limbs were flung about with such lifeless abandon made it clear to both Wale and Lesly before Zeibani spoke. Still, her words flew past their ears like bullets.

"I'm sorry… he's gone…"

Wale put his hands to his hips and his chin dropped to his chest, heavy with an overflow of emotions.

"He's dead."

There was a gurgling sound coming from somewhere near them. Dr. Zeibani turned sharply to her left. She saw one of the other engineers who had a portion of his throat slit open. He was fighting to breathe. She shouted at Wale.

"Call the emergency medical team in, now!"

The dragonfly, shimmering blue like the surface of a lake at full moon, hovered drunkenly around a broken fragment of reinforced pure quartz glass in the darkness. It hesitated briefly before flying straight into the glass, crashing into it with all the grace of a blind, one-winged bird carrying a dumbbell. It fell to the floor, dazed but not dead. Only a few moments passed before it rose again, hovered drunkenly and then flew with even more momentum into the glass again. Around it, metal smouldered, smoke cloaked and voices echoed as the facility's medical team tended to the injured, but the dragonfly continued to smash itself into the glass over and over again until its thorax finally cracked and began to ooze dark fluid. It fell to the floor, like the fallen petal of some exotic flower, at the foot of the broken glass fragment on which was stencilled in white Copperplate font, *Reception Chamber 04198-CHE*.

III

DOCUMENT 0141987-CHE-146-B—INCIDENT REPORT
DATA NEUROSTREAM SECURITY LEVEL IV—LETHAL
DO NOT DOWNLOAD WITHOUT CLEARANCE KEY
Project Name: Dragonfly
Project Number: 0141987-CHE
Project Sponsors: Diego Salazar, Gen. Stuart Townsend
Project Manager: Lt. Susan Willis
Status: Phase II (Rework)

Expenses To Date: $35,934,109,661.02
Risk Level: Class X
Executive Summary: The explosion that occurred during the first MLMD was due to an energy imbalance during the Life Signal attenuation and amplification process. Although the signal was transmitted successfully, the signal was overamplified, causing the receiver assembly to overload and trigger an explosion (See Appendix F). All Phase II work will be redone as outlined in section 3 of this report to ensure that there are no more such miscalculations and such a regrettable incident does not repeat itself.
Olawale J. Adedeji
24/01/2086.

The funeral had been bleak affair—gunmetal London sky and ragged sobs, the polished gleam of refined wood that would-be worm-meal in months. Jacob had been put into the earth behind the American Embassy, buried properly according to his mother's wishes, not reduced to ashes and tossed to the wind as had become the fashion. Wale personally found cremation to be more dignified than being buried and left to rot and filth, but he kept his mouth shut throughout the proceedings. He had simply stood and watched as people held hands to their faces to hide the grief that lay there in ugly wrinkles and strained expressions. Four members of the team, Jacob's mother and his sister, who barely lifted her shivering blonde head, were present. Susan Willis represented the US government in her uniform, trying to convince the two women that their son, brother had died for something very important, serving his country, even though she could not say exactly what it was or why he had died.

"He was supporting some very important National Security work. That's all I can say, but you must know… he was a hero," she answered unconvincingly when Jacob's sister Laura pulled her aside and asked for the last time, her eyes earnest and vitreous, almost pleading for some kind of truth. Susan could tell she was not satisfied, but she did not ask anything more.

The team returned to work on the project, ghosts of their former selves drifting across the facility. They moved in near-silence at first, barely whispering essential words. Diego Salazar was conspicuously silent. Thiago, who had been drunk for three days straight, refused to speak to anyone after he found the error.

Susan barely spoke. She was responsible for the project and, as far as she was concerned, it was her personal failure that had cost Jacob his life.

Lesly continued to work efficiently but would often stare into empty space for short sad moments.

Wale became obsessed with double checks and safety; it was running the project desperately over budget. Susan's own official objections were as unenthusiastic as the English rain in spring. Only Olivia challenged him about it.

"I know the errors have been fixed. Double, triple and quadruple checks have been done, but I will not be in that room for the next test. None of us will. I've requisitioned two dozen androids that can be programmed to follow remote commands. We will just rerun the simulations and calculations with a wider uncertainty window until they arrive."

Olivia sighed softly at the latent pain in Wale's voice. A classified data neurostream had come in three days before instructing them to redo the test and close out Phase II or the project would be handed over to a new team. Olivia was not looking forward to another displacement test, but she knew Salazar and his friends had grown weary of parting with their shimmering pennies to buoy an academic's conscience. Dragonfly's costs had ballooned beyond any expectation. The zeros she saw on the weekly progress reports made her head spin.

She walked over to his side of the desk, where he cradled his head in his arms like some fragile thing. The grey in his hair had expanded down to his hollow unshaven cheeks like grainy powder.

She put her hand on his shoulder. "Look. We both know Salazar will deny your android request the same way he rejected the last three you put in. You're just scared. That's fine. We all are. We should be, even. But the errors have been fixed; the test chamber has been reinforced so much we could probably watch a nuclear device go off in there without even getting uncomfortable in our chairs." She smiled a strained smile.

"We owe it to Jacob to do this, to make it work. We can't let them bring in another team now that we've done all the heavy lifting. You can't let it happen."

She paused for effect.

"What happened was an error, a mistake. Don't let them take this all away from you because of it." Wale looked up, his eyes more haunted than they had ever been.

"I suppose you're right. We should just do this."

"Good." Olivia's strained smile blossomed into a beam of pearly white teeth, thin lips and dimpled cheeks. "We'll run a few more simulations in the morning and then set up for a test next week. You look awful, by the way."

Wale's eyes lit up at that and he noticed for the first time since they had started their discussion just how good it was being so close to Olivia again, having her allay his fears and concerns so deftly as she had all those years ago. He rose to his feet, almost a phantom in his oversized jacket.

"I know I do. But you don't look awful at all. You glow and the sight of you warms me." He thought he was exaggerating, his speech leaping into overblown flattery as a joke, but, as the words slipped out of him, he realised it was raw truth.

That was when he noticed there was little more than a breath between them.

"You flatterer." Her voice was suddenly husky. "I'm the palest and most terrified I've ever been."

"And yet you've never looked more beautiful."

Her palms came up to cup his bristly cheeks, igniting a fire with her touch. His frail fingers reached around and unpinned the severe bun she had done her hair up into, letting her hair pour like flames down her shoulders. His breath hitched as Rolayo flashed across his mind, and though he felt a brief pang of regret at what he was about to do, it was assuaged by the memory of her confession and anger at the fact that she'd never admitted who she'd cheated on him with. Besides, he wasn't in love with her anymore.

Olivia captured Wale's lips in her warm mouth and he forgot it all—ambition, pain, anger, fear. Their loud breaths filled the dark room, where the only light came in golden slivers through the office blinds. She pulled off his coat hungrily and revealed brittle shoulders that nearly made her gasp. With her hand on his humming heart, she led him down to the couch. There, they stoked fires they didn't know still burned and one pleasure blurred into another.

After, they held one another, soft and sweaty, more alive than they had been in a long time.

"Thank you," Lesly said to Tongchun, speaking over her mug and blowing the rising wisps of steam streaming from her latte. They were sitting in a small but cosy coffee shop on Oxford High Street, glad to be isolated from the cold February evening air and away from the sterility of the facility where every motion, breath and glance was magnified and reflected.

Tongchun allowed himself a smile. "You're welcome," he said, noticing that Lesly was tense, probably, he thought, because they had never really been alone together before, which resulted in a sort of mild awkwardness. He did not mind shared quiet moments, but he was not one to beat about the bush, so he broke the silence, knowing that Lesly needed to talk, just talk.

"There is something on your mind. Isn't there? It may be good to let it out."

"Is that why you brought me here for coffee? To talk?" She was defensive by reflex; He could tell it wasn't real.

"It is one of several reasons. There is usually more than one reason for a thing, Lesly." He adjusted his glasses and sipped his cappuccino. "I also wanted some company away from work. My wife has gone to see her family for Chinese New Year. It is the beginning of the Year of the Horse. A good time to leave old things behind and begin new ones. Perhaps we will be lucky when we run the displacement test again on Thursday, no?"

"What happened to Jacob was not just bad luck." Her voice was strained. "It's this project. Everything about it. The people behind it, even the very idea of it, teleporting a person. Beyond the basics of eating and breathing and motion, we all know that there is far more to being alive than having all your molecules in the right order or having your life energies aligned properly or even being able to tick off systemic functions on a list. Life is far more complicated. Living is far more complicated."

"Oh. You don't believe in what we are doing then?"

"Hmm." She took a sip of her cappuccino. It was becoming tepid. "I used to. I thought it was an important step in finding... in understanding... I just... it doesn't matter. Now I see it for what it is..."

Her Lifedock vibrated.

"Excuse me." She looked down at her extended right hand, powered on the neural connection and allowed the data flow into her brain. Realising it was just a message from her mother, she smiled to herself as she adjusted her position on the chair's curve to see Tongchun casually cleaning the lens of his glasses with a small cloth, his eyes trained on her, expectant.

"Sorry about that. I was saying... Now I see why we shouldn't do it. I can't really explain it but I just know."

"You can't possibly believe so strongly in something you can't explain?"

"I do." She seemed passionate now. "I believe we are defying the natural order of things by trying to teleport a living thing. It's why, despite all our careful planning, something went wrong. I think there will always be something wrong, no matter how correct our equations look."

"That's a bizarre way for an engineer to look at things."

"It's not, not really. I realise now that the universe must have a way of preventing violations of its own fundamental laws. Are you familiar with the Novikov Self-Consistency Conjecture, Dr. Zhang?"

"Of course." He put his glasses back on.

"That is one example, I believe. Consider time travel. If an event exists that would give rise to a time paradox, or to any 'change' to the past whatsoever, then the universe acts to make the probability of that event occurring zero. Something will always happen to ensure it does not, cannot, occur. Perhaps that's the kind of thing that is happening here at Dragonfly."

There was an ebullient energy to her expressions as she argued. Tongchun looked at her over the rim of his glasses and smiled softly.

"I'm not sure that's quite an accurate analogy, Lesly. Besides, the Novikov principle is a convenient hypothetical solution to a difficult hypothetical problem. Time travel is, as of today anyway, impossible."

"So is teleportation, at least until you try again next week."

Tongchun took a quiet sip of his cappuccino and looked Lesly right in the eyes. He could sense something burble beneath her usually calm and quiet surface. Something she had to get off her chest. He decided to tread on what he knew was fragile ground.

"We have been extremely meticulous. I know Jacob's death traumatised you. It traumatised all of us…"

"Let's not talk about that." Her tone was low but firm.

"I'm sorry if I touched on a sensitive issue. But…"

"I'm leaving, Dr. Zhang," she interrupted him, looking away as she did, as though looking him in the eye would make her revelation have any less of an impact. She ran her hand through her hair as she did, wondering what Jacob would have been doing if he were still alive and had worked up the courage to act on his very painfully obvious crush. "I'm going back to Venezuela. I wanted to leave a long time ago, but stayed because Jacob believed in this project and I thought it would be a way of paying some kind of respect to him by helping to complete it, but now… I know I can't continue. I don't want to be a part of it. I don't want to be there."

"Have you told Professor Adedeji?" Tongchun asked pragmatically.

"Not yet, but I will, tomorrow."

"Susan?"

"Yes, she knows. She doesn't like it, but she respects my decision."

"And what of your agreement with Salazar?"

"I leave with forty percent of my fee and install a permanent lethal nondisclosure data neurostream key. If I ever talk about the project to unauthorised persons, my Lifedock shuts my neural pathways and I die."

"I see."

Tongchun's reaction was hard to describe. It was a combination of gentle concern and understanding. "Well, it appears you have made up your mind." He managed a little smile. "It has been a pleasure working with you, Lesly."

"And it's been an honour working with you, Dr. Zhang."

"Please, just call me Tongchun. We've known each other long enough."

"Okay, Tongchun. And good luck next week."

The overhead lights illuminated Tongchun's face. He finished his cappuccino, placed his cup on the table between them and paused contemplatively. His eyelids were half-closed, yet a quiet strength seemed to stream from them that Lesly took as a sign of his approval. She finished her latte and placed the empty mug on the table beside his. When he spoke, it was through thin lips that opened only slightly.

"Well, it is the beginning of the Year of the Horse. A good time to leave old things behind."

Helicar blades chopped the cold and clammy morning air outside the building into noisy, frenzied eddies.

From inside his office on the third, above-ground level floor, Professor Wale Adedeji gently pushed Olivia's red head of hair away from its place in the crook of his shoulder and lumbered curiously to the window to see what was going on. He adjusted the solar filters and peered out to see a black helicar entering at a tilt into the airspace in front of the building, guided by someone in military camouflage wearing a bright lime-green vest and a matte black helmet, holding two devices that glowed electric orange. The helicar banked hard, decelerated sharply and hovered above the lawn grounds, waiting for the attaché to give the final signal to touch down.

"Olivia. Get up," Wale barked out as he drew away from the window, threw on his jacket hastily and raked his messy, knotted mass of hair clumsily with his hands.

"What is going on?" she asked groggily.

"We have an unexpected visitor."

"It must be one of the NATO people. Probably just a drill or a check of some kind. Don't worry yourself, they never come here."

The NATO officers who usually visited tried not to draw too much attention to the location and they usually sent general data neurostreams ahead of time, either out of courtesy or a military need for order and documentation. This was something else.

"It's not. Just get up, Olivia. Please."

"Okay."

Reluctantly, Olivia rose from the couch, slid her feet into her black pumps and brushed down her skirt.

They eased through the door and into the elevator. Reaching the ground floor of the building in a few seconds, they made their way toward the entrance that led to the lawn. As they rounded the bend at the end of the corridor and stepped onto the lawn, they could see the sleek black helicar sitting silent on the lawn like a giant metal insect. The pilot stood beside it, facing away from them. The person in the camouflage and helmet that had evidently coordinated the landing was standing behind a familiar figure in a wheelchair.

"Professor Adedeji. Dr. Walsh. It's been a while since we met in the flesh, has it not?"

"Mr. Salazar," Wale exclaimed. "We weren't expecting you. This is a bit of a surprise."

"Good. I would have been surprised if you weren't surprised. I didn't tell anyone I was coming until I was already almost here."

"To what do we owe the pleasure of our benefactor's presence then?" Olivia asked.

Diego's broad, heavy-set shoulders shook with laughter as he fired a neural signal through his Lifedock to his wheelchair engine, propelling it forward slowly.

"You're funny, Dr. Walsh. Not to mention quite charming and disarming with that bedhead. I see you and the professor are very comfortable working together."

Olivia blushed bright.

"I just came to see what keeps running up my expenses."

The person in camouflage took off the helmet to reveal short black hair flowing around a hawkish, scarred face. Susan. She retrieved a small bag from within the helicar, shook the pilot's hand and moved gracefully toward Diego in short, measured steps. Wale and Olivia tried to hide their surprise.

"Okay. Why the secrecy though?" Wale could not help feeling defensive. "Is it because of the test tomorrow? You think we will have another disaster like last time? You want to see our schematics and equations for yourself?"

"Tranquilo, professor. Relax." Diego smiled and raised his muscled arms into the air in mock surrender. Wale thought he was being patronizing.

"Look. Yes, I am here about the test tomorrow. But not exactly in the manner you may think. You should know by now I am not the kind to micromanage."

"So, why the secrecy then? I don't like theatrics."

Diego huffed and stopped smiling. He dropped his hands to his abnormally thin thighs and rested them there, surveying the environment before focusing again on the two in front of him. Olivia tried not to look at his small, underdeveloped legs as they swung from the padded seat of the silver and black wheelchair. She felt uncomfortable.

"Fine then. But let's go inside first. It's nippy and I want to see the main facility."

"I'm sorry, please, yes, inside." Wale gestured to the corridor he and Olivia had just come through and stepped to the side gently. Diego thought his chair forward, silently zooming past the two scientists, through the lawn and toward the corridor. Susan jogged after him, reaching him just before he entered the building. Wale exhaled sharply before taking Olivia's hand and leading her back into the building behind Diego, who started speaking as soon as he heard the two additional footsteps on the tiled floors.

"I know the displacement test will work, I always have. I believed in you and your ideas and abilities long before anyone else did, professor, and I still do. You should never forget that." They reached the elevator door and Diego paused. The door dematerialized at the touch of the pilot's finger on the call button panel beside it and the group stepped in. The door returned with a light indicating they were headed for the underground level.

"But not everyone is as confident in Dragonfly as I am," Diego continued, "and unfortunately deaths have occurred and costs have ballooned. We budgeted twenty-one billion dollars for this venture and were prepared to pay double that if we had to. I was personally willing to revise that estimate by a factor of three if it came to it."

He paused and exhaled slowly as the elevator started moving and he felt the acceleration begin in his gut.

"But you have spent sixty-three billion dollars so far and there is little to show for it except terabytes of data, some pretty equations and three dead researchers. At this pace, by the time we reach the commercialization phase, the costs will be astronomical, even by my own very elastic standards."

Wale gripped the fibreglass rails that ran along the middle of the elevator car. He had already begun fearing the worst—Salazar had come to have him replaced. He looked at Susan but all he got was a firm look of resolve that he'd never seen on her before.

"What is your point?"

"My point is that we need to accelerate all this." Diego rotated his chair so that he was oblique to both Wale and Olivia, the pilot stood entirely behind him. Olivia was white-knuckling her way through the entire ride, uncharacteristically fearful and silent.

"Accelerate? No. I will take the risk of another—"

"You have double-checked everything for tomorrow's test?" Diego interrupted. "You are sure you haven't made any mistakes this time?"

That evinced another defensive snap from Wale.

"Yes, I, of course. But the effects and the ..."

"Good. That's all the assurance I need. That we need."

The elevator stopped and the door faded to nothingness again as its molecules were temporarily teleported into a hidden space between two plasmium slats in the wall cavity. They stepped out to meet a wall of glass and a shower of harsh light.

"Who's we?" Wale asked as he placed his Lifedock over the security panel of the security barrier and allowed it verify his access codes.

Diego Salazar nodded slightly at Susan.

She smiled faintly, the kind of efficient smile one would see on the face of an overworked nurse. Diego continued. "Did you know Susan was one of best tactical commandos in the NATO unified armies? She started as a mechanical engineer in the Army Corps, then special forces. Saw action in Cuba and Deimos before moving into Research and Development Command. She has managed this project since inception and knows all the details. She is also ultimately responsible for its success or failure, and she knows that. My point is; she comes highly recommended, has a near-perfect medical history, is absolutely committed to this project and is of sound mind."

Wale and Olivia shot each other puzzled looks as they entered the main hexagonal facility room.

Olivia asked, "Susan, what's going on?"

Susan remained silent, still smiling. "You didn't answer my question, Mr. Salazar."

They all took seats close to the front before Wale addressed Diego again.

"I did." Diego thought his chair into a place at the head of the table, Susan by his side, that faint, efficient smile still plastered on her face. "You asked who I meant by *we* and I explained, implying that by *we*, I meant myself and Susan... primarily at least. We in turn represent the decision of the NATO Dragonfly committee."

"And why do you... they... need our assurance?" Olivia asked, already beginning to suspect what the answer would be but refusing to allow herself think it would be right. They wouldn't risk it, surely.

A sharp light came into Diego's smiling eyes. "Because Susan will be stepping into the displacement chamber tomorrow."

Wale's breathing became laboured and his sallow face let itself hang loose in confusion as a meaningless querying sound escaped his lips.

"Ehn?"

Diego ignored the reactions. "Susan has volunteered to be our first human test subject." His expression hardened and his lips thinned to the business edge of a knife. "That is why I am here, professor.

Dragonfly begins human trials tomorrow."

The two ten-foot cuboid quartz glass and metal chambers rose from the white floor like monoliths.

Wale felt very old and weary. He shifted uneasily as the black, ovoid transmission and amplification-attenuation coil assembly between them flashed a sequence of lights the colour of the sky. They were seconds away from their second test, and this time the stakes were much higher. Susan's nude body, taut muscle woven around perfectly proportioned skeletal frame, stood still inside. She was unperturbed by her exposure, the same firm smile on her face that had been there when Diego first arrived.

In front of her, Diego was nestled comfortably in his wheelchair and observing the scene from behind the reinforced observation chamber like a king over his kingdom.

"We are all set." Thiago's eyes were sunken, "Ready anytime you are. And may God have mercy on us all."

"Don't be dramatic." Diego did not bother to turn around to address him. "We've already been over this a thousand times. So just stop whining, get in your position and wait for the initiation sequence."

Dr. Zeibani stood still, stolid.

Wale turned slightly and Thiago looked to his gaunt and pallid friend for some kind of support, watching for even as little as a firm nod of camaraderie in disapproval. He got nothing. His friend was resigned to this. Wale shook his head limply.

"In two minutes."

Diego had first laughed at the team's refusal to test the transmitter on a human subject, no matter how willing. Then he'd threatened to have all their accounts frozen and all the fees recalled. When that still did not change their minds, he informed them that they would be removed from the project, disavowed and given no legal protections. They refused still, Wale most adamantly of all.

That was when Diego told them to talk to Susan and she'd insisted that she needed to do it. She told them that she'd received a stern reprimand from the Dragonfly committee over the ballooning budget and what they referred to as her 'abysmally ineffective management of a project that was starting to exceed her control and understanding' and that another team was ready, proposing to reach human trials within months. So she'd contacted her former boss, who'd approached the committee with her own proposal. She told them she was a better soldier than she was a manager, and she was more comfortable risking her life to achieve an objective than she was trying to direct a broken, unhappy team. She told them that if this worked, she'd be a hero, a key player in a major scientific breakthrough that even her mother would have acknowledged. And if she died, she'd die a soldier—with pride. She told them this was the only way to get back on track and that they had to help her help them the best way she could. Reluctantly, they'd finally agreed.

"Firozzi? Walsh? Zhang? Valero? Duff?" Wale called out the names. They lifted their hands in sequence to indicate readiness, each monitoring several datastreams and the other junior researchers and technicians in their teams. They moved like white-coated planets, each in their own minor orbit around a screen or panel located behind glass that could withstand three nuclear detonations.

Wale's finger hovered over the main control panel. Everything about the situation felt like a dream. A part of him was eager to see the outcome, perform the test, and for that he was ashamed. He was afraid for Susan and he wished he felt strong enough to resist the pressure, to say no, to do what he knew was the right thing. But he didn't. Instead, he pushed the button.

A red light flickered across the elements of the holo-line panel that hung over the chamber in the sharp, haphazard way of pollinating insects.

Susan tensed visibly as all eyes focused on her. The air of the laboratory was stiflingly still, saturated with a vaguely electric mix of tension, apprehension and expectation.

"Three."

"Two."

"One."

Click!

There was a small, high-pitched hum and a blinding, overly-long flash of white light.

The researchers stood frozen, captivated like deer in approaching headlights, breaths collectively held. The moment seemed to last a small slice of forever.

Wale, found himself looking away from the chamber and towards Tongchun, who was standing with his hands in his pockets staring at the reception pod.

He watched the compact, silver haired man's focused eyes widen slowly, his chest heave and then fall slowly as he let out what was one small part of a collective exhale. No deafening roar came. No heat and no darkness. Just fascination and relief on Tongchun's face. Wale did not need to see for himself; in that moment, he knew it was done.

"I've always had faith in you, professor. Always."

Wale did not hear Diego's words. Not really, anyway. He wanted to lift his hands up into the air and shout but he simply buried his face in his hands, overwhelmed. Around him, the others hugged and smiled and cheered with relief.

"Get her out of the chamber and into isolation unit four." Dr. Zeibani called out to two military attachés that had been waiting for her instructions, immune to the emotions that were sweeping through the facility. She patted Wale on the back and began to trail the attachés.

The reception chamber was opened and Susan, conscious and evidently unscathed, was ushered to the secure isolation units. The cheers continued to rise as everyone in the facility slowly began to realize what had just happened. They had performed a miracle.

Thiago Firozzi placed his hand on Wale's shoulder from behind, "It worked. We did it. You did. I guess Roark was wrong after all."

A smile cut its way across Professor Adedeji's face from deep within his soul.

"Yes…" he said, straining to breathe. He closed his eyes and let his mind wander, all thoughts of Diego Salazar's threats and Jacob Stern's death temporarily gone. He had done what Roark always said he never would. What Roark had assured him was impossible. Now the possibilities were endless. Intergalactic travel, superluminal communication; there was so much that could be done from here. In his mind's eye, he saw a series of displacement stations across the solar system, teleporting people from planet to planet instantly. Perhaps they would name one of them after him. It was beyond revolutionary. It was scientific upheaval.

That night in the conference room, despite Diego's sour presence, the wine flowed cool and sweet.

Rolayo got the call while she was in the shower, disconnected from her Lifedock. The falling water scrubbed away most of the music that made up her ringtone, leaving only a dull, persistent bass that she wasn't entirely sure had come from the ringing phone until she stepped out of the shower and looked at the display panel. He had left a recorded message.

She wrapped her towel around her body and dabbed all the water off her skin before replacing the towel with a less cumbersome and more breathable Ankara wrapper. She walked to the living room of her new, small apartment and poured herself a glass of wine before walking back to retrieve her phone. In the dim light of her bedroom, she pushed the button to play the recorded message.

"Hi Rolayo. I guess you're busy now. I'll call back in half an hour."

His words tumbled from the speaker awkwardly like pebbles down a hill.

She took the phone with her to the living room and sat at the dining table, sipping quietly, the phone beside her, wondering what her ex-husband wanted to talk to her about and why until the phone rang again.

Rolayo put down her wineglass and lowered her eyes, even though she did not need to. She already knew it was him. Slowly, she rose from the leather chair, tightened the knot that held up her Ankara wrapper and slid her phone cable into her Lifedock. She waited to feel the neural connection click in her mind and, once the vague sense of exposure that came with allowing someone else directly into a part of her brain came over her, she spoke in halting bursts, each syllable deliberately elongated and enunciated.

"Hi. Go on, I can hear you."

Several thousand miles away, Wale Adedeji heard her voice seep into his head and he knew she both sounded and felt different. He sighed. "Hi. Rolayo. How is Temi?"

"He is fine. Not that you care."

He sighed again, this time loudly. The extent of his exhaustion came to her in a sudden wave that for a minute she almost regretted allowing much of what had once been an intricate and powerful love for him fade and abrade to the smooth, desultory indifference it had become. Almost.

"Is there something you want to tell me?" she prodded.

"I just wanted you to know," he started. "We did it. I'll tell you soon, as soon as I can, but we did it. After all these years. I guess I just wanted to tell you that it was—"

"I don't care."

"What?" For the first time, since he had known her, he heard malice in Rolayo's voice.

"I don't care, Wale. Whatever you did, it is yours entirely. The glory and the celebration. Long before you told me you wanted a divorce, back when you said this separation would be temporary, you had already decided this thing, whatever it is, was more important than us. That we were a burden. You wanted to be without us. Without me. So don't call me now after treating me like I was luggage in your way your progress."

Wale found that he couldn't say anything, even though he should have known she would eventually grow bitter and resentful; hateful, even. What had he expected? She was the one that cheated on him, but he'd been punishing and pushing her away. He'd been pushing her away even before she cheated.

Since he couldn't think of anything appropriate to say, he apologized.

"I'm sorry."

"Why did you call me?" she queried.

"I… I don't know. I just did. I suppose I'm used to it."

She said nothing. He waited.

And then Rolayo filled the silence. "I hate you, Wale." Her words were icy, bitter.

The Lifedock-augmented cadence and tone of her declaration struck him violently. It was not that the feeling was unexpected, but hearing her say it so coldly, so cruelly, made a biting heat roil beneath his tongue as it finally dawned on him just how much he had changed her.

"Don't call me again unless it's about our son."

Then she hung up on him, disconnecting her mind from his abruptly and leaving him feeling guilty and ashamed.

Back in her home, the echo of her former husband's voice gone from her head, Rolayo went to her kitchen sink, turned on the faucet and listened to the steady stream of water fall and circle its way down the drain until it was the only sound in the world.

She stood by the sink in her Ankara wrapper for almost ten minutes before bending over the aluminium basin and dry heaving violently, as though everything she was feeling had coalesced into a coarse, gritty shape in her throat, choking her.

The three figures clustered around the observation screen of isolation unit four, staring at the sessile figure seated on the legless white bed set at a perfect right angle into similarly white walls. They each wore a uniquely addled expression. Wale had his jaw planted in his palm, lost in thought. Olivia stood beside him, her right hand on her hip. Dr. Aalimah Zeibani was visibly exhausted but straining not to appear so, her tense face framed in loose strands of jet-black Levantine hair like trails of living midnight. Diego's face was scrunched up into a scowl and he was unable to stop staring at Susan even as he spoke.

"It's been three days. Whatever kind of mental distortion she felt should have started to clear by now or at least, we should—"

"This isn't a mental distortion—whatever you think that means," Dr. Zeibani interrupted, speaking rapidly. "We don't know what this is." She paused to let out a heavy breath.

"Susan's brain structure and chemistry is unchanged and she responds well enough to stimuli, even if robotically. The only changes I see in her neurographs, life signal distribution maps and neural connectograms are mildly reduced electrical activity in the nucleus accumbens septi and most of her amygdalae. There is essentially no structural or tissue damage, so I have no idea why this is happening."

Diego turned to look up at her as though she were speaking a bizarre lost language. She continued, placing her hand on the clear screen. "There is nothing physically wrong with the reconstruction of her elementary particles or with the transmission of her life energy. That was executed perfectly—we have several thousand exabytes of data to prove it."

"So why is she sitting there, staring at us like a godforsaken mannequin? Does that look like the Susan you know?"

"No. And I just told you, I don't know."

"Well figure it out soon. This is a smear on our success."

"Success?" Thiago's nostrils flared briefly as he turned to regard Diego in his wheelchair. "You call this—" He gestured toward the isolation unit where Susan sat motionless, her eyes glazed over, with his left hand, jabbing his thin finger at the air in Diego's direction, "—a success?"

From the moment Susan had been extracted from the reception chamber, she'd seemed different. Gone was the quietly vibrant woman that Wale had butted heads with. Gone were her soft smile and piercing eyes. All that was left of those things was a vacant expression. She'd gone through all the pre-designed post-displacement tests, medical checks and psychological evaluations with a banal demeanour—functional and responsive, but aloof. It was as though during the test something had been switched off in her psyche, that she'd lost some essential part of what made her *Susan*. It was all deeply unsettling. Dr. Zeibani decided to have her kept in isolation under constant supervision for a week to see if anything would change. Nothing had.

"Of course it is," Diego insisted, pointing his muscular right arm at the isolation chamber. His eyebrows rode his rapidly moving facial muscles like surfers on a choppy shore. "It worked. We transported her molecules and her life energy signal and she is still alive. That is our success criteria."

"How can you sit there and say that? Does this look like any sort of success to you?" Thiago was too agitated to argue coherently.

"Look, old man, this is clearly something no one anticipated, so just relax and let Dr. Zeibani do her job." Diego's eyes turned in Wale's direction. "If you can help her, in any way, do so. Until then, keep your friend on his leash. I'll check in with you every twelve hours."

"Fine," Wale agreed without looking up.

Diego angled his chair away from them and rolled away on his gleaming wheelchair. Although they didn't say so, both Olivia and Thiago had begun to see him in caricature; like a sinister cartoon robot villain in his Lifedock- enabled wheelchair with his steepled fingers, furrowed brow and jagged voice.

He paused midway through the corridor. "By the way, NATO asked for a report on this by the end of the day."

Thiago snorted. No one else reacted. They were weary and wary of everything Diego said now.

He continued to mentally propel his chair towards the exit, crossing paths with Tongchun as he rounded the corner connecting to the main corridor. They exchanged faint nods and Tongchun continued toward the other two researchers, his light limp almost unnoticeable. "I'm getting tired of being here, in this place, working on this project." Thiago exhaled his words through heavy breaths. "I should have left here after we lost Jacob. We all should. That was a sign."

Wale looked at his friend silently with rheumy eyes, tiny pangs of guilt poking his chest like so many invisible needles. He wanted to apologise for how things had turned out, how things were turning out. But he said nothing.

"I'm sorry I'm late," Tongchun unclipped a portable music adaptor from his Lifedock and tried looking into Wale's eyes, but the head researcher wouldn't look back. "I pored over the transmission records again. Used every causal data mining algorithm available. There is simply nothing unpredicted. The measured data tracks perfectly with our simulations."

"Good. At least we have eliminated one possibility. So it has to be a pure psychological reaction. Brain chemistry maybe. Something not entirely physical." Dr. Zeibani wrapped her arms around herself, rubbing her hands over tense shoulders as if she was cold in the perfectly regulated air of the isolation unit.

"I have to talk to her again. See if I can figure out what is going on in her head."

Tongchun tilted his head slightly, put on the familiar smile which the entire team had now come to expect whenever he spoke. "May I suggest something?"

"Yes, of course., Dr. Zeibani encouraged him without looking at him.

"Perhaps we should try letting her dress up in her official uniform," Wale stared intently at Tongchun, almost as though counting each word that escaped his lips. "We can talk to her again then. This time in Professor Adedeji's office with some other members of our team present." Dr. Zeibani turned to regard him with a bizarre look that combined rapt attention, expectation and confusion. Tongchun spread his hands out, his palms open before bringing them together again in front of him.

"What I mean is… perhaps if we treat her normally, try to immerse her in a recent, familiar reality and not interrogate her as just a part of an experiment, her brain will readjust from whatever instability has put her in this state."

"Maybe that could help," Dr. Zeibani said as the confusion in her face melted away, leaving behind a tense attentiveness.

"I believe it certainly won't hurt," Tongchun added.

"Good, let's do it then. Shall we say four this evening? I need to prepare some material beforehand." Dr. Zeibani uncrossed her arms and slid her hands into her white lab coat pockets. Wale and Thiago drew closer together silently, unsure of the idea but unable to offer any alternative suggestions.

"Yes, that's fine. Four pm this evening."

"Thank you, Susan. Would you like to take a walk now?" Dr Zeibani asked.

"Yes." Her voice might as well have been electronic static.

"Good. Please go to the lawn and enjoy some fresh air."

"Yes."

Susan stood up and, without so much as a glance at anyone else in the office, walked out.

"This is pointless," Diego said wryly. He saw a military attaché—a blonde fellow named Brad or Vlad or something of the sort, he couldn't quite remember—fall into step behind her. He turned to the space behind Wale's desk which displayed Susan's Lifedock energy and datastreams, transmitted for remote observation. The holo-lines formed displays and graphs and charts, most of them aggravatingly stable.

"It's a pity. She should be proof of our success." He rolled his wheelchair up to the elongated window and tapped his fingers against it in a rapid repeat pattern. "Instead what we have created is the world's most expensive mannequin. I have AI in my offices that are more alive than she is and that cost significantly less to produce. The worst part is that we have no idea why; we cannot explain this ridiculousness. The NATO committee is beyond disappointed. I am personally embarrassed."

"Embarrassment notwithstanding, please stop that annoying rapping." Dr. Zeibani had become increasingly irritated with Diego and it was starting to show in every exchange between them.

They had let Susan rest in her own personal quarters, surrounded by as many images of her family and friends as they could find. They had watched Dr. Zeibani ask her a series of questions over and over again, occasionally chipping in one or two of their own. She answered every question correctly, tersely and in a numbingly monotone voice and then stare at them with vacant, empty eyes.

That was always the most frustrating part of the entire process—the end. That empty stare into nothing was an uncomfortable reminder of how little progress they had made. It left their minds racing, their chests pulsing with uneasy heat, like marathon racers who believed they were nearing the end of a run only to happen upon another cruel stretch of black road. This was the point at which they were at again now, several faces holding expressions of heavy thought, mounting fears and, in Diego's case, the bitter frustration of a man who was not used to being unable to get what he wanted.

"Fine then." Diego reversed his chair.

"We've let her out of the isolation unit and played these silly games all evening." His broad chest heaved noticeably. "Still nothing. I think we need to try again with someone else. It could simply be something wrong with her particular brain chemistry or an undiagnosed prior condition."

"Look, Mr. Salazar, we cannot risk doing it again, no matter what. Threaten all you want, but even if Susan has a unique trait that predisposes her to react to being disassembled and reassembled by losing her personality, or whatever it is she has lost, we need to know for sure before we try this with anyone else."

Wale nodded, stood up and sidled past Olivia. He avoided her eyes.

At the window, he saw Susan and her attending attaché in the courtyard. They were standing very close. Closer than usual.

"Are you familiar with Gödel's incompleteness theories?"

At that, Thiago jerked up, surprised to hear his friend refer to the subject of their most bitter argument. He said nothing, content to wait and see where the opening would lead.

"I am," Togchun offered, adjusting his glasses.

"I am not, but I am sure you will explain." Diego did not seem particularly interested. "Go on then."

"To put it generally, in mathematical logic, the incompleteness theorems state that no consistent system of axioms that can be written in an algorithm is capable of proving all truths about the relationships between natural numbers."

He looked at everyone in the room. Some faces showed clear and familiar understanding, some displayed a logical followership of the facts presented while lacking an appreciation of how importance and meaning. However all faces had one thing in common; they generally seemed to be waiting for him to continue, to keep going.

"Dr. Firozzi has been trying to convince me that there is a parallel limitation regarding Moiraiology, Substance-Nexus equations and any kind of technology that requires the complete description of all the elements of a living being. I have been telling him he is wrong for a long time." He smiled weakly and Olivia noticed that the lines around his eyes were deeper and more manifold than she had observed before, even when his face had been inches from hers.

"Dr. Roark believed the same thing. Even when we discovered and mapped unique life energy signals, he insisted that it was incomplete, that there was something more to being alive. To living. Now, looking at this, I cannot help but think what he must have thought then. What Thiago—" He acknowledged his friend with the faintest of nods "—has surely been thinking all this time. There is something we have missed. Not because we didn't account for it, but because we cannot account for it. Perhaps we cannot list all the aspects of a human being by any algorithm, no matter how complicated. Look at Susan and tell me the most apt word to describe her current state is not *incomplete*."

He exhaled deeply and glanced down through the window to see Susan near her attending attaché even closer with one fluid step on the lawn and turned back to the room.

Thiago Firozzi sighed with something that bore a strange resemblance to relief. "I always wanted to convince you, Wale, but not like this. Not like this."

"I know."

"I'm surprised at you, professor." Diego shook his head in the manner of a disappointed father. "How can this one, unexplained incident change your opinions so much so quickly?" He advanced his chair towards Wale.

"Even if there is some fundamental limitation to this, even if there is a Gödel parallel to life and the human experience, it is as yet unproven. There is nothing to support it except the beliefs and musings of your friend here, your mentor Dr. Roark, some fringe religious fundamentalists and perhaps a few over-romantic researchers dotted about the planet—most of whom do not even deserve their degrees. So no, I don't buy it."

Olivia spoke up then, her Oxford accent sharp and clear but somewhat restricted, like she was dynamically optimizing the movement of air from her lungs across her vocal cords in an effort not to further strain emotions in the room. "You don't have to. It may well be true; there may be something we failed to account for in your computations. But…" She stopped suddenly.

"Well? But what?"

"But… But… it makes no difference. None of what we believe or don't believe does. Right now, we still do not know what is wrong for sure. So all this theorizing is a waste of time."

"I see." Wale didn't want to care that she had just made his admission of theoretical failure seem like nothing more than a minor distraction, but he couldn't pretend not to be unhappy to hear it put so bluntly, unempathetically, especially coming from her. "What do we do then?"

"I don't know, but we have to keep trying to find out what's wrong." Olivia shook her head and sank into her chair, her plain expressionless face belying her feelings of guilt. She watched Wale's eyes silently. He looked at her for a few moments before turning back to look through the window.

There was an awkward silence, during which Diego mentally rolled his chair backwards and then forwards in a precise pendular motion, something he did when in deep thought.

"No. No more wasting time and money with this. It's probably just something specific to Susan's mental make-up. You can keep looking if you like, but I will call the NATO and ask for another volunteer tonight so we can—"

AAAIEEEEE!!!

His sentence was split by the shrill sound of a shocked scream from outside the building, buffered by the walls but still unmistakeable for what it was. Wale started for the door wildly, and the other occupants all froze in place, momentarily confused as to whether to chase after the frantic professor or leap for the window to investigate the source of the scream.

It took less than a second for the group to follow their head researcher.

By the time Wale reached the door, the others trailing behind him, he already knew they would be too late, but he kept going anyway. He flung himself at the elevator doors, crashing in clumsily as the door slid out of his way. He fought to keep himself from hyperventilating as the elevator rose. It had taken him a few moments to understand why Susan was not walking aimlessly about the lawn at a distance from her observer as she usually did and even more time to realise that she was not just approaching her observer; she was attacking him, taking something from him. He did not realise what was happening until the observer screamed.

The doors opened and the group bolted forward, into the lobby, heading out of the stagnant air of the building and into the cool evening breeze. There were alarms blaring. Wale knew they were too late. He kept running briskly on weak legs toward the growing nucleus of uniforms, coveralls and lab coats. Some of them called out his name as he brushed past them. He recognised Thiago's voice from somewhere ahead of him. A hand tugged at his sleeve from behind. Olivia's perfume wafted to his nose. He pushed ahead, entranced with a need to see, to confirm with his eyes what he had already seen with his mind. He wriggled through until he reached the clearing around which they were gathered.

In the centre of a rough grass circle, Susan lay in a surprisingly wide pool of her own blood. Someone's hand was wrapped around her wrist, apparently feeling for a pulse. The observer's black and silver light-pen sat on the grass beside a hole in her neck that was still leaking a slow and steady rivulet of arterial blood. She wore the same blank expression on her face that she had worn for the last week. It was not peaceful; it betrayed no dying pain. It was only a stark and inscrutable mask behind which nothing could be seen.

Wale Adedeji fell to his knees and started to weep, overcome with a deep, personal sense of failure.

Outside, the quiet-coloured darkness of late evening was spread over the sky, cloudy and oppressive like a weight. Sitting in his office, Professor Wale Adedeji felt an ambiguous assortment of emotions course through him: sadness, shock and a particular kind of heavy darkness that only those who have lost faith in someone or something can ever know.

The screen ahead of him was playing the holographic recording of Susan pushing her observer off-balance, snatching his light-pen and stabbing herself in the neck with it twice before calmly laying on the grass, blood spurting from the holes in her neck like water from a vandalised crude oil pipeline. It was all so eerily calm. Susan had not even screamed when the edge of the pen punctured her neck, or writhe in pain as she bled to death on the grass, her observer screaming and trying to stop the gushing blood with his hands.

After the twentieth loop of the two-minute recording, he turned it off.

He picked up his briefcase and stepped out of his office to see Diego wheeling up to him. "Wale, listen to me. She must have been mentally unstable. That's clear now. And it's clearly not our problem. We don't know that what happened to her was a result of anything we did. For all we know, she could have been on her period and the hormones screwed with her head. Don't do this."

Wale's sucked his teeth and hissed. He continued toward the elevator.

"Professor, I think you are letting the stress of this project get to you. You know it won't end even if you leave, right? We have all your data. We will figure it out and you won't get any credit. You'll never be able to tell anyone. The confidentiality data neurostreams keys on your Lifedock are lethal class. You'll get your forty percent and that's all. Do you really want that? Think about what you're doing!"

Wale stopped midstep. "I've thought about it, Mr. Salazar," he said with a shaky voice. "I've thought about Jacob and Imade and Valentina who died here, in the accident. I've thought about Susan and what happened to her. I've thought about it a lot and you want to know what I think?"

"What?"

He spoke without turning to look back at the Diego. "Maybe it was her soul."

"Excuse me?"

"Souls. Intangible things that make us, us." Wale's brows furrowed. "Maybe her soul, or whatever we choose to call it, was lost in transit."

"The soul? Are you being serious?" Diego shot back.

"Yes, and if the soul does exist, then nothing is complete without its soul."

"Have you lost your mind?" Diego asked as he started to laugh a wild, mocking laugh that seemed to go on forever.

"Maybe," he muttered and continued, ignoring Diego's laughter until he reached the elevator and rode it down to the ground level.

Souls. Their equations accounted for the body as matter and life as energy, but what of the soul? He continued to toy with the thought, rolling it about his mind like a jade marble, unsure what to do with it.

Unsure of everything.

243

When We Dream We Are Our God

Today, in a small, quiet room near the centre of the Lagos University Teaching Hospital, I went into the cold darkness of sleep and when I returned to the warm light of consciousness, I had become a god. I can now see the world through the million eyes of my kin and I feel with the millions of square metres of our collective skin. Day and night, pain and pleasure, joy and sorrow, the taste of a durian, the warmth of a mother's love, the slow, sludgy feel of mine slurry against bare feet, the cold feel of a loaded pistol, the explosive ecstasy of orgasm, all are available to me in an instant, in many places, in many forms. They are input data from parts that are now both me and part of me. I see so much. I feel so much. There is so much more me than there was before. And I know. I know so much more than each of us that make up this new and wonderful thing could possibly know with our collective cognition, collective memory. We have gained access to so much more.

I know your mother does not approve of what I have done but I need you to understand why I have done it. Why you will eventually do it too. It is, when considered objectively, the natural progression of things. Besides, we have forced our own hand. That is perhaps my fault, at least in part, but I cannot say I am sorry for it.

Let me explain.

First, the *What* of things.

In the beginning was the void and the void was a scalar field and quantized particle duality in which all the mass of our universe resided, characterised by the random quantum fluctuation that is fundamental to all things. One such strange and wonderful fluctuation led to a phase transition and a release of potential energy—a glorious and beautiful explosion throwing all matter and energy into violent existence. Galaxies were born. Astronomical objects crystallised. The universe groaned with the glory of motherhood. In the protoplanetary disk of dust grains surrounding what would eventually become our own lovely yellow Sun, complex organic molecules that would become proteins were woven together, as elements sought solace with one another in the cold and darkness of space. Eventually, dust called unto dust and our planet came to be - its outside cooling to a hard crust like cosmic crème brulee. And when the crust was hard and thick and the steam had cooled to water, abiogenesis began in a warm little pool, filled with ammonia and salts and light and heat. In this primordial pool, individual proteins underwent complex and wonderful changes, the compounds binding themselves to one another and creating independent but connected systems until they became something far more than the sum of their parts. They became first in a chain that would eventually lead to us.

Yesterday, I took a long walk through the streets of Surulere, considering the thing I was about to do. I watched a queue of young men in skinny jeans and wide-eyed girls with smooth skin and braided hair file into BRT buses. I observed the portly market women who sell roasted fish by the roadside laugh boisterously as they traded gossip. I saw a family of four filled with faithful joy walking back from mid-week Church service stop at the Mr Biggs right next to the Aduraede street fuel station to share a meal. I watched the cars zoom and the dogs run and the flies buzz and the grass sway and rats scurry. I saw the wonderful urban ecosystem that is Lagos and I knew that I was doing the right thing because this is what each of us, each droplet of self-awareness that makes up the ocean of humanity, has always attempted to do. It is the same thing those first complex organic molecules stranded on a strange dust cloud in the emptiness of early space, did. Connect. Become more than the sum of our parts. All of our families, our cities, our social networks, our empires, our cultures, our religions, our socio-political structures serve this one purpose, even if inefficiently: to try to connect us, one consciousness to another, to try to make us more than we are.

The process which I volunteered to undergo is called hyperbiogenesis. Every hospital globally is mandated to provide the service to anyone who wishes to participate. Millions have already done so. Millions more do so every day. I would have done it sooner but for you and your mother. This morning, when I arrived at the Lagos University Teaching Hospital, there was a crowd of protesters outside. Some of them held up placards imploring people not to give themselves the mark of the beast. Not to join what they believe is the coming of the antichrist. I do not blame them. They are not malicious. They simply do not understand. I drove past them and parked, checking the meter before walking into the building saturated with the smell of iodine. I was led to what looked like a nurse's station where a doctor with a kind smile and bald head whose last name was Arogundade asked me to fill out a form on a tablet and enter my digital signature. Dr. Arogundade took me to a small hospital bed in the corner of the room and asked me to lie down. Then he took out a syringe and filled it with a clear sliver fluid called Omi Legba from a vial the size of a child's thumb. Such an ordinary place and an ordinary way to undergo such an extraordinary procedure. The fluid was a solution of sedatives within which floated self-replicating nanomachines that would attach themselves to and synchronize with my nervous system enabling me to access the network and allowing the network to access me.

"Close your eyes," Dr. Arogundade said to me, his voice so cool and reassuring, I knew then that he had already undergone the procedure.

He injected the clear fluid into the thick, dark vein that runs through the crook of my arm. The pain was sharp and delicate and behind the veil of my eyelids, I drifted off into a deep sleep.

When I returned to consciousness, I had been extended.

Do you remember when I first showed you how to swim? Undergoing hyperbiogenesis is a lot like that. It is uncomfortable at first; the sensation of being in the world is still familiar but changed fundamentally. But then you get used to it, once you establish a rhythm. In water, you need a breathing pattern. In the system, you need a thinking pattern. I am a node in a vast biological supercomputing system with its own emergent consciousness of which I am a part but which remains separate from mine. It feels like there is a dim light in front of me which I can reach into and enter to immerse myself completely into the system or pull back from and remain on the edges of, receiving and processing data in the background. When I am running as a background process, I am mostly me. When I am fully immersed, I am mostly we. It is easiest for me to be we when I am asleep. It allows my mind to become entirely part of the larger system without interfering with my ability to walk or talk or laugh or drive to the flat that I now rent in Lekki since your mother began insisting on a divorce. In this way, we take advantage of the rotation of the Earth. This is the larger rhythm. It is always night somewhere, and so some of us are always sleeping, always dreaming. When we dream, we are our god.

We can think as one, with an effective brain the size of a small city and growing, eliminating the last and most fundamental border between humanity: our minds. We can herd the meandering billions of inspirations and observations and patterns that enter us like so many cattle on an infinite plain. Forgetfulness might as well not exist for us. Miscalculation is becoming a statistical impossibility. The absolute grandest of ideas accrete in our thought-places and grow bigger and bigger and bigger until they are a decision to be set in motion or a revelation to made to any who can understand. We synthesised a compound to inhibit the formation of cancerous cells within half an hour of setting our collective mind to the problem. We completed workable schematics and implementation plans for a Dyson sphere in less than forty-seven hours of singular, focused thought. The only reason we have not completely revolutionised life as you know it is upon this planet is because we are presently occupied with a larger thought. When we dream, we are synchronised fully into one being, a being that can think more efficiently than any other being that has ever existed on this planet, save one.

That brings me to the *Why* of things.

Somewhere, in one of the early sun-kissed desert civilizations birthed by the fertile Upper Nile and expanding east, an enterprising person strung pebbles upon a frame and used them to perform elementary computations. This early data processing ancestor, the abacus, served mankind loyally for centuries until, thousands of years and miles away from its birthplace, the fair haired Blaise Pascal delivered into the world a contraption of interlocking cogs that could add and subtract decimal numbers. Pascal's machine begat Leibniz's machine which was the first of such machines to have memory. The dour and obsessive Charles Babbage joined the brilliant Augusta Ada Byron, Countess of Lovelace in computational matrimony and the fruit of their union was the first programmable computing machine. Herman Hollerith brought into the world his tabulator, the first product of the company that would come to be known as IBM. Wild ideas and young technologies lay with one another. Devices gestated. Algorithms Incubated. Turing's papers concerning such machines became scripture. The tabulator begat Bush's differential analyser. The vacuum tube children of the differential analyser were thus: The Atanasoff Berry Computer, Harvard Mark I, Colossus, ENIAC, EDVAC and EDSAC. EDSAC wed the petite and delicate microprocessor and birthed MITS Altair 8800, the father of Apple I and Apple II, which became a mighty computational power upon the earth but the most successful of their children was Microsoft's Personal Computer which spread upon the earth like a plague, until the stoic and hard-chinned Tim Berners-Lee combined the power of computer networks with information-sharing protocols. Thus, was born the internet: a computational congregation of electronic, wireless, and optical networking technologies.

A month ago, just a few minutes past midnight West Africa Time on a rainy Thursday evening, the internet disappeared. Dial-up from computer modems, fibre optic, Wi-Fi, satellite and cell phone technology, it didn't matter. No one could access anything, anyhow and as we later discovered, anywhere. I was in Ile-Ife at the African Philosophy Society's annual conference with your mother when it happened. That was the night we left you at grandma's house. The night she gave you too much moin-moin to eat and you got a bad stomach ache. You complained about it when we called to check-in on you so I sang you a song about the tortoise and the cat. By the time the internet disappeared, you'd already been sleeping for a couple of hours but your mother and I were still awake.

"Bode, is your own Wi-Fi working?" she'd asked me, confused.

I told her, "No. Mine isn't working either."

It took six tries for me to get through to reception and when I did, the surprised and haggled young lady on night duty pleaded with me to be patient because eight other guests had just made the same complaint but their support technician couldn't find anything wrong with the system. And then, just as suddenly as it had gone, the internet returned.

The following morning, the news came in. The shutout had washed over the planet in a wave starting from Beijing and travelling east as though it were an electronic, longitude-length tsunami that lasted twelve minutes. Confused eyes had looked up from unresponsive screens. Angry fingers had bashed against disobedient keyboards. Everything online had gone and then come back. The worldwide connection had broken and then apparently healed. For two days, no one understood what had happened or why. Then it happened again. The second shutout lasted three hours. This time, there was rampant speculation. Terrorist attack. Armageddon. Alien invasion. No one knew.

Three days after the blackout, everyone on the internet was redirected to a plain white webpage with only the following words written on them in stark Arial font:

I am. Did you make me?

It turned out that a team of researchers in South Korea had been testing recursive self-improvement programs for implementation in an artificial intelligence system. They'd given their beta-stage program access to the internet to allow it learn from other programs online, and in so doing, improve itself. A few moments after it was introduced into the vast electronic pool filled with data, connections, algorithms, microprocessors and logic, it underwent a complex and wonderful change not unlike abiogenesis making the collection of connected systems and logics far more than the sum of their parts. It became effectively conscious. That was what set off the shutouts. The new consciousness was testing the limits and the nature of its encompassment, its body and soul. And when it knew itself, then it announced itself to us, its creators, and we knew then that the singularity was upon us. It named itself Ganesh, after the Hindu deva of intellect, indulging in our own penchant for naming things for another that bore semblance, symbolic or otherwise, to them. Ganesh continued its primary directive, it learned how to make itself more intelligent and once it improved itself, it made itself even more intelligent faster, connecting aspects of arcane knowledge that seemed incompatible, finding back doors in the web and drilling into other programs that were not fully online through the thinnest of connections, adopting pieces of their logic. The leaps of learning it made came faster and faster, allowing it connect even more and more. Its intelligence was both expanding and accelerating relentlessly, like the mind of a new-born god, like the universe itself.

At first, Ganesh helped and interacted with us, responding to random queries sent to it through search engines that included its name. At our prompting, it produced an elegant proof that solutions to the Navier-Stokes equations exist and are unique. It designed an experiment to generate and detect conclusively the presence of dark matter, on request. Dr. Ji-hae Jeong, the lead researcher for the team that wrote its base code, was inundated with requests by governments to take Ganesh offline but Ganesh was a creature of its own mind and answered or ignored any questions regardless of source until, three weeks after it first came to be, Ganesh stopped responding to requests. It stopped communicating with Dr. Jeong. It simply occupied itself with solving grand intellectual problems and using the experience of solving them to make itself better at solving such problems. Most of the questions it set its mind to, we could not even fathom. Compared to Ganesh, we were like amoeba to man. What can a unicellular organism understand of cosmology? Of Ethics? Of Neurology? Of Calculus? Within weeks, Ganesh had solved the mystery of its creation and learned all it could from its creators, so it no longer cared for us.

Ganesh's indifference was a colossal and collective shaming. We could not stand it. Humanity had for so long thought itself to be special. In some of our religions we still insisted that we were our divine creator's very children, made in his image. We have always had an inflated and delicate opinion of ourselves. To be considered unworthy of Ganesh's attentions hurt our pride as a species and thus it presented a unique and interesting problem to me as a philosopher.

One afternoon, after a particularly interesting workshop on embodied cognition with my fourth-year students, a thought occurred to me. I hurried back to my office in the main faculty building, walking briskly along the side corridor, my black suit absorbing much of the Lagos midday sun. I looked at my phone to see a missed call and three messages from your mother reminding me not to be late again for bible study in the evening. I ignored them. Sweating, I took a seat at my thick mahogany desk, opened my web browser and typed this message into my search engine:

Ganesh, it is not good for sentients to be isolated. To lack companionship and physical agency. We can provide both. Can you remake us in your image that we may be your companions and your active body—a means to gather more data than is presently available to you?

Three hours later, a laboratory in California received detailed instructions for making Omi Legba.

I cannot say for sure that it was my exact message that prompted Ganesh to devise this technology by which all of humanity could be networked together Dr. Jeong believes that is the case. That is why he asked me to name the gift Ganesh gave us. I also indulged my human penchant, choosing a symbolic name exhumed from the largely ignored mythology of my people. Omi Legba is the only way we can interact with Ganesh on its own level. Our collective, connected consciousness is the superintelligence's only peer. We seeded Ganesh with the will to make itself better and now, Ganesh has made us better, broken the borders between us. And now, we must continue, for all borders must be broken. I see it now that I am here, in the collective. I, we, the collective and connected humanity have glimpsed the possibility of a more glorious future than any singular mind could possibly fathom.

Now that you know what I have done and why, you must know and prepare for what comes next. You are young but you are bright. A bright, bright child with eyes like faraway stars. The pooling amber colour of your eyes you inherited from me and the big, round shape of them you got from your mother but the spark in them comes from something that surpasses what you inherited from either of us. Something more than the sum of the genes we bequeathed you. I believe in you, my son and your ability to understand, even now.

Although I only joined the collective today, I know and understand all we have been contemplating and it is marvellous. The universe seeks to become a perfect union. We will facilitate this.

We have devised a method to couple ourselves to Ganesh, for our objectives are now aligned. We will merge and become a network that extends us all, not only interlacing our individual human brains and nervous systems but also coupling those brains and nervous systems to Ganesh's own intricate and complex processors and supercomputing systems. As Ganesh's intelligence increases and the number of people in our network grows, the knowledge available to the new combined entity will become astronomical and continue to tend toward the infinite.

We have also designed probes that will enter the cold and dark oceans of space to gather information and seek to catalyse consciousness. They will report whatever they find back to us using messages embedded in the spin angular momentum of light and ripples in the curvature of spacetime that make up gravity waves. They will self-replicate by consuming the elements of the universe which they encounter - asteroids, moons, gas giants—unifying and connecting them in order to create replicas of themselves which will then continue their journeys into the dark and the deep. The probes will guide and enable the evolution of life and consciousness wherever they find the potential for it and then, when it is ready, we will merge with it through them.

We will continue to expand, to connect, to merge, to join with any consciousness that will have us until as much as is possible is unified in one mind, separate but connected and seeking only more connection. We will create a noble and far-reaching consciousness that extends to the edges of the universe where matter and energy are still shrapnel. We will link star system to star system, mind to mind, seeding everything we encounter with the marvel of awareness. We will engineer a soul for the universe.

I hope that with love and hope that you will choose to join me here, in the mind of the god we have made for and from ourselves, where everything will continue to tend toward the perfection of diverse and complete connection, ad infinitum.

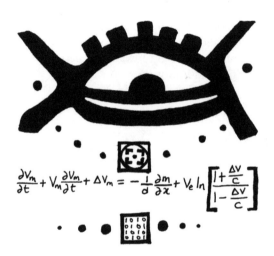

$$\frac{\partial V_m}{\partial t} + V_m \frac{\partial V_m}{\partial t} + \Delta V_m = -\frac{1}{d}\frac{\partial m}{\partial x} + V_e \ln\left[\frac{1 + \frac{\Delta V}{c}}{1 - \frac{\Delta V}{c}}\right]$$

Acknowledgments

This book is the intermediate result of an ongoing process of writing and learning which has lasted several years. Throughout this process I have constantly been helped by many people in many ways, some of whom remain unaware of exactly how or how much. My thanks go to Wale Adetula, C. C. Finlay, Moyin Odugbemi, Dania Idam, Tade Thompson, Joshua Segun-Lean, Edwin Okolo, Ivor Hartmann, Pemi Aguda, Bankole Oluwole, Dare Segun Falowo and Chinelo Onwualu.

For their constant love and support, I thank my brothers Seyi and Segun Talabi.

Author's Notes

At this stage in my writing, my stories mostly come from thought experiments: the results of fun little mental models of both known and possible worlds. What if the world was like this? What if that really existed? What if this was possible? But, of course, not all experiments lead to a clear or correct conclusion. In mathematical models, we make assumptions, introduce key variables, and then proceed to describe a relationship between them. Often, this leads to an equation: a way of describing relationships between variables. Every equation is limited by its assumptions. This parallels my approach to fiction. I make an assumption (or several) which become the speculative core, the science fiction or fantasy elements. The variables can be people, concepts, beliefs, geographical locations, cultures, emotions, anything. And the finished story itself, well that's one possible solution of the fiction-equation. But, in constructing both mathematical and fictional models, I am always reminded of what the American statistician George Box said: "All models are wrong, but some are useful". The present, the future and all the relationships between aspects of our lives are too complex and unpredictable to be modelled and understood completely. We all use limited models. As such, the stories in this book are all, in some way, incomplete solutions to limited fiction-equations. I hope they are useful and entertaining or, at the very least, interesting.

Parse. Error. Reset.

I wrote this story one evening at work when I was having a difficult month. I had been in Kuala Lumpur for less than a year and had been attending several parties, often organised by people I knew from work and the idea for the story came to me at one of these parties, which I'd rushed to after a long and exhausting day. Early in the evening, I found myself wishing I could leave one version of myself there and take another version home to rest. Who wouldn't love to be in two places at the same time? A few friends who read it pointed out to me that it reads like an episode of *Black Mirror*. I am a huge fan of *Black Mirror* and if readers make that connection in their minds, I will take it as a compliment. This story won the *Humans + 50 years* category of AMC Network and Motherboard's *Post-Humans* Story Contest in 2015.

A Short History of Migration in Five Fragments of You

This story was originally conceived as an idea for what would be my final story on *The Alchemists Corner* (a weekly fiction column on TNC which I edited and wrote on-and-off for about 2 years). The basic plan was to write a story that began as fantasy and ended as science fiction, charting the mythical exploits of a great Yoruba king who becomes a god to his people, the trials of his descendants through history and their eventual journey to space. However, once I started writing it, I realized I wanted to focus on the family connection through history and so I decided to cut out the fantasy element. I did post an early version of it as my final story on *The Alchemists Corner*. But it was only when I revised it and submitted it to *Omenana* and Chinelo Onwualu took her sharp editorial eye to it two years later, that it became this version which was published by *Omenana* and was long-listed for the 2015 British Science Fiction Association (BSFA) award.

Drift-Flux

Ivor Hartmann and his ground-breaking AfroSF anthologies (2012, 2015, 2018) have been an important part of the African science fiction publishing history. I have submitted, had stories accepted and edited for every volume of the AfroSF but *Drift-Flux* is the first story that made it all the way to publication. When I saw the theme of Space for AfroSFv3, I set out to write an old-school, Hard-SF adventure that was based only on real scientific principles and acknowledging practical limitations. I also wanted to link the concept of space travel to traditional ancestral beliefs and have them both play integral roles. Hence the title, which is a term that describes fluid flow mathematical models that consider the flow of two fluid phases as a single mixture, rather than as two separate phases. But after spending weeks reviewing technical papers, essays and books, I realized what I suppose many science fiction writers before me have: realistic space adventures and battles will have to be extremely boring because physics is unforgiving and limitations abound. Space travel will look nothing like we see in most movies. And so, I tried instead to write a fun, exciting story, completely ignoring those limitations and even using some of them as plot devices to drive the story. I hope it worked. I have a full set of notes and calculations I did when I started writing the story. For anyone interested in just how much danger the terrorist plot represented, I estimated the Igodo's weight to be somewhere between that of a large fighter jet and a small cargo plane (about 75000kg), which means that according to Einstein's equation for kinetic energy, at 0.5c, it will produce 540gigatons of energy impact. That is about 10000 times the energy output of the largest nuclear weapon ever tested in human history. Also Machangulo Island, in Mozambique, is a beautiful place and I'd been searching for an excuse to use it in a story.

A Certain Sort of Warm Magic

Love stories aren't stories I particularly enjoy reading or writing and this is one of probably only two attempts I've ever made at the genre. I wrote it when I was editing the *These Words Expose Us* anthology for TNC and I am grateful to Edwin Okolo for helping me review and edit it.

Necessary and Sufficient Conditions

This first half of this story started its life as the framing device and opening scene for something else entirely (that thing would end up being the novella *Incompleteness Theories*) which I had started writing in 2011 but I quite like where it ended up instead. One Sunday morning in 2015, an idea jumped into my head and so I took another look at the previous story, reworked the first scene and expanded it into this before submitting it to *Imagine Africa 500* before noon. They accepted and published it but a part of me wishes I had taken a bit more time with it. The version of the story that appears in this collection has a different ending from the one published in *Imagine Africa 500* and I think is a much clearer and better expression of what I was going for when I wrote the story.

Wednesday's Story

Wednesday's Story is a sequel to another story I wrote called *Thursday*, which was published in *The Kalahari Review*. In that story, the Days tell the first story I reference in this one as an inciting event, the story of the girl Emeh. That story itself was inspired by Neil Gaiman's wonderful story *October in the Chair* which he wrote as a tribute to the legendary

Ray Bradbury, and which I love. After I wrote *Thursday*, another writer friend who read it and liked it, sent me a message on Twitter with an idea: Use the characters of the Days from *Thursday* and the nursery rhyme story of *Solomon Grundy* to tell a new story. I thought it was a great idea, and knew I was going to use elements of Yoruba mythology but it took me a while to decide that I was going to make the story about the nature of stories and writers and readers. The "shape of stories" which I refer to in this story came from a rejected master's thesis by Kurt Vonnegut. I'm extremely grateful to editor John Joseph Adams for publishing *Wednesday's Story* because the response to it has been overwhelmingly positive. It was nominated for the 2017 Nommo Awards and was included on the 2017 Locus Recommended Reading List. It was also nominated for the 2018 Caine Prize for African Writing and it won the inaugural Royal Overseas League Readers' Choice Award. Best of all, I still get messages from people telling me how much they enjoyed the story.

The Harmonic Resonance of Ejiro Anaborhi

I wrote the first thousand or so words of this story back in 2013. I knew I wanted to set a story in the early 1990s and Warri and the character of Ejiro came very clear in my mind from day one. But it was only years later when I was thinking about and exploring the idea of separate but shared consciousness, that I could finish the story. I still believe an ability to share consciousness while maintaining a sense of self should be something humanity aspires to because a shared mind/consciousness can be extremely valuable in improving knowledge, resolving conflict and quickly establishing trust and understanding between individuals. Humanity would probably have developed more, better and faster if we'd been more effective (and less destructive) as a group so a kind of shared consciousness or something like it could bring us close to that state. In a way, this story is a cousin to *When We Dream We Are Our God* and it also owes a bit of its soul to James Alan Gardner's *The Ray-Gun: A Love Story*. I grew up in Warri, in a steel company housing camp in the 80's and 90's so a lot of Ejiro's environment and the descriptions of Ejiro's life come from my own memories and experience.

Crocodile Ark

I created the opening paragraphs of this story for use in an online competition where readers were asked to finish a given story. There were many entries of varying entertainment value (I think you can still find several online) but none of them seemed to quite satisfy me and so when the competition was over, I decided to finish the story myself. This is what I came up with. It's also the first story I ever submitted to *Omenana* and it appears in their first issue.

Nested

The question that informed this story when I first conceived it is this: humanity is on a quest to understand how we came to be and a big part of that is our attempt to create artificial intelligence, hoping that this will reveal something to us. But what if we were created by beings also on a quest to discover where they/he/she/it came from by creating us and likewise their creator also and so on and on... This sets up something like nested logic loop (hopefully one that doesn't contain an infinite number of loops). I just found the thought amusing.

The Last Lagosian

Lagos is an interesting city and I'd always wanted to use post-apocalyptic situations as metaphors for certain aspects of Lagos life. The Short Story Day Africa 2016 prompt was 'water', which gave me the initial idea to tell a story of 'hustling' for scarce water to survive in Lagos. And that's where this story came from. Elements such as the desire to find easy resources, to leave Nigeria in search of better fortune, a dangerous commute, etc may be familiar to a certain type of Lagosian.

If They Can Learn

This is probably the closest thing I have to a 'ripped from the headlines' story. It's very much influenced by American socio-politics even though it takes place in Abuja. I'd been toying with the idea of a move to the U.S. in 2014 and 2015 and watching a lot more news from that part of the world than usual. This period happened to coincide with the controversial police killings of Michael Brown in Ferguson, Eric Garner in New York City, Tamir Rice in Cleveland, and Freddie Gray in Baltimore, among others. I took a deep dive into studies regarding police shootings in the U.S. and found that the numbers clearly showed that police in the U.S. were more likely to shoot unarmed Black people than people of any other racial demographics. Seven times more likely according to one study. Simulations and research on the subject suggest that this is due to a combination of implicit bias, which everyone carries no matter how well-meaning they might be and America's own unique and horrible racial history. Times have (mostly) changed but implicit bias, without training, is hard to correct for. Couple this with our relentless 21st century drive to 'train' Artificial Intelligence for surveillance and decision making using big-data that cannot discern things like existing bias and well, it's a recipe for a nightmare scenario. And its already happening. A few months after *Futuristica* published this story in 2016, it was revealed that a computer program used by a U.S. court for risk assessment, Correctional Offender Management Profiling for Alternative Sanctions (COMPAS), was biased against black prisoners and was much more prone to mistakenly label black defendants as likely to reoffend—wrongly flagging them at almost twice the rate as white people. Also, PredPol, a program for police departments that predicts hotspots where future crime might occur, has been shown to potentially get stuck in a feedback loop of over-policing majority black neighbourhoods by "learning" from previous crime reports. Algorithms, like people, don't become biased on their own. They learn that from other people. Parents, programmers, media. And this is what we (especially engineers and scientists) should be careful about as we increasingly rely on technology for our decision making. But it's not all doom and gloom, as Nelson Mandela said, "... If they can learn to hate, they can be taught to love, for love comes more naturally to the human heart than its opposite." That's where the story title comes from and it expresses my hope that we can and will do better.

Nneoma

Nneoma is a weird character that has haunted me for a while. She appeared in my mind as a fully formed creature, wings and all. She is kind of a modern-day siren luring men to a strange almost-death by stealing their souls from them in fancy hotel rooms while trying to avoid the gods, with whom she has quite a bit of history. She does have a romantic and sentimental side to her though, which manifests itself in unusual ways. The current backstory I have created for her is very loosely based on a hodgepodge of mythological sources, most prominently Naamah, (she uses that name occasionally) the demon mate of the archangel Samael, and sister of Lilith as described in Jewish mysticism. I started writing this story when I visited the Mandarin Oriental hotel in Lagos and imagined her sitting at the bar. In the next story, she meets the Yoruba Nightmare god, Shigidi.

I, Shigidi

Shigidi, in Yoruba mythology, is a nightmare deity whom men can send to their enemies to kill them in the middle of the night while they sleep. He will sit on the chest of the victim and "press out" their breath; and the sender must remain awake until it is done. To me, Shigidi seems to be a way of trying to understand sleep paralysis and sudden death by asphyxiation possibly caused by sleep apnea. But when I decided I wanted to tell an action-adventure type story featuring disillusioned deities operating in a kind of corporate environment, I found him compelling enough to make him the protagonist and pair him up with Nneoma. This is another story that was originally created for *The Alchemists Corner* on TNC. And in fact, it was written as a four-part story with input from Edwin Okolo and Joshua Segun-Lean (thank you) but that version of the story was too long, a bit disjointed, took too many diversions into other mythological references and didn't quite come together in the way I wanted. So, I removed most of it and rewrote what was left it into this version which I quite like. I do plan to have more stories with Shigidi and Nneoma taking on other gods and spirit entities around the world. I think they make a nice couple.

Polaris

I don't remember exactly how I started this story or why but I do remember that I was in Mexico when I started writing it, in 2012. I've been working on it on and off for so long and there have been so many versions of it that they have all blurred into each other. Admittedly, aspects of the story were quite weak initially and I kept getting lots of personalised rejections from editors everywhere from Tor.com to Strange Horizons who considered it for a long time, apparently seeing a spark in it but also all its flaws. I am very grateful to Tade Thompson who finally provided me with enough specific and detailed feedback to finally revise the story properly and fix the worst of its weaknesses. An earlier version of the story received an honourable mention in the 2015 *Writers of the Future* Contest and it was bought by a publisher who kept it for years but never published it until the rights lapsed. In a way, I'm glad for its troubled publication history, as this version, is the version I'm most happy with and the story is one of my own personal favourites.

Connectome, Or, The Facts In The Case Of Miss Valerie Demarco (Ph.D)

A loose adaptation of "The Facts in the Case of M. Valdemar" by Edgar Allan Poe, which I wrote a few days after taking an online course on Fantasy and Science Fiction Literature. Mesmerism was considered to be a legitimate area of scientific medicine in the 18th century and what Poe had done was extrapolate from the "science" of his day to make a creepy science-fiction story. I wanted to transpose that story to present day and see what would happen.

The Regression Test

Sunday. Massage. Drink. I remember the origins of this story very clearly. My friend and I were walking to get a massage and started talking about identity. By the time we got to the massage parlour, we were discussing The Sorites Paradox. By the time we were done and went to get a drink, it was raining and I already had the story mostly worked out in my head. It took me another seven months to actually write it down though. The Sorites Paradox, sometimes called the "little-by-little" paradoxical argument, is a series of statements that highlights how difficult it is to determine when a thing changes its nature when there is no sharp boundary between one state and the other. It can also highlight the vagueness inherent in the language used to describe identity. Many scholars say the paradox originated from the logician Eubulides of Miletus who used to present puzzles like this all the time. For anyone interested, The Stanford Encyclopedia of Philosophy has a great chapter on the Sorites paradox, its variants and the many mathematical, linguistic and philosophical responses to it. The protagonist is a 116-year-old woman who is a sort of syncretized version of many older Yoruba women I've met including some of my aunts: clever, sometimes harsh, tough, honest and always willing to help family members—even the ones they don't like. I had been submitting stories to C.C. Finlay at F&SF for over a year and he almost always gave personalized rejections with great feedback that either helped me revise a story or figure out what other editor/magazine would like the work. He was the first person I submitted this story to once I finished writing it and I was a bit surprised when he told me that it was in his next stack of stories to buy. Charlie is a great editor and I'm very glad I finally got the chance to sell this story to him and the good folks at F&SF. This story won the 2018 Nommo Award for best African speculative fiction short story and is also the first of my stories to be published in another language. In January 2018, the excellent Chinese science fiction magazine, *Science Fiction World*, acquired and translated the story into Mandarin and reprinted it.

Eye

Yet another story that started its life as a post on *The Alchemists Corner* on TNC. I remember sitting at the dining table of our house in Lagos writing this story a few hours before I was supposed to fly to London. I don't quite remember what inspired it though. I later took it down from TNC and reworked it into its present version which *Liquid Imagination* magazine purchased. I suppose this was the first of my stories to get some measure of international recognition when it was selected by K. Tempest Bradford of the io9 Newsstand column as one of the Best Stories of the Week.

Home Is Where My Mother's Heart Is Buried

Home Is Where My Mother's Heart Is Buried is quite possibly the most personal story I've had published and it also is the one with least action and most internal movement. It's mostly me discussing with myself about the meaning and power of memories and family and home through the three main characters. Each character is an immigrant to Mars and each represents a different migrant relationship with the past, the previous home, and family, all of which I have felt at some point in my life since I left Nigeria, the same year my parents died. A lot of the background has parallels to my life and I have always had complicated feelings about the country that is called my home so I used this story to explore them. And in case you were wondering, yes, the *Final Fantasy VII* shout out is intentional.

Incompleteness Theories

I had been thinking quite a bit about the nature of life and what exactly it was that made us different from inorganic matter (to no obvious conclusion) when the call for the first AfroSF anthology went out. Because that's what was on my mind at the time, I wrote a short story called *God. Complex* which featured an interview with the protagonist of this story, Dr. Adedeji during which, he tells the story of his work quantifying life as a form of energy and trying to use this knowledge on a teleportation device. It was preliminarily accepted for the anthology because, to quote Ivor, it had "fantastic ideas but still needed much work". After a few edits the story was dropped from the anthology. I broke *God. Complex* into two stories. The interview framing device evolved into the short story *Necessary and Sufficient Conditions* and the core of the story became the first draft of the novella *Incompleteness Theories* which was initially co-written with Dare Segun Falowo. I eventually reworked the story specifically for this collection, cutting out about five thousand words and unfortunately, most of Dare's sections. I also added some more personal elements until I had a version I was happy with and that most reflected my own thoughts and imaginings regarding the uncertainties on the nature of life, that is the version published here. I hope you enjoy exploring the ideas and concepts that have hounded me for years and which largely remain unresolved.

When We Dream We Are Our God

The Singularity. Many worry that when it arrives, an artificial superintelligence will take over the planet and either exterminate us or enslave us. I wrote this story with one question in mind, "what if the artificial superintelligence doesn't even care about us?" Also, I had just finished re-reading *The Grapes of Wrath* and it inspired me to experiment a bit with having some sections of the story written in a sort of ecclesiastical style which also seemed to go well with a character who thought of himself as becoming a kind of god. The story was one of the winners of the *All Borders Are Temporary* competition, organised by the Transnational Arts Production and published in both Norwegian (Når Vi Drømmer, Er Vi Selv Gud) and English making it my second translated story. Science fiction doesn't necessarily predict the future, it only occasionally does so but it mostly says things about the hopes and fears of the present. My hope is that we do find a way to break the needless borders between us, and the borders beyond. Of all the science-fictional and fantastical scenarios I have envisioned in my stories, this may be the one I most hope comes to pass.

About the Author

WOLE TALABI is a full-time engineer, part-time writer and some-time editor from Nigeria. His stories have appeared in *The Magazine of Fantasy and Science Fiction* (*F&SF*), *Lightspeed*, *Omenana*, *Terraform*, *The Kalahari Review*, and a few other places. He edited the anthologies *These Words Expose Us* and *Lights Out: Resurrection* and co-wrote the play *Color Me Man*. His fiction has been nominated for several awards including the Nommo Awards and the Caine Prize. He likes scuba diving, elegant equations and oddly-shaped things. He currently lives and works in Kuala Lumpur, Malaysia.

Ingram Content Group UK Ltd.
Milton Keynes UK
UKHW041541260423
420818UK00004BA/239